Arthur Griffiths

French Revolutionary Generals

Arthur Griffiths

French Revolutionary Generals

ISBN/EAN: 9783337227494

Printed in Europe, USA, Canada, Australia, Japan

Cover: Foto ©Andreas Hilbeck / pixelio.de

More available books at **www.hansebooks.com**

FRENCH REVOLUTIONARY GENERALS.

BY

MAJOR ARTHUR GRIFFITHS,

Late 63rd Regiment,

AUTHOR OF "THE ENGLISH ARMY," "CHRONICLES OF NEWGATE," ETC. ETC.

LONDON: CHAPMAN AND HALL,

LIMITED.

1891.

CONTENTS.

CHAPTER V.
DUMOURIEZ.—V.

CHAPTER VI.
HOCHE.—I.

CHAPTER VII.
JOURDAN.—I.

CHAPTER VIII.
HOCHE.—II.

CHAPTER IX.
MARCEAU.

CHAPTER X.
MARCEAU AND JOURDAN.

CHAPTER XI.

HOCHE.—III.

CHAPTER XII.

HOCHE.—IV.

CHAPTER XIII.

JOURDAN AND MARCEAU.

CHAPTER XIV.

JOURDAN.—II.

CHAPTER XV.

JOURDAN.—III.

CHAPTER XVI.

HOCHE.—V.

CONTENTS.

FRENCH REVOLUTIONARY GENERALS.

CHAPTER I.

DUMOURIEZ.—I.

THE DECLARATION OF WAR IN 1792.

THE war which the French Revolution had rendered almost inevitable, was actually declared in April, 1792. The despotisms of Europe could not tolerate the establishment of a new democracy in their midst. All absolute monarchs dreaded the extension of revolutionary ideas through their dominions. Some had special reasons for taking up arms against France. Prussia in particular hungered for more territory, and hoped to arrange with Austria for the further plunder of Poland. The Emperor of Austria was more pacifically disposed, and would still have left diplomacy to settle the quarrel. But the quixotic Gustavus III. of Sweden was eager for the fray, and Catherine of Russia, ever bent upon aggrandisement, promised him material help to further her own wily views. The proximate cause of war, however, was the congregation of the French *émigrés* upon the frontier. Their presence especially in the cities of Trêves and Coblentz, to the number of twelve or fifteen thousand, was a circumstance of alarm and annoyance to the revolutionary Government. They were

B

continually recruited by fresh fugitives, and were in a state of continual ferment and hostility to the authority that had driven them into exile. At length Dumouriez, for the moment at the helm of Foreign Affairs, peremptorily demanded their dispersion. He declared that unless a satisfactory and practical answer was returned within a certain date, France would consider herself at war. Austria hesitated, and France, in the person of its new rulers, would brook no delay. Failing the assurances required, the French Assembly formally declared war at a late hour of the night of the 20th April, and thus rushed into a struggle destined to last for nearly a quarter of a century and convulse all Europe.

Hostilities followed close upon the declaration of war. At this time the forces destined to come into collision were posted as follows: Austria had 40,000 men in Belgium, and 25,000 on the Rhine. These numbers might easily have been increased to 80,000, but the Emperor of Austria did no more than collect 7,000 or 8,000 around Brisgau, and some 20,000 more around Rastadt. The Prussians, now bound into a close alliance with Austria, had still a great distance to traverse from their base to the theatre of war, and could not hope to undertake active operations for a long time to come. France, on the other hand, had already three strong armies in the field. The Army of the North, under General Rochambeau, nearly 50,000 strong, held the frontier from Philippeville to Dunkirk; General Lafayette commanded a second army of about the same strength in observation from Philippeville to the Lauter; and a third army of 40,000 men, under Marshal Luckner, watched the course of the Rhine from Lauterbourg to the confines of Switzerland.

The French forces were strong, however, on paper only. The French army had been mined, as it seemed, by the

Revolution and had fallen almost to pieces. The wholesale emigration of the aristocrats had robbed it of its commissioned officers, the old experienced leaders whom the men were accustomed to follow and obey. Again, the passion for political discussion, and the new notions of universal equality, had fostered a dangerous spirit of license in the ranks. The bonds of discipline were loosened; the private men had grown insubordinate, argumentative, prone to canvass freely the character, conduct, and opinions of officers who had but recently gained their epaulettes, to despise them as no better than themselves, and to cavil at the orders they gave. While the regular regiments of the old establishment were thus demoralised, the new levies were still but imperfectly organised, and the whole army was unfit to take the field. It was badly equipped, without transport, and without those useful administrative services which are indispensable for mobility and efficiency. Moreover, the prestige of the French arms was at its lowest ebb. A long and enervating peace had followed since the last great war, in which the French armies had endured only failure and ignominious defeat. It is not strange, then, that the foes whom France had so confidently challenged, counted upon an easy triumph over the revolutionary troops.

The earliest operations fully confirmed these anticipations. A brief reference to them must be given here, to make what follows intelligible. France after the declaration of war had at once assumed the initiative, and proceeded to invade Belgium. Here the Duke Albert of Saxe-Teschen, who commanded the Imperialist forces, held his forces concentrated in three principal corps: one covered the line from the sea to Tournay; the second was at Leuze; the third and weakest at Mons. The total of these troops rose to barely 40,000, and Mons, the most important point in the general line of defence, was the least strongly held.   An able strategist gathering together 30,000 men from each of the French armies of the Centre and North, would have struck at Mons with all his strength, cut Duke Albert's communications with the Rhine, turned his inner flank, and rolled him up into the sea.   But no great genius as yet directed the military energies of France. Lafayette, it is true, strongly urged the concentration of 50,000 men at the confluence of the Sambre and Meuse, whence he might have marched upon Brussels.   This project, which is distinctly creditable to Lafayette's military judgment, was not adopted, nor was Rochambeau's proposal to act strictly on the defensive.   It was Dumouriez who finally decided on the plan of campaign.   Although only Foreign Secretary at the time, he was consulted, on the strength of his professional antecedents, of which more directly.

By Dumouriez's advice, the French armies were ordered to advance against the Austrians by several lines.   Four columns of invasion were to enter Belgium; one was to follow the sea coast, the second to march on Tournay, the third to move from Valenciennes on Mons, and the fourth, under Lafayette, on Givet or Namur.   Each, according to the success it might achieve, was to reinforce the next nearest to it, and all, finally, were to converge on Brussels.   At the very outset, however, the French encountered the most ludicrous reverses.   Their columns fled in disorder directly they came within sight of the enemy.   Lafayette alone continued his march boldly towards Namur; but he was soon compelled to retire by the news of the hasty flight of the columns north of him.   The French troops had proved as worthless as their leaders were incapable; whole brigades turned tail, crying that they were betrayed, casting away their weapons as they ran, and displaying the most abject cowardice and terror. Not strangely, after this pitiful exhibition, the Austrians—

all Europe, indeed—held the military power of France in the utmost contempt.

"Do not buy too many horses," said the Prussian Minister to his emissaries, who were preparing for the coming campaign on the Rhine. "The comedy will not last long ; this army of lawyers will soon be annihilated, and by autumn we shall be on our way home." The King of Prussia was encouraged by the manifest disorganisation and worthlessness of the French forces to expect an easy victory, and it is more than possible that, had the allies acted with more promptitude at this juncture, France would have been speedily overthrown. If a weak fraction of the Imperialist forces could thus put the whole French army to rout, surely the combined forces of Austria and Prussia would carry all before them, and would find no obstacle to a rapid triumphant march on Paris.

But now the national danger stirred France to its inmost depths. French spirit was thoroughly roused. The country rose as one man, determined to offer a steadfast, stubborn front to its foes. Stout-hearted leaders, full of boundless energy and enthusiasm, summoned all the resources of the nation to stem and roll back the tide of invasion. Immediate steps were taken to put the defeated and disgraced armies of the frontier upon a new footing. Lafayette replaced Rochambeau with charge from Longwy to the sea, his main body about Sedan ; Luckner took the line from the Moselle to the Swiss mountains, with head-quarters at Metz. A third general, destined to come speedily to the front, also joined the army as Lafayette's lieutenant. This was Dumouriez, who, wearied and baffled by Parisian politics, sought the freedom of the field. Within a month Lafayette played into his hands by his defection from the revolutionary cause. Lafayette endeavoured, but in vain, to use his military authority to restore order and the King. He misapprehended, however, the temper of his troops, which was decidedly in favour of the popular movement. Disappointed, and deserted by all on whom he had counted, Lafayette fled to the Austrian camp. His defection came at a most critical time. The enemy was close at hand, and in overwhelming strength; a hundred thousand men with large trains of artillery were already on French soil. Longwy had fallen, Verdun was in danger, and the French forces, weakened and disseminated along a wide extent of frontier, were actually without a head. The French Government in that crisis put its trust in Dumouriez, and appointed him Commander-in-Chief. It fell to his lot, as we shall see, to stave off disaster and lay the foundations of French military success.

It has been claimed, and with justice, for the French revolutionary epoch, that it developed and brought to the front military genius that otherwise must have remained unknown. Caste prejudices had long forbidden any but the nobly born to hope for command in the French army. Promotion from the ranks was altogether denied to the common soldier; only an aristocrat could bear the King's commission. The Revolution not only swept away these invidious distinctions; it did far more. The exodus of the officers into voluntary exile left innumerable vacancies and an almost endless vista of advancement to those who remained, however lowly their status or inferior their grade. Yet more: the Revolution abolished all seniority, all ancient notions of precedence, and plainly promised preferment to all capable of winning it. Men were now to be judged by their performances; they stood or fell by the success or failure they achieved. It was a rough-and-ready, rule-of-thumb process, which might act hardly on the unlucky, but it kept back the incompetent and as surely hurried forward the real leaders of men. The defeated general ended his career upon the guillotine; another took place to conquer or face the same fate. The alternative was too often between rapid glory and a shameful death. Thus by the severest form of natural selection none but the fittest survived. But in this way France was well served.

"The flight of the aristocrats," says Jomini, "had opened a vast field for ambition. Soldiers came to lead armies who no one dreamed could command a battalion. There was a limitless field of choice. Levies *en masse* summoned every citizen to arms; amongst the recruits were men of every class and of every variety of talent, all enthusiastically eager to adopt a profession that gave free vent to their patriotism, and at the same time offered to bring them rapidly to fame and great honour."

When in the bitter days of his last captivity Napoleon I. mused over the troubled epoch in which he had been a principal actor, he expressed his astonishment at the number of great generals the Revolution had produced. To use his own language, it was as though nature had vindicated her rights, and every prize had been thrown open to general competition in a nation of thirty millions of souls. Most of these prominent military leaders were of obscure origin, and had been private soldiers in the ranks. Ney was the son of an old soldier, who threw up a small appointment in the mines to enlist as a private hussar. Massena's father was a *marchand des vins* in Nice; Massena began life as a cabin boy, enlisted, took his discharge, re-enlisted, and became a general of brigade within a year. Soult was of still humbler origin; he too enlisted, and served slowly through all the non-commissioned grades, to jump in twelve months from captain to general of brigade. Lannes was the son of a livery-stable keeper, and was at one time apprenticed to a dyer.   He was only half educated, but he rose twice within four years to the rank of general, the second time in Italy under the approving eye of Bonaparte. Augereau, the son of a mason, enlisted and was drummed out of his regiment, to re-enlist and rapidly achieve the highest rank.

Remarkable as are these and many similar cases of rapid advancement won by undoubted personal merit, they are, with one exception, outdone in the persons of the generals who first led the French Republican troops to victory. The careers of Hoche, Marceau, Kleber, and Jourdan, sufficiently prove that neither gentle birth, nor mature years, neither long and varied service, deep reading, nor great practical experience are indispensable to the development of great military skill. How they prospered by sheer weight of natural talent for war it will be my business to show; but before dealing with these, the most notable of the Republican generals, it will be necessary to dispose of the man who preceded them in point of time, and was the single exception to the general rule of Republican advancement.

Dumouriez was educated on the old lines; he belonged to the old school of French officers, he had seen much service in various parts of the world, and he was already more than fifty years of age when he arrived at supreme command. But it was under his orders that many young generals whose fame ultimately far surpassed his, gained their first laurels, and it may fairly be said that Dumouriez's campaigns paved the way to their greater successes.

CHAPTER II.

DUMOURIEZ.—II.

EARLY LIFE AND CAREER, TO HIS APPOINTMENT AS COMMANDER-IN-CHIEF, AUG., 1792.

CHARLES FRANÇOIS DUMOURIEZ was born at Cambrai on the 25th of January, 1739. He came of a noble family, and his father, a man of education and good parts, who had been a military officer, assisted in the education of his son. The younger Dumouriez had to thank his father for his acquaintance with modern European languages, mathematics, classics, history, and that fluency in the expression of his ideas, which made him in after life an inveterate memorialist and pamphleteer. Whilst still in his teens, Dumouriez appears to have expressed a desire to become a monk, but he soon abandoned that idea, and eagerly embraced the profession of arms. He accompanied his father, who was employed as a war commissary, to the campaign against Frederick the Great in 1757, and early displayed his military proclivities. While serving as a volunteer when Cherbourg was captured by the English, he won a commission by his gallant conduct in the field. A year later he was severely wounded at the relief of Munster, and was again wounded the day before the battle of Clostercamp. He had on this occasion a narrow escape of his life, and was only saved from death by a musket-ball by a book which he carried in his pocket. His wounds and his intrepid conduct gained him distinction and advancement. In 1761 he received a troop of horse, and two years later the cross of St. Louis. When peace came, the regiment to which he belonged was disbanded, and for a time his active energies were checked. But he could not settle down into a peaceful, humdrum life, and he roamed about the world in search of adventurous employment. He went first to Corsica, carrying credentials from the Duc de Choiseul. He offered his services to Paoli, but they were declined. He returned then to Paris, and busied himself in an intrigue intended to procure independence for Corsica. Failing in this he was for a time discredited, but soon afterwards regained the Duke's favour, and proceeded with recommendations to Spain. There he became a hanger-on of the Marquis d'Ossuno, the French Ambassador. He visited Portugal, and the trip supplied him with materials for two of his earliest memoirs on the attack and defence of that country. To another memoir, previously drawn up, upon the affairs of Corsica, he owed his recall to Paris and his appointment as Quarter-master-General to the French army despatched to that island. According to his own account—and it must be borne in mind that for those early services we are solely dependent on his own account—he contributed largely to the success of the campaign. He certainly displayed gallantry; for his courage was never in question at any part of his career. Whether his counsels, which he continually thrust upon his com-manders, had any appreciable effect upon the operations, may be doubted. A passion for giving advice was a trait early developed in his character, and through the whole of the active part of his life he was perpetually inditing memoirs, drawing up suggestions, and acting as advocate and mentor to every one he came across. The Corsican campaign brought him promotion to the rank of lieutenant-colonel, and he returned to Paris, to be presently employed by the Duc de Choiseul on a new mission. He was sent to Poland, as minister, he declares, but his enemies assert that his duties were those of a spy.

Dumouriez was to support the party conspiring to depose Stanislas and attack Russia, and with this object he endeavoured to introduce reforms into the Polish army, and, of course, drew up a memorial for the best plan of a campaign. But dark days were now at hand for him; the Duc de Choiseul was disgraced, and the Duc d'Arguillon, his successor, was no friend. Dumouriez having submitted to Louis XV. a long memorial, suggesting the employment of a foreign legion to assist the King of Sweden, he was sent, unknown to the Duc d'Arguillon, to Hamburg, to report upon his own scheme. But he was surrounded by the French Minister's spies, and was speedily arrested and consigned to the Bastille. His imprisonment was not long protracted, nor does it appear to have been very irksome, and he employed the leisure it afforded him, to write a couple of military treatises, translate some Italian poetry, and project some more ambitious literary work. At the end of six months he was transferred to the Castle of Caen, in Normandy, where he married, and remained a prisoner at large until the accession of Louis XVI. He then demanded to be legally tried in Paris, and the reply was unconditional release. Presently he was quite taken into royal favour, and selected to assist in instructing the French army in the newly introduced Prussian drill.

In 1778 he was appointed commandant of Cherbourg. His prolific pen had won him this advancement. He had prepared and submitted to the King a lengthy memoir, demonstrating the supreme fitness of Cherbourg for a naval arsenal and fortified seaport on this side of the French coast.   Louis XVI. recognised the value of this document, and wrote across the margin, "Dumouriez, Commandant of Cherbourg."   He had here a fine field for his superabundant energies, and he set to work with a will. He may fairly claim to have laid the foundations of Cherbourg's greatness.   He laboured incessantly to improve the harbour, strengthen the fortifications, and develop its resources.   During the ten years that he remained commandant, the population of Cherbourg was nearly trebled.

It was not to be supposed, however, that a man of restless, intriguing disposition, ambitious, self-sufficient, and ever eager to push himself forward, would remain a passive spectator of the political troubles that were now to shake France to its very core.   Dumouriez seems very early to have adopted the Liberal principles of the day ; he became and long remained an adherent of the Orleanist faction.   He was strongly in favour of the assembly of the States General, and his pen was constantly at work upon all the burning questions of the hour.   He paid many visits to Paris during 1788, but he was present at his command when the news reached Cherbourg of the taking of the Bastille.   Dumouriez now threw off all disguise, and openly avowed himself a Republican.   He accepted the appointment of commandant to the newly raised National Guard, and he strongly urged other commanders in the neighbourhood, not to oppose the formation of a National Militia.   A little later, his pay having been stopped, he resigned his command, and transferred himself to Paris, where for some time he played a double part, now presuming to give advice to the King, now joining the Jacobin Club and accepting missions and other employment from the most advanced Republican party.

In 1791 he was promoted, when fifty-two years of age, to the rank of major-general. Having gained this position, he became a still more devoted adherent of the Revolution, and he proceeded to Nantes, where he obtained command of the twelfth military district. He now speedily showed that he was no true friend of the King. Two days after Dumouriez's arrival at Nantes, Louis XVI. fled from Paris. The news spread consternation in Nantes, but Dumouriez promptly dealt with the crisis. He forced the officers whose allegiance was supposed to be all the King's, to take an oath of obedience to the nation and the law, and then sent dispatches to Paris, declaring his intention of collecting all available forces and marching to the succour of the Constituent Assembly. The King's recapture rendered this demonstration unnecessary, but Dumouriez had gained credit for his exuberant patriotism, and the time was approaching for him to take a more prominent part in the revolutionary struggle.

Next year his promotion to lieutenant-general deprived him of his command at Nantes, but he could not at once return to Paris owing to his pecuniary difficulties in the West. From these he was released by the liberality of M. Delessert, who brought him to Paris, hoping, it is said, for his influence among the Jacobins, with some of whom he was now intimately allied. He betrayed rather than befriended Delessert, and soon afterwards replaced him as Foreign Minister, having been specially selected for the post, it is said by the Jacobins, who counted upon his resolution to assist them in declaring war. His soldier-like promptitude quickly cut through the meshes of diplomatic chicanery, and, as we have seen, speedily brought about a rupture with Austria. He held office as Foreign Minister barely three months.

Dumouriez was not thoroughly in accord with his col·leagues, and they differed more especially with regard to the King.   He seems to have been anxious to save Louis XVI. unnecessary humiliation, and he certainly disapproved of Roland's peremptory letter calling the King too strictly to account.   This led to his estrangement from the Girondists, and the breach became wider by Dumouriez's opposition to the two decrees, one for expelling the non-juring priests, the other for the formation of a large military camp in the neighbourhood of Paris.   When Louis, driven to despair, sought Dumouriez's advice, he recommended the dismissal of the obnoxious Ministers.   The difficulty was to replace them. But new Ministers were found, and Dumouriez accepted the post of Minister of War.   He remained in this only four days.   The dismissal of the Ministers had raised a storm in the Assembly, and Dumouriez was denounced as the creature of a tyrannical King.   But he had the courage to tell the Assembly many plain truths, and in the teeth of a storm of execration, he bravely persisted in reading a long memoir which, with great promptitude, he had prepared, concerning his department.   Girondists and Jacobins alike vowed vengeance against him, and threatened to send him before the court of Orleans for trial as a traitor.   But his undaunted demeanour cowed his enemies, and after calmly signing and depositing his memoir upon the table, he coolly walked out of the Chamber. His firmness was approved of by the King; but estrangement speedily followed.   Louis was prepared to sanction the formation of the camp, but he still opposed the harsh measure against the priests.   None of the Ministers would countersign his resolution, or convey it to the Assembly. All preferred to resign.

Dumouriez now resolved to withdraw himself from political strife, and to leave Paris for the front.   There is nothing to show by whose orders Dumouriez proceeded to join the army in the field. It is possible that as he was War Minister he issued instructions to himself, but it is certain that his departure was known to and approved of by the King. As an officer of high rank, long standing, and practical experience, it was right and proper that he should wish to take part in the defence of his country. Whatever difference of opinion may exist as to Dumouriez's political conduct, his character as a soldier now and at all times stood high. He may have failed, as we shall see, to prove himself a great commander, but he had sound, soldierly instincts. He was an energetic administrator, and his personal gallantry has never been denied. He appears to have done good service, too, even during his very brief tenure of the post of Minister of War.

The memoir already referred to, which caused such a disturbance in the Assembly, was an able and exhaustive document, setting forth fairly the chief flaws in the existing military organisation of France. It criticised severely the ridiculous procedure of the Assembly in decreeing fresh levies of troops without providing funds for their support; it pointed out that what the army needed was not new regiments, but the reinforcement and organisation of those already enrolled; it revealed the ruinous condition of many of the fortresses, and charged the authorities with culpable neglect in concealing the fact, and failing to put them right. Dumouriez seems also, during a short stay at the War Office, to have inquired closely into the system of contracts, and to have introduced new checks upon the methods of obtaining supplies. Moreover, he found time to write to all the generals on the frontier, and gave his views at length upon their future operations. He hastened the march of reinforcements from Paris, and, as he says, signed his name fifteen hundred times while in office.

Dumouriez was now to find a more suitable field for his energies, more congenial employment for his indefatigable spirit.   But his *début* with the army was scarcely encouraging. He proceeded direct to Marshal Luckner's head-quarters at Valenciennes. Luckner was now supreme along the whole line from the Rhine to the sea, and Lafayette, at the head of the Army of the Centre, was nominally under his orders. Only nominally, for Lafayette was strong, and Luckner, a poor creature just verging on his dotage, liked to be led by others. Lafayette hated Dumouriez, and made no secret of it. Thus hostile influences prevailed at Luckner's head-quarters, and Dumouriez was speedily made to feel them. He was badly received by the Marshal, and snubbed by the staff; he was accorded none of the honours due to his rank; they gave him no orderlies, no guard of honour, not even the countersign for the day. He remained for many days as a private person in the camp, and was denied any command of troops by Luckner, although, as second senior lieutenant-general, he was entitled to the left wing. The excuse was that nothing could be done till Lafayette's return from Paris, whither he had gone to strike a blow in favour of the King. He failed, and coming back to Valenciennes, was received with great military honours by Luckner. Dumouriez, having no post assigned to him, was absent from the parade. A day or two later, however, he was selected to command the camp at Maulde—an important point covering the rich plains between Valenciennes and Lille, but weakly held by three or four thousand men.

The Austrians were before it in much greater strength, and Dumouriez felt that he had been sent there in the hopes that he might encounter a serious check. He held his own, however, and throwing himself with his customary vigour into his work, so harassed the enemy and beat up their advanced posts that they refrained from attacking the camp. He strengthened his position materially, and protected the frontier by a chain of fortified outposts. Above all, he kept his troops continually employed, and by inuring them to fatigue, and enforcing a strict discipline, gave them the confidence of seasoned veterans. In the campaigns that followed, the regiments which had served in the camp of Maulde were always noticeable for their steady conduct. Dumouriez, while in command at Maulde, took a curious step with the idea, he says, of raising the courage of his troops. Two of the daughters of a retired cavalry sergeant named Fernig, who resided at Mortagne, had come out, of their own wish, to accompany the French detachments. When they were engaged at the outposts, these young girls, one of whom was only twenty-three, the other barely seventeen, gentle, delicately-nurtured creatures, faced cheerfully the hardships of campaigning. Their courage was conspicuous, and Dumouriez put them forward on all occasions as an example for his troops. They accompanied him to Champagne when he became Commander-in-Chief, and took part in all the actions fought in the Argonne, as well as in the invasion of Belgium. The National Convention granted them a pension in recognition of their gallant services, but they forfeited this at the time of Dumouriez's flight, for they followed that general across the frontier.

While Dumouriez was thus engaged in minor operations around and in front of Maulde, great movements were in progress at Paris. The waters were fast closing over the unhappy Louis, and his position became hourly more critical. It was evident that the friends advancing to his rescue must hasten their movements, or they would be too late.

The concentration of the allies upon the frontier was proceeding rapidly. An invasion became imminent; already the Prussians were close to the Rhine, and the Austrian forces had assembled about Spire. It was necessary for the French to make preparations to meet attack. These were entirely of a defensive character, and some changes were made in the commands. Lafayette's attitude had raised the suspicions of the Government, and it was thought safest to keep him as near as possible to Paris. For this reason he replaced Luckner at Valenciennes, while the latter was sent to command at Metz, and generally from the Moselle to Switzerland. Dumouriez was kept under the orders of Lafayette, and although exercising at times a more general supervision over the northern frontier, was still chiefly employed as commandant of Maulde. His force, however, was increased by twenty-three battalions and six squadrons, and he spent his time, as before, in seeking diligently to improve and perfect his troops. He continued to practise them incessantly in outpost duty, and arranged that all in turn should be engaged. Every detachment as it went out was furnished with maps, and with ample and special instructions under the general's own hand, and he himself frequently superintended the operations. He thus kept in check the Austrians, who had been reinforced on this side in order to make a diversion for the principal line of invasion by the centre. Nothing decisive occurred, but Dumouriez gained experience and proved his skill as a partisan leader, whilst his men, thus constantly employed in the minor operations of war, became the nucleus of an excellent army.

While thus employed, Dumouriez received intelligence of the catastrophe of the 10th of August, and the imprisonment of the King. He does not appear to have been very deeply affected by the news. He thought more of the enemy in front of him, and neither he nor the troops under him were disposed to take part for or against the King. But when Dillon sent him a copy of the oath which Lafayette wished to be administered to all the troops, Dumouriez refused to take it. In his opinion the King was made prisoner by one of two factions contending for supreme power, and to administer an oath swearing allegiance to the King would be to range the army on the side of the party that had succumbed. This must have led to civil war, always terrible, but infinitely more so when a foreign invader was close at hand. For these reasons he refused to act upon Dillon's instructions, and published his reasons in the papers. His adhesion to the Government of the hour gained him great favour, and no doubt led to his subsequent selection as Commander-in-Chief. The National Assembly was much incensed at the attitude taken by Lafayette with regard to the oath, and dispatched Commissioners to all the armies who upheld its authority. Those sent to Lafayette were immediately arrested by that general, who now declared openly for the King, and announced his intention of marching direct upon Paris. Lafayette acted hastily as usual, and without judgment, seeing his mistake too late when his army openly vented its dissatisfaction at the arrest of the Commissioners. After pausing irresolute for five days he realised that he was powerless, and suddenly escaped across the frontier. This was on the 19th of August. On the 14th, the Commissioners sent to General Dillon had arrived at Valenciennes. They were still hesitating whether or not to entrust Dumouriez with the command when a courier arrived direct from Paris, announcing Lafayette's defection. The same message brought instructions to Dumouriez to assume general charge of the armies on the frontier of France.

It was time to take vigorous action. On the day previous, the 18th of August, the enemy's forces had entered French territory.

CHAPTER III.

DUMOURIEZ.—III.

THE ARGONNE.

THE invasion of France, although at last an accomplished fact, had been carried out by the allies in a very leisurely fashion. Austria and Prussia had entered into a defensive alliance as early as February, a couple of months, in fact, before the declaration of war, and it was understood that the Prussians would take the field at once. But, although an army was collected about Magdebourg in May, it was not until the end of July that any considerable part of it reached Coblentz. By that date the Austrians, but in no great strength, were at Spire. A plan of campaign had been arranged at Vienna, and the chief command entrusted to the Duke of Brunswick, but the King of Prussia also accompanied his army into the field. Everything encouraged the allies to adopt a sharp and vigorous offensive. They might, in the first place, make their attack while the French forces were still without organisation or confidence in themselves. Much time would be needed to bring up reinforcements, and perfect the discipline of the new French levies. A rapid advance, therefore, offered the allies dvantages greatly superior to slow, methodical war. It was indeed essential that they should achieve a rapid and early success. Delay must give strength to their enemies. Victory could be most easily obtained in the days when the French soldiers still distrusted their leaders and themselves, and while the veterans who attacked them still enjoyed unquestioned the prestige of traditional prowess. A prompt initiative was still further encouraged by the faulty disposition of the French forces at the commencement of the campaign. They were dispersed over a wide front, and could only concentrate slowly and with difficulty to oppose the enemy and reinforce one another. The weakest part of the whole line, the centre, was that which covered the shortest and most direct road to Paris ; a determined enemy might thrust himself along it before the distant flanks could render effective assistance. The rapid advance of an enemy by this route would take all the isolated corps on the frontier in reverse, and oblige them to fall back hurriedly, but with no certainty that they could by any concentric movement effectually cover the capital, for the enemy would be nearer Paris than they. Again, such a retreat would surrender utterly the whole of the intervening country. Briefly recapitulating, the centre was clearly the most advantageous line of invasion. It was the nearest to the allies, and yet the shortest and straightest to Paris ; it was based on two strong fortresses, Mayence and Coblentz, and it broke through the weakest point of a long line, the extremities of which could be afterwards beaten in detail. Moreover, authentic intelligence had reached the Prussians, through the emigrant Marquis de Bouillé, that the chief French fortresses on this side, Longwy, Montmedy, and Verdun, were in too dilapi-·dated a condition to offer a prolonged resistance. The Duke. of Brunswick seems to have fully realised the advantages. offered by this line, and adopted it, almost as a matter of course. He too was eager, it is said, for decisive and immediate action. He foresaw the dangers of delay, perceiving that the French, unless quickly overcome, might yet rally and exhibit a desperate and unconquerable tenacity. On the other hand, the Duke was not well inclined for war; he was solicitous for his military reputation, which had been somewhat too cheaply earned under his friend and comrade, the great Frederick, and which might easily be imperilled or lost in fresh campaigns.

However excellent the conception of the plan of campaign, its execution was dilatory and full of faults. The general idea was as follows. Demonstrations were to be made along the whole line; the Austrian army, in Belgium, was to make a diversion on the northern frontier; 5,000 emigrants were to menace the French frontier from Switzerland to Philippsburg; Count d'Erbach was to do the same from thence to the Sarre. Meanwhile, the main body, consisting of Prussians, Hessians, and 12,000 emigrants, under the command of the brothers of the French King, was to concentrate at Trèves, then ascend the left bank of the Moselle, mask or capture the fortresses of Luxembourg, Longwy, Montmedy, and Thionville, attack Verdun, and march thence by the Verdun-Chalons road on Paris. Prince Hohenlohe was to cover the left of the advancing army by menacing Metz; on the right, Clairfayt, with a corps of Austrians from the army of Belgium, was to cover this flank, and, crossing the river Chiers, between Montmedy and Sedan, then masking the fortresses on this side, to march on Rheims and Paris by the Fismes-Soissons road. These movements were commenced early in August. On the 5th the Prussians crossed the Moselle; on the 18th May they were at Montfort, and on the 19th, having taken twenty days to march 120 miles, they reached Tiercelet, in France. On this day Clairfayt came up abreast with the line, but Brunswick, finding that the Austrians were only 18,000 strong, instead of 50,000, objected to advance further.   The personal authority of the King of Prussia, however, now interposed to overrule this decision, and, on the 20th, Longwy was invested.   It surrendered on the 24th.   The campaign had commenced brilliantly, and Brunswick for the moment held all the cards in his hand. The French forces were disseminated, dispirited, and without any recognised leader.   Lafayette was gone, and the army knew little of Dumouriez, except that it vaguely distrusted and disliked him.

Vigour and determination on the part of the allies might now have terminated the campaign.   Everything depended upon Brunswick's promptitude and skill.   Four courses were open to him.   He might fall with all his strength upon the disorganised army of Sedan, which had so recently lost Lafayette, its chief; he might continue his march on Paris by seizing the defiles of the Argonne; he might concentrate to his left and crush Luckner at Metz; or he might sit down before Thionville, Luxembourg, and Metz, thus suffering the campaign to degenerate into a slow affair of sieges.   The first was undoubtedly the wisest, and offered, if promptly executed, the most decisive advantages.   It was a supreme chance unexpectedly offered by the curious vicissitudes of war.   Lafayette's defection had left his army leaderless, demoralised, and disheartened—an easy prey.   Brunswick could have brought an overwhelming force to crush it utterly. His march on Paris would then have been practically unopposed.   The third plan was, however, that decided upon; one which had no merit but that of cutting through the French line, while it had the dangerous defect that one, probably two unbeaten armies, hourly regaining courage and fresh strength, were left close behind on each flank to harass the lengthening communications of the invading foe. Brunswick adopted it, no doubt, against his better judgment, and this is in some measure his excuse for the unenterprising tardiness with which he carried it out. It was not until the 20th August that he arrived at Verdun, and he lingered before that fortress until the 2nd September, when it capitulated. On that date the position of the allies was as follows : the main body at Verdun; Clairfayt at Stenay, behind the Meuse; the Hessians at Longwy; a corps of Austrians at Thionville; the emigrants in the Black Forest and at Trèves.

Let us turn now to the French, and see how matters stood with them. Their armies, towards the end of August, were, as I have said, greatly disseminated. The Army of the North, 30,000 strong, was dispersed along the frontier, between Lille, Maulde, and Maubeuge. In the centre, round about Sedan, was the army abandoned by Lafayette, about 23,000 strong, occupying a position far too extensive, and in a state of complete demoralisation. Kellermann, who had succeeded Luckner, commanded the army at Metz, 20,000 strong. Custine occupied Landau, with 50,000 men; and General Biron was in Alsace, with 30,000. The full measure of the danger which menaced France by the advance of the allies, was not at first realised by Dumouriez. For some days after his appointment to the supreme command, he still contemplated an invasion of Belgium, and he was making preparations for this his favourite project, when the news of the surrender of Longwy, and the investment of Verdun, aroused him to the paramount importance of meeting the enemies' advance. He started, therefore, for Sedan, without, however, abandoning entirely his designs against Belgium; and the tenacity with which he clung to this project strengthens the impression that the measures he subsequently took for holding the Argonne did not originate with himself, but were forced upon him by orders from Paris. He acted, however, with commendable promptitude, and soon made his influence and authority felt. This was the brightest period in Dumouriez's career. It cannot be pretended that he proved himself a general of the first order; he had no profound insight, intuitive or acquired, into the principles of strategy, and he was wanting in the instinct that seizes at once upon the decisive points of a battle-field or theatre of war. But it would be gross injustice to deny him a high place among generals of the second rank. He was by this time a veteran soldier, who had seen many wars in many lands. He had never commanded an army in the field, but he had been actively employed from his earliest youth. He was resolute, energetic, indefatigable; although now past middle age he enjoyed robust health, and his active, compact figure, somewhat below the middle height, with his easily-animated face and bright eyes, proved him capable of the greatest physical exertions. He never spared himself; he was for ever on the move, personally directing the operations he commanded, and always forward in the field.

On his joining the army at Sedan, on the 28th August, Dumouriez found it disaffected, mutinous, and greatly prejudiced against himself. It had degenerated into an undisciplined mob; the men were sullen, disobedient, insubordinate, the officers timorous, and exercising no sort of authority or control. The new general was greeted openly with contemptuous shouts. "This is the scoundrel who has brought about the war," they cried. Dumouriez grappled boldly with the difficulties of the situation; he took immediate steps to vindicate discipline, to introduce a firm system, and oppose the enemy's advance. A small force was at once detached to reinforce Verdun ; this detachment was too late, but the direction of its march proved useful in the operations that soon followed. Larger measures were now imperative to meet the enemy, and Dumouriez called a council of war, before which he frankly explained the exact state of affairs. The danger was pressing ; it was impossible, he declared, to remain inactive. What should be done ? Opinions were divided ; one party, headed by Dillon, an old officer, actually senior to Dumouriez, but now under his orders, was for retreat on Chalons and behind the Marne—a retreat which, in the demoralised condition of the French army, would probably have ruined it completely, while it would certainly have surrendered to the enemy, without a blow, the rich districts of Lorraine and Champagne, and thus solved satisfactorily his most difficult problem, that of providing his vast numbers with sufficient supplies. Others were for the invasion of Belgium, a project Dumouriez had never abandoned, and which he clung to still, although he would have us believe that he now favoured the defence of the Argonne. To forestall the enemy there, and hold him in check, would force him to fight his way inch by inch from starvation to plenty, and give France time to gather up her strength. Kellermann supports Dumouriez's claims as originator of the project, but there is not wanting evidence to show that the orders to occupy the Argonne actually came from Paris. This would exonerate Dumouriez from the responsibility of the measure, which some writers, especially Gouvion St. Cyr, have condemned. St. Cyr is of opinion that the enemy should not have been opposed in front, but suffered to advance across the Marne, and thus induced to expose his communications to flank attack. As a general rule, the principle of declining to meet an invasion by frontal defence is sound, because the assailants may thus force on a pitched battle, the best move possible for themselves; but in the present case there were many and preponderating arguments against retreat. To hold the Argonne was really the safest course to pursue, and whether or not Dumouriez planned it he adopted it heartily, and set about carrying the scheme into effect with energy and decision, boldly proclaiming that he intended to make it a new Thermopylæ for France.

A few words as to the scene of the coming operations must be given here to make what follows intelligible to the reader. The forest of the Argonne, which divided Champagne from the Three Bishoprics, extends from Sedan forty miles south beyond Sainte-Menehould to Passavant. It is a difficult country, intersected by many streams and deep ravines, and so cut up by marshes and ponds that it can only be traversed safely by five principal passes or defiles. The first leads from Sedan to Rethel, through Chêne-Populeux; the second passes through Croix-au-Bois; the third through Grandpré, coming from Stenay and going to Rheims; the fourth passes through La Chalade, intermediate between Varennes and Sainte-Menehould; the fifth and last contains the high road from Verdun through Chalons to Paris, which passes through a long defile at Les Islettes. An invading army must use one or more of these routes, and his progress might be seriously hampered by a defending force, which forestalled him at and disputed these issues with tenacity and skill.

The season was already far advanced; a check in the Argonne prolonged into the autumn would oblige the allies to retire, or winter where they were, amidst great scarcity, and experiencing great difficulty in bringing up supplies. A success of this kind would, moreover, give the French that leisure for further preparation so imperatively required.

Dumouriez decided to occupy the position of Grandpré, in the very centre of the Argonne. He had two roads available to Grandpré : one circuitous, round the edge of the forest, through Chêne-Populeux and Vouziers, the best and safest, but also the longest, and to take it would give the enemy a chance of forestalling him at Grandpré. The second road, lying between the forest and the Meuse, was the most direct, but to move by it was to make a dangerous flank march in the presence of the enemy, for Clairfayt with the Austrians was at Stenay, and could easily have struck at him on the march. He resolved to use both roads, sending his artillery and baggage round by Vouziers, and moving his main body direct on Grandpré. To open the road, he directed Dillon with a strong division upon Mouzon, and that general was engaged on the 31st with Clairfayt's advanced guard. Dumouriez, under cover of this, marched from Sedan upon Beaumont on September 1st. On the 2nd, he pushed Dillon on to St. Piermont, following by himself more leisurely, to allow the artillery and baggage to get ahead. On the 3rd, Dillon marched through Buzancy to the Aisne and crossed it.

On the 4th, Dillon took his whole army to Grandpré, and got into position on the heights between the Aisne and the Aire. Dillon, continuing his march, reached the same day the defile of La Chalade, and occupied also that of Les Islettes, where he found a detachment under General Galbaud, who had been sent to reinforce Verdun. This daring flank march, carried out in sight and touch of the enemy's advanced posts, was effected skilfully and without any accident. Dumouriez's position at Grandpré was excellent; his front was covered by the Aire, beyond which, strong detachments occupied Bessu and St. Juvin as advanced posts; on his extreme right and rear, Dillon held the defiles of La Chalade

and Les Islettes, while on his left a division under Dubouquet occupied Chêne-Populeux, and a detachment, 1,000
strong, held Croix-au-Bois.   Thus, in less than a week,
Dumouriez had seized every passage through the Argonne,
and, safe in a strong position about the centre, waited for
reinforcements.   These were in full march towards him,
from north, south, and west : 16,000 men were coming from
Flanders, while Kellermann with 22,000 men had left Metz
on the 4th, and was moving round through Pont-à-Mouson
to Bar-le-duc.   Dumouriez might thus count very shortly upon
showing a front with 60,000 men.   Meanwhile, the allies
were slowly advancing.   Verdun had fallen on the 2nd of
September, but it was not till the 5th that the allies crossed
the Meuse, and then they moved only a couple of miles
along the Chalons road, where they remained till the 11th.
Their advanced posts were pushed through Siply as far as
Damballe, where Dillon got touch of them when marching on
Les Islettes.   A portion of the Prussian cavalry had reached
Varennes, and Clairfayt had pushed on through Dun and
Romange.   The Hessians were behind in reserve at Longwy.

Brunswick's delay was forced upon him by the necessity
of baking bread, and waiting for his flank columns to come
up, but it was fatal to the success of the invasion.   Now at
length he heard of Dumouriez's evacuation of Sedan, and that
the French were strongly posted at Les Islettes.   He seems
to have despaired at once of pushing forward on this flank,
the nearest and most direct road to Paris.   He resolved
instead to extend his right, and threaten the enemy's left ;
it was his intention to threaten Grandpré from Mont Faucon
and Landres, while Hohenlohe covered the movement from
Clermont and Varennes, and, more to the right, Clairfayt and
Kalkreuth made strong demonstrations towards Briquenay.
He was at Landres on the 12th, and there he remained till

the 17th. He did not deserve to succeed; but nevertheless, the enterprise of one of his generals, and Dumouriez's strange neglect, now threw victory almost in his hands. The French general, through some misunderstanding—and he blames himself for the error—had weakened the post at Croix-au-Bois until it was held by barely a hundred men. On the 12th, Clairfayt, manœuvring boldly to his right front, fell upon Croix-au-Bois and seized it, thus compromising dangerously the left of the French position. Dumouriez, realising his danger, at once dispatched General Chazot with a couple of brigades, some guns, and cavalry, to recapture the post at all costs. On the 14th, Chazot's columns drove the Austrians out of Croix-au-Bois, but Clairfayt, hurrying forward reinforcements, speedily forced Chazot back across the Aisne to Vouziers, and thus cut him off from Grandpré. At the same time, Dubouquet was attacked at Chêne-Populeux, and obliged to retire on Alligny, whence he retired on Chalons.

Dumouriez found himself all at once in a most critical position. The detachments under Chazot and Dubouquet had reduced the force at Grandpré to barely 16,000 men. He had before him the whole strength of the Prussian army, and Clairfayt was established upon his left flank. Had the latter general followed up his advantage vigorously, the French army was lost. Again the enemy's dilatoriness, no less than his own fortitude, saved Dumouriez. He resolved, with great presence of mind, to extricate himself from his difficulty by refusing his left and withdrawing to a new position at Sainte-Menehould. Here he hoped to reunite his scattered forces and remain strongly posted, even at the risk of surrendering the road to Paris. He meant then to change his base to Vitry, and thus support it by the rich country to the south.

Dumouriez expected to be better able to harass the enemy's

communications than they could his, and, having come to this resolution, he executed it with great promptitude and daring. He sent his artillery round by Rethel, through Rheims to Sainte-Menehould; Chazot and Dubouquet were to follow by the same road, and so were the reinforcements coming from the north. Kellermann, who had displayed inexcusable tardiness, was implored to hasten his march on Bar-le-duc, and all possible reinforcements were called up from Rheims towards the Suippe. At the same time, Dillon was directed to hold out at all costs at La Chalade and Les Islettes—the key and pivot of the whole operation. Dumouriez kept his intended retreat a profound secret, and the enemy, who had sent in a flag of truce to gather intelligence, learnt that there was no sign whatever of withdrawal in the enemy's camp. Yet the same night Dumouriez broke up and fell back across the Aisne, covered by a strong rearguard. The weather was most tempestuous, with storms of blinding rain, which effectually concealed the movements in progress. By eight a.m. on the morning of the 18th of September, Dumouriez's army was in position at Autry, on the left bank of the Aisne, while the rearguard was falling back across the river, and breaking up the bridges as it retired. Again misfortunes overtook Dumouriez, and the success of this skilful retreat was nearly jeopardised by a fresh disaster on his left. Chazot, who was to have left Varennes at midnight, did not start until dawn. On reaching Vaux, his columns came unexpectedly upon a body of Prussian cavalry, and, being seized with a sudden panic, broke and fled. The cavalry charged promptly, and so completely routed the division that the French, crying that all was lost, fled in great numbers as far as Rheims. Some of the fugitives came across Dumouriez himself, who was at a loss to understand what had occurred. Happily Mirando, who commanded the rearguard, still showed a bold front, and Chazot's division was eventually rallied with no greater loss than that of its baggage. The retreat was continued, and the army reached Dommartin that evening, where it spent the night under arms. Next day it marched on Sainte-Menehould, and, on the morning of the 17th, took post there as follows: the right on the Aisne, at Neuville-au-pont; the centre behind the villages of Maufrecourt, Valmy, and Dampierre; the left on the Auve, covered by the marshes which abound on this side. This new position, like the first, was equally intended to gain time. Dumouriez was anxiously expecting reinforcements, and hoped that Beurnonville, coming from the north, and Kellermann from the south, were now near at hand. But unfortunately for him, both these generals, having heard exaggerated accounts of the disaster at Vaux, had fallen back, the first towards Chalons, the second to Vitry. Dumouriez's situation was now one of great jeopardy. He had barely 25,000 men in line, 6,000 of whom were cavalry, and the enemy was in great strength in front. But once again he was saved by the slothfulness of the allies, and repeated peremptory orders to Beurnonville and Kellermann had the effect of so hastening their movements that they both reached Sainte-Menehould by the 19th.

Throughout these trying days, Dumouriez displayed praiseworthy constancy and courage. The army he commanded was still raw and undisciplined, easily cast down, apt to be startled by shadows, as at Vaux; any sudden surprise rapidly degenerating into a rout. He was not well supported by his lieutenants; none of them possessed his fortitude. While at Grandpré, five general officers had come to him protesting against the position, on account of its unhealthiness, and urging him to withdraw his forces. Dumouriez replied that he would ask their advice when he wanted it, and so silenced their clamour. But the protest openly indicates the spirit abroad. No doubt his men were greatly harassed by their long marches, they were suffering from sickness and many privations. Their discontent soon broke out into open mutiny, which was only quelled by the personal appeal of the general to their patriotism. At the same time Dumouriez laboured incessantly to augment his supplies. He drew largely upon the resources of the neighbourhood, and by all other means in his power, by menace, exhortation, by purchase with assignats, or by forcible requisition, gathered together the sinews of war. He had the satisfaction, however, of knowing that, badly as his army was provisioned, the enemy were infinitely worse off. The difficulties of supply, added to the inclement weather, were already beginning to tell seriously upon the Prussian and Austrian troops.

As usual, Brunswick had followed up the retreating French very leisurely. Prince Hohenlohe had advanced on the 15th, on hearing that the French had evacuated Grandpré, but the main body did not leave Landres till the 18th. On the 20th it arrived at Ville-sur-Tourbe. Brunswick wished, it is said, to manœuvre now along the right bank of the Aisne, reopening communications with Clermont and Varennes, and threatening the enemy's communications at Bar-le-duc. This would have cut the French communications with Vitry, and rendered the position at Sainte-Menehould untenable. But the King of Prussia, hearing that there was much activity in the French camp, concluded that Dumouriez intended to fall back on Chalons; and eager to intercept his retreat, the allied forces were directed to make a sweep round to the westward, as far as Somme Tourbe. This change in the direction of the allied march was made by the King of Prussia, without consulting the Duke of Brunswick; and the King, although assured that the enemy stood firm, and had received reinforcements, continued to push hastily forward, still confident that the French were in full retreat. On the morning of the 20th, the advanced guard, which was now under the command of the Duke of Brunswick in person, was at Somme Bionne. The morning was thick and foggy, and nothing could be seen for a distance of more than twenty yards; but the heads of the advance were soon engaged, and the King of Prussia, more than ever certain that the French were retreating along the Chalons road, hurried forward to intercept them. This assumption was confirmed when the fog cleared off, and the French were seen in force around the heights of Valmy. These French troops were the corps commanded by Kellermann, who had come up on the previous day, and had been ordered by Dumouriez to take up a post south of the Auve.

Kellermann did not comply with these instructions, but crossed the stream and advanced to the heights of Valmy. His centre was posted about the middle of the hill, near the mill, on his right were posted Stengel and Beurnonville, and his left reached towards the Auve. The Prussians, advancing in force, formed up in line of battle on the opposite plateau of La Lune, which overlooks Valmy, and massed their artillery on these commanding heights. Brunswick also extended his right across the Chalons road, and seized Gizancourt, which outflanked Kellermann's left. The action commenced by a sharp artillery fire on both sides as early as 7 a.m.; the Prussian guns were well served, and about 10 a.m. caused great confusion in the French line near the mill, where two ammunition waggons were blown up. Kellermann's presence restored order, but the Prussians maintained their fire, and soon afterwards formed up their columns for attack. They advanced on the mill of Valmy, but were met by the French, whose loud shouts of " Vive la nation," and determined bearing, imposed upon the attacking columns, and they retreated in disorder. Kellermann's position was hazardous, but his right was made safe by the advance of Stengel, under Dumouriez's orders, and the left would have been equally so had not Chazot, whom Dumouriez had ordered to take Gizancourt, hesitated, and allowed the Prussians to forestall him at this important point, whence their guns enfiladed Kellermann's line. But that general stood firm, and a second advance made by the Prussians, late in the afternoon, was checked as easily as the first. The battle, which was nothing more than a cannonade—it is known in history as the Cannonade of Valmy—was ended without exchanging blows. But although the opponents never actually joined issue, the result of the battle was important. It was the first action in which the French had successfully stood fire, and the negative victory had a great effect upon the *morale* of the two armies. It raised the courage of the French, and drove the allies to despair. The Prussians abandoned the attack without being worsted, but their retreat was an acknowledgment of defeat. Kellermann was able to fall back that night to the position he should have occupied before the fight, behind the Auve. He had lost control of the Chalons road, but he could still threaten it; the Prussians continued to hold Gizancourt, and Clairfayt occupied Valmy.

The position of both the opposing armies was now far from satisfactory, but that of the allies was the worse of the two. They had both so manœuvred that they faced to their proper rear; their right had become their left, and the left the right. The communications of the allies, however, were long and very circuitous, reaching round through Grandpré to Varennes, from which the French at La Chalade were but six miles distant, and the main body only a short day's journey. Dumouriez, at Sainte-Menehould, faced instead of covering Paris, but he had the advantage of drawing his supplies from Vitry and Bar-le-duc, and he could, if hard pressed, fall back upon Metz. He did not lose confidence, therefore, and boldly resolved to hold out where he was. The central Government was less courageous, and fearing to lose its only army, sent urgent instructions to him to retire behind the Marne; being alarmed for Chalons, Rheims, and the capital itself. But Dumouriez boldly declined to obey orders. He declared that he could not renounce what he conceived the safest and strongest course, because he was threatened by the enemy's hussars. Rheims, he said, was protected by an army of 10,000 men, and could take care of itself. The event proved that Dumouriez was right. No doubt the general was fully informed of the desperate plight into which the scarcity of supplies, the inclement season, and the greatly extended line of communications, had thrown the enemy in front of him. The allies were starving; their only rations were hay, and chalky water; a deadly dysentery raged in their camp, and all alike, from the King to the meanest man, were sick of the campaign.

The arrival of convoys instilled vigour for a time, and the King of Prussia was for renewing the attack on the French posts, but to this the Duke of Brunswick was now resolutely opposed. He saw that there was nothing to gain by a victory, and everything to lose. To retreat with a beaten army, incapable of forced marches, through the difficult defiles of the Argonne, at all of which he might be forestalled by an enterprising foe, meant simply the annihilation of his army. He saw clearly that the French had at last gained confidence from their success, and that every hour was increasing their strength. Brunswick has been blamed for his want of vigour at the outset of the invasion, but it must be admitted that the persistence with which he advocated a retreat, even at the risk of his military reputation, saved the allied army from a crushing and overwhelming disaster.   Whether the escape of the allied forces was favoured by the indulgence of its enemy will never be ascertained, but it is well known that secret negotiations were opened after Valmy with Dumouriez; and although there may be no good ground for accusing the French general of taking bribes, as his enemies would have us believe, it may reasonably be supposed that he would be glad to see the invaders evacuate French soil.   But the facility with which the allies withdrew from the Argonne would be unintelligible except upon the supposition that Dumouriez, from motives which remain obscure, and which may not have been quite disinterested, had entered into an engagement not to greatly vex their retreat.   The dilatoriness and neglect of so active a commander is not to be otherwise explained.

Brunswick's retrograde movement was begun on the 30th September, and was known to Dumouriez, but he took no immediate and sufficient measures to stop it.   He was content to send his columns to pursue the rear feebly, instead of checking the van by promptly seizing the eastern issues of the Argonne.   Beurnonville, with twelve battalions, was directed on Autry, and Chazot was to march through Sedan towards Longwy.   Dillon was to recapture Clermont and Varennes, a movement which Kellermann was anxious to reinforce, but Dumouriez sent him to Somme-Suippe, quite in the other direction.   This pursuit was conducted in a very leisurely, incomplete fashion.   Beurnonville made an empty demonstration across the Aire; Dillon only pressed the allies hard as they fell back from Clermont and Varennes.

By the 3rd of October, they had threaded all the defiles,

and on the 4th, they crossed the Aire. On the 7th, they
passed the Meuse, Clairfayt occupying Stenay, Hohenlohe
Verdun, and the main body retiring on Longwy. Now, when
they had almost eluded his grasp, Dumouriez sent Kellermann *viâ* Clermont past Verdun to Etain, whence he was
to strike in at the enemy's line of retreat, whilst Dillon and
Beurnonville harassed their rear. Kellermann might have
accomplished great things ; the Austrian army was terribly
weakened, and further to its rear, Custine had just captured
Mayence.· But the lieutenant was not more active than the
Commander-in-Chief ; he lingered by the way so long that
the allies reached Longwy on the 21st, after a most toilsome
march, and having suffered the most terrible losses by the
way. Dumouriez himself had abandoned his army to
hasten to Paris. He has been greatly blamed for leaving
his command, just when his presence was most needed to
follow up success. But he still ardently desired to invade
Belgium, and he thought that a newer and finer opportunity
had arrived. It was to concert' measures for this invasion
that he now proceeded to Paris, and his journey thither is
another proof of his inferiority as a strategist. Granted that
the conquest of Belgium would be an immense service to
France, it would have been best and safest effected by
Brunswick's utter defeat. Had the French succeeded in
sweeping him away, and reached Coblentz, they would have
rendered the position of the Austrians in the Low Countries
untenable. Brunswick would have been quite unable to
resist Dumouriez, who, reinforced by the garrisons of Thionville, Sedan, and Metz, could have marched on Trèves at the
head of 80,000 men. Custine too, with 20,000 more, could
have easily descended the Rhine, and seized Coblentz and
Cologne. But Dumouriez had not the true insight of a great
commander, and he failed to understand what line of opera-

tions promised him the readiest and most decisive results. He could not perceive the strategical weakness of the Austrian defence of Belgium, and in planning his campaign, he neglected to strike at its most vulnerable point. This was on their left; the side on which lay their only line of retreat, by Namur, through Liége to Cologne. At this moment, the French army of Champagne was nearer Namur than the Austrians, who were mainly about Tournay; yet, as we shall see, although admirably placed to strike directly against the Austrian line of communications, Dumouriez was at great pains to bring his forces from Champagne, a long way round, to make a frontal attack.

CHAPTER IV.

DUMOURIEZ.—IV.

THE INVASION OF BELGIUM AND BATTLE OF JEMAPPES.

AT the time when the French invasion was imminent, the Austrian forces in Belgium were still under the command of Duke Albert of Saxe-Teschen. It was open to him to cover the whole frontier from the Sambre to Tournay; or he might give up the country to the left of the Meuse, and concentrate between Liége and Namur. The first was the least safe, but it fell in with the instructions of his Government and the Austrian military views of the day, so he adopted it, holding his forces dispersed along a very wide front, from Ypres to Namur. The line was further extended beyond the latter point by Clairfayt, who was on the march to reinforce him from the Meuse. This dissemination of the Austrian forces offered Dumouriez a great opportunity. By acting rapidly and with all his strength against his enemy's left, he might strike in at the weakest and most vulnerable point, then roll up each Austrian detachment in turn from Namur from the sea. He preferred, erroneously, to break up his own forces and advance along four distinct and widely separate lines. General Valence, with 24 battalions and 12 squadrons, was to move from Givet towards Namur, to prevent Clairfayt's junction with the Duke. This, strategically the most decisive operation, was never properly executed. Difficulties of supply delayed the march until it was too late to exercise any effect upon the campaign. D'Harville with a second corps was to march from Maubeuge upon Charleroi, join Valence, and cut off the Austrian communications through Liége. The third and principal advance was that of the centre column, 25,000 strong, under Dumouriez in person, which was to move from Valenciennes to Mons, engage the enemy wherever he might be encountered, and push on to Brussels. The fourth column to the left, under Labourdonnaye, 18,000 men, was to menace Tournay, and oblige the Austrians to extend still further their line of defence.

Dumouriez came from Paris on the 20th November, fortified with ample promises of support in men and material, promises destined to be never even partially fulfilled. His army was lamentably ill-found; it was destitute of everything, especially of warm clothing and great-coats, now greatly needed as winter was near at hand. But by strenuous exertions on the spot he ministered to the more immediate necessities of his men, although to the last he continued hampered by the difficulties of supply. But there was much, nevertheless, to favour his enterprise. He had great numerical superiority ; the spirit of his troops had been raised by recent successes ; he could choose his own line of operations, and the people of the invaded country were certain to be on his side. Had he adopted a more judicious plan of campaign, he might have compelled every Austrian in Belgium to lay down his arms.

On the 28th October, Dumouriez, having directed Labourdonnaye to demonstrate towards Ath on the left, and Harville on the right to approach him by Hou, near Maubeuge, collected a great part of his army between Quaroble and Quievrain, in advance of Valenciennes, meaning to march on Mons, where the Duke Albert occupied a position carefully selected beforehand, and fortified to resist attack. The right rested on Jemappes, the centre on Cuesmes, the left on Berthaimont, a suburb of Mons. Two villages, Quarcignon on the right front and Siply on the left, were held each by a battalion, and the broken ground in front of the position was filled with Tyrolese marksmen. On the left wing General Beaulieu was in command; the centre and right was under Clairfayt, who had joined the Duke early in November. The chief fault of the Austrian position was its extent, which was too great for the numbers, differently stated at from 15,000 to 20,000, holding it. Moreover, the decisive tactical point on the left was the most weakly held. A marshy stream, the Trouille, ran behind the position, and forbade retreat, except through the town of Mons. The slightest reverse on this flank would have cut Clairfayt from this fortress, and closed to him the road to Brussels. Dumouriez, as we shall see, missed the chance thus offered him by the enemy's faulty dispositions, and his victory at Jemappes was in consequence far from decisive and complete.

On the 3rd and 4th November, the French, after a sharp fight, drove in the Austrian outposts, and their advanced guard occupied Wasmes and Framenès. On the 5th, Dumouriez made his dispositions for the attack of the enemy's position. The left wing was charged with the assault of Quarcignon and the entrenchments in front of Jemappes. The centre, under the Duc de Chartres, supervised by Dumouriez, and supported by the infantry and cavalry reserves, was to storm Cuesmes; on the right, Harville, who had occupied Siply, was to outflank the enemy's left at Berthaimont. The action was commenced at daylight, about 8 a.m., on the 6th November, by a sharp artillery fire along the whole front. Dumouriez took post on his left wing, where he saw General Ferraud, after some hesitation, carry the village of Quareignon. Then directing that general to continue the advance on Jemappes, while General Rosière turned it by a long outflanking movement, the Commander-in-Chief rode to his centre, to await there the development of his two flank attacks. But Beurnonville and Harville both hung back. The first contented himself with opening an artillery fire on Beaulieu, in Cuesmes and Berthaimont, and the latter remained perfectly inactive at Siply. At 11 a.m., Dumouriez determined to press forward vigorously with his centre and left. To the latter he sent his aide-de-camp, Thouvenot, whom he trusted implicitly, and who, on this occasion, fully justified his chief's confidence in him. The halting columns of Ferraud and Rosière asked only to be led, and gaining a fresh impulse under the energetic guidance of Thouvenot, speedily made themselves masters of Jemappes. Dumouriez, who had waited for the successful development of the left attack, now bore with all his strength upon the opening in the slopes between Jemappes and Cuesmes.

Here, however, the French narrowly escaped reverse. Drouet's brigade was thrown into confusion by the un-expected onslaught of a body of Austrian cavalry, and turned back. The wavering brigade affected the next in line. Many columns halted irresolute, suffering severely, when all were rallied, the first by Dumouriez's valet-de-chambre, the rest by a royal prince. As Jean Baptiste Renard checked the flight of Drouet's brigade, so the Duc de Chartres reformed and gave fresh courage to the shaken line, and all went forward again to the attack.

While matters were thus in doubt in the centre, Dumouriez, according to his own account, rode off to his right, meaning to use it as might be necessary, either in prolonging the attack against Cuesmes or in covering the Duc de Chartres' retreat. Other accounts deny Dumouriez the credit of initiating the tardy advance of his right, which in any case did not commence until 11 a.m. When Beurnonville was half-way across Cuesmes, he had left a gap between his infantry brigades, into which Clairfayt promptly thrust a portion of his cavalry. At this moment Harville, from Siply, mistaking friends for foes, assailed the rear with a heavy artillery fire. Beurnonville wavered, and disaster was imminent, but Dumouriez again assures us—which others deny—that he placed himself at the head of the shaken columns and checked the cavalry attack. The check occurred, whether or not it was under the personal leadership of the general-in-chief, and the forward movement of the French right was maintained. This advance decided the day. Its direction threatened the weakest part of the Austrian position, and Clairfayt, in the centre and right, was now quite unable to hold his own. He had lost Jemappes, and the frontal attack under the Duc de Chartres had been completely successful. He was forced to retire in all haste behind the Trouille; only the left, protected by the firm front that Beaulieu still showed at Berthaimont, drew off through Mons. Harville had been ordered to take ground to his right, and occupy Mont Palisel, so as to intercept the enemy's retreat; but, after having failed to take part in the action, he failed also to secure the full benefit of the victory. The Austrians themselves seized this position, and held it until the beaten army had withdrawn across the Haisne to Soignies and Tubise.

The victory of Jemappes caused a great sensation through Europe. " The thunder of the battle echoed all over the

Continent," says Jomini. It had been thought that the French were incapable of winning a pitched battle, and Jemappes came as a surprise. Yet it was hardly a first-class affair. The French troops displayed much gallantry and their leader some tactical skill; but the chief credit is really due to the Austrians, who with inferior forces, engaged at a long distance from home, along a faulty line of operations, managed to draw off without overwhelming loss. A great captain would have crushed them completely; but, as has been said, Dumouriez was not a past master in the craft of war. A Napoleon would have seized at once upon the tactical point, and, leaving a few battalions to hold the enemy about Quareignon, would have concentrated all his strength against Cuesmes and the Austrian left, thus sweeping the whole line, taking the redoubts in reverse, and jeopardising the Austrian retreat.

Dumouriez has also been blamed for not reaping the full fruits of his victory by a more vigorous pursuit. He defends himself, in his memoirs, by declaring that his army was completely worn out. It had been manœuvring for four days consecutively, and on this, the day of battle, the men had had no food. A further and still more unfortunate delay, till the 12th, followed at Mons, but this, he says, was also unavoidable, on account of his destitute condition. He was without provisions, money, or means of transport. Some supplies were, however, raised locally, and loans were obtained from certain Belgian bankers and wealthy ecclesiastical establishments. By the time the French army pushed on, Duke Albert had drawn detachments to him and showed a new front at Tubise, with 28,000 men.

On the 13th, Dumouriez engaged the Duke's rearguard at Anderlecht, and, on the 14th, entered Brussels, which the Austrians had already evacuated. Here he again halted to provide for the wants of his army, which were now terrible ; it was starving, shoeless, and in rags. The military chest was empty, and it was not easy to raise funds. The difficulties of supply were greatly increased by the attitude of the Executive Government in Paris, which ignored Dumouriez, and entrusted the control of contracts to a committee, independent of him. He raised money, however, on his own responsibility, but was again thwarted in Paris, and his engagements disavowed. There can be no doubt that the Government would have been glad to see Dumouriez make the country support the war, but the system of requisitions was not yet introduced, and Dumouriez evidently shrank from adopting it.

From this period dates the general's constant conflict with the Jacobins. He had, no doubt, grown somewhat overbearing. He had saved the country by· expelling the Prussians, and his recent victory at Jemappes had tended to greatly increase his arrogance. Already he seems to have entertained ambitious projects. His troops were now, as he thought, devotedly attached to him, and he was encouraged to hope that he might yet interpose with a strong arm and put an end to the troubles in Paris. His haughty language to the Convention and his defiant attitude raised the deepest suspicions. Already Marat, who hated him, had declared publicly that Dumouriez would desert like Lafayette. It may be doubted whether Dumouriez was as yet aspiring to play the part of a General Monk, and it is certain that in these days he paid more attention to political intrigue than to his military plans. He had halted in Brussels until the 18th of October, when he marched to Louvain, thence on Liége, which he entered on the 28th, but kept his army outside lest the rich district should tempt it, now nearly broken by hunger and nakedness, into excesses. At the same time, a force had been detached to besiege Antwerp, which surrendered on the 26th, and General Valence, seconded by Harville's division, took Namur on the 2nd of November. These detached operations so far weakened him that he was unable to press the retreating columns vigorously; but on the 6th, Clairfayt, who had succeeded to the command, fell back behind the Erft, and Dumouriez entered Aix-la-Chapelle on the 8th.

The French general had now along the line of the Meuse some 60,000 men, which he proposed to employ, as he tells us, part in the siege of Maestricht, and part to drive the Austrians across the Rhine. It may be doubted whether he seriously contemplated the latter measure, although it might easily have been accomplished, and would have soon put a serious obstacle between him and any renewed attack on Belgium by the Austrian forces. He declares that the orders he received from Paris forbade both the above-mentioned operations; but this is directly contradicted by the despatches of Pache, the French War Minister, who desired him on no account to let go of the enemy until it was beyond the Rhine. This operation formed part, moreover, of a general movement in which Beurnonville from Trèves, and Custine from Mayence, would have joined. So far from carrying out the wishes of the Government, Dumouriez proceeded, on the 12th of December, to put his army into winter quarters. The main body was at Liége; on the left, Mirandeau commanded from Longres to Ruremonde; the advance was at Aix-la-Chapelle, with posts pushed forward to the Roer.

CHAPTER V.

DUMOURIEZ.—V.

THE INVASION OF HOLLAND — BATTLE OF NEERWINDEN —
DUMOURIEZ'S FLIGHT.

DUMOURIEZ spent the winter months intriguing in Paris. He arrived there on the 1st of January, and, according to his own account, kept his room, where he was busily engaged upon military reports and a lengthy protest against the committee of contracts. He declares, too, that he laboured strongly to save the King, or at least to defer his trial; but that he was quite unsuccessful. Everywhere, he tells us, he found consternation or apathy. He could not perceive the slightest movement, private or public, in favour of the unfortunate Louis XVI. On the other hand, Dumouriez's enemies insist that he was in close correspondence with the Orleanist faction during his stay in Paris, and his subsequent conduct in the Low Countries rather encourages the accusation. Again, according to his own account, he was confined to his room by illness on the day of the King's execution; while others declare that he was an unconcerned spectator of it, and it is certain that he still retained the confidence of the Jacobins, who seemed to think they could not do without him. At the end of the month he returned to his army, charged to undertake the invasion of Holland.

E

The death of the King had brought two new enemies, England and Holland, into the field. Pitt had plainly told the French Ambassador that friendly relations could only be maintained with France, if she would keep within her own territory and refrain from insulting other Governments, destroying their tranquillity, or violating their rights. On the 1st of February, 1793, Brissot reported to the Convention that the English Court wished for war, which was accordingly declared. Fresh levies had been decreed, and on the 19th of January all available forces had been already directed on Antwerp, the proposed base of operations against Holland. The enterprise was most hazardous, for the French were by no means masters of the territory they occupied. The Austrians were gathering fresh strength about Cologne, the Prussian army had entered Cleves, and an Austrian corps was advancing to reinforce it in its intention of succouring the Dutch; Maestricht still resisted the French, and thus the line of invasion was threatened through all its length.

Dumouriez, however, did not hesitate; he knew that if he fell back he would pay the penalty with his head, and he already cherished a vague ambition of making himself supreme in the Low Countries, whence he could dictate terms to the Jacobins in Paris. His columns crossed the frontier of Holland on the 17th of February; on the 22nd he himself left Antwerp with his guns. On the 26th he took Breda, and his army occupied the line of the Beesbosch opposite Dordrecht. But now his further advance was checked by the news of disasters in Belgium, and, leaving Thouvenot to command in Holland, Dumouriez hastened in person to Louvain. The Prince of Saxe-Coburg had assumed command of the Austrian forces, and under him Clairfayt, with a corps of 30,000 men, had advanced across the Erft towards the Roer. On the 1st of March he had forced the passage of the latter river at Juliers, had attacked the French outposts at Aldenhoven and carried their entrenchments. Next day he drove the French out of Aix-la-Chapelle, and compelled them to retire upon Liège. The Austrians now advanced along their whole line, and forced the French to evacuate Ruremonde and Tongres, to raise the siege of Maestricht, and fall back, first on St. Tron, then on Tirlemont, and finally on Louvain, where Dumouriez joined them on the 13th of March.

The rapid advance of the Austrian forces spread dismay amongst the French from the front back to Paris. Amidst loud outcries against "treason" and "traitors" the Convention suddenly displayed terrific energy. It decreed a new levy, ordered every soldier of every rank to rejoin his regiment, and expressed its firm resolve to utilise to the utmost the vast resources of the country, to purge its soil of invaders, and hold out to the last extremity. The French army in Belgium, disheartened by its reverses and hasty retreat, was already disorganised and out of hand. The appearance of Dumouriez, however, worked wonders, and he spared no effort to restore confidence and good order.

The enemy, fortunately, had remained inactive until the 15th; the Prince of Saxe-Coburg having as yet formed no definite plan of action. He was, in fact, a little surprised at his rapid success, and it was not until that date that he decided to co-operate with the English for the purpose of driving the French out of Holland. The Duke of Brunswick was now sent towards Grave, Beaulieu to Namur, while he himself remained cantoned round Tongres. The delay had, however, given Dumouriez time to make fresh dispositions. The French army was reorganised into a centre and two wings, with an advanced guard and a reserve; the right under Dampierre was at Hougarde, the left at Diest, covering the communications and the retreat of the army. On the 15th, the Austrian advanced guard surprised Tirlemont, and both flanks of the French fell back in consequence upon Louvain. Dumouriez, convinced that it was necessary to resume the offensive in order to restore full confidence in his troops, advanced his right, and drove the enemy out of Tirlemont on the 16th. On the same day, the Austrians, moving from St. Tron, found the French at Goidsenhoven, and attacked it vigorously with their advanced guard, but without success.

This combat raised the spirits of the French army, and decided Dumouriez to risk a battle. He has been blamed for this on the grounds that his troops were not sufficiently disciplined or steady to retreat in good order if defeated; but he really had no choice between the offensive and a defensive battle in a good position. The first little suited the temper of the French troops, and Dumouriez was, therefore, right to attack. His great fault, however, was that he did not draw together the whole of his forces and concentrate them on the decisive points. On the 17th, he formed his army in order of battle—the right towards Heylissem, whence the line extended towards the Tirlemont-Maestricht road, the left resting just beyond it at Orsmael. The enemy was drawn up in two lines—the left along the heights behind Oberwinden, and the right across the same high-road beyond Hal towards Leau. The Austrians had 39,000 men, the French 45,000. The Archduke Charles commanded the right of the advanced guard, Clairfayt the left, which was covered by the little Gette, and the villages of Oberwinden, Neerwinden, and Mittelwinden; the village of Leau, on the extreme right, was not occupied.

Dumouriez's plan of attack was based on the supposition that the enemy's chief strength was on the right, covering the road by which he drew his supplies; hence he determined to throw all his strength against the left. He formed his army in eight columns: three under Valence on the right, two under the Duc de Chartres on the centre, and three more commanded by Miranda on the left. One of Valence's columns was to outflank Oberwinden, the second was to attack it by the front, the third to attack Neerwinden. When these attacks had succeeded, Valence was to swing his whole corps round, pivoting on his left, and take a new position on the flank of the enemy, facing the high-road. The Duc de Chartres was then to attack the right and left of Neerwinden with his two columns. On the left, Miranda was to thrust in two columns between the road and the right of the Austrians, while the third was to occupy Leau on the right of the village of Oberwinden.

The village and the heights above Mittelwinden were at first carried by the French, but were again lost, and were the subject of a fierce dispute throughout the day. Clairfayt met this attack with vigour, and soon recaptured Oberwinden, while Valence's third column, having taken Neerwinden easily, through a misunderstanding again relinquished it to the Austrians. The Duc de Chartres again seized it for the French; but the Austrians being strongly reinforced, and supported by a concentric fire of artillery, the French were once more driven out. Dumouriez now in person directed a fresh attack upon Neerwinden with the whole of his right; but, finding it strongly defended, he was compelled to fall back and reform his line a hundred paces to the rear. He was now sharply handled by the Austrian cavalry, which in its turn was repulsed. This ended the battle on the right, where, however, the French held their ground, and were prepared to renew the attack on the following day.

But matters had not gone so well upon their left. The

Prince of Saxe-Coburg, seeing that the French had concentrated their efforts against his left, adopted a similar design against the same flank of the enemy. It was a dangerous manœuvre, as success on the side of Oberwinden would have exposed the Austrian right more dangerously the more they prospered. Nevertheless, very early in the day Miranda's two columns had been easily and completely routed by the Archduke Charles, who was greatly superior to him in numbers. Fortunately for Dumouriez, this success was not followed up by any movement of the victorious columns upon the centre and right of the French, which they would have taken completely in flank. Dumouriez knew nothing of Miranda's failure, except that fire ceased in that direction soon after noon. He supposed this meant that Miranda's columns had gained the position in front of him, and not that they were in full retreat. Accordingly, he spent the evening before the village of Neerwinden, and only at nightfall, when his suspicions had developed into real alarm, did he ride across to hear what had happened. Finding the Austrian hussars in occupation of the bridge of Orsmael to his left, and Miranda in Tirlemont, he now gave hurried instructions to take up a position upon the heights before the great Gette, so as to secure the retreat of his right and centre, which were still surrounded by the victorious enemy, and had the river in their rear. This ended the Battle of Neerwinden.

Dumouriez has been rightly blamed for massing his principal force against the strongest part of the Austrian position, while he weakened his left unduly, and exposed it to defeat by superior numbers. He should rather have endeavoured to turn a flank, the left for preference, so as to have threatened the Austrian communications. But fortune was this time against him, and he had no alternative with his beaten army but to issue instructions for a general retreat. Next day, covered by Dampierre, he withdrew his right and centre across the little Gette, and occupied the position between Goidsenhoven and Hackenhoven. That night he crossed the great Gette to the heights of Cumlich, behind Tirlemont. These movements were executed in good order, and on the 20th he continued his retreat.

Dumouriez's idea now was to form a line of posts, extending from the mouth of the Meuse through Antwerp, Courtrai, Tournay, Mons, and Namur, and await reinforcements within it. The Austrians continued to press his rear, and there was a skirmish between them and the French at Louvain on the 22nd, on which day Dumouriez commenced to treat with the Austrian General Mack, with whom it was agreed that the French should be permitted to retire behind Brussels without being actively pursued. Hostilities were still continued, however, as this convention was not very generally known. On the 25th Dumouriez was at Brussels, and on the 26th he left it. General Harville abandoned Namur and retreated on Maubeuge, while the Army of Holland was brought back to Courtrai. Dumouriez is described as being in a state of violent agitation; his high hopes were shattered, his ambitious designs frustrated by his recent defeats, his popularity was on the wane, and the Jacobins doubted his good faith. Yet he dared to think still of turning his arms against the Government of his country, and in a second interview with Mack, openly avowed his hostility to the National Convention. He was now to all intents and purposes a traitor, and the arrangement entered into with Mack was distinctly treasonable. It was settled between the two generals that Dumouriez should evacuate Belgium and march upon Paris; the Austrian army was to back him up, but without invading France, and the strong places in Belgium were to be held by mixed garrisons, partly of Austrians and partly of French. This treachery was suspected, although not positively known. Two representatives of the people, Danton and another, had already been sent to Dumouriez to demand explanation of an intemperate letter addressed by the general to the Convention, and Danton's report, which was handed in on the 31st of March, declared that they had no doubt of the general's treasonable machinations. Four other emissaries came back possessed of the same opinion, and at length the Convention dispatched six Commissioners to summon Dumouriez to its bar. Meanwhile, Dumouriez had taken up a position intermediate between Lille, Condé, and Valenciennes, which he hoped to overawe. The regular troops and the artillery were said to be on his side, but the national volunteers were against him. On the 31st of March, six of the latter appeared in his tent with the words "The Republic or Death" chalked on their hats, and resolved, as it seemed, to take the general into custody. Dumouriez promptly arrested them, and feeling that it was time to act, sent one general to seize Lille, and another to secure Valenciennes. Both projects failed, and on the 1st of April, Dumouriez moved to St. Amand, where the day following the Commissioners from the Convention found him, surrounded by his staff, and supported by a strong body of Austrian cavalry. The Commissioners insisted upon Dumouriez's immediate submission to the authority of the Convention. He stoutly refused, and they declared him suspended from his command and under arrest. "This is a little too much," cried Dumouriez, calling in a detachment of Austrian hussars, by whom the Commissioners were made prisoners and sent as hostages to the Austrian head-quarters. The news of this arrest greatly agitated the French army, but Dumouriez still seemed to think the bulk of it was on his side. He passed freely to and fro between his own camp and that of the Austrians, a proceeding highly distasteful to his own men, although a great portion of the French line remained faithful to him to the last.

On the 4th of April, having narrowly escaped death at the hands of a hostile body of volunteers, he spent the night with the Prince of Saxe-Coburg, drafting a proclamation to the French army, announcing their alliance to give France a constitutional king. Next day, Dumouriez, followed by a troop of Austrian dragoons, rode into the camp of Maulde. He was received with loud murmurs, and passing on to St. Amand, learnt that the artillery had risen against him, and that whole divisions were rallying round Dampierre at Valenciennes. The plot, in a word, had completely failed, and Dumouriez saw at once that all was lost. Followed by Colonel Thouvenot, the Duc de Chartres, the two Mesdemoiselles Fernig, and a few others, he returned to the Austrian camp; and " thus ended," says Jomini, " the stormy career of a man to whom it would be unfair to deny talent, varied knowledge, strong character, and who did good service for France in 1792." We must not judge Dumouriez by ordinary rules. He was carried away by ambitious passions, at an epoch when heads were easily turned. He misjudged the political situation in France, his strategical operations were constantly false, except in the Argonne, but it may be taken for granted that in ordinary times he would have proved a good minister and a capable commander.

The remainder of Dumouriez's life was spent as an exile from his native land. He lived principally in England, where he died in 1823, at the advanced age of eighty-four.

CHAPTER VI.

HOCHE.—I.

EARLY CAREER.

THERE was a young soldier serving in Dumouriez's army when it was shaken with doubts as to which part it should take in the general's quarrel with the Convention. His name was Lazare Hoche, and he was at that time a simple captain, acting as aide-de-camp to General Leveneur, who commanded the camp at Maulde. A staunch Republican, strongly imbued with new ideas, Hoche was unswervingly loyal to the Convention; and it may be gathered from his language, a day or two after Dumouriez's defection, that he had contributed largely to the decision made by the troops.

Hoche's determined attitude singled him out as a suitable messenger to carry the details of what had occurred to the Convention. Arrived at Paris, the young man was closely interrogated by the leading statesmen of the day; he was asked by one of them, Couthon, to give his views upon the defence of the frontier, and the report he drew up is the more interesting, because it contains the first enunciation of the principle that victory must be sought in manœuvring in masses, instead of frittering away strong forces in small detachments at many points. The firmness, sound sense, and abundant intelligence of this young man, marked him out for rapid advancement. He was, indeed, one of the first to benefit by the great changes introduced by the Revolution in the French military system, and was destined to be promoted within a few months from a subordinate grade to the rank of general commanding-in-chief the Army of the Moselle. Brought to the surface in these days of universal chaos and confusion, he owed it to his own natural talents, his indomitable energy, his great force of character, and his unfaltering devotion to his country, that he became one of the most prominent personages in the revolutionary epoch. But in order to fully appreciate this extraordinary man, " general, organiser, administrator, politician, statesman, who displayed all the attributes of greatness, and who when he died was only twenty-nine," we must trace him from his early days long antecedent to the date when he obtained rank and command.

Hoche was of obscure origin ; his father was a kennel-keeper to the King at Versailles. Born on the 24th of June, 1768, he received a scanty education, and at the age of fifteen entered the royal stables as groom. But seized with an ardent desire to see the world, he enlisted as he thought into a colonial corps, only to find that the recruiting sergeant had deceived him, and that he was engaged to serve in the French guards. He seems to have taken naturally to his military exercises ; he soon passed his drill, and being consumed with a constant desire for self-improvement, he spent every spare hour in manual labour ; he dug in the gardens, drew water from the wells, wove caps for sale, and laboured incessantly to obtain funds for the purchase of books which he read and studied the whole night through. An eager, ambitious youth, ready to work and play, and on occasion quarrel. To his dying day he bore upon his forehead the scar of an ugly gash received in a youthful duel. Tall, erect, of martial bearing and distinguished appearance, he was so fine a specimen of a soldier that the story goes, some lady of the Court singled him out in the ranks with the remark, "There is the making of a general in that fine young man!"

Although the guards sided with the people at the outbreak of the Revolution, Hoche was not present with his regiment at the capture of the Bastille. But with his comrades he was afterwards engaged in acting as police in Paris; they mounted guard over Louis XVI. at Versailles, and frequently helped to keep order in the theatres at night. He was now sergeant-major, and the company to which he belonged was so remarkable for the steadiness of its drill, that the War Minister, Servan, rewarded Hoche with a commission in the regiment of Rouergue. He served with this regiment under Dumouriez in the defence of the Argonne, and greatly distinguished himself at the retreat from Grandpré, where he helped to rally the troops fleeing from the stampede at Vaux. He was present at the Cannonade of Valmy, and later, at the Battle of Jemappes. When the Austrians again assumed the offensive, and drove the French out of Aldenhoven, he was entrusted with the withdrawal of the artillery and stores from Liége. He accomplished this difficult task in the very teeth of the enemy, without losing a single gun, and so gained the approval of General Leveneur, who witnessed his intrepidity, and made him his aide-de-camp on the spot. From this moment dated a close intimacy between the general and his young *protégé.* General Leveneur, who was a man of good family, although he had adopted the revolutionary ideas, speedily became attached to Hoche, being much impressed by his strength of character, his quick intelligence, and his firm will. He constituted himself Hoche's mentor, taught him the manners of good society, and practised him in writing military essays, to give him a facility in expressing his ideas, thus preparing the young man for the high functions to which he might yet be called, and for which he already displayed great natural aptitude. Hoche was with Leveneur at the Battle of Neerwinden, where that general commanded one of Valence's columns, that employed in the attack on Oberwinden. Hoche had two horses killed under him, and was himself wounded in the fight; yet he was again on duty within a day or two, covering the retreat of the French across the Dyle. Here he had another horse killed under him, and he led the troops on foot.

His attitude when Dumouriez deserted has been already mentioned, and his visit to Paris. For a moment Hoche's fortunes were clouded, and he was arrested as the friend of his general, Leveneur, who had fallen under the displeasure of the Jacobins. But his patriotism was too clearly shown by the memoir he had drawn up at Couthon's request. The reading of this document before the Committee of Public Safety gained him not only immediate enlargement, but selection for active and responsible employment. Hoche was now promoted to the rank of major, and appointed adjutant-general to the garrison defending Dunkirk, a fortress at this time hardly pressed by the Duke of York, at the head of 40,000 men. It was insufficiently held with some 7,000 men, when twice that number would hardly have sufficed to occupy its extensive lines. Its fortifications were incomplete, the garrison was demoralised by recent defeats, while the sailors of the flotilla of boats entrusted with the defence of the sea front, had mutinied on the appearance of the enemy and taken refuge in the harbour. Hoche at once gave a new energy to the defence; his courageous spirit was communicated to

General Souham, who nominally commanded, although Hoche was really supreme, and under his active control the works were strengthened, discipline restored, the sailors returned to their duty, and the garrison gained fresh life.

"The place shall be burnt rather than surrendered," writes Hoche to the Committee of Public Safety. A few days later he writes that, although reinforcements were needed, the garrison could wait. Yet Dunkirk was in sore straits at the time. While the Duke of York attacked by the sea front, Marshal Freytag, with another army at Hondschoote, covered the siege. On the 5th of September, however, the French generals Houchard and Jourdan, advanced to fight Freytag, whilst Hoche made a vigorous sortie upon the Duke of York. Freytag was beaten back on Furness, and had the Duke of York been more vigorously pressed by Houchard, he must have laid down his arms. He just managed, however, to beat a hasty retreat, and was compelled to raise the siege of Dunkirk. For his gallantry and fortitude Hoche was rewarded with the rank of general of brigade. Dunkirk continued his headquarters, and from this point he was directed, about the end of October, to recapture Furness and Ostend. His first attack was unsuccessful, and he was on the point of renewing it when he was suddenly called away to other and more important functions. The Committee of Public Safety, acting under the advice of Carnot, had advanced him to the rank of general of division, and appointed him, at the early age of twenty-six, to the command of the Army of the Moselle.

Carnot was, at this time, practically the military dictator of France. When the Committee of Public Safety had been called into existence by the defeat of Neerwinden, it found itself without the special qualifications to direct and control the vast military forces it soon gathered to its hand. Carnot, a simple captain of engineers, but a scientific officer of acknowledged reputation, and a staunch patriot, was presently joined to the committee to act as its professional adviser. He speedily became *de facto* irresponsible and almost autocratic War Minister. France, at the moment, was in supreme danger. Victorious foes hemmed her in on every side, threatening her with complete subjugation and dismemberment. Her frontiers had been violated at many points; some of the principal fortresses on the north had already fallen; the west was ablaze with the fierce—seemingly unquenchable—insurrection of La Vendée; Toulon was besieged and must shortly surrender; Mayence and Valenciennes were in the hands of the enemy; Lyons had closed its gates against the Republicans, and was a focus of civil war. The crisis was desperate; only the most summary measures could save France. The nation must rise to the occasion. A demand for a *levée en masse* was heard on every side. The Committee of Public Safety caught up the echo and gave it legal, tangible form. A decree was quickly passed and promulgated, putting into permanent requisition the services of every Frenchman until the enemy was expelled from France. Every living soul was to lend his aid. The able-bodied were to go out and fight; the married men were to forge weapons and organise supplies; the women were to make uniforms and tents, and nurse the wounded; children were to scrape lint and make bandages; the aged and infirm were to be carried into public places to excite the warlike spirit by speech and gesture. All public buildings were to be converted into barracks; horses, saddlery, and harness belonging to private persons were to be pressed into the public service; the cellars even of private houses were to be searched for natural deposits of that saltpetre so urgently necessary for the manufacture of gunpowder, the chief sinew of war.

France responded nobly to the call. Some idea of the

exertions made will be obtained from the figures shewing the rapid growth of the French forces in 1793. These in February that year, were barely 200,000 strong. In May that number was exactly doubled. On the 15th of July the total had reached half a million. By December it was increased to 628,000, and by the autumn of 1794 there were a million of men under arms. The organisation of these vast legions fell upon Carnot. The great army thus hastily got together was still an inchoate, heterogeneous mass of human beings, without any systematic military organisation. The *personnel* was of the most varied character; old soldiers and conscripts stood side by side in the ranks, next volunteers raised under various conditions and at various times, and amidst the *débris* of foreign legions and bodies of irregulars. The great bulk of the infantry was still formed in battalions, some of which consisted of veteran troops, many more were composed entirely of newly enlisted recruits. The uniforms differed throughout the army. Some regiments of the line still wore the white coats which had been the fashion under the kings of France; the new levies were partly in peasants' blouses, partly in the blue and red—the new Republican colours. Carnot first introduced uniformity in clothing and appearance. He too established a new regimental organisation, and first formed the demi-brigade, consisting of three battalions; he adopted a new system of tactics, and was strongly in favour of manœuvring with the heavy columns, intended primarily to give the young French troops confidence, and subsequently employed always as the surest formation for tactical success. Carnot did yet more. He reformed and reconstituted his own arm, the engineers; he gathered together the numerous independent companies of volunteer gunners into an admirable and compact body of artillery; he managed, too, to improvise a tolerable force of cavalry. Horses were very scarce, but his agents purchased largely abroad, and others were obtained by urgent requisitions peremptorily enforced at home. Possessed of no small administrative capacity, he laboured hard to provide for the equipment and supply of the troops. But the civil departments of the War Office could be only developed slowly, and for many a day to come the French armies in the field continued to be badly fed and indifferently clothed. Carnot was indefatigable, and his self-sacrificing, unwearied efforts gained him the approval even of his enemies. His organisation and manipulation of the armies of the Republic has, very properly, been deemed one of the most astonishing feats in history. The great end was only attained by the almost superhuman exertions of the man whom Napoleon styled "the most sincere, honest, and indefatigable spirit that figured in the revolutionary epoch." Opinions are divided, however, as to Carnot's qualifications as a leader of men. Napoleon, while conceding him all the virtues of a great citizen, declared that in military science his ideas were false. Jomini, on the other hand, thought that Carnot's instructions to the generals commanding armies—and he personally addressed them all—displayed no little military genius. "Had Carnot been more practised in the field," says the same authority, "and had he learnt to take a wider view of strategical operations, he might have claimed rank against the great captains of the world; as it was, he at least rivalled Louvois in the art of conducting war from the closet."

CHAPTER VII.

JOURDAN.

EARLY LIFE AND SERVICES DOWN TO WATTIGNIES, OCTOBER, 1793.

THE various campaigns conducted by the generals of the young Republic are much intermixed, and often overlap each other in point of time. It was necessary, therefore, to elect whether historical or biographical continuity should have the preference. The latter might give greater unity and completeness to the portraiture, but it would complicate the narrative, it would entail needless repetitions, and might militate against a clear exposition or ready comprehension of the operations in progress. I have decided, therefore, in the present memoir to follow the sequence of events, and trace the progress of the French arms from year to year, as they failed or prospered under the different leaders whose lives have been selected for illustration.

Before accompanying Hoche to the Moselle, then, we must deal with movements which took place at an earlier date, in 1793. While Hoche was still the active spirit of the defence of Dunkirk, another general, his senior in years, but also young, was gaining earlier laurels against the enemies of France. This was Jean Baptiste Jourdan, who in

September, 1793, succeeded Houchard in command of the
Army of the North. Some account of the life and services of
this new general, whose advancement was as rapid as that of
Hoche, will appropriately follow here. Jourdan, like Hoche,
was a man of the people ; he was born of bourgeois parents at
Limoges in 1762, and at his father's death while still in his
teens, he was put to serve behind the counter by his uncles, who
were silk-mercers at Lyons. Young Jourdan chafed at the
tyranny of his relations, and, when barely seventeen, enlisted
in the regiment Auxerrois, which he soon afterwards accompanied to America, where he served for some six years. In 1784
he was invalided on account of the weakness of his constitution, and returning to France, he paid a first visit to Lyons ;
but his cross-grained uncles refused to take him back. Thence
he passed on to Limoges, hoping to find friends in his native
place. On his way he called in at a garrison town to see an
old comrade, and presenting himself at the gate, a seedy, sickly
youth in threadbare uniform, he overheard a stalwart trooper
say : " That poor devil of a foot soldier will never wear the
breeches of a Marshal of France."

Jourdan, in after days, when he had achieved this, the
highest grade in the military profession, delighted to repeat
the story and laugh over the falsity of the trooper's predic-
tion. At Limoges he found employment in a linendraper's,
and presently gained his employer's daughter in marriage.
He now started on his own account, and opened a small
mercer's shop, where for some years he presided, displaying a special aptitude for business, and always conducting
himself with great probity. He seems to have imbibed ideas
of personal freedom while serving in America, and he eagerly
embraced the revolutionary cause in 1790. He took an
active part in the organisation of the National Guard at
Limoges, and, at the time when veteran soldiers were scarce,

his previous services readily gained him the rank of lieutenant of chasseurs.

In 1792, when the invasion of France stirred the patriotism of the people, Jourdan was appointed to the command of one of the newly raised battalions of volunteers. With this he served in the Army of the North, and took part in Dumouriez's campaign against Belgium, being present at both Jemappes and Neerwinden. He soon distinguished himself, not alone by his fortitude and coolness in the heat of the fight, but by his steadiness, subordination, and love of discipline ; somewhat rare virtues in those days, and greatly esteemed whenever they were encountered. These solid qualities speedily gained him promotion, and in 1793 he passed straight from chef-de-bataillon to the rank of general of brigade. Two months later, he was appointed general of division, and was under Houchard when that general advanced to raise the siege of Dunkirk. Jourdan showed great enterprise in the combat of Rexpœde, where he forestalled the enemy and nearly captured Freytag, who commanded the Austrian forces. In the action of Hondschoote Jourdan commanded the centre, and carrying the village of that name, forced the enemy to retire. He was wounded severely at the moment of his success, and he was not engaged in the operations which immediately followed. He thus escaped the censure which brought the unfortunate Houchard to the guillotine ; a cruel fate, the punishment not of retreat, but of winning an important victory, without completely destroying the enemy. Houchard's downfall was Jourdan's elevation. Carnot, who was present with the army at Hondschoote, had formed a high opinion of Jourdan's military capacity. Satisfied that the French Army of the North needed a young and vigorous, no less than a skilful leader, he recommended Jourdan to the Committee of Public

Safety for supreme command. Carnot's influence was naturally great with a young man like Jourdan, whom he had himself raised to command. Hence, when he pressed upon the general the necessity of submitting some plan of operations, Jourdan yielded, although he himself wished for a short breathing space to improve the organisation of his army. But the Committee of Public Safety was eager to take the offensive. Jourdan therefore proposed to advance from Lille on one side, and Maubeuge on the other; and the plan was still under consideration when the Austrians solved the difficulty, by crossing the Sambre and advancing in force to invest Maubeuge. The Prince of Saxe-Coburg had under his command an army of 65,000 men and 40 guns; 15,000 would have been sufficient to mask Maubeuge, and with the balance he would have been strong enough to crush the French in the open field.

Coburg, however, threw all his strength upon Maubeuge, and the place was in great danger. It was defended by 20,000 men, part in the garrison under General Ferrand, and part in an entrenched camp under General Chancel. Its fall would have given the Austrians a new base, and would have opened another short and direct road upon Paris. It was essential, therefore, for the French to raise the siege. Jourdan, fully alive to this, collected an army of 45,000 men from the camps of Cassel, Lille, and Gavarelle. He left as many more to cover the frontier as far as Dunkirk. He could, besides, call upon the Army of the Ardennes, although he was never reinforced from this side with more than 5,000 men. The danger of Maubeuge brought Carnot in person to Jourdan's side; he was accompanied by another representative of the people, Duquesnoy, and the three agreed to push on at once to Avesnes. The advance of the French decided Coburg to draw the Duke of York towards him from the Lys to the Sambre, and Clairfayt was directed, with his corps of observation, 25,000 strong, to oppose the progress of the enemy. On the 14th of October, Jourdan and Carnot reconnoitred the Austrian position, and found them occupying a line of wooded heights reaching from Wattignies on their left, to St. Remy and Monceau on the right. Clairfayt was in the centre, with about 13,000 men, and an advanced guard was pushed forward to St. Waast. The wisest course for the French general to pursue, would have been to throw his whole weight upon Wattignies, which was weakly held by General Terzy, crush him, and forming a junction with the defending force in Maubeuge, fall with the 60,000 men thus united upon whatever forces he might find before him. Jourdan seems, however, to have been loath to let go of the Avesnes road, which was on his left, and which was his line of communication with Guise, and besides, the direct road to Paris. He feared to be outflanked on this side and driven back on the Ardennes. Labouring under this apprehension, he preferred to attack by both right and left. It has been asserted that these tactics were forced upon Jourdan by Carnot, and it is certain that Carnot was very partial to the attack by both wings. Jourdan in his memoirs declares that he alone designed and carried out the operations which relieved Maubeuge, but it seems probable that the general yielded to the personal influence of a powerful person like Carnot, who was at that moment the supreme chief of all the Republican armies. Whoever is responsible, there can be no doubt that the plan of battle decided upon was faulty, and deserved to fail.

At daybreak on the 15th, the French columns advanced to the attack. They consisted mainly of new levies; the ranks were filled with recruits, many of them bare-footed and in blouses, others still wore the wooden sabots of the peasant, and many carried aloft on their bayonets big loaves that they had brought with them from their village homes. Their only military knowledge was in handling a musket, but all alike were fired with wild enthusiasm. They sang songs as they marched to the front, some preferring the "Ca Ira" and the "Carmagnole," others the "Marseillaise," and all alike shouting "Vive la République!" On the left, Fromentin's division soon drove in the Austrian advanced guard on Monceau; on the right, Duquesnoy, passing through the woods, forced the enemy out of Dimont and Dime, and approached Wattignies. This movement of the wings accomplished, Bolland in the centre assaulted Dourlers, which was strongly occupied by the enemy, who held his reserves behind it, and a great body of cavalry. The attack was made with tremendous spirit, but the enemy rallied on its reserves; the Austrian cavalry charged the French left flank, and the attacking columns fell back in disorder. Carnot was obstinately resolved to carry the centre, and he ordered a fresh advance; but the second attack was not more successful than the first. It was unsupported, too, on the left, for Fromentin had wandered away to his left into the open country towards Bertaimont, where he was promptly routed by the Austrian horse. The right had remained inactive before Wattignies, and thus ended the day. That night a council of war was held, and it was decided to renew the battle next morning by throwing the whole weight upon one flank.

Some say that Jourdan was for reinforcing the left, and Carnot the right wing; the latter was clearly the proper course to pursue, for it was on the right, opposite Wattignies, that the key of the Austrian position lay. Happily for the French arms, an attack by the right in force was chosen as the principal operation of the following day. Early on the 16th,

Duquesnoy was reinforced with 7,000 men. As dawn broke, the right wing, 22,000 strong, was collected opposite Wattignies. A thick fog obscured the landscape, and Coburg knew nothing of the movements behind this impenetrable screen. Believing, from the persistence of the French attacks upon his centre, that this was the point most menaced, he made no dispositions to strengthen his left, where Terzy, with insufficient force, had now to make head against a concentrated attack. Fromentin and Bolland, on the left and centre, were to make strong demonstrations from their front about the same time that Jourdan and Carnot, opposite Wattignies, prepared for the principal attack. The fog lifted about 1 p.m., when the Austrians saw for the first time strong columns of French advancing upon their left. The assault was twice checked by a heavy fire; but the third attack, led in person by Jourdan and Carnot, drove the Austrians at the point of the bayonet from the village to the heights of Glarus. Behind here the Austrians made a last stand, and the French were nearly routed, through the misconduct of Gratien's brigade, the flank of which became exposed to the attack of a large body of cavalry, sent at the eleventh hour by Coburg to secure his left. Carnot and Duquesnoy promptly rallied it; Gratien, its leader, was cashiered on the spot, and the brigade, resuming place in the line, pressed forward to share in the final charge, which now completed the French success on this side. The centre and left had also prospered, and only on the extreme right, where the forces coming from Philippeville and belonging to the Army of the Ardennes, had retreated before the Austrian General Haddick, had Coburg's forces encountered anything but disastrous defeat.

The Austrian Commander-in-Chief, although joined by the Duke of York, now felt that his position was critical. He would be greatly outnumbered if Jourdan effected a junction with the garrison, and he prudently decided to withdraw at once behind the Sambre. His defeat was no doubt a surprise to him. With easy assurance he had waited attack, and so fully did he believe in the strength of his position that he is said to have declared: "The French are great Republicans; if they can drive me out of this I will become a Republican too!" But he found it impossible to withstand the reckless courage of his assailants, and afterwards admitted that the French fought like madmen, "enragés." But the victory of Wattignies ought to have been far more decisive. Through some misunderstanding, or a want of enterprise, the garrison of Maubeuge did not attempt to co-operate with Jourdan. Had Ferrand and Chancel issued forth to attack Coburg's retreating columns, the Austrian army would have been annihilated before it could recross the Sambre. The whole weight of this negligence fell upon Chancel, who was accused of treason, summoned to Paris, tried, and promptly guillotined, after the encouraging practice of those days. The victory of Wattignies, followed as it was by the immediate relief of Maubeuge, was hailed with acclamations of joy throughout France. It delivered the country from its most pressing danger, and entitled Carnot and Jourdan to the gratitude of their countrymen. The Committee of Public Safety were not satisfied, however, and wished to follow up their success by a winter campaign against the Allies in Belgium. Their forces were scattered for some time after Wattignies, and Jourdan might have overwhelmed Clairfayt, at least, had he pushed forward upon Charleroi. But he was ignorant of the exact position of his enemies, and, after hesitating for several days, lost his opportunity. He really had no heart for further operations just then. His army greatly needed rest and reorganisation. He shrank from a winter campaign with ill-armed and poorly-clothed men, many of them undrilled; hence he advised the maintenance of a cautious defensive until the spring, and proposed to spend the winter in the reorganisation of the army. This advice was eventually adopted by the Committee of Public Safety, but with a very bad grace. Jourdan's army was withdrawn to Guise, there to occupy an entrenched camp, while the drill and discipline of the new levies was proceeded with. Jourdan himself was recalled to Paris, and for a moment was in danger of losing his head. The order for his arrest was actually issued, but, through Carnot and Duquesnoy, his two friends, he escaped with the loss of his rank and command. He retired to Limoges, where he quietly resumed his trade as a linendraper; and the only vengeance he permitted himself was the placing prominently at the end of his shop his uniform of a general officer and the sword he had worn at Wattignies.

Jourdan was succeeded in the command of the Army of the North by Pichegru, who had recently been actively engaged with the Army of the Rhine, in conjunction with Hoche. The operations of these two generals, which were proceeded with in the winter, must now be described.

CHAPTER VIII.

HOCHE.—II.

WHEN Hoche took command of the so-called Army of the
Moselle, it occupied the line of the Sarre. It was in a state
of utter disorganisation, spread over a frontier of seventy
or eighty miles, without strength or consistence, and scattered about in small bodies, contrary to all military rules.
Regiments and corps were mixed up anyhow, and none was
certain to which division or brigade it belonged. The men
scarcely knew their commanders; all seemed broken
down with disasters, and were as destitute as they were
disheartened. They were nearly in rags, many were shoeless,
and starvation was so often the rule, that the men broke out
into terrible excesses, and pillaged the neighbourhood far
and near. Hoche's despatches to Paris are full of the deplorable condition of his army. "I want shoes and shirts,"
he writes. Again: "We are very short of hay; the horses
of the artillery and cavalry are reduced to half rations. The
soldiers of the Republic ask only bayonets and bread." "I
shed tears of blood," he cries in the middle of his campaign,
"to see myself checked for want of ammunition. My men

are brave and well-behaved; but, in the name of the Republic, send clothes and equipment to its defenders." But Hoche was not satisfied with urgent appeals to others for support, he himself strove hard to remedy the evils from which his army suffered. He commenced by restoring discipline with a strong hand; in a stirring appeal to his troops, he promised them speedy relief from their distress, while by instituting a system of forced contributions from the district he provided for their immediate needs. He put the soldiers upon their honour, and implored them to protect their good name by driving from amongst them the cowards who brought them into disrepute by their excesses. They were warned that they must make great sacrifices, but told that they were certain to succeed, if only determined to conquer.

Hoche never doubted his soldiers; with his officers he had more trouble. Within a day or two of his arrival on the Sarre, he laments his being so badly supported. Pitiful intrigues prevailed throughout the army to a despairing extent. He could not trust the officers nearest to him in rank; they were always working against him, he said. But he never despaired. The seniors were, if necessary, boldly replaced by young and intelligent juniors; an entirely new staff was selected. By this happy combination of vigour and eloquent entreaty, he quickly got the army into good working order, and at last he writes: "The machine begins to turn, very soon it will be in full blast."

The Committee of Public Safety had in Hoche a general after its own heart; it could not be more anxious to drive the enemy from France than he was. His unflagging administrative energy was only equalled by his desperate eagerness to engage. His ardour is to be seen in his language to his generals. To one he writes: "When you get your orders, swoop down like an eagle on

its prey." To another : " Attack, comrade, attack, and strike
the enemy. I depend on you." Again : " Do not wait for the
signal to commence ; push on vigorously as far as you can
go." "March forward ! Don't you know that there are
still guns to be captured ? " " Remember that, with bayonets
and bread, we can conquer the whole of the brigands
of Europe." "I forbid you," he writes to General Vincent,
"to correspond with the enemy otherwise than with round
shot and steel. The letter you sent to me yesterday begs to
be informed who commands this army. I will give the
answer, myself, in the field."

It is to be regretted that such spirited outbursts should
have been very frequently disfigured by the coarse language
that was just then so greatly in vogue. At first many
questionable expressions flowed freely from Hoche's pen ;
but he readily listened to the correction of his old friend and
mentor, General Leveneur, who, from his retirement to
Normandy, upbraided the young general for his license, and
begged him to write in his own firm and elegant style. With
such a chief, the Army of the Moselle rapidly recovered confidence. It believed thoroughly in Hoche. The estimation in
which he was held by his troops is well expressed by a young
officer, one of his staff, who about this time thus describes
his new chief :

" Be of good heart, defenders of our country ! We shall
speedily emerge from our torpor. Our new general is young,
like the Revolution ; vigorous, like the people. His is not
the limited vision of the man he succeeds. His glance is
bold and far-seeing, like that of an eagle. Be of good
heart, my friends, he will lead us as Frenchmen should be
led."

Hoche speedily justified this glowing encomium ; a week
or two sufficed to change completely the spirit and condition

of the army. He joined about the 1st of October, yet on the 17th of November he was ready to advance; all the necessary measures had been completed on that date. He writes :

"If I can believe my presentiments, the best cause will triumph. I could scarcely survive a defeat; but if I have that misfortune, I should wish my bleeding corpse sent to Paris and exhibited to the people, to stir them to make one last effort, before which all tyrants should succumb."

The winter campaign now resolved upon was intended to strike a blow at the Austrians and Prussians in turn, and raise the siege of Landau. The allies seemed to attach no importance to acting in combination; they kept their forces separated by considerable distances, and operating on different lines. The Duke of Brunswick, who commanded the Prussian army, was in position about Blies Castel, on the western slopes of the Vosges, and communicated with Wurmser through Deux Ponts and the Pass of Pirmasens. Wurmser, with the Austrians, was between the eastern slopes and the Rhine, in front of the lines of Weissenberg. The Duke of Brunswick was about to go into winter quarters; but he wished first to seize the fortress of Bitche, which commands one of the four passes through the Vosges. He failed in this just before he heard that the French were on the move, and he resolved therefore to fall back at once on Kayserslautern; a retreat accomplished without Wurmser's knowledge. Wurmser, finding his right uncovered, was compelled to take up a defensive position behind the Motter, his main body about Haguenau. On the 17th of November, Hoche, at the head of 35,000 men, crossed the Sarre and attacked the Prussians, who were still in position between Bisingen and the Blies. Hoche, on the right, struck at the Prussian left, as it advanced along the valley of the river;

but the attack was met by a change of front, executed by General Kalkreuth, and the French were repulsed. The French centre had made no more than a demonstration ; the left, under Ambert, wandered out of the action as far as Tholey, and was not engaged. Next day the Prussians continued to retreat, followed by the French. Hoche now occupied Blies Castel, and next day Ambert, whose flank march had disturbed the enemy as far as Trèves, rejoined the main body by Ottweiler and Neukirchen. Hoche, by no means disheartened at his first failure, determined to push on, and bearing against the extreme right of the Prussians, gain Kayserslautern. This decision was tardy, for the enemy had time to concentrate ; it must not be forgotten, however, that Hoche was only at his début as a commander in the field. He knew little of the country or of the troops, and being but imperfectly informed of the movements of the Prussians, he had unavoidably lost much time, between the 22nd and the 27th, by misdirected marches. He had wasted time, too, in searching for Brunswick towards Pirmasens and beyond ; after which, finding no trace of his enemy, he had fallen back on Deux Ponts, whence he decided to advance on Kayserslautern.

On the 27th, Ambert was again sent off to make a long detour to the left by the Potzberg on Otterberg. Hoche, with the centre, followed as far as Kibeberg, he then moved on Rodenbach, while the right, under Taponier, marched direct by Landstuhl on Kayserslautern. Brunswick's position was very extended ; his centre was at Kayserslautern, while his left reached as far as Anweiler, to join the Austrian right. He was strong enough, however, to disdain Hoche's attack, and he had two excellent lines of retreat. But Ambert's march made him uneasy, and he sent Kalkreuth, therefore, to hold Otterberg.

On the 28th, Ambert, after a most difficult march, reached

the Lauter, and was soon engaged with Kalkreuth. He was checked, but again advanced, to be once more repulsed, while Hoche, having lost his way, was unable to give any assistance with the centre. Taponier on the right was not engaged. At night Hoche withdrew behind the Lauter, but resolved to renew the fight next morning, supporting the left with the main body.

Accordingly, on the 29th, Ambert was sent round by the left, while Hoche assailed the redoubts in front of Kayserslautern. His columns, decimated by a murderous fire, failed to make any impression, and they presently retired. Ambert, meanwhile, wandering amidst thick woods, had taken no part in the action, and he was recalled to the centre, which he fortunately rejoined in the night, thus escaping destruction from a Prussian division which marched unexpectedly that night from Lautereck on the right to Ponnaye. On the 30th, Hoche began a fresh action ; he attacked the road again in force, but was beaten back, while on his right Taponier had much difficulty in holding his own. Brunswick being now reinforced on his right, Hoche found himself outnumbered and outflanked, and was compelled to retire. Ambert covered the retreat, which was executed in good order, and without interference.

Hoche now fell back and occupied posts at Pirmasens, Hornbach, and Deux Ponts. He had undoubtedly been defeated, in spite of the most strenuous efforts to win ; he might well anticipate reproof and recall, possibly a shameful death, but the Committee of Public Safety did not withdraw their confidence from him. Hoche was a staunch Republican, and Carnot was his friend. Carnot wrote him, a letter at once wise, forcible, and dignified, in which he declared that the Committee did not judge men by results, but by the efforts displayed to secure success. He urged the general to undertake a fresh compaign, either along the Sarre or in the valley of the Rhine, and promised him reinforcements. Hoche answered bravely to the appeal; he already realised that it was impossible to relieve Landau by Kayserslautern, and he promptly adopted another plan of operations, which promised better results, and which proved his genius for war. He saw that in his present position he greatly outflanked the Austrian right, and he determined to strike at that vigorously and at once. For this purpose he proposed to use a couple of divisions, reaching out a hand by them to Pichegru and the Army of the Rhine. This operation, excellent in itself, would have been far more decisive had Hoche employed his whole force for the purpose. He might have directed not 12,000 but 30,000 men upon Reichshoffen, and when combined with Pichegru, the French would have been strong enough to crush Wurmser completely.

While Hoche had been actively engaged against the Duke of Brunswick, the Army of the Rhine had given Wurmser no peace. That general, after the Prussian retreat upon Kayserslautern, had taken up a strongly intrenched position behind the Motter, which the French attacked repeatedly between the 24th of November and the 9th of December. On the latter date the Austrians, who had succeeded in holding their own, were compelled to draw in their line of defence, and the French left at Pfaffenhofen had touch of Taponier's columns. This general, forming Hoche's advanced right, had been engaged with Wurmser in the valley of Niederbrunn on the 8th, and having made substantial head had continued his advance. He attacked Reichshoffen on the 15th.

The Allies were now aroused to the danger which threatened their centre, and for some days past had been concerting measures to meet it; but the want of unity of command led to divided councils, and want of energy in movement. Brunswick, who might easily have forestalled Hoche's flank movement by carrying the whole of his forces from Kayserslautern towards Weissenberg, a shorter road than that which Hoche had to travel, had been satisfied to arrange with Wurmser to attack the French on the 15th. This was again postponed to the 18th, and still further delayed by stormy weather. The impetuous French, however, disdainful of the elements, made a fresh assault on Freschweiler; Wurmser was forced to throw back his right, and Brunswick at length decided to reinforce it. There were fresh conferences between the allied generals to arrange a counter attack, but their leisurely, matter-of-fact movements were speedily upset by the ardour of the young Republican general, determined at all hazards to succeed. Hoche had reinforced his advance under Taponier, on the 22nd of December. He had fallen upon the Austrian right at Werdt, and advancing under cover of the fog, with five divisions, had carried the Austrian position, captured many guns, and forced the Prussian division in support to retire. Hoche's success at Werdt compromised Wurmser's position on the Motter. The Austrian general would have been in great danger had Pichegru delivered a frontal attack while Hoche assailed the flank. But Wurmser was able to draw off without accident, and on the 24th he occupied the lines of Weissenberg. By this time the armies of the Moselle and Rhine had joined forces, and Hoche, who had been invested with the supreme command, pushed forward to strike a fresh blow before the Allies recovered self-possession. Their position extended from Lauterbourg on the Rhine to the Upper Lauter on the extreme right, which was held by the Prussians. It was intended to attack the French on the 26th of December. Hoche again forestalled them; the right wing of the Army of the Rhine attacked, and carried Lauterbourg. Messent's division, with other divisions of the centre, marched on Weissenberg, whilst the rest of the Army of the Moselle operated against the Prussian right. The French gained an easy victory, the Austrians retreated in disorder, but were saved by Brunswick, who placed himself at the head of the Austrian reserves and held Weissenberg for a time. The Austrians continued to retreat, and on the 30th they crossed the Rhine at Philippsburg, leaving the Prussians on the left bank to get back as best they could. The Duke of Brunswick after Weissenberg evacuated Kayserslautern, and retired on Mayence. Hoche might have pressed their retreat more vigorously, perhaps, but Landau was relieved, and the Palatinate was cleared of the allied troops.

Hoche was but indifferently recompensed for these achievements. He was made the victim of political intrigues, and had to bear the brunt of the schism between the civilians who, representing the executive power with the armies in the field, sought, after the manner of the old Aulic Councils, to control the operations of war. There were four of these busybodies in the Vosges; two of them members of the Committee of Public Safety, St. Just and Lebas, who had been despatched from Paris with extraordinary powers and had used them with ruthless severity. They acted with the Army of the Rhine, · and had practically superseded Lacoste and Baudot their predecessors, who transferred themselves to Hoche, and the Army of the Moselle. On the junction of the two armies, Lacoste and Baudot hastened to give the chief command to Hoche, although St. Just intended it for Pichegru. St. Just, not wishing to create dissensions at a critical moment, allowed the appointment to take effect, but under protest, and the moment Weissenberg was won despatched a special courier to Paris with the news, giving the whole credit to Pichegru, who had really done his best to ruin the operations. He had been consumed with jealousy of his young colleague, and had withheld cordial co-operation and support. Hoche made a manly appeal to him, but he did not deign to reply. "We serve the same country," wrote Hoche to Pichegru on arriving on the Sarre. "I am anxious to second you to the utmost; I have not hesitated to send you troops sufficient to enable you, with those from the Ardennes, to operate vigorously; you can count on me, then, as a friend and comrade." After Hoche's elevation to the chief command, he writes to the representatives: "The Citizen Pichegru has given me no news of himself for the last six or eight days. You know him better than I do; but he seems to me much annoyed at your having preferred me to the command." Hoche continually writes to the same effect: "I have no news of Pichegru." The Army of the Rhine would probably have done little, but for the active energy and opportune arrival of that of the Moselle. Hoche found it much disorganised, *tout en désarroi*, its chief knew little of the whereabouts of its various units, and it was so short of ammunition that Hoche had to supply it from his own limited stock. Yet it was to this army and this leader that the success of the campaign was attributed. Hoche naturally protested. He claimed loudly to be at once acknowledged as the man who had really commanded at Reichshoffen, Werdt, and Weissenberg. In a letter to the War Minister, he openly declares: "You know you have been deceived: that Pichegru was only at Werdt for half-an-hour, and that he was not at Weissenberg on the 6th, for a day later he was still at Haguenau, five-and-twenty miles to the rear." A few days later, Hoche met Pichegru, who had not the chivalry to repudiate these unmerited honours, and "apostrophised him in a way to make his blood boil. There was not even a tinge of colour in his cheeks." "What a man!" is Hoche's comment.

The truth was vindicated; but Hoche, in so sturdily defending his rights, fell into disfavour with the committee. St. Just was implacable; and he visited upon Hoche the whole responsibility for the delay to advance upon Trèves, delay caused really by Pichegru's neglect of the orders he received. As soon as Hoche had gone into winter quarters along the Sarre and the Blies, he was superseded in the command on the pretence that his services were required by the Army of Italy. It was pointed out to him that to reorganise it, and lead it to victory, would be a great and enviable task. He left the Army of the Moselle with profound regret, but in his farewell general order, he announced that the service of the Republic summoned him elsewhere. Then he prepared to throw himself, with characteristic energy, into the new duties he expected would be entrusted to him. On his arrival at Nice, even before he unbooted or changed his travelling dress, he spread out the maps of his new scene of operations, and commenced the study of the theatre of war. His military genius fixed at once upon the plains of Lombardy, as the true field of battle. "Here," he cried, "we shall most effectually measure our strength with Austria." While thus employed, General Dumerbion was announced, bringing, to Hoche's intense surprise, an order from the Committee of Public Safety to place him in arrest, and send him under safe escort to Paris.

Hoche was practically a prisoner, when the generals, who were to serve under his orders, came in to pay him their respects. They were indignant at the scurvy treatment of the victor of Weissenberg, and promised him assistance if he was disposed to fly across the frontier. But

Hoche stoutly refused, and, escorted by two gendarmes, started for Paris. He was taken straight before the Committee of Public Safety, where he saw and spoke to St. Just. "What do you want?" asked St. Just abruptly. "Justice," replied Hoche. "You will get what you deserve," was the reply, and in the same breath an order was issued to convey Hoche to the prison of the Conciergerie. He remained there calmly, expecting the worst, for nearly six months, when he was released on the fall of Robespierre. Directly he was set at liberty, he wanted to hasten to Thionville to join his young wife, a girl of humble origin, belonging to that city, whom he had romantically married the previous year. He desired, he said, to withdraw altogether from active employment; but his friends strongly combated this resolve, and persuaded him to seek fresh employment. He did so, and was appointed forthwith to command the Army of Cherbourg.

In this mission he was occupied for three years, and when it was completed by the suppression of the Chouan insurrection, and the pacification of La Vendée, he was already on the high road to fame. But before following Hoche through this eventful period of his career, it will be necessary to detail other operations which come first in point of time, and to give some account of the civil war in the west of France. It had already been in progress for nearly a year, and had afforded another young general of the Republic an opportunity of gaining distinction. Some account of Marceau should procede the description of the operations in which he was engaged in La Vendée.

CHAPTER IX.

MARCEAU.

EARLY LIFE, ETC.

FRANÇOIS SEVERIN MARCEAU was born at Chartres on the 1st of March, 1769, where his father was an *employé* in the bailiff's office of the town. His childhood could not have been happy, for neither father nor mother treated him with much affection. He found a home, however, with an elder sister, through whose kindness he also obtained an indifferent education. Some of his biographers assert that he was sent to college, where he learnt little. "When he was offered a book he asked for a sword; a camp not a college," says his panegyrist, " would have suited him best ! " And it is certain that, when he entered as a clerk into a lawyer's office, he revolted at the employment, and preferred to enlist. At the age of sixteen he joined the regiment of Savoy Carignan, as a private soldier, and devoted himself earnestly to acquire the rudiments of his profession. He showed himself very diligent, not only in perfecting himself in his drill, but in higher military studies. He read all the military books he could obtain, and studied tactics, castrematation, fortification, geometry, and mathematics. His industry and steadiness soon gained him the approval of his superiors, and promotion to the rank of sergeant in his regiment. He

was on leave in Paris in July, 1789, when the masses rose to
attack the Bastille ; Marceau joined in the crowd, and acted
at the head of a detachment destined to oppose the regular
troops marching on Paris.   After this, in common with all
soldiers who had served at the taking of the Bastille, he
obtained his discharge, and returning to his native town,
became soon afterwards drill instructor of the National
Guard of Chartres.   From this he was promoted captain
of Chasseurs, and was further advanced to the post
of commandant of a battalion of volunteers, raised
in the department of Eure-et-Loire.   With this battalion he proceeded to the frontier in the summer of
1792, and formed part of the garrison of Verdun when
besieged by the Prussians.   Marceau is said to have been
violently opposed to the capitulation forced upon Beaure-
paire, an indignity which that unhappy commander resented
by blowing out his brains.   It fell to Marceau's lot, however,
as the youngest field officer in the garrison, to be the bearer
of the capitulation to the King of Prussia.   He was taken
with eyes bandaged into the Prussian lines, and is said to
have gained the pity of the King himself from the manly
sorrow he displayed.   The whole of the superior officers who
took part in the defence of Verdun were arrested as traitors,
Marceau with the rest, and it might have gone hard with him
had he not found a protector in his brother-in-law, who was
now a member of the Convention.   Marceau was soon afterwards transferred to the German Legion, serving under
Westermann in La Vendée, where he was destined to give
the first proofs of his capacity in war.

At this time he was barely twenty-three years of age, and
he is described as a fine, handsome young man, somewhat
below the middle height, with a slender, graceful figure, but
full of activity and strength.   His countenance was noble,

he had a clear, honest brow, bright eyes, and a firm mouth ;
- but his face is said to have worn an habitual air of sadness,
which gained him the interest and sympathy of all who saw
him.

The insurrection had been raging in La Vendée for some
months before Marceau went to the West. The measures of
the Revolutionary Government had long stirred up bitter discontent amongst the Vendeans ; but the West did not rebel
until after the execution of the King, and even then it
might have remained tranquil but for the new law of conscription. Now the whole district which lies south of
the Loire, from Saumur to Niort, and thence to the sea, rose
en masse. The villagers of seven hundred communes rushed
to arms, in overt resistance to the Republican Government.
They were animated by a fierce religious enthusiasm, stirred
up by the local clergy, whose dearest principles were
threatened by the Revolution. They were led, too, by their
old seigneurs, to whom they owed an hereditary attachment,
although one or two of their most prominent generals who
gave their forces organisation and won their chief victories,
were men of low origin. There was much to favour the
insurgents ; the country in which they fought was specially
suitable for a guerilla warfare. Dumouriez, when serving in
the West, had already noticed it, remarking that it was the
country he would choose if he had to head a civil war. It
was traversed by only two good high roads, and the whole
surface was cut up by hedges and ditches, which impeded progress for artillery and regular troops, but which offered
excellent cover for the Vendean marksmen. The latter
were mostly excellent shots, they knew their country by
heart, and they could go anywhere, easily surmounting all
obstacles by the aid of their long jumping poles. All
this contributed greatly to their early success, which was

further assisted by the inexperience and incompetency of the Republican generals, and the constant discord which existed amongst them.

At first the Convention was at no great pains to suppress the insurrection. It was satisfied to collect a flying column of 6,000 men at Nantes to overawe the country; but the capture of Chollet, on the 15th of March, 1793, followed by that of other places, and the general activity of the Vendeans, necessitated more serious measures. An army was organised under General Berriger, who took the field in April, and was speedily defeated. By this time the Vendeans had three armies in the field, each from 10,000 to 12,000 strong. They had been successfully engaged at Thouars, and Fontenay, and early in June they advanced with 40,000 men upon the Loire, determined to drive the Republicans out of Saumur. This town was captured on the 7th of June, and after such a success it would have been easy to have marched upon Paris. The Vendeans were not, however, well advised; they preferred to strike at Nantes, which was near at hand, thinking it would give a centre and focus to the insurrection, and open up communications with their friends beyond sea. Now the Convention, aroused to the dangers which threatened it from the West, resolved to send a more imposing force to quell the insurrection. Troops which could be ill-spared were drawn from various parts of the frontier; a portion of the army, which had its head-quarters at Niort, and was to co-operate with another at Tours, was placed under the command of General Biron. It was in this army that Marceau was serving under Westermann. While Biron was getting his troops into some sort of order, the Vendeans had moved on Nantes by the right bank of the river, but had been repulsed by General Canclaux, who held it with a weak force, and they had again retired upon Saumur. Biron was strong enough to have advanced in mass upon Saumur, but he preferred to spread out his forces along a wide front, hoping thus both to overawe and conciliate the country. The French forces, acting on many different lines, gained some small success; but the Vendeans rallied round Chollet and beat General Santerre, who had come up from the Loire. The representative, Bourbotte, was with this force which fled before the Vendeans, and he bravely strove to rally the fugitives and show a new front. But he, too, was carried away by the crowd, unhorsed, and nearly lost his life. At this moment, a young officer who was near rode up, to his own great risk, and eventually saved him by giving up his own horse. The author of this gallant act was Marceau, who thus repaid good for evil, for Bourbotte had wished, not long before, to send Marceau a prisoner before the revolutionary tribunal at Tours. Marceau was in disfavour because he had sided with his chief, Westermann, against Rossignol, the Sans Culotte general, supported by the Central Government.

This incident is vouched for by various authorities, although Marceau's presence at Chollet, when he belonged to a division engaged much more to the South, is not explained. He might, however, have been detached on special duty; but in any case, a month later he was serving as Adjutant-General to the division stationed at Luçon, which within a few weeks had had half-a-dozen different commanders. We get glimpses of the young soldier, always foremost when there was fighting to be done. He was in the disastrous action at Chantonnay, where Lecomte commanded the division in Tunck's absence, when that general was suspended. Lecomte was surprised by 15,000 Vendeans on the 5th of September, and attacked before he could get his troops into position; they fought bravely enough, but two battalions turned tail.   Marceau was sent post-haste to rally the fugitives.   With this object he drew up two fresh battalions on the left of the high road, and brought up a couple of light guns and some cavalry.   While thus engaged two other battalions on his left broke and retreated in disorder, thus exposing the French left.

The enemy were, however, checked for a moment by the firm front shown by one battalion, and Marceau, perceiving this, promptly ordered the cavalry to charge.   They refused, and in spite of all Marceau's courageous efforts, displayed a most shameful cowardice.   Soon after this the Vendeans broke through the centre of the Republicans, who, thus separated into two parts, took to flight.   Only two battalions remained with the general, and under cover of these, aided by Marceau, who had reached him by riding right through the enemy's lines, Lecomte withdrew his shattered forces. Out of 6,000 men, barely 1,800 gained Sables-d'Olonne, and the whole of the artillery, transport, and supplies, fell into the hands of the enemy.   Although thus decimated and disorganised, the division of Luçon was quickly reorganised.   It was defeated at Chantonnay on the 8th of September, and on the 19th, the general commanding reports that, assisted by Lecomte, its chief, and Marceau, its adjutant-general, the little division was once more in a position to take the field.   It was destined to be speedily and actively employed, at first under a new leader, Bard, and subsequently under Marceau himself.

The operations for the coercion of La Vendée were now to be greatly enlarged.   Two independent armies — one styled the Army of Brest, under Canclaux; the other, the Army of Rochelle, under Rossignol, were to be employed for this purpose.   Veteran troops were to be sent into the West, and the whole garrison of Mayence, which had been allowed to leave that fortress with full honours of war, were transferred bodily to La Vendée. The operations of Canclaux and Rossignol. were badly conceived, and may be dismissed with a brief statement of their failure. The Committee of Public Safety began to realise that they must proceed on other lines if they were to suppress the insurrection. Carnot's influence—for that enterprising patriot had by this time joined the Committee—was no doubt instrumental in this, and it was clearly understood that some other remedy than denouncing the treason and incapacity of the various leaders must be tried. In a speech of Barrère's the steps to be taken were clearly pointed out.

"For many representatives, substitute one; for many generals, a single leader with a united army : one mind, one will is needed to extinguish the rebellion."

In consequence of this, the Convention acted vigorously ; it recalled all its commissioners except Bourbotte and Thurreau ; it appointed General Lechelle to the supreme command of the Army in the West; but retained Rossignol under him as chief of the Army of Brest, and at the same time it issued an extraordinary proclamation to the Republican troops, requiring them to exterminate the rebels without fail by the end of October. Lechelle, it may be stated at once, was quite incompetent as a leader, his only merit was that he was a man of the people, and had once been a private soldier. Some idea of his ignorance may be gathered from Kléber's story, given in his "Memoirs," about the capture of Noirmoutiers, an island to the south of the Loire. Lechelle asked : " What's that ? Where is it ? "

Yet he had once commanded at Rochelle, and, as a general in the field, he ought at least to have studied his maps. His ridiculous incompetence was made more apparent as the campaign proceeded ; but his first measures, intended to concentrate his strength for the coercion of Upper Vendée, were reasonable enough. Kléber, in fact, was behind Lechelle, and Kléber had already given proofs of military capacity hardly inferior to that displayed by Hoche, Jourdan, or Marceau.

Some account of a general whom Napoleon afterwards highly esteemed, must be introduced here. Kléber played a prominent part in the early revolutionary wars. He was constantly and actively employed, although the chief command seldom fell to him. Like many of his great comrades, he sprang from the people. His father was a mason of Strasbourg, who died early, and his mother re-married a master carpenter. There was nothing remarkable in Kleber's childhood except a hasty, imperious temper, which involved him in perpetual quarrels with his playmates. He was a precocious lad, unusually tall and strong for his age, and his abilities were of the best. His predilections were so strongly shown towards drawing and geometry that, after a short apprenticeship at the bench, his step-father, the master carpenter, sent him to study in Paris. He became a skilful architect, and returned to establish himself in Strasbourg, when an accident threw him into the society of certain Bavarian youths, whom he accompanied to Munich, where he entered the military school. Here he so distinguished himself, both in his studies and field exercises, that he attracted the attention of the Count de Kaunitz, son of Maria Thereśa's minister. Count de Kaunitz carried him off to Vienna, where he entered the Austrian service, hoping to see active service against the Turks ; but for eight years he ate out his heart in garrison life, always in junior grades.

Returning to his native town on leave of absence, he determined to resign his Austrian commission, and soon after he obtained the appointment of inspector of buildings at Belfort. Kléber spent many years at Belfort, and was actively concerned in the erection of many of its principal edifices. He was there when the Revolution broke out, and took a prominent part in the quarrel which ensued between the people and the garrison (the regiment Royal Louis), which was still devoted to the King. Kléber's promptitude and presence of mind in protecting the local authorities, saved Belfort from bloodshed. Soon afterwards the old soldier—he was now thirty-seven years of age—enrolled himself in a battalion of volunteers raised in the Upper Rhine, and was appointed adjutant-major. He became, from his experience and practical knowledge, a leading man in the battalion, and rapidly rose in rank. He was engaged on the frontier at the time of the retreat of the Prussian army, before Dumouriez, from Champagne, and after that was shut up with Custine in Mayence. He took an active part in the protracted defence of that fortress, and was for the moment involved in the discredit that followed its surrender. The Convention arrested and would have guillotined every officer of rank who had belonged to its garrison ; but when the facts of the defence were made public they met with honour instead of a disgraceful death. Custine was made the solitary victim. He lost his head ; but the rest of the Army of Mayence was declared to have deserved well of the Republic, and was sent intact to help in the subjugation of La Vendée.

Lechelle's first orders were that Marceau with the division of Luçon, should march upon Mortagne and Chollet, while the division of Mayence with Kléber, crossing the Loire at Nantes, was directed on the same side. The Vendeans at this time were divided amongst themselves, and a portion of their forces under Charette had gone off on an expedition against Noirmoutiers, leaving only Generals Bonchamp and D'Elbée united to make head against the enemy. These leaders were to rendezvous at Mortagne on the 13th, but they were forestalled by the division of Mayence, and fell back on Chollet. The division from Luçon, under General Bard, passed through Mortagne on the 15th, with orders to push on to Chollet. This order was given by Robert, Lechelle's chief of the staff, who told Bard that he would find other troops before him on the road. But no troops were sent on, and the neglect nearly sacrificed Bard's advanced guard. It was commanded by Marceau, the adjutant-general of the division, who, as he advanced, was suddenly assailed by a sharp fire. He thought at first that this proceeded from his friends mentioned by Robert, but the extension of the fire soon proved that it came from the enemy. Marceau was retreating when Bard came up and helped him to rally his troops ; but Bard was now seriously wounded, and the command of the entire division devolved upon Marceau. He was still sorely pressed, and would probably have been overcome but for the timely aid offered him by General Beaupuy, who now came into line. The fight continued for the rest of the day, but as the Republicans brought their other reserves, the Vendeans were driven back with heavy loss upon Chollet.

The day had been long and trying, the Republican troops were worn out with continuous marching, and in the sharp action the various units had been thrown into much confusion. But Kléber, who practically commanded, for Lechelle, although in the neighbourhood, never shewed himself under fire, drew up the army in two lines on the heights opposite Chollet, and in this position waited for daylight. Kléber himself spent the night at a bivouac fire in a field near the road, and it was here that he first made acquaintance with Marceau—an acquaintance commenced under rather unfavourable auspices, which was yet destined to develop into

a close and most affectionate friendship. Kléber had already
earned a high reputation, and young Marceau was eager to
know him. At ten o'clock that night he came to Kléber's
bivouac fire, full of enthusiasm, to pay his respects. The
elder soldier reproved him sternly. " You had no right to
leave your post; go back to it at once," said Kléber. "You
can make my acquaintance by-and-by." Marceau was
naturally much hurt by this reception; but Kléber made up
for it next day, and so plainly showed Marceau that he
respected and trusted him, that the young fellow frankly
forgave him. In the next battle, a couple of days later,
Kléber fully admitted the excellence of Marceau's dispositions when in command of the centre of the line.

On the 16th, the Republicans took position at Chollet, on
a line of heights extending from Chollet on the left to the
Angers road on the right. The left was held by the
Mayence division under General Haxo, with that of Luçon
in the centre. Vimeux commanded on the right, Beaupuy
with the advanced guard was in front of the left. The force
under Bressiure and Chalbos had arrived and took post
behind the left. The position of the army was faulty, but
it was hardly held for defence, as the Republicans intended
to advance on the 17th; but, on the morning of that day, the
Vendeans, although torn with dissension amongst themselves,
determined to make a last and more vigorous attack upon
their enemy. Beaupuy found himself hard pressed in the
afternoon and asked for help. Kléber, who again seems to
have issued orders instead of Lechelle, sent back for one of
Chalbos' brigades to reinforce Beaupuy; but before it could
arrive, Haxo was also engaged. The brigade sent by Chalbos
now came up, and facing round at the first sight of the
enemy, fled, so that the left of the Republican position
would have been lost but for the steady conduct of the 109th

regiment, which advanced boldly, headed by its band, and restored the fight in the centre. Marceau had also repelled a first attack, but was again assailed. The second time he allowed the attacking columns to approach within half a musket shot, then suddenly opening his ranks, showed his artillery well posted, which immediately delivered a murderous fire. Arrested by the sudden discharge, their ranks decimated, the Vendeans broke and retreated, hotly pursued by Marceau, who drove them down the hill. On the right, Vimeux had not been seriously engaged, and he easily held his own. As night fell, the Vendeans drew off, badly beaten along the whole line. They had fought obstinately, but nevertheless they failed.*

The result of this day, so disastrous to the Vendeans, was important to Marceau. His gallant conduct gained for him the acting rank of brigadier-general, conferred upon him on the spot by the representative of the people. A few days later, he was advanced to a more responsible post as chief of the staff of General Lechelle. It must not be supposed, however, that Marceau was able to exercise any appreciable influence over his new chief. General Lechelle was persistently deaf to the wiser counsels of his subordinates, and continued to show his incompetence to the last. He ought to have followed up the victory of Chollet without a moment's loss of time. No doubt his men were weary and footsore, but he had a great chance of totally crushing his beaten foes, for, all next day, the Vendeans were in a most dangerous position, retreating through the gorge of St. Florent, with the Loire at their back. When, after thirty-six hours' rest, Lechelle

---

* In the account of the Battle of Chollet I have followed Kléber's own description, as given in his "Memoir," in preference to that of Jomini, which differs greatly. Jomini's account can hardly be more trustworthy than that of a general who was present in person.

pushed forward a reconnaissance to St. Florent, the enemy had disappeared. The defeat at Chollet had been followed by further discussion, and, after much debate, the Vendeans decided to abandon La Vendée, and, crossing the north bank of the Loire, throw themselves into Brittany. They had crossed the river in great haste, a beaten army, destitute of ammunition and supplies, greatly embarrassed by the helpless crowd of old men, women, and children, fugitives whom they were compelled to convoy from place to place. There were ninety thousand souls in the retreating force, and of this at least thirty thousand were non-combatants. The movements of the Vendean army for the remainder of the campaign followed none of the regular principles of war. It was without base or communications, and wandered to and fro in a strange and most irregular fashion, retreating, advancing, now pointing north to the sea-coast, now south to regain its native province, undertaking crude, isolated operations with no settled plan of action, beyond that of dealing with the immediate difficulties that surrounded it.

On receiving news of the retreat of the Vendeans across the river, Lechelle called a council of war. Jomini says that he was anxious to follow up the enemy vigorously across the river, and engage him wherever he could be found. This is not vouched for by other authorities, and in any case he yielded to other opinions, deciding that the army should break up into two portions, one of which was to move on Nantes, the other on Angers. Kléber took the former road, and passing through Nantes, marched on Rennes and Château-Gonthier, to which latter place Beaupuy with Westermann also proceeded *viâ* Angers. The Vendeans were found in force at Laval, where Westermann's scouts came upon their advanced posts on the 24th October.

It was now the general wish of the various Republican

commanders that the enemy should be attacked forthwith, and a council of war, from which Lechelle, the general-in-chief, was absent, assembled to arrange a plan. Having learnt that the town of Laval lay on both sides of the river Mayenne, but that the castle and heights on the right bank were the key to the position, Kléber and Marceau were agreed with the rest to attack by the right, and Marceau rode back to Château-Gonthier to convey the opinions of the generals to Lechelle. But the general-in-chief disdained the advice of his subordinates, and proceeded to follow a plan of his own. The mass of his army was on the left bank, and by the left bank he resolved to advance "majestically and in mass," as he put it. The orders he sent to the divisional commanders were ridiculous in the extreme, and to propose the attacking of a position by a single line, which was approachable by many, was to blindly tempt disaster. Moreover, the enemy had but to push a strong force along the right bank as far as Château-Gonthier, and cross the river by its bridge, to establish themselves upon Lechelle's only line of retreat. Beaupuy, accompanied by Marceau, commanded the advance, and they came upon the enemy drawn up in line of battle at Antrain, before Laval. Kléber, who followed, was arranging for a general attack, when Lechelle, who still kept to the rear, interfered, and having first halted a division intended to make a flanking movement, then gave the order for retreat. Beaupuy was now sharply attacked by the enemy, and, being unsupported, was soon driven back. The Vendeans promptly following up their success, the Republicans were overpowered, and the retreat soon degenerated into an irremediable rout. The Mayence division bravely strove to show front; but soon the whole Republican army streamed away to the rear, the Vendeans pursuing hotly into Château-Gonthier. The Republicans continued their retreat as far as Angers, where, destitute, discouraged, and diminished to half their strength, they took post, covered by the river Oudon. At the same time, a column which had moved on Laval on the other bank, through Craon, retrograded on Rennes. Lechelle blamed his troops unjustly, who retaliated, and when he asked with bitter scorn, "What have I done that I should command such cowards?" replied: "Why should we be commanded by such a miserable hound?"

His last act was to denounce Kléber to the Committee of Public Safety, and to accuse the division of Mayence of treason. The first entailed Kléber's suspension, as we shall see by-and-by, and the latter the breaking up of the division of Mayence. But Lechelle's treachery did him no good, for soon afterwards he died at Nantes, it was supposed by his own hand.

Meanwhile great efforts were made to reorganise the army at Angers; it was formed into two divisions, with a reserve, and Marceau assumed command of the advanced guard. The Vendeans had benefited little by their victory at Laval. They wasted the precious days immediately following in doubt what to do, whether to march on Rennes, Paris, or the sea-coast. At this moment two English emissaries arrived, promising help from the British Government, and it was thought best to secure some sea-port, as a means of communication with these new allies. Granville was soon selected for the purpose, and the Vendeans now marched on it, not by the most direct road, through Fougeres and Avranches, but making a long detour through Dol and Pontorson. This delay allowed Granville time to prepare for its defence, and the Republican army to advance and concentrate afresh at Rennes, where it joined the Army of Brest, Rossignol taking the chief command. The Vendeans were soon in difficulties again. They had advanced upon Granville, but were unable to take it by a *coup de main;* the Republican forces pressed them on every side, an army was advancing on their rear from Brest, and Rossignol was at their flank. They were compelled to retreat, and once more occupied Dol. The Republicans advanced slowly to Antrain, and while here learnt from Westermann that the Vendeans were in great distress at Dol. Rossignol now resolved to attack them, and there was a sharp fight in front of Dol on the 20th, when the Vendeans gained an advantage on their left against Westermann, but were checked by Marceau on their right. Marceau was weak in numbers; but his coolness and the excellence of his dispositions gave him the advantage, and he beat off his enemy easily. As night approached, however, he could not pursue, and Müller's division coming up, the latter, as senior, took command. The story goes that Müller and his staff were all intoxicated, so that further operations were rendered impossible. The position of the troops, too, was dangerous, and Marceau, flying to Kléber for advice, decided to retire to a position which Kléber had reconnoitred that morning, and the strength of which had not escaped the quick eye of Marceau himself. Next day a fresh action commenced, the Vendeans advancing to the attack. Rossignol's army was posted behind the Couesnon; Westermann's brigade was on the other side of the river, and this was attacked in such strength by the Vendeans that it was speedily overwhelmed. Its defeat exposed the right of the position, and threatened the rear. This rendered withdrawal inevitable; but the Republican troops, already shaken, could not execute the movement with self-possession. A general retreat followed, and soon panic reigned supreme. The whole of Rossignol's army fled towards Antrain, where Marceau alone showed courage and presence of mind. Collecting together a handful of troops, without reference to battalion or brigade, with this small force he long and stoutly defended the bridge. But Marceau, too, was overpowered, and the retreat now became a regular stampede. The Republicans fled to the rear in every direction, some to Fougeres, others to Rennes, and beyond, and the disastrous defeat ended in the loss of 5,000 or 6,000 men.

The beaten army collected at Rennes on the night of the 21st, where Rossignol had already arrived. His incompetence, like that of Lechelle, was always fully proved. No one was readier to admit this than himself; he confessed to the representatives of the people that he was unfit to command an army. "Give me a battalion," he said, "and I shall do my duty. Here is my resignation." The representatives refused to accept it; they told Rossignol that he was the "oldest son, the cherished child of the Revolution," and that he would continue so, even if he lost twenty battles. They insisted on his remaining supreme, and promised him the advice and assistance of the most capable military generals. " On them shall depend the responsibility of success," he was told, "and woe to them if they lead you astray." Full of this extraordinary design, they entrusted Kléber with the task of selecting Rossignol's military advisers. That general naturally shrank from the delicate and invidious task. He knew that he must excite jealousy and dissatisfaction; but, as he tells us, "the good of the service outweighed all other considerations." He accordingly recommended Marceau to command all the troops; Westermann, to command the cavalry; Debily to command the artillery. He gives his reasons for choosing Marceau. " He was my friend, and I knew that he would undertake nothing without previous arrangement with me. Marceau was young, full of intelligence, courage, and tenacity. I was there myself, calmer and more self-possessed, to check his eagerness if it went beyond bounds. We swore never to separate until we had brought back victory to our arms."

These recommendations were accepted, and Marceau at once exercised his authority. In a short space of time he reformed the divisions, named their commanders, gave each his appointed place, fixed the daily routine, constituted reserves, and generally saw to the discipline and organisation of the army. His position was not an easy one. He was liable to be blamed for failure, and was without full power to avoid it. Within a few days he was threatened, in common with his friend Kléber, with the guillotine, on a charge of dilatoriness in hastening to the relief of Angers ; yet the delay was traceable entirely to Rossignol, who would not allow the army to march until he joined it. But on reaching that place, Marceau found himself in a less dangerous position. Despatches were received there from Paris by which he was appointed to the supreme command, *ad interim*, of the Army of the West, and until the arrival of General Thurreau, who, at the moment, was serving in the eastern Pyrenees. The same despatch contained an order for Kléber's suspension, and Marceau, with true friendship, would have refused the command, if it separated him from his comrade. Fortunately, he received a second letter, containing permission to hold over the suspension, and to continue to employ Kléber in any post where his services might be useful. Marceau sent at once for his friend, and told him that although he was nominally the chief, Kléber should really command. " I will take all the responsibility," said Marceau, " but you shall really lead. All I ask is the command of the advanced guard at the time of danger." Kléber accepted the noble offer, declaring that if the worst came to the worst, they would mount the guillotine together.

Once more the Vendeans neglected their opportunity. They had not taken advantage of their victory at Antrain, although it opened to them the road back to the Loire. A movement in force through Rennes upon Nantes would no doubt have been successful, and the return southward was now the more necessary, because the Vendean soldiery were in open revolt, clamouring to go back to their homes. This discontent caused their next move, which was on Angers, accomplished leisurely and without difficulty through Laval. But they were not more successful in their descent upon Angers than in their attack on Granville. They had to deal, too, with a new general, a young and vigorous leader, with a natural capacity for war, of a very different stamp to the incompetent commander he succeeded.

The attack on Angers having failed, the Vendeans could only cross the river higher up, at either Saumur or Tours. They considered it dangerous to attempt either passage, and, after fresh discussions, decided to move forward again upon Le Mans. They hoped to find friends there, and perhaps reach a hand once more towards the coast and Brittany. Marceau meanwhile, hearing of their failure at Angers, hastened after them. The division of Cherbourg under Tilly was directed on La Flêche and the river Loire ; Kléber was to follow the right bank of the greater Loire to cover Saumur; while Westermann and Müller, under Marceau himself, marched on Baugé, pursuing the Vendeans from behind. The Vendeans reached La Flêche, and found it occupied by the Republicans ; but they gained possession of it by a stratagem, and slowly retired on Le Mans, an open city, which they entered without difficulty. Here they found abundant supplies for their sick and helpless followers, and their army rested and recovered spirits. But on the second day of their occupation, Westermann's hussars appeared in the outskirts of the town. Marceau at the head of three divisions was approaching. Müller, commanding the leading division as usual, gave way before a vigorous sortie; but Marceau, coming up with the Cherbourg division, rallied him. Marceau would now have awaited the arrival of Kléber before he attacked the town. Westermann, however, too impetuous to wait, insisted upon continuing the advance. "My position is in Le Mans. The enemy is wavering, we must take advantage of it." The cavalry charged forward, and Marceau was bound to support them; they gained the centre of the town and occupied a great square, where Marceau took post for the night, carefully watching all the streets that opened into it. But his position was one of some peril; he was alone in the heart of a great city with a single division, and might be surrounded and crushed before reinforcements could reach him. He sent two pressing messages to Kléber to come up, and Kléber is said to have remarked on receiving the first message, "Marceau is young, he has acted foolishly, and he ought to be made to feel it; but we must hurry forward to his rescue." Kléber arrived at Le Mans about daylight, where he relieved the worn-out troops that had captured it, and found that the enemy had evacuated the town. Active pursuit soon showed that they were retreating on Laval; Westermann's cavalry gave chase, and a terrible carnage followed. The Vendeans must have lost in this retreat at least 10,000 men, and as many more women and children, with the whole of their artillery and baggage. This butchery was indefensible; but Marceau can hardly be responsible for it. It is certain that he was most anxious to save and shelter the helpless, and in one particular instance gave his personal protection to a young lady whose friends were massacred, and whom the soldiers had seized. Marceau saw that she was conducted to a place of safety in Laval, but here she was speedily discovered, denounced, and guillotined. At her trial she confessed that Marceau had wished to save her, and that general was forthwith accused of treason. It might have gone hard with him; but the case fell into the hands of the representative Bourbotte, who, to his credit, remembered that he owed his life to Marceau, and the accusation was quashed.

Marceau was not disposed to allow the Vendeans any rest. He soon heard that they had made no halt in Laval, but were heading back on Château-Gonthier, with the evident intention of making once more for the Loire. His information was that they were pointing for Ancenis, and he accordingly sent instructions to the generals in command at Saumur, Angers, and Nantes, to be on the look-out for the enemy, and prevent him at all hazards from crossing the river. At the same time, with the main body of his own army, he continued to press them from behind.

It was perfectly true; the Vendeans had again marched southward, and had reached Ancenis on the 16th of December. But, whilst they were hastily constructing rafts to cross the river, Westermann's indefatigable cavalry overtook them, and the Vendeans hastily fell back northwards to Niort. Marceau was now at Château-Briant, whence he moved more to his right to Derval, so as to interpose between the enemy and Rennes or Redon, in case the hunted Vendeans headed for either of these places. Thence he pushed on Kléber to Blain, which the Vendeans had actually occupied, and which, at the approach of the

Republicans, they evacuated, to fall back on Savenay, Westermann still at their heels. Marceau pushed Kléber forward in support of Westermann, who seized the Nantes road and drove the enemy back from Savenay. The Vendeans made a desperate resistance, and, as the main columns came up before daylight, Marceau renewed the attack with all his strength; the enemy's right and left were both beaten, and Marceau, at the head of the centre, entered Savenay in triumph. The enemy was completely routed; escape was impossible. The river closed the left, deep marshes on the right; but the Vendeans fought to the bitter end, like men who refused to survive defeat. A few laid down their arms, others broke and fled into the woods, many more were slaughtered as they ran. This sanguinary battle practically ended this particular period of the Vendean war. The result fully bore out Marceau's not unjustifiable boast.

Marceau had already been much crossed and thwarted by his successor Thurreau, who as early as the 10th of December was at Alençon, and might, if he had chosen, have assumed command before the battle of Le Mans. But Thurreau let others win victories, and passed on to Angers, where he sought only to upset the excellent dispositions made by Marceau to prevent the enemy from recrossing the Loire. He went still further, and coolly reprimanded Marceau for daring to act without awaiting his orders. Thurreau desired him to cease operations until he, the general-in-chief, was present. Marceau's reply was characteristic: "I am in front of Savenay. To-morrow at dawn I shall attack the enemy and destroy him. You had better make haste if you want to see the end of the war." Thurreau reported the circumstance to the War Minister, and added that he was on his way to Nantes to hold Marceau to account for his insubordination. Marceau had already reached Nantes on the 24th of December, two days after Savenay, and, with Kléber, had been enthusiastically received by the people. Thurreau arrived on the 1st of January, and a stormy scene ensued. Marceau demanded an apology, with the alternative of a duel, but Thurreau refused to fight with an officer under his command.

"Had you been a brave man," was Marceau's taunt, "you would have joined us while there was fighting to be done. In any case, until I resign my command to you, I am your equal."

Thurreau's answer was to send Marceau back to Château-Briant under arrest, where he fell ill, but was soon afterwards passed on to Paris. It was during this visit to Paris that Marceau was first introduced to Carnot. The story is told in Carnot's "Memoirs." Marceau's brother-in-law, Sargent, took him in when Carnot was seated at his desk writing. At the mention of Marceau's name, Carnot looked up sharply, and said, as he examined the young soldier keenly:

"You are very young to win battles."

At this date, Marceau was only twenty-four.

Another story told of Carnot and Marceau may be given here. A year or two later Marceau had several horses killed in action, but had failed to obtain reimbursement from the State. His repeated applications having been ignored, he asked his brother-in-law to speak to Carnot. The Minister at once called for the subordinate who dealt with these claims.

"Why," asked Carnot, "has not General Marceau received payment for the horses he has lost?"

"Because his applications were not quite according to form," was the reply.

"The general is not so particular about having horses killed under him," said Carnot. "Send him his money at once. Our new general must be mounted; the Austrians are to be beaten again."

It is with his services in the campaigns on the northern and eastern frontier against the Austrians, under the command of Jourdan, that I shall next deal.

CHAPTER X.

MARCEAU AND JOURDAN.

THE beginning of the year 1794 saw a marvellous change in the relative condition of the belligerents. Aroused to extraordinary enthusiasm, France had become one vast camp; the whole flower of the nation was in the field, and no less than 700,000 combatants were ready to take the offensive. Along the northern and eastern frontiers were four considerable armies; that of the Rhine, 45,000 strong, with as many more garrisoning the strong places; the Army of the Moselle, 60,000; that of the Ardennes, 35,000; and, lastly, that of the North, 160,000, holding the whole line from Maubeuge to Dunkirk. Against these forces the Austrians had 60,000 men under Saxe Teschen, on the Upper Rhine; Beaulieu commanded 18,000 in Luxemburg; the Prussians, under Hohenlohe, had 65,000 at Mayence; and the Austrian army in Belgium, under the Prince of Saxe Coburg, numbered 150,000.

There was, as usual, a want of concerted action amongst the allied leaders; but after much discussion a plan had been devised by the Austrian General Mack, as chief of the staff, which, stated briefly, was that Coburg should march on Paris, while the Prussians advanced on the Meuse to protect his flanks. The chief fault of this plan was that it tied down the Allies to a particular line of invasion, without reference to the enemy's movements or position. It would have been wiser to have concentrated wherever the French were found to be strongest, and attack them persistently, following up every success boldly and without intermission. This was the more necessary, because the French were actually superior in numbers, and, under the active supervision of Carnot, were also determined to take the initiative. Carnot had laid down a general idea for the coming campaign, the main principle of which was that it should be offensive all along the line, but decisive only at two or three particular points. The heaviest work was to fall upon the Armies of the North and East, which Carnot intended to combine under one head. He was most anxious, he wrote, to make these operations decisive. "The war can only be determined," he said, "by winning great battles." It was useless to beat the enemy partially ; if only half destroyed he could easily recover, and make a fresh attack the following year.

In spite of these wise resolves the early operations of the French along their northern frontier during this year were mostly abortive and ·unsatisfactory. The blame has been visited upon Pichegru, who commanded the Army of the North, and who was, probably, no great general. It was clear that now, as in Dumouriez's time, the weak point of the Austrian line was towards the centre and left, and that the proper course for the French commanders was to concentrate their whole strength, and strike at Charleroi. Instead of this it was resolved to operate by both flanks, and expose each army to be beaten in detail should Coburg choose to avail himself of his central position.

Pichegru's left wing was more successful than it deserved to be. Moving against Menin and Courbrai, it won the battle of Turcoing when it ought to have been overwhelmed on its exposed right flank, and driven with its back to the sea. Pichegru persisted in his mistaken plan, and drew to himself more and more strength from his centre. At the same time his right wing, joined to the Army of the Ardennes, was ordered to cross the Sambre and march on Mons. The direction of the latter movement was judicious, and it should have achieved more. The French were numerically superior on this side, having 60,000 men against 30,000 Austrians, but their generals, Desjardins and Charbonnier, were quite unfitted to command an army in the field. They were overawed, too, and continually harassed by the ruthless St. Just, who tried his best, by his ignorance and obstinacy, to ruin the operations in progress.

Both Kléber and Marceau were actively employed in these movements, the first having no special appointment, the latter in command of the advanced guard of the Army of the Ardennes. Three times the French crossed the Sambre, and were unsuccessfully engaged with the Austrians. On the 10th of May, 1794, they forced the enemy back and attacked his camp upon the right bank. On the 13th, they were driven back across the river. On the 20th of May, they again passed the Sambre, and were again defeated, this time so effectually, that but for Kléber, who had been sent on a foraging expedition to Frasnes, far north of Charleroi, and who had retired in good order, the French right wing would have been lost. But now Carnot had realised the importance of this line of attack, and felt that the force employed here was insufficient to secure success. He had already sent orders to Jourdan to move on the Sambre, with the whole Army of the Moselle, reinforced by 15,000 men, and, uniting himself with the troops under Desjardins, to take the supreme command on this side. " This manœuvre," says Jomini, "one of the most skilful and fortunate of these early campaigns, decided the fate of the Low Countries."

At this moment, the Army of the Sambre was nearly disorganised; the men were in rags and barefooted, worn out with hunger and fatigue, ammunition was short, and guns were needed to replace those used up or lost in the recent disasters. But St. Just, reckless and precipitate as usual, insisted upon a fresh attack. In a council of war, he ended the discussion by loudly declaring, " The Republic must have a victory to-morrow. Choose which you will have, a battle or a siege." It was dangerous to oppose him; hesitation would have entailed the guillotine. Accordingly, it was resolved to cross the Sambre for the third time, on the 26th of May. To encourage and show a good example to the rest of the army, an especial advanced guard was organised of nine picked battalions and four cavalry regiments, the whole under the command of Marceau. But on the morning of the 26th, these troops, which had been for forty-eight hours without food, refused to march, and were only won over by the exhortation of Kléber, who seeing that the leading battalion was from Alsace, harangued it in German. Marchiennes was attacked but without success, but the Austrians presently evacuated it, upon which the French crossed the river and invested Charleroi. One division laid siege to the place, covered by another and Marceau's advanced guard, posted above Charleroi. On the 3rd of June, however, the Austrians, who had been reinforced again, fell upon the French divisions and forced them to raise the siege, the retreat across the river being happily secured by the bold front which Marceau showed.

Next day Jourdan with his army arrived, and the French forces upon the Sambre now numbered 80,000 men. Jourdan spent some days in organising his forces; but on the 12th of June he crossed the river for the fourth time, and again laid siege to Charleroi. One division opened trenches, protected by the rest of the army, which was drawn up on a wide front from Trasegnies, where Kléber commanded through Gosselies, Ransart, Lambusart, to the woods of Copieaux on the right, where Marceau was in command, holding the bridge of Samines. The Prince of Orange had succeeded Kaunitz in the command of the Austrians, and he resolved to risk a battle to relieve Charleroi. Jourdan felt that his line was too extended, his position insecure. It was impossible for him to maintain a front of twenty or thirty miles without being forced at some point, yet he was unable to close in; and fully alive to the danger, he saw no way out of his trouble but to take the initiative and attack. Orders were issued for a forward movement on the morning of the 16th of June; but as his columns began to march, they met the Austrians advancing towards them. Jourdan at once halted, and then retired, preferring, if obliged to fight, to engage on ground that he knew. The action commenced in a thick fog, and was soon in active progress along the whole line. The Austrians made some impression in the centre, but had failed against Gosselies when the fog had lifted, and displayed the French right in full retreat. Marceau had been attacked vigorously by Beaulieu, and his two divisions had given way, retreating hastily across the Sambre in spite of their general's efforts to rally them. This defeat uncovered Jourdan's centre, and he at once ordered a general retreat. It was covered by Lefebre's division, which stood fast for a time. The beaten army had but one line of retreat, across the bridge of Marchiennes, and it might easily have encountered a serious disaster, but for the success which Kléber had achieved on the left. Trasegnies had been lost and won, and Kléber was on the point of pursuing his beaten assailants, when he saw that the French centre was pierced and in full retreat. Kléber now fell back quickly, and occupying a strong position on the heights above Marchiennes, gave Jourdan time to withdraw. At the same time the siege of Charleroi was raised.

The French defeat was attributed to the scarcity of ammunition; but there can be no doubt that Jourdan's position was defective. He was not discouraged, however. The ferocious St. Just was behind stimulating him to fresh efforts, and on the 18th of June, the French, for the fifth time, crossed the Sambre and resumed the siege of Charleroi. The Austrian army had disappeared. Coburg, believing the French to be utterly discouraged by the defeat on the 16th, had not only failed to reinforce the Prince of Orange, but had withdrawn him towards the right to make a fresh attack on Pichegru. Pichegru anxiously demanded reinforcements, and St. Just would have sent him 30,000 men, but Jourdan stoutly refused to spare a single soldier. A furious argument followed; the general continued to brave St. Just, and triumphed in the end. Fortunately the events of the next few days fully justified this refusal, or Jourdan's head would have paid the penalty. But now Coburg, hearing that the French were again across the Sambre, began to be seriously uneasy at these persistent attacks upon his left. He abandoned all thought of attacking Pichegru and hastened back towards the Sambre with all his available forces. Charleroi had already fallen; it capitulated on the 25th of

June under the stern menaces of St. Just, who sent an ultimatum to its commandant, declaring that the French general had been directed to assault the place, and put the whole garrison to the sword, if it did not surrender within an hour. The same evening it capitulated, and the garrison was permitted to march out with all the honours of war. The gates had barely closed behind the Austrians when guns were heard in the distance; this was Coburg, who had arrived in the neighbourhood of Fleurus, and who wished to inform the garrison at Charleroi that help was at hand.

Jourdan now knew that he had to deal with a very powerful enemy. He expected to find the Austrians superior to him in numbers, and he thought it best to await attack in a carefully chosen, strongly fortified position, that subsequently known as the battle-ground of Fleurus. It was not perhaps perfect, being far too long, while he had the river in his rear; but it was the best that offered, and he occupied it with judgment and care. Daurier was on the extreme left near the river; next came Montague, who was in front of the wood of Monceau, at Trasegnies; in the centre, Morlot was at Gosselies; Championnet at Heppignies; Lefebre at Lambusart with an advance as far forward as Fleurus; Marceau held the right in front of the wood of Copieaux. Kléber was behind the centre about Jumet, where he could act, either to reinforce that part, or the left flank; Hatry's division, released by the fall of Charleroi, was at Ransart in reserve behind Fleurus on the right. The French position was thus a semicircle, with Charleroi for its centre. Coburg, who had plenty of time to arrange his plan of attack, decided to move in five columns, striking at various points of the French position, and practically on a larger external semicircle. He would have shown better generalship in making great efforts against the right extremity of the

French line ; it was unnecessary to do more than demonstrate against the French left, as any development of strength upon this flank jeopardised the whole field of battle, and exposed the French line of communications with Louvain.

The action commenced on the 26th of June. At daylight the Prince of Orange, moving round by a long detour, seized Anderlues and Fontaine-l'Evêque, but Daurier continued to hold him in check. General Latour pressed hard on Montague, and forced him to retreat from Trasegnies through the wood of Monceau, to the heights of Marchiennes above the river. In the centre Quasdanowich approached Gosselies, driving in Morlot's advanced posts, while Kaunitz did the same at Heppignies. Montague's retreat becoming known to General Jourdan, he hastened to despatch Kléber to his support. That general promptly cleared the woods of Monceau, and saved Marchiennes. Latour had, moreover, sent scouts to the very walls of Charleroi, and finding it in the possession of the French, had already felt it wiser to retire. In the centre, Morlot held his own, while to his right Championnet, who had had to deal with Kaunitz, and who was in an excellent position, holding a strong redoubt armed with 18 guns, stoutly resisted all attack for some hours, and would have continued to resist when he heard that Lefebre to his right had yielded to the persistent attacks of the Archduke Charles. This was all a mistake. Lefebre was holding his own, but Championnet, dreading defeat, had already withdrawn his guns from the redoubt on Heppignies and was moving to the rear, when Jourdan, who as general-in-chief was stationed mostly about the centre of the position, rode up, and promptly restored the fight. He saw at once, with true military insight, that it was essential to stand fast here ; he accordingly brought up at once a strong brigade of Kléber's division and six squadrons of cavalry ;

with these he arrested the retreat, and presently, by a happy onslaught of his cavalry, drove back the enemy. Lefebre, although still unbeaten, had been compelled to evacuate Fleurus, but he held Lambusart obstinately, although his position had been imperilled by Marceau's misfortunes on his right.

The two divisions of the Ardennes under Marceau had occupied points in front of the wood of Copieaux, from which they had been driven by a vigorous attack of Beaulieu ; their retreat soon became a flight back to the river. Marceau, alone and in despair, still held a small handful together, determined to die at his post, but Lefebre supported him by extending his right, and sent Soult as chief of the staff, who persuaded Marceau to hurry after his defeated columns to rally them and bring them again to the fight. Beaulieu seeing his advantage pressed forward to attack Lambusart, which he presently carried. But Jourdan was again on the spot, and he immediately reinforced Lefebre with a portion of Hatry's division from Ransart. A fierce struggle ensued ; the French using all their strength to recover Lambusart. Marceau assisted in this with some of his reformed battalions, and eventually Lefebre succeeded in driving the Austrians out of the village. By this time the Prince of Orange had heard of the surrender of Charleroi, and he issued orders for a general retreat. . He seems to have lost heart, although a slow, concerted, com-bined attack upon the centre might yet have won him victory. He could hazard his whole army to save a small town, but he dared not strike a last bold blow to beat his enemy ; in fact, when the battle was still undecided, he gave up the fight. His retreat began on both flanks, the centre line holding fast; but this too fell back, and the French remained masters of the field. They did not pursue, being short of ammunition, and the victory was in consequence somewhat incomplete; but its results were exceedingly important to the French, no less for the increased prestige it gave their arms, than for the opportunity it offered them for accomplishing the conquest of Belgium.

Jourdan's army was now admirably placed to strike at Coburg's communications through Namur and Liége. Nothing could have saved the Austrians but a prompt concentration of the allied forces, and this Jourdan might easily have prevented by forestalling them at Namur. The most decisive results might have been thus secured by the French if Pichegru with the Army of the North were now promptly joined to Jourdan to assist in this decisive advance. But the Committee of Public Safety made the grave strategical error of suspending Jourdan's movement to the right, and of directing him instead on his left. He moved, therefore, towards Mons, where he was to join Pichegru, instead of towards Namur, where Pichegru, moving by Ath, should have joined him. Jourdan appears to have been alive to the mistaken course he was compelled to follow; but his protests were ignored, and he was unable to more than partially menace the Austrian line of retreat. Coburg was now behind the Dyle, covering his communications with Cologne. Brussels was abandoned, and the two French armies of Jourdan and Pichegru entered it on the 9th of July. It was too late for them to cut off the Austrian retreat; but they were strong enough to have fallen upon the Allies, now separated, and to have overwhelmed them in detail. But further offensive movements were checked by the Committee of Public Safety, which directed the French armies to merely occupy a defensive line between Antwerp and Namur, until the French fortresses, still in the hands of the Austrians, should be recaptured.

About the middle of July, however, Pichegru proceeded

to operate against the Duke of York, without obtaining any marked success, while Jourdan followed the Austrians to Louvain, whence Coburg, hard pressed, retired behind the Meuse, which he held from Ruremonde to Liége, the centre on Maestricht. The French followed. For another six weeks no further operations were undertaken by them, notwithstanding the enormous preponderance of their forces over those of the Allies. This delay was quite inexcusable. Jourdan was hardly to blame, as his orders were positive to await the fall of the fortresses which Scherer besieged; but the Committee of Public Safety should not have tied his hands. Nor can the Allies be excused for not availing themselves of the opportunity that offered of operating against Jourdan's left, about Maestricht, and of separating him from Pichegru.

Early in August, however, the successes gained by the Army of the Moselle, roused the Committee of Public Safety to fresh exertions. Pichegru advanced against the Duke of York and forced him back behind the Aa, whilst, as Scherer's task was completed, he joined Jourdan, who was now in a position to operate upon the Meuse. But nothing was done before the 14th of September, on which date the Austrians, now under the command of Clairfayt, occupied the whole line of the Meuse, from Ruremonde to Liége, with the left thrown back, extending from Liége to Sprimont, and covered by the Ourthe and Ayvaille. It was against this left that Jourdan now resolved to deliver his principal attack. Kléber was directed to make strong demonstrations against the centre and right, and this had the immediate effect of obliging Clairfayt to draw his reserves towards the threatened point. A few days previously three French divisions, one of them Marceau's, and all under the command of Scherer, had crossed the Meuse at Namur and Huy, and advanced to the Ourthe. Passing this river,

Scherer established himself on the banks of the Ayvaille, where Jourdan joined him and decided to force the passage of that river ; Marceau, with his division, was to cross and carry the heights of Halleux, manœuvring against the right of the enemy's position ; a second division advanced against Sprimont in the centre; whilst a third, crossing at Sognes, was to seize the village of that name, and turn the Austrian left. Latour, who commanded the Austrians in Sprimont, found that his advanced posts could not stand in the centre and right ; but on his left at Sognes, the French found more difficulty, although they eventually made good their passage. Latour, unhappily for himself, allowed these French columns to form up for attack, instead of falling upon them as they deployed. He could not resist their impetuous onslaught, and he speedily found his left flank turned. Retreat was now inevitable, and Scherer, manœuvring against the Austrian right, forced it back towards Verviers.

Had Jourdan now followed up this advantage with the divisions of his centre, which might have taken Clairfayt's main position at Robermont, behind Liége, in reverse, the Austrian army would have been cut in two, and would probably have suffered complete defeat. But Jourdan, knowing well the difficult nature of the country about the lower Ourthe, was reluctant to commit a large force too hastily amidst its defiles. That night Scherer halted behind the Vesder, and next morning Jourdan, finding that the Austrians had entirely abandoned the Meuse, falling back from all their positions towards Bolbec and Aix-la-Chapelle, reinforced his right, and continued to menace the enemy's left.

Clairfayt, becoming anxious for his communications with Cologne, at once retired, and took up a new position behind the Roer. His right was still at Ruremonde, his centre at Juliers and Aldenhoven, his left at Duerin under Latour, and his whole front was covered by the rapid Roer, a river rarely fordable, whose right banks, occupied by the Austrians, commanded the left, while the most important points had been strengthened by entrenchments.

Jourdan's army was in front of the river, the centre at Aix-la-Chapelle, the right at Cornely Munster, and the left thrown back to the Meuse, where Kléber, with four divisions, was about to lay siege to Maestricht, under instructions from Carnot. Clairfayt, however, seemed resolved to hold the line of the Roer instead of retreating on the Cologne. Jourdan, however, took upon himself to postpone the siege of Maestricht, and merely leaving a force to mask it, used all his strength to drive Clairfayt behind the Rhine. Collecting his forces, he sent Scherer on the extreme right to force the passage of the Roer at Duerin; next him Hatry was to cross at Altorp, while the divisions of Championnet and Morlot, with a reserve of cavalry, were to advance against Aldenhoven, and carry everything before them as far as Juliers, which place they were to blockade. Lefebre, more to the left, was to cross at Linnich; while on the extreme left Kléber, with two divisions, was to cross opposite Rathem and deal with the enemy as far as Ruremonde. Each commander had positive orders to push forward with all vigour, without wasting time or concerning himself with what was in progress to right or left of him. This plan of attack was meritorious enough, but it was accepted at too great a distance from the enemy's position, and a reconnaissance would have shown Jourdan that the configuration of the country permitted him to greatly reinforce his right without injury to his general scheme.

On the 2nd of October the French army was early in movement, but a fog hindered the development of its attack until about 10 a.m. The French centre was the first engaged. Clairfayt seemed disposed to hold Aldenhoven at all cost, but Championnet soon drove the Austrians out of it, and advanced to the plateau behind, where they had constructed numerous redoubts. There the Austrians made a stand for some time ; but the movement of Lefebre on the left towards Linnich menaced one flank, and that of Hatry's division on the right, marching towards Altorp, threatened the other. Clairfayt, therefore, abandoned his entrenchments, and fell back, pursued by the French cavalry, to the very glacis of Juliers.

Meanwhile the brunt of the fighting had fallen upon the French right. Scherer had started at 11 a.m., but as all his divisions did not come up at the same time, he postponed his attack for some hours, wishing to operate simultaneously with all his force. At three o'clock, however, he sent Marceau to pass the river by the ford at Merweiler with one brigade, while the other attacked Duerin in front. Mayer was to attack the centre at Linnich, whilst the third division was to make a long detour and outflank the Austrian left. Marceau encountered a most determined resistance, but made good his passage ; his brigade assaulting Duerin was also stoutly opposed. He was more successful about 5 p.m. ; but he had still dealt only with Latour's advanced posts, and that general was strongly posted above him with a numerous artillery. It was at this moment that Jourdan, deeply concerned for the success of his right, directed Hatry to lean to that side and reinforce Marceau. But it was too late in the day for Hatry to give any effective assistance, and his division actually took no part in the day's work ; the direction of its march, however, had been useful in bringing about the evacuation of the redoubts in the rear of Aldenhoven. Marceau had thus to hold Duerin practically alone, which he did till nightfall. On the left Lefebre and Kléber had been also fairly successful. The first had advanced on Linnich with the results already mentioned; but he did not actually cross the river until the following day. Kléber had commenced his movements at daybreak, but had met with stout resistance at Rathem. He had been unable to use a bridge prepared for him; but his troops, ruffled by opposition, had flung themselves into the river and gained the passage at the bayonet point. Kléber supported this bold advance with his guns and drove away the enemy. This was the end of the day's fighting, which was greatly in favour of the French. Their centre was across the river at Juliers, the right was firm at Ducrin, and on the left Kléber had gained a foothold on the right bank at Rathem, where, constructing a bridge during the night, he passed over his whole corps. These successes along the whole front forced Clairfayt to withdraw behind the Rhine: a retreat effected in the night without accident, and so quietly that it was not till daylight on the 23rd, that Jourdan found that the enemy was gone.

Jourdan's victory was extremely creditable to him. His dispositions were good, although not exactly perfect; but he was wrong to fight before he had thoroughly reconnoitred his ground. This precipitation exposed his right to be beaten, and Scherer was in the more danger from having to pass the river at three separate points. Marceau in consequence found himself exposed, with only a single division, to the full strength of Latour. Jourdan would have shown better generalship had he concentrated his whole force at one point covered by demonstrations at many others. As it was, the left wing contributed little to the result of the day; it was really uselessly employed, for the Austrians about Ruremonde would have been lost the moment Latour gave way on the left. Nevertheless, the battle of the Roer obtained the most decisive results; it decided the fate of Belgium, which was now lost entirely to the Austrian power. Clairfayt's retreat behind the Rhine abandoned it completely to the French. Nothing could be more remarkable, indeed, than the contrast between the position of the Allies at the end and at the beginning of 1794. In the early part of the year they hemmed France closely in, and owned several fortresses on French soil. When the year ended, the Austrians had no hold upon the left bank of the Rhine, but Mayence and Luxembourg. The siege of Maestricht had been resumed by Kléber directly after Clairfayt's defeat, and had speedily succumbed. Coblentz had been captured by Marceau a few days after the victory on the Roer; that young general had pushed forward with characteristic impetuosity under the orders of his chief, and had carried the Austrian entrenched position before the town at the point of the bayonet. The successes of the French were completed by Pichegru's advance against the Duke of York, who retired behind the Meuse, and Holland was once more conquered by the French. A series of doubtful operations, during which victory had leant to either side, had been engaged in between the Prussians and the Army of the Moselle. Hohenlohe had won a battle at Kayserslautern; but Clairfayt's retreat changed the aspect of affairs, and the Prussians also withdrew behind the great river.

At the close of 1794, Jourdan's army held the left bank of the Rhine, from Bingen to Dusseldorf, while the Army of the Moselle, now commanded by Kléber, closely besieged Mayence in spite of the difficulties of the winter season. Luxembourg was also blockaded, and the French were triumphant all along the line.

CHAPTER XI.

HOCHE.

WE left Hoche about to take command of the Army of Cherbourg. At this moment, there were three Republican armies engaged in the west; that of Cherbourg; the second, of Brest; and the third, that of La Vendée under Thurreau, at Nantes. Marceau's successes had crushed the Vendeans, and the atrocities perpetrated by Carrier and Thurreau had for a moment put an end to that part of the western insurrection. But other provinces of France still defied the Republic. In Brittany, where the Vendeans had looked for aid and missed it, an irregular warfare had sprung up, chiefly through the exertions of Depuisaye, which threatened to give infinite trouble. Depuisaye was a Royalist, who saw in Brittany the germs of a new resistance. This province had enjoyed under the ancient *régime* the privilege of immunity from taxation, especially in salt, and a large contraband trade had always flourished between it and its less fortunate neighbours. The Revolution having abolished this distinction, the swarms of smugglers, with the Custom House officers who had watched them, were both thrown out of employment. They both hated the new Government, and making common cause, readily took up arms against it. Organised in small bands, they ravaged the whole country, attacking gendarmes, and detachments of troops, stopping the public conveyances, pillaging and plundering on every side. Moving rapidly and secretly, and concealing themselves in the forests that covered the country, they easily defied pursuit. This insurrection was known as that of the "Chouans," a name derived, according to some, from a family that soon made itself conspicuous; by others, from the cries used by the insurgents to recognise each other, which resembled the hooting of the night-owl, in French, "chat-huant," whence the transition into "Chouan" was easy. It was against this formidable, because elusive organisation, that Hoche was now to act.

He reached his new command in September, 1794, at a moment when Depuisaye had crossed over to England to seek support in men, money, and munitions of war, from the British Government; with what result we shall presently see. Hoche meanwhile set himself to work with his customary vigour to grapple with the difficulties of his new command. His first acts were to address himself to the inhabitants of the rebellious districts, and to make himself known to his officers and men. The first he endeavoured to win over by appealing to their patriotism. They were Frenchmen and fellow-countrymen, he reminded them, and he was loth to coerce them by force of arms. He issued proclamations—which, as he told the Committee of Public Safety, would prove more effectual, he hoped, than the fire of sixteen-pounders—calling upon them to return to their allegiance and lay down their arms.

"I have not come," he said, "to annihilate the population, but to make the laws respected. Let every one lay down his arms and return to his own occupation. To all who remain quiet I promise peace, protection, liberty, and an ample guarantee of all properties and rights."

But threats followed in case persuasion failed, and he plainly warned all inclined to prefer the name of Chouáns to that of Frenchmen, that he was resolved to put down insurrection with a strong hand. He next made himself known to his army. In a circular letter to the generals and other officers in command, he urges them to maintain and improve discipline, promising them that all who co-operated loyally would find in him a sincere friend and brother. He assured the soldiers, by general orders, that he hoped soon to gain their confidence, and that he would be ever ready to do them justice and to minister to their wants. But he also gave his whole army to understand that he meant to conduct operations on a new and more vigorous plan. He was resolved, he said, to stamp out the spirit of disorder; to put an end to the outrages and oppression practised by his soldiers upon the people. A small, well-disciplined army, he was convinced, would serve his purpose better than any number of ill-conducted men.

"I do not want any more men," he wrote to the Committee of Public Safety; "the 22,000 I have are quite enough. I can do all that is necessary with them."

These energetic measures for reorganising his troops speedily gained Hoche high favour in Paris. He was deemed by the Committee of Public Safety the man for the occasion, and to his command of the Army of Cherbourg was now added that of the Army of Brest. Hoche would gladly have escaped from this new burden; but he could not well refuse, and he proceeded to Rennes dejected and anxious, fearing to ose in this new charge the reputation he had already gained. He found the Army of Brest in a worse state than that of Cherbourg. It was disorganised, mutinous, and wastefully

K

administered.   The troops oppressed the unfortunate people with a hateful military tyranny.   But Hoche promptly applied the same remedies.   He did more.   Fixing with true genius upon the real cause of the failure of all military operations, he at once ended the excessive dispersion of his troops.   The army had been broken up into small detachments, stationed in the various villages and towns.   Hoche, although winter was approaching, resolved to collect them together in strong bodies and establish them in military camps.

"The system of camps," he wrote, " can alone end the ridiculous war we have been waging, and waging without success."

Life under canvas might be severe ; but its hardships must be borne with soldierly fortitude.   Republican troops should display the virtues of self-restraint, and fly from drunkenness and self-indulgence.   Not that Hoche was austerely intolerant of the soldiers' common weakness.   He knew how dreary was their life, and he could forgive them for yielding at times to excess; but he was stern and implacable when drunkenness interfered with duty, and the strictest performance of duty he vigorously exacted from all. He appealed more particularly to his officers to set a good example to their men.

"I strongly urge you," he writes to one, a friend, " to be always most active, always on the alert ; remain as near as possible to your camp; never miss a parade ; and go frequently round your posts at night."

Such vigorous measures soon bore fruit.   Disorders ceased, and the inhabitants no longer looked with terror on the " Blues," the new sobriquet of the Republican troops.   Nor, while thus protecting the well-disposed, did Hoche neglect the pursuit of the disaffected.   To deal with the ubiquitous rebel bands he organised movable columns from each of his camps. These were to issue every two or three days and beat up the neighbouring district—now this side, now that—for eight or ten miles round. General activity was the result of these orders, yet the Chouans still continued to make head against the Republican troops. Animated and encouraged by the liberal promises of Depuisaye, who constantly communicated with them from London, they maintained their harassing, irregular warfare, scouring the country, subjecting all who acknowledged the Government to their vexatious depredations. Some towns were cut off from supplies; some were attacked; the friends of the Republic lost their lives; and Hoche was bitterly upbraided for having withdrawn the protection of the troops. In the midst of this renewed rebellion, the National Convention tried a more humane plan for terminating the Western insurrection. A general amnesty was offered to all Vendeans and Chouans alike who would lay down their arms. In Brittany these overtures were at first contemptuously rejected; but Hoche soon won over some of the Chouan leaders, and opened negotiations with others. The movement towards pacification thus begun was further encouraged by the attitude of the leaders of the Royalist cause, who began to think that intrigue might succeed where force had failed. Hence they issued instructions, pressing the most notable amongst the insurgents to make their submission and accept the proffered peace.

Charette, in La Vendée, was already treating with the Republicans; in Brittany, Cormatin was engaged to do the same. The latter was a General of Chouans, who had been sent through the provinces of Brittany, Maine, and Anjou to preach submission to the Republic. But he himself had no sincere intention of accepting peace; on the contrary, he hoped to seduce the Republican generals, and had already made overtures to Humbert. He tried Hoche also, but failed signally with this straightforward, simple-minded soldier. Outwardly, however, Cormatin, as well as Charette, submitted themselves to the Republic, but secretly they encouraged the insurrection, and the country continued in the wildest disorder. The Chouan bands still robbed, and plundered, and murdered on every side.

In the early part of the year 1795 the same reports arrived from all parts of the district. Amnesty and supposed pacification had not put a stop to brigandage. Hoche, on the 14th of March, writes : "From all I can hear, and all I can see, there is no sign of peace. The projects of the Chouans, so far as I can ascertain them, are enough to make a well-meaning Republican sick. They desire to goad the towns into insurrection by cutting off their supplies, to intercept communications, assassinate patriots and public functionaries, seize arsenals, organise a numerous army, and spread terror everywhere."

He was not deceived by the pretended submission of the leaders, but protested, after a meeting which he had witnessed between them and certain representatives sent from Paris, that he was convinced of their bad faith. He felt certain that a fresh struggle was imminent, and was anxious to prepare for it. But now he was vexed and thwarted at every turn by these same representatives, a score of whom had been dispatched by the Convention to watch over the interests of the Republic in the west. They were all ignorant busy-bodies, who fought and squabbled amongst themselves, issued contradictory orders, and continually interfered with Hoche in the exercise of his command. Not only were various districts differently administered : here peace prevailing ; there the inhabitants continually harassed ;

but each representative took upon himself to march and countermarch the troops without reference to the general-in-chief.

Hoche complains one day that three battalions he wanted at one spot were detained at another by a representative through false alarms. Next day one of these "burlesque legislators," as Hoche calls them, denuded Cherbourg of all its garrison, and left that important fortress defenceless against hostile attack. Again, 3,000 men were detached from a force of 12,000 on the march to join Hoche, and kept at Alençon, without consulting him.

His vexations are best told in his own language : "I am sorry," he writes to the Committee of Public Safety, "to have to make such a report to you, but when fifteen or sixteen persons give me contrary orders, I think it my duty to inform the Government of the fact. I beg of you, while directing me to submit my operations to the two, four, or six representatives accompanying my army, to order the remaining ten or twelve scattered about at various points, to refrain from initiating movements, especially when circumstances do not require it."

No wonder that Hoche was disheartened, that he wished to resign his command, and implored the Committee to employ him elsewhere. The Committee replied that he possessed their full confidence ; yet it lent a ready ear to evil report, and even permitted itself to reprimand Hoche for any casual disorder, such as the plunder of the diligence, for which he could in no way be held responsible. We can sympathise with him in his protest against such unworthy treatment.

"The position of a general," he writes, " whose army is split up into squads of from sixty to one hundred men over a surface of 40,000 square miles, is assuredly

not brilliant; it becomes miserable, if, while he redoubles
his efforts to do his duty, he is accused of weakness and
negligence by a Government to which he is devoted."

That Hoche's measures were sound was soon to be
established beyond doubt. Active preparations were now
in progress in England for the despatch of a flotilla to the
French coast, and it was of the utmost importance to be
ready to meet any hostile descent. Hoche naturally desired to hold his forces well in hand in the centre, whence
he could direct them in strength upon a given point. But
the orders which he issued for concentration were resisted
and misconstrued. He was upbraided and denounced on all
sides. All the representatives in the districts now denuded
of troops complained bitterly that the general's disposition
tended to favour the Chouans. They did not hesitate to
accuse him of disloyalty, declaring that, despite the critical
condition of the districts, he had withdrawn battalion after
battalion, their sole support against brigandage, to collect them
around his own person, and neutralise them entirely. These
complaints at length deprived Hoche of the confidence of the
Committee of Public Safety; but it would not supersede him,
much as he desired to resign. It was satisfied to take from
him the command of the Army of Cherbourg, and leave him
at the head of that of Brest alone. It was fortunate for the
Republic that this command was left to Hoche. Important
events were close at hand in this neighbourhood, and Hoche
was the best able to deal with the emergency.

Negotiations with the Chouan leaders had never flagged
all this time, and they culminated at length in a treaty
signed at Mabilais, on the 20th of April, 1795. This submission was by no means general, and it was certainly not
real. Hoche was soon in a position to show the Committee
of Public Safety, that it was all a sham. The Chouans scorned

to submit to the Republic or accept its terms; they still kept together in numerous bodies, armed, and wearing uniform; their foraging parties still committed great depredations; they made a large collection of stores, and enrolled numbers of fresh recruits. These attempts were directly traceable to the encouragement they received from the other side of the Channel. News had by this time reached Brittany, that friends in England were on the move. Depuisaye's mission, although jeopardised by the treaty of Mabilais, had been entirely successful. He had explained away the pacification as a ruse, a sham submission, behind which a newer and larger movement would be organised.

Pitt seems to have believed in Depuisaye, and to have given him encouragement and support. An extensive expedition was prepared at Portsmouth, consisting of sixty transports, escorted by six gunboats, six frigates, and six sail of the line. The convoy was to carry a force of 5,000 men, recruited amongst the emigrants in England, or the Channel Islands, and amongst the French prisoners of war. Large quantities of stores of food, clothing, and equipment, were put on board the transports, to be utilised in arming and organising the insurgents, as soon as the descent was made. The Chouans, not strangely, were emboldened at the prospect of approaching succour. Everywhere, as Hoche puts it, they organised war, everywhere broke their word, proving that they had fooled the Republic, and were waiting only for the appearance of the English, to exterminate its friends. The coming invasion was talked of openly, and the expulsion of the Republicans deemed the only sure way of obtaining peace. It was idle to talk of pacification, when the Chouans were more actively hostile than ever. Cormatin's arrogance knew no bounds; he posed as a dictator, issuing passes and safe-conduct, and insolently offering even Hoche his protection.

"Cormatin's conduct," says Hoche, "is abominable, his language is that of a convict." Cormatin himself dared to address the Convention with great hardihood, complaining that the conditions of the treaty were broken, that he and his colleagues were treated as enemies, and taxed with collusion with England, although he repudiated the aspersion. Even then Cormatin was guilty of double dealing; he was secretly in correspondence with the insurgents, who had obstinately resisted the Republican overtures, and on the 23rd of May, a number of compromising letters of his were secured. This led to his arrest, together with that of other chiefs. Hoche, meanwhile, had been operating vigorously against the insurgents whenever they could be found. The number of movable columns was increased to thirty-six, and frequent engagements took place. The troops were successful on every side. "Would that our enemies were not Frenchmen," pathetically remarks Hoche. Humane sentiments seem to have been continually uppermost in his mind. His opponents, especially Depuisaye, have endeavoured to asperse his character, declaring that Hoche waged a war of assassination, and displayed an insatiable thirst for blood; but such cruel truculence was surely foreign to his character. We have only to read the words in which he indignantly protested against the barbarous act of which his troops had been guilty when they decapitated a Chouan general, Boishardy, and carried his head in triumph through the streets of Lamballe. "I am indignant at their conduct," he writes; "these wretches wish to repeat the horrible scenes as of La Vendée. I consider it a crime against the honour, humanity, and generosity of Frenchmen, and insist that all concerned in this atrocity should be at once arrested." There were malcontents, who declared that they would resist this order, but Hoche was not to be opposed. His firmness and impartiality in enforcing discipline were the admiration of his subordinates ; they respected a leader who strictly maintained his authority, while he never spared himself. Hoche's personal gallantry, according to an eye-witness, often led him to shoulder a musket, and march at the head of a company of grenadiers when they were beating up the disturbed districts.

But now a new and more dangerous enemy than the Chouans was close at hand : the English invasion was imminent. For weeks past the English fleet had been cruising off the French coast, and as long back as the 15th of May Hoche had himself observed thirty-three sail of the line off Brest. The expedition, however, did not leave Portsmouth until the 10th of June. The flotilla was commanded by Admiral Warren ; the French troops on board the transports were under the command of the Count d'Hervilly ; and Depuisaye accompanied the expedition to organise the insurgent Chouans as soon as the landing had been effected. The English ships anchored in Quiberon Bay on the 26th of June, a squadron summoned the island of Belle Isle, and the remainder, accompanied by the transports, were clearly resolved to cover disembarkation. News to this effect reached Hoche from various parts of the coast, and the danger long expected now actually arrived. There appears to have been a want of unity amongst the council of the invaders. D'Hervilly and Depuisaye were not exactly in accord ; the latter seems to have better understood the nature of the enterprise they were undertaking, and strongly urged a bold plan of campaign. Disdaining common precautions, he wished to take advantage of the confusion caused by the sudden appearance of the expedition, rally the Royalists to their standard in all parts of the country, and acting without any regular plan of operations, spread themselves everywhere, seize all the principal cities, then gathering together a force of 100,000 men, advance to the Mayenne. Occupying this line, with the right resting on La Vendée, and the left on Normandy, they might laugh at the opposing Army of the West, and threaten Paris itself. This plan was too bold for d'Hervilly, who, although a soldier of experience, had none of the qualities of the great leader. He obstinately refused to agree to Depuisaye's proposal, and as each held tenaciously to his own views, the question was referred to England for decision. Delay at this critical moment was naturally most injurious to the invasion, which, to ensure success, should have been followed up with the utmost promptitude. Complete inaction, however, would have been intolerable to all parties, and it was resolved, pending further instructions, to seize and hold the peninsula of Quiberon. This narrow neck of land runs out like a breakwater far into the ocean, and continued by the islands of Houat and Hoedic, forms a magnificent bay, well sheltered from the Atlantic. It is about six miles long, and from two to two-and-a-half miles wide, with a sandy surface but a rocky coast, on which, on the western side, are one or two havens. The principal defence of the peninsula was the fort of Penthièvre, situated half-way between each extremity, and this stronghold Depuisaye seized at once. He converted it into an arsenal, to which were transferred the great stores of war material and provisions, brought from England by the fleet.

Quiberon became thus a strong place of arms, covered by the cross-fire of the English gunboats, which were anchored on both sides of the peninsula, and the command of the sea gave Depuisaye's emissaries access to any part of the mainland. The moment the landing was effected, all Brittany was agitated by the news. The country arose; the Chouans put in practice their usual tactics, blocking the roads and destroying the bridges; they forced many of the large towns to declare for the invaders, and general consternation prevailed. It is more than probable that a vigorous offensive on the lines suggested by Depuisaye, would have been crowned with immediate success. The alarm spread even to Paris, and the Convention in great distress saw no better method of grappling with the difficulty than by dispatching two of its most prominent members to the scene of danger.

Hoche, however, without this questionable support, was quite equal to the occasion. He had already received, with the news of the approaching invasion, authority from the Committee of Public Safety to concentrate his forces. He had been told that the distinctions between the western armies would cease under the exigencies of common defence, and that the generals were to support each other. Hoche, the moment he had heard of the landing at Quiberon, had taken the necessary measures; he established his headquarters at Vannes, as near as possible to the enemy, and issued his orders thence to Chérin, as chief of the staff, who was at Rennes. Reinforcements were to be sent to him from every side; the commandant of Brest, having provided for the safety of the fortress he was to defend to the death, was to reach a hand by occupying Quimperlé and l'Orient. Dubayet and Canclaux, the generals commanding the Armies of Cherbourg and La Vendée, were pressed to send him large reinforcements. All this Hoche ordered with great sang-froid; "du secret et du calme" are the watchwords repeatedly quoted to his generals. He had no fears for the result, and wished the Committee of Public Safety to make their minds easy; all he wanted were men and material. "I have no guns of position," he writes Chérin, "get them for me from anywhere you can; send me all the troops you can hunt up, I want good artillery officers, and one or two engineers. Try hard to keep your communications open, and get plenty of cartridges made."

Hoche's energy met with speedy reward. On the 30th June, three days after the landing, he occupied Auray, close to the neck of the Quiberon peninsula, with 2,000 men ; thence he established his communications with l'Orient. In the four following days, reinforcements reached him from all sides, and on the 5th July, at the head of 13,000 men, he advanced towards the enemy. On the 6th he prepared to attack. The enemy's regular regiments occupied the village of Quiberon, the advanced posts were formed by Chouans in front of Penthièvre, and across the peninsula, from sea to sea. Hoche, by turning their left, threatened to take the right, about Cornac, in reverse, and the Chouans were compelled to retire. They evacuated the heights of Ste. Barbe, which Hoche occupied in his turn. Next day Hoche writes Chérin, " I hold the Anglo-emigrant Chouans in Quiberon like rats in a hole. I hope to be rid of them in three or four days. I am without a secretary, without an aide-de-camp, without adjutant-general, without paper, almost without food." Nor was his position on the heights of Ste. Barbe absolutely safe. The night he arrived there, the Chouans had made a sortie in force and had attempted to drive him back ; but the attack had failed, and Hoche lost no time in making his position more secure. He threw his posts further forward and began entrenching himself, constructing on each flank a strong redoubt. He sent to the rear for spades and pickaxes, for workmen, and guns of any calibre. The work was pushed forward with unflagging zeal under his own eyes. " You must neither eat, drink, nor sleep, until your twenty-four-pounder battery is completed," were the orders he gave the officer in charge. His energetic spirit soon communicated itself to his men ; officers and soldiers, stripped to their shirts, worked side by side, and the position at Ste. Barbe was no longer in peril. The chief dangers that remained were within his own camp ; his troops, cut off from all supplies, were starving, and the soldiers, goaded to despair, broke their ranks and took to pillage, setting at defiance the most rigorous orders. A mutiny was imminent, when Hoche arrived on the scene, and quelled it by cutting down two of the ringleaders with his own sword.

Meanwhile the condition of the invaders was becoming more and more desperate. There was constant discord between the Chouans and the emigrants. The former complained that they were left to bear the brunt of the fighting ; that being unsupported when attacked, they were driven from Carnac and Ste. Barbe ; and that independent operations on the mainland would have been successful had one or two regular battalions been sent across the water to support them. The Chouans were still further exasperated by the refusal of the leaders to allow their families, the helpless women and children who had accompanied the Chouans into the field, to take refuge in the fort of Penthièvre. The discontent rose to its height when the Chouans were offered half rations, with the alternative of enlisting in the regular regiments.

These quarrels would have ended in blows had not Depuisaye removed the Chouans by sending two large bodies, one to Sarzeau, the other near Quimperlé, both on the main land. These detachments were intended to rouse the country, and make diversions against the flanks of Hoche's position, while the others attacked in front. Hoche was at Dal, preparing to follow up the Chouan columns, when he learnt from Ste. Barbe that the enemy meditated attack. The 16th was, in fact, the day agreed upon for the combined movement from Quiberon, and on the mainland. A Chouan force had been sent during the night by the Count de Vauban to land near Carnac and outflank the Republican position, while the main army, in four grand columns, advanced against the front. General Humbert was in command at Ste. Barbe, his orders were to withdraw his outposts within the entrenchments and to await attack. As he executed these instructions the emigrants, thinking him in full retreat, attacked boldly and approached within pistol-shot of the entrenchments, when all the batteries suddenly opened a most effective and frontal fire. The Royalists, taken aback, wavered, and at this moment they were charged by the Republican cavalry, and driven back. Their retreat soon degenerated into a rout, and few would have escaped had not active pursuit by the Republicans been prevented by the cross-fire of five English gunboats. A little more, and Royalists and Republicans would have entered the fort of Penthièvre together. This misfortune spread consternation amongst the invaders ; it unsettled the minds of many of the soldiery, who, recruited in the English prisons, had only joined the Royalist cause to escape from hateful durance. Numbers of these deserted to the camp at Ste. Barbe. They crept away below the rocks on the sea-shore at low tide, braving the fire of the gunboat employed expressly to prevent desertion.

Coming in day after day, they brought the latest news from Quiberon, telling of the dispersion of the Royalist forces, of the discontent that prevailed in their ranks, of the slackness with which the outpost duty was performed ; above all, of the weak points in the line of defence, through which a daring assailant might gain access to the works. Fortified by the information he thus received, Hoche, who had returned to Ste. Barbe at the close of the late action, resolved to make a night attack upon the fort of Penthièvre. At the last moment he found a deserter ready to guide a column along the western shore, the most dangerous side of the peninsula, where the restless Atlantic waves dashed perpetually upon the rocks, and produced what is locally termed "a savage sea."

Hoche's plan of attack was detailed in the orders he issued on the 19th of July. General Humbert was to advance along the eastern shore towards the village of Kerhostin, leaving the fort of Penthièvre on his right, and the English fleet on his left. He was to pass the fort, then wheel sharply to his right, and storm it in rear. General Botta was to follow Humbert and seize the village of Kerhostin. Both these generals were directed to give no quarter to officers or non-commissioned officers, but to offer it to all soldiers who laid down their arms. General Menage was to help Humbert by driving in the enemy's outposts to the right of the fort; but the instructions to this general were altered on the receipt of the intelligence already referred to, and it was he who, at the head of the right column, was to brave the dangers of the "savage sea."

He was told to wade through the water until he reached the base of the rocks on which the fort was actually built. These he was to climb as best he could, and take the fort by escalade. Eleven at night was the hour fixed for the march of the various columns, and they started punctually, but in the teeth of a terrific gale. The fierce wind drove rain, and sand, and sea-surf into the faces of the troops and nearly blinded them. They were drenched to the skin, and, in the fury of the elements, could not hear the word of command. Humbert's columns soon became mixed up in dire confusion, and the proper direction of advance was lost. Hoche alone kept his head clear. In the midst of the storm, when the

confusion was at its worst, he coolly gossiped on trivial subjects with the representatives of the people and his generals,
and, having thus imparted his own self-possessed spirit to
others, issued fresh instructions for advance.   The dis-
entangled columns resumed their march and rapidly approached the fort, which gave no signs of anticipated
danger.   Suddenly, however, the centre column, which was
nearest the fort, was overwhelmed by a heavy fire, and soon
afterwards the left under Humbert, while struggling with
the tide, was similarly assailed.   The guns of the fort did
great execution, and the Republicans fell back disheartened.
Hoche, seeing that a surprise was impossible, gave orders
to retire.   He placed himself at the head of a battalion
of grenadiers to dispute the ground should the enemy
make a sortie, and to give time for his shaken columns to
withdraw.

The retreat had commenced when a messenger arrived
from Menage.   He had captured the fort !   The right
column had surmounted successfully the difficulties of the
march, and, reaching the base of the fort, had formed up and
climbed the rocks, although the slope was slippery and precipitous, to the height of fifty or sixty feet.   Some of the
more adventurous got up by digging their bayonets into the
fissures of the rock, and thus gaining the ascent, they in
turn dragged up their fellows.   The escalade was effected
without noise ; the garrison had no thought of danger from
this side, and the commandant, who was making his rounds,
was the first to bear the brunt of the Republican attack.
Menage's men fell upon him and killed him before he could
give the alarm, then, bursting into the fort, they overpowered
it, taking the defenders in reverse, while they turned their
guns, and slew them where they stood.   The gates of the
fortress were at once opened to the column, which had been

directed to support Menage ; and soon afterwards the good
news brought Hoche himself to the spot.

But although the fort was captured, the fighting was not
over ; there was still the entrenched camp and the army of
emigrants on the extremity of the peninsula. The Royalists,
however, made no stand in the entrenched camp, and Hoche,
without opposition, followed up his success. Humbert continued to advance along the left; another column pursued
on the right ; Hoche, with his grenadiers, was in the centre.
At the same time the fort of Penthièvre was dismantled,
and, to guard against all possible disaster, its guns were
turned towards Quiberon.

By this time Depuisaye, whose headquarters were a mile
and a half from the fort, had learnt that it was lost, and his
first idea was to collect all his remaining forces to recapture
it. But panic had already taken possession of the Royalists ;
a crowd of fugitives, momentarily increasing in number, was
pressing towards Quiberon. Already anxious eyes were
turned towards the English fleet. A general wish to re-
embark prevailed ; but the ships were anchored far out in
the offing, and Admiral Warren seemed unaware of the disasters in progress on shore. Several messengers were sent
off to him, and at last Depuisaye went in person, thus laying
himself open to the charge of having abandoned the troops
which he commanded when the danger was greatest. The
Comte de Sombreuil, who had only landed three days
previous, now became the leader of the unhappy Royalists,
and he endeavoured, as best he could, to show a front against
the advancing Republicans. Hoche was the first to come up,
when a number of Sombreuil's men passed over to the Republican side. Humbert and Vallelaux continued to advance
on the left and right, and Sombreuil retreated upon Fort
Neuf, a simple breastwork, into which the Royalists, com-

batants and non-combatants, huddled pell-mell. By this time the English fleet had got under way, and the *Lark* frigate, approaching Quiberon, swept the front of Fort Neuf with its fire.   Hoche now resolved to carry Fort Neuf at all cost, when Rouget de l'Isle* deprecated the bloodshed that must follow.

"What else is to be done ?" asked Hoche sternly. "Unless the fort is stormed at once the emigrants will escape to the ships, and my retreat will be cut off by the fleet." Rouget de l'Isle still implored clemency, and Hoche at length permitted him to go forward and summon the Royalists to surrender, with the indispensable condition that the English men-of-war should at once cease fire.   "If I have a single casualty," cried Hoche, "the Royalists are all dead men." The details of what followed are somewhat complicated ; but it seems certain that Sombreuil gave himself up on con‑ dition that his men should be treated as prisoners of war. He appears to have first pressed Hoche to allow the emigrants to re-embark, but this was beyond the general's power to grant. He then asked for their lives, forfeited by the law of the Convention, which condemned to death every emigrant found fighting against France ; but this concession was also clearly beyond Hoche's power, and Sombreuil must have misunderstood him by supposing that he had entered into such an engagement. Many of the Royalists took this view, and some of them, rather than trust themselves to the tender mercies of the Republicans, cast themselves into the sea and swam off to the fleet. At this time, the ships were still firing on the shore, but Sombreuil's capitulation becoming known, they drew off.

* The author of the "Marseillaise." He was present throughout the operations against Quiberon, and his narrative is one of the best contributions to the literature of the campaign.

The prisoners were directed to the fort of Penthièvre, whence they passed on to the towns on the mainland. Sombreuil remained with Hoche, who soon afterwards presented him to a representative of the people. Next day, Tallien started for Paris, carrying full accounts of the overthrow of the invasion, and on the 27th, he made an eloquent speech before the Convention, describing the whole affair. It is said that he left Brittany with the full intention of pleading for the lives of the Royalist prisoners, but that on his arrival in Paris, he learnt that he was suspected of Royalist leaning, and that he resolved to abandon them to their fate. In any case they were arraigned without delay before a military commission, and presently sentenced to death. Sombreuil was tried on the 27th, and was greatly surprised to find that he was not alone. He protested that he had surrendered on condition that his companions should be treated as prisoners of war; but he was told that no capitulation could be permitted to traitors taken with arms in their hands. He died next day, and, within a short interval, some seven or eight hundred emigrants were also executed. This has been called a shameful breach of faith, and the chief blame has been visited by some upon Hoche. There can be no doubt that the emigrants believed that they had surrendered conditionally; but in the agitation of the moment they must have obtained a wrong impression of what passed. What Hoche insisted upon was, that arms should be laid down on pain of extermination. Rouget de l'Isle, who was present, declares that there was never a question of capitulation. Hoche, in a letter subsequently published, confirms this:

"Had any of my men cried out that the emigrants were to be treated as prisoners of war, I should have contradicted it on the spot."

This denial made subsequently, when suspicion rested on his conduct, is corroborated by an act of Hoche after the fall of Fort Neuf. Returning to Penthièvre he found four or five emigrants in hiding there, who begged for their lives. Had any capitulation been made, Hoche would simply have included them in it. Instead of this, he first proposed to plead for them with the representatives, and then, apparently doubtful of the result, desired one of his companions to find disguises for them and smuggle them off to the fleet. This would have been unnecessary, had the lives of all the emigrant prisoners been guaranteed.

There are not wanting other proofs of Hoche's clemency. He was greatly distressed at the prospect of a similar fate to that of the emigrants overtaking the Chouan prisoners, to the number of 5,000, and begged hard that they might be spared the utmost rigour of the law. The Convention, at his instance, distinguished between the degrees of their guilt, and this further wholesale butchery was avoided. Again, months later, Hoche, in La Vendée, called one of his generals to the strictest account for a supposed breach of faith to prisoners taken and shot.

The massacre of the Royalists, whose place of execution near Auray is still known as the "Martyrs' Field," was undoubtedly an act of ruthless and barbarous severity; but the responsibility in it rests with the French Government and not with Hoche.

CHAPTER XII.

HOCHE.

THE Quiberon disaster had not extinguished utterly the hopes of the Royalists. Brittany might be crushed, but La Vendée was ready to rise again. England, it appeared, was not discouraged. A second and more formidable expedition would speedily be organised and despatched to the French coast. This time one of the Royal Princes, the Count d'Artois, would be in command, and the previous errors of divided leadership, and the absence of any prominent personage, would be avoided.

Meanwhile Warren's fleet still carried a freight of arms, the balance of the vast stores landed and lost at Quiberon, and these were thrown into La Vendée, when two partisan leaders of some note were prepared to renew the insurrection. These were Charette and Stofflet : the first a naval officer who had held somewhat aloof from the disastrous operations ending in the defeat of Savenay; the latter the friend and colleague of the first Vendean chiefs, with whom he had shared the Vendean triumphs and reverses beyond the Loire. Charette and Stofflet, unfortunately for their common cause, were not in close accord.   Stofflet was under the influence of the Abbé Bernier, one of the most remarkable characters of the insurrection, whose fierce spirit and burning eloquence had gone far to organise resistance and maintain the war.   Bernier and Charette had quarrelled; hence disunion and divided counsels, fostered ere long by jealousy, for the Royal Princes patronised Charette alone, and recognised him as the Royalist commander-in-chief.

These deplorable differences were inimical to the Royalist cause at the time fortune seemed most to favour it.   The want of enterprise of the Count d'Artois was another, and a still more fatal error.   The new expedition brought him in due course from England to the French coast, accompanied by an imposing array of transports and a fresh consignment of military stores.   The moment was well chosen.   Public opinion in Paris was hostile to the Convention; and France, weary of the Revolution, would have welcomed back the Bourbons with any prospect of a settled Government.   Had the Count d'Artois raised his standard on the mainland, and, by his personal authority and prestige, rallied round him the torn and conflicting factions in the insurgent provinces, he might have marched upon the capital at the head of 100,000 men.   But such a daring policy was foreign to his nature.   He had established himself upon L'Ile Dieu, a rocky island off La Vendée, with four or five thousand adherents and a quantity of stores. Hither came the most encouraging messages and the most ample promises of support.   Yet the Count d'Artois did nothing.   After waiting a month for Charette's co-operation, which was denied him because that general was hard pressed elsewhere, the Royal Prince, hesitating to risk his fortunes in France, re-embarked and returned to England.

In these new troubles the Executive Government relied entirely upon Hoche. His success at Quiberon had now fully established his reputation, and, for the moment at least, silenced all detractors. Among the narrow-minded politicians who had canvassed and criticised his conduct were some who went the length of suspecting his loyalty to the Republic, but one Boursault, a representative, had the good feeling to congratulate him on his victories over the Royalists and to apologise for previous mistrust. Hoche's reply gives us a good insight into the general's character and temper. "To those who do not know me," he writes, "my countenance may seem icy, but my heart is as fire in the matter of liberty. I have done my duty; I find my reward in my own heart and in the esteem won from worthy men. May my conduct undeceive all who, like you, citizen, have been mistaken in me."

The noble tribute to Hoche's high qualities paid by Tallien, in his report on the affairs of Quiberon, no doubt helped to secure him the confidence of the Convention. "I must do ample justice to the behaviour of General Hoche," he says. "Boldness of conception, self-possession in the midst of every kind of opposition, courage, intrepidity, forethought, energy, and firmness, all these qualities he displayed that day;" and Savary, afterwards Duke de Raguse, the historian of the Vendean War, corroborates this testimony by declaring that Tallien's eulogium was well deserved. The Convention speedily gave proof of their good opinion by appointing Hoche to the supreme command of the Army of the West, with special instructions to deal offensively with Charette. This new mission rescued Hoche when he was almost in despair. The renewed disturbances in La Vendée had already brought the three Republican generals together in conference at Nantes, when, much to Hoche's dissatisfaction, it had been resolved to remain inactive until the arrival of reinforcements expected from the Pyrenees. " What a miserable ending to our conference ! " . . . . he cries. " Am I then doomed to see our troops rotting perpetually in cantonments, to the disgrace of our arms ? Are we to linger till the rainy season (it was now late in August) before we commence operations in La Vendée ? Yes, I assert for the second time that delay will be our ruin, that to wait for the troops from Spain before resuming the war is to sacrifice the campaign by anticipation."

But now Hoche had full powers to act as he wished, and he lost no time in following up Charette. In the midst of this the English fleet reappeared with the Count d'Artois, and fresh measures had to be taken to intercept communication with the shore. Hoche kept his troops constantly on the move, and gave the Vendeans no peace. But after the defection of their Royal leader, they abandoned hope and fought only with the courage of despair. The pressing need for active pursuit had passed away, and Hoche sought some more humane and yet more effectual plan for ending this unhappy civil war.

In a masterly State paper addressed to the Committee of Public Safety in October, 1795, he set forth his views, the result of a close and thoughtful examination of the country, its people, and the character of the war. The Vendeans, he urged, must be encountered differently to others. The whole population was in arms ; all alike—men, women, and children—now looked on the Republicans, the hated *bleus*, with horror. They had lost everything ; their country was completely devastated, and so barren of resources that all supplies must be drawn from the base by convoys, imposing endless escort duty, in which men and provisions were constantly cut off. Campaigning was most hazardous, the woods and broken country favoured ambuscades, close pursuit after attack was impossible, as the enemy dispersed rapidly and got out of sight; if overtaken, they had concealed their arms and pretended that they were harmless peasants, anxious only to till the soil. It was clear, declared Hoche, that such a country could never be subjugated by force alone. Diplomacy must also be tried, and he proceeds to indicate the proper line of action in another paper addressed now to the Directory, which had replaced the Committee of Public Safety as the executive power. Hoche strongly insisted first upon the necessity of dealing with the leaders of the insurrection. These were of two classes, the priests and the aristocracy. The first he would detach from the movement, by offering them and their religion protection; the troops, both officers and men, were to assist at the church services, and at the same time treat the priests with reverence and respect. With the nobles, sharper measures were to be employed. Hoche deemed them the real obstacle to pacification; he could not think that the country could ever be quiet so long as they remained in it; they must be removed; either they must submit and go, or if they remained and still resisted, they must perish. These chiefs, he wrote, must be got rid of anyhow, by bribery, if by no other means, only if taken with arms in their hands, they must suffer the extreme rigour of the law. But Hoche would not be satisfied to put down all active opposition; peace could only be secured when the people had surrendered their arms. This he would bring about by summary treatment: all the cattle of a commune should be seized, and only restored when those who owned them had given up their weapons. All the grain should follow the cattle, if the first requisition were not obeyed. He felt sure that after disarmament, the country would be quiet, provided only that the troops were kept within bounds, and discipline strictly maintained. But how, asks Hoche, were excesses to be prevented, when the soldiers suffered such cruel privations? He enumerates a few of them. In one month, 3,000 men had gone to hospital for want of shoes and clothes; another 3,000 men were forced by nakedness to remain in their cantonments. In the previous winter, nearly the same number had died of hunger; and in one commune alone, that of Nantes, 900 horses had perished. While the Vendeans were most active, he describes his army as "without headgear, without shoes, without clothes, without money, surrounded by enemies. Such is our deplorable position." All this time, the purveyors and commissariat officers were making their own fortunes; contractors of all kinds were rolling in wealth, robbing the State and the soldiery, and living riotously on their ill-gotten gains. Hoche wished to make a clean sweep of them; to let the army provide for its own needs, through requisitions raised in the rebellious localities, which would thus relieve the Republic of the burthen of supporting the troops employed in restoring order.

These were sound and sensible proposals, and Hoche believed in them fully. But despairing, perhaps, of their adoption, unless more strongly urged, he sought and obtained leave to proceed to Paris to give further explanation of his views. After conferring once or twice with the members of the new Government, he quite won them over, and returned to his command armed with ample powers and enjoying the full confidence of the Directory. A decree, dated the 28th December, 1795, invested him with the supreme command of the three Armies of the West, which were henceforth to be united in one; and at the same time set forth in a series of articles the plan to be pursued for the termination of the war. The most important of these were that all the insurgent communes should be considered in a state of siege, that they should be obliged to pay the expenses of the war so long as it continued ; passports might be given to any Vendean leaders who would forthwith leave the country ; all arms should be seized without distinction ; at the same time the Republican troops were to treat the inhabitants well, and all generals and other commanding officers were warned that they would be held personally responsible for pillage or assassination committed by those under their orders. Hoche at once made these articles public throughout the army, and accompanied their promulgation with detailed instructions that prove him a far-seeing and able administrator. He pointed out to the subordinate generals that they must be firm, vigilant, but circumspect, carefully avoiding any suspicion of abuse of authority. He inculcated the most perfect harmony between the various authorities, civil and military, and he regulated in the most precise manner the method of levying requisitions. This was to be done by the military authorities, without the intervention of agents or employés ; every five days the War Commissaries were to send in a statement of the provisions seized, and the paymasters of the cash received, which were forwarded to the War Minister in Paris. On the other hand, the chief intendants prepared regularly the necessary demands for supplies and men, which were submitted to the War Minister, returned promptly to the West, and met by drawing upon the stores collected locally. " By this simple system," wrote Hoche, "accounts can be kept easily ; we shall administer without difficulty to the wants of the troops, and shall be able to move them about without being hindered by the thousand-and-one difficulties arising from the want of clothes, boots, or horse-shoes." To the disturbed districts he spoke in firm, nay menacing terms. "Remember," he told them, " the cost of your rebellion will fall upon yourselves. It is you who must support the large legions you dare to oppose. But you shall be relieved of the burden when you choose; you will get rid of us by obeying the laws of the Republic, and laying down your arms; only by continuing the war, the burden will increase by the arrival of more troops." He continued to lay the greatest stress on this last measure. The disarmament of the insurgent communes was the only sure way of securing peace. The country, he felt convinced, would never submit whilst it possessed the means of furthering the insurrection. " As long as the chiefs have the means of making war," he writes to the Directory, "rest assured they will make it." The unflinching sternness with which Hoche enforced this salutary measure, soon won him the hatred of all classes. He was not to be deceived by pretences; and when one of his generals had blindly accepted a sham submission, he boldly broke the compact, and was roundly abused for his pains. Some false and foolish people denounced him to the Directory as dishonouring the Government by his breach of faith, and renewing the reign of terror by his relentless severity. His indignant reply to these charges is worth recording. They had said that certain Vendeans had fulfilled the obligations imposed upon them, and laid down their arms. " How many ?" demands Hoche, " 1,200 muskets out of 5,700. Yet they assert that peace was made, and its conditions fulfilled. Citizens, in the name of God, put me under surveillance. I am hot-tempered; but nothing is so loathsome to me as injustice, and falsehood I detest." Even on his own side Hoche encountered unmeasured disapproval. A number of the reddest Republicans, the former colleagues of the infamous Carrier, denounced Hoche to the Government, accusing him of keeping patriotic friends at a distance and taking advice only from the local landowners, many of them ex-leaders in the Vendean army; they declared that the disarmament was all a sham, and that Hoche in his heart favoured the Royalists' cause. These charges were followed by still more bitter complaints from the Vendeans, who found a mouthpiece in a member of the Corps Législatif, and accused Hoche of laying waste the country, of robbing loyal subjects, killing their cattle, and of putting an end to agriculture in one of the most fertile and productive districts of France.

Hoche's fortitude was hardly equal to these repeated attacks. He relied much on the confidence reposed in him by the Directory; but he hardly hoped that they would continue to support him against these slanderous denunciations.

"No, citizen!" he writes to Carnot; "to resist would be impossible; pray Heaven that my downfall may be easy! I expect it."

But he was not always disposed to yield without protest; and to one more than usually dishonouring accusation, he replied by demanding a court-martial, at which his conduct might be fully inquired into. The annoyances to which he was subjected were not limited to criticising the general himself; his enemies descended to more despicable vengeance, and paid some scoundrel to creep into his stable and put out the eyes of three of his four chargers. No wonder that Hoche at this period wrote to his friend, Chérin, that he was heartsick and disgusted.

"I must go away from this; to remain here longer will kill me. I have again asked the Directory for leave or my recall."

But now, at the moment of his greatest despair, he found support. The Directory reassured him of their full confidence, endorsed his orders, and invested him with a still further authority. It realised at last that

Hoche must be following the right road to pacification. This explained the hostility his measures encountered on every side.

Through all this period of harassing opposition and vexatious intrigue, Hoche had not slackened in the prosecution of the measure upon which, next to disarmament, he counted most. This was the vigorous pursuit of the Vendean chiefs still in the field. Only three of any consequence remained. These were Stofflet, Bernier, and Charette. The two last had already had an interview with Hoche, and had talked of submission; but Hoche had sternly refused to agree to their terms. They might have submitted unconditionally, being alarmed at the rapid progress made by the Republican troops, when a message arrived from the Count d'Artois conveying promotion and honours to both. They now sought, although still in treaty with Hoche, to stir up a fresh insurrection; and proofs of this fell into Hoche's hands. The general at once prepared to cope with the rising. He announced that 30,000 men would occupy Anjou and Poitou, being quartered on the country; and that 15,000 men from Brest and Cherbourg would speedily follow them. He had not nearly so many troops available; but he desired to overawe the people. With the same object, he dispatched movable columns to beat up all parts of the country; and accompanied one in person. These measures succeeded, and few followers responded to Stofflet's appeal.

The people were sick of fighting; they no longer looked upon the Republican troops with dread, and they prayed only for peace and quiet. Some went further, and, believing that the Abbé Bernier was stimulating Stofflet into prolonged resistance, were ready to betray him. A peasant offered to lead a party of Republican troops to where Bernier could be found. The enterprise was undertaken, and Stofflet, not

Bernier, was captured and shot. Bernier, for the moment, disappeared; but Charette had still to be dealt with: a man of boundless resolution, fertile in experience, of unwearied activity, absolutely fearless, and whose allegiance adversity could not shake. Hoche was no less determined to kill, capture, or subdue him. He pursued him perpetually, sent after him his best officers with the *élite* of his men. His letters are full of earnest exhortations to activity.

"Start at once," he writes to one officer, "and do not come back without Charette's head."

"Charette has with him 6,000 louis d'or," he writes to another. "Promise them, give them to any one who will take him dead or alive. Do not abandon him even at the mouth of the tomb."

"We must have cavalry," he writes to a third. "Form three movable squadrons of fifty or sixty men each, and march them night and day after Charette."

"Do not give him a moment's breathing time," he writes again; "assemble all your men from every side. Kill your horses. Horses will not matter if you only succeed. Try any stratagem; disguise hussars and soldiers as peasants, wearing a white cockade."

Amongst the number of enterprising officers, all equally anxious to make this important capture, there was one Travot, who distinguished himself most. He was indefatigable. When one column was worn out he put himself at the head of another, and continued the pursuit without intermission day and night. Charette, fearing surprise, no longer slept under any roof. He carried a peasant's bed into the woods and passed the night there, without even lighting a fire, lest the smoke should betray him. Sometimes he pretended to submit, and Hoche would agree, promising to allow him to pass over to Jersey, or, to go to Switzerland if he preferred it.   Then Charette would declare that nothing should persuade him to yield. He told the handful of officers who still clung to him, that he released them from their oath ; that they might leave him ; but that he would remain alone under the white flag. On one occasion he drew his sword and threw away the scabbard.

"They may break it off at the hilt," he said ; "but I will never surrender it to the enemies of my king."

As time passed on, the chase never slackened, but Charette still continued to avoid capture. The country, so perfectly familiar to him, helped him greatly with its forests, marshes, streams, and rivers, of which Charette knew every ford, as he did every path through the woods. The little faithful band, however, that still clung to him, became woefully reduced in numbers. Travot, constantly at his heels, cut off a dozen here, a score there. At last Charette took refuge in the West, where the insurgents were devoted to him ; but still he lost his followers, and still he made head, resolutely determined not to yield, even though left single-handed. Towards the end of February, Trayot once more defeated them, and Charette for the moment disappeared. He was not heard of again till the end of March, when a small force came up with him at the head of some fifty men, and routed him easily. Charette fled, hotly pursued at the bayonet point ; "he ran like a rabbit," says the report of the officer in command, and once again he got away into the woods. Travot now surrounded them, and drew them from end to end for four whole days. Still there were no signs of Cha-rette, when a peasant was seized and was forced to confess that he was hiding in a marsh close by. Here they laid hands on him, but Charette broke away, only to fall into a ditch, from which he was extracted insensible. When he came to himself, he asked who had taken him. "Travot," was the reply. "So much the better," said Charette ; "he alone was worthy." News of the capture was speedily transmitted to Hoche. "We are wild with delight at the capture," wrote the officers, and Travot was forthwith rewarded with the grade of general of brigade. Charette was at first treated with much consideration, but at Nantes, to which he was transferred for execution, they led him through the streets in triumph. He was shot in the Place Viarme the following day.

The capture of Charette permitted Hoche to treat most of the Western departments with less rigour. The state of siege was raised, and requisitions ceased. This clemency and the more settled condition of the districts served to reassure the people. They were absolutely sick of the war, and infinitely preferred to return to their more peaceful occupations. Hence, the few and comparatively obscure leaders who, succeeding to Stofflet and Charette, still strove to keep the insurrection alive, found that no one joined their standards. The most prominent of these was D'Autichamp, to whom Bernier had attached himself, believing that his youth and energetic spirit might develop him into a capable chief. But Bernier himself soon despaired of the Royalist cause. Although appointed agent-general for the King with the British Government, he declined the post, and claiming a passport from Hoche, took refuge in Switzerland, after which the leaders remaining in La Vendée, including D'Autichamp, also made their submission. Thus ended the Vendean War, which had desolated the country for nearly three years ; and its successful termination was undoubtedly due to the military energy and statesmanlike policy of Hoche.

But Hoche's task as a peace-maker was not yet finished. La Vendée was tranquillised, but Brittany was still in arms. Depuisaye had returned there after the defeat of Quiberon, and resuming his old tactics, had rallied the Chouans and got three fresh armies into the field; with wonderful skill and persistence he had woven together a new organisation, inspired his followers with fresh spirit, obtained promises from London of further support, and by his unwearied efforts revived the spirit of the Chouans. But at the moment when, with renewed strength, they looked for better days, the collapse of La Vendée set Hoche free to deal with them with all his forces.

He at once directed his Vendean army to cross the Loire to co-operate with that of Brest, addressing them in the inflated language so much in fashion with the French generals of those days. " Hasten," so runs his order of the day, " ye bulwarks of my country, destroyers of the Vendean hydra! Hasten to embrace comrades who are worthy of you, and with whom you will triumph! Sound the charge from Orne to Finisterre, from Nantes to Granville!"

An impassioned proclamation was at the same time issued to the people of Brittany, warning them that they could not hope to succeed. Were they as brave as the Vendeans, whose passage of the Loire was a feat from which any other people would have recoiled? What leaders had they? Men of talent like d'Elbée, Bonchamps, Stofflet, and Charette— brave men who knew every inch of the country in which they fought, and were masters of every stratagem and ruse in war? With all their advantages, the Vendeans had failed utterly; four winter months had sufficed to end the war. " You," he tells the Bretons, "are but half armed; your ammunition is only got by treachery and tricks which cannot be repeated, for your agents are arrested or in flight. . . . Take care, our legions are approaching. Make haste to repent; lay down your unhappy weapons, come over to us, and live under the same laws."

Hoche was not the man, however, to be satisfied with mere words. He impressed the necessity for prompt action upon his lieutenants. They were to form a number of movable columns, repeating the tactics which had already succeeded so well, and "stick night and day to the heels of the Chouan chiefs." Night marches and unvarying good conduct towards the inhabitants, these were the most effective weapons to be used against "Royalism;" to which he adds, drawing again on his Vendean experience, "I cannot remind you too often that general disarmament is the sole end we have in view." Hoche's counsels had now great weight, and deservedly, with the Directory; so when he urged that, as in La Vendée, the priests should be won over, the Government willingly agreed, and not only in this matter, but to the extent of approving fully all the arrangements he made. The general saw personally to the execution of his orders; his activity was unbounded; to-day he was at one end of the province, the next at another. The various movable columns started simultaneously, and were almost immediately successful. The Chouan bands could not stand before them; their leaders, emigrant nobles mostly, who knew little of the country, were soon taken or killed, while others submitted, and Depuisaye found himself left almost alone. He soon saw that discretion would be the better part of valour, and withdrew to Jersey, hoping to renew his enterprise at some more favourable opportunity. Depuisaye's disappearance was the death-blow to the Chouan insurrection. Hoche, too, never relaxed his pursuit while any fugitives remained together; he patrolled the coasts, and prevented any new disembarkation of emigrants. Little by little peace and quiet were re-established in the land, and the military once more gave way to the civil law. Hoche voluntarily surrendered his dictatorship to the civil authorities, although he continued to watch carefully against the exercise of any revengeful party spirit.

But he was now meditating another and a still more ambitious campaign. The invasion of Ireland, planned and attempted unsuccessfully by Hoche, will be treated on a later page.

CHAPTER XIII.

JOURDAN AND MARCEAU.

JOURDAN'S CAMPAIGN ON THE RHINE, 1795.

THE victories of the French Republic in 1794, had reduced
the number of its enemies. Prussia had made peace and
withdrawn from the contest, so had Spain ; England and
Austria alone remained in the field. The first was still
determined, under the vigorous policy of Pitt, to oppose
the establishment of the French Republic; the latter was
still yearning after her lost possessions in Belgium, smarting
under recent defeats, and bound to recover her lost prestige
by a vigorous prosecution of the war. The whole brunt of
coming operations would fall upon her, but she was backed
up by large subsidies from England, and readily agreed to
keep a force of 200,000 men in the field. The Emperor
employed the winter of 1794–5 in gathering his forces
together, and preparing to oppose the passage of the Rhine.
Clairfayt commanded the Imperial forces, which occupied a
long line reaching from about Düsseldorf to the Neckar. A
second large army was being collected in the Black Forest,
under Wurmser, but it was not ready to operate until late in
the summer of 1795.

The winter had been full of trials for the French : the

Republic was almost at the end of its resources, collapse had followed the tremendous efforts made to repel its enemies, its treasury was empty, it had no credit, and the assignats it issued were scarcely worth the paper on which they were printed.   More than this, Robespierre in his fall had dragged down Carnot with him, and although the latter had been replaced upon the Committee of Public Safety by another soldier, Letourneur de la Manche, Carnot's restless and indomitable spirit was much missed in the military councils of the state.   " His precise, frequently luminous, and always energetic letters, were succeeded by vague instructions, devoid of sound judgment, which kept the Republican Generals inactive, because they could not be readily understood." *   The distress of the armies in the field was unparalleled, the troops were once more starving, barefooted, almost without clothes ; they plundered where they could, privation drove thousands to desert.   The numbers steadily diminished, and in six months Jourdan's army alone had dwindled down from 100,000 to 60,000 men.

Jourdan had remained absolutely inactive for many months. He had been ordered to prepare for the passage of the Rhine, yet all this time, although the French were masters of Holland and Belgium, he was kept without a pontoon train. In May, through inconceivable carelessness, three bridges of boats across the Wall and the Rhine had been broken up, although it was certain that within a few weeks they would be again required.   Jourdan had collected a few pontoons during the previous campaign, but they remained on the Meuse, and he was without horses to bring them up.   He wanted horses, indeed, most. terribly, for every part of the service ; his artillery and cavalry needed remounts sorely ; his transport trains were so ineffective for want of animals to

* Jomini vii. 180.

drag them, that he could not move more than seven or eight days' march from his base. No less than 25,000 horses in all were required to complete the various services. Jourdan laboured hard on his own account to supply the needs of his army. Boats for bridge-making were collected on the Wall and the Meuse, and lest these should be unable to ascend the Rhine, he ordered a number more to be sent down the Moselle to Coblentz. But all these operations, carried out with extreme difficulty without administrative agents, and in the teeth of local opposition, wasted much time. Spring passed, and summer was far advanced, without much furthering the preparations for a new campaign, the plan of which, as a matter of fact, had not yet been decided upon by the French Government. All that had been secured was the possession of Luxembourg, but Mayence, a fortress of the highest importance, commanding both banks of the Rhine, still kept the Republicans at bay. Kléber, who had helped to defend it against the Russians two years previously, had been charged with its reduction—a task unwillingly undertaken, because he knew he was without the means of securing success. It was strongly garrisoned, and supported by the near neighbourhood of two considerable armies. Nothing less than complete investment or a regular siege could have subdued it, and Kléber was without sufficient numbers, or the heavy guns, to carry out either operation. Hence the Austrians continued to hold Mayence, and the French efforts were limited to a simple blockade.

In August, 1795, when the French Government had at length resolved upon resuming the offensive, the position of the opposing armies was as follows : Jourdan, commanding the Army of the Sambre and Meuse, as it was still called, occupied the banks of the Rhine from Düsseldorf to Bingen. Pichegru, who had surrendered the command of the Army

of the North to Autry, and was now at the head of the Army
of the Rhine and Moselle, occupied Alsace. and the Palatinate
from Landau to Bâle ; he had also charge of the blockade of
Mayence.   Clairfayt was opposed to Jourdan, watching the
whole length of the river from Düsseldorf to Mayence.
Wurmser, in front of the Black Forest, faced Pichegru, and
held his forces between Rastadt and Fribourg.   Jourdan had
upwards of 80,000 men, but Clairfayt's army was rather
more numerous.   Pichegru and Wurmser were pretty well
balanced, and had each from 70,000 to 80,000.   The strategical position of the Imperialists was decidedly superior to
that of the French ; the rivers Mayn and Neckar, running
at right angles to their front, gave them excellent lines of
communications with their base on the Danube ; the two
fortresses, Düsseldorf and Ehrenbreitstein, covered their
right, which was further protected by the neutral territory
of the Elector Palatine, between Duisbourg and the river
Angerbach ; three other fortresses, Mayence, Mannheim, and
Philippsburg, covered their centre ; and their left rested on
the Black Forest.   Mayence, astride of the great river, gave
them the enormous advantage of being able to operate at
will by both banks of the Rhine.   The French, on the other
hand, were on the wrong side of the river, which could only
be successfully crossed by the construction of a bridge—
always a delicate and difficult operation, since the enemy can
fall with superior numbers upon any force thrown over for
the purpose.   Moreover, a great distance separated the two
armies, and there was no close accord between the two
leaders, although both of them took their orders from the
central authority in Paris.   This authority, however, was at
a distance, and possessed but a meagre capacity for directing
military operations.

It had been directed that Pichegru should cross first, somewhere below Brisach, but this was deemed hazardous in the presence of Wurmser; besides, Jourdan was the earliest ready, and had wisely concluded that by taking the initiative, he would attract the attention of the Austrians towards him, and render Pichegru's enterprise the more easy. On the 2nd of September, Jourdan ordered General Hatry to make strong demonstrations towards Neuwied, to occupy the attention of the enemy at this point, and threaten at the same time the communications of Clairfayt's right to the Lahn. At the same time he made all his arrangements for crossing the river below Düsseldorf, selecting a re-entering bend near Urdingen for the purpose. He could occupy both flanks of this bend with his artillery, drive the enemy from the right bank, and, collecting his forces in the apex of the bend, cross safely.

But this operation was to be preceded by a crossing lower down the stream. Jourdan had persuaded the Prussian authorities in occupation of the neutral territory to allow him to pass through it, and thus the Count d'Erbach found his flank turned when he thought it secured by the neutral zone. General Lefebre accomplished this piece of successful chicanery on the 8th of September, and d'Erbach, after contemplating the defence of the Angerbach, rapidly retired, followed by Lefebre, as far as Angermonde. At the same time General Championnet approached Düsseldorf, and bombarded the city from its left bank. Its commandant, Baron Hopesch, promptly capitulated, and opened the passage of the river to the French. A little later, General Grenier effected a crossing in the bend of Urdingen, covered by the fire of eighty guns on the two flanks ; but, as he was the last to cross, the success of Lefebre on his left, and of Championnet on his right at Düsseldorf, rendered his undertaking easy of accomplishment.

D'Erbach's position was now extremely critical. Jourdan's army was well across, threatening d'Erbach's communications with the main body, and the latter was compelled to retreat on the Sieg, by Elberfeldt and Schwarline, where he joined the Prince of Wurtembourg, and with him made a stand. But he was again driven back through Altenkirchen on the Rhine, by the French army, reinforced by a division which had crossed at Cologne. At the same time Wartensleben, who had been posted at Neuwied, fearing that he might have to face the whole French army and fight with his back on the Rhine, also retired behind the Lahn. Hatry, having nothing in front of him, now threw a bridge across at Neuwied, and joined Jourdan, with the divisions of Bernadotte, Poncet, and Marceau.

On the 20th of September Jourdan had reached the Lahn, and was posted on its right bank, with his left at Wetzlar and his right on Nassau. He had succeeded in his operations, but his position was somewhat perilous: his army was squeezed in between the neutral territory of Hesse Cassel on his left and the Rhine on his right. He was a long way from his base at Düsseldorf, and without the means of transport for drawing up supplies. His troops, whose discipline had been greatly relaxed by long months of inaction and distress, now became almost unmanageable under the fresh privations they were called upon to endure. They broke out into terrible excesses, and Jourdan was so ashamed of his army that he threatened to resign his command unless he was invested with new and stronger powers of suppressing misconduct.

Before undertaking the offensive, Jourdan doubted almost whether effective operations could now be combined with Pichegru, and already he began to concern himself for his line of retreat should he be compelled to recross the Rhine. To secure repassage at more than one point, he directed Düsseldorf to be garrisoned and fortified against a *coup de main*, and at the same time ordered Neuwied to be covered by a bridge-head and other entrenchments. These were prudent and not unnecessary precautions, yet the chances of the campaign were so far on his side. Fortune, moreover, was about to favour the French still further. Jourdan's advance had brought Clairfayt into the field, bent upon defending the line of the Lahn, and prompted him to urge Wurmser to draw near. Wurmser at once moved towards the Neckar, thus relieving Pichegru from his fears of the active interference of that general. Pichegru accordingly, although tardily, descended the Rhine. He had been at first disposed to cross it about Oppenheim, and thence stretch a hand towards Jourdan; but the Committee of Public Safety, fired by the easy capture of Düsseldorf, now desired Pichegru to make a dash at Mannheim with all his strength. Strange and undeserved success attended this enterprise, which Pichegru undertook with only one weak division. Mannheim sur-rendered directly it was summoned, and the French thus unexpectedly gained possession of a strong place of arms, admirably situated as a base for new and decisive operations. Had the two French armies, the whole available forces of both Jourdan and Pichegru, been now rapidly concentrated between the Mein and the Neckar, they might have pushed in between Clairfayt and Wurmser, beaten each in detail and cut both off from their base. Within a dozen miles of Mannheim lay Heidelberg, a point of vital importance to the Austrian armies, seated astride of the great Rhine road by which Wurmser was advancing, and commanding a second great road through Heilbronn by which the Austrians com-municated with home. Heidelberg, moreover, was Clairfayt's general magazine and store-house; its capture by the enemy must have inflicted irreparable loss upon the Austrians. Clairfayt was fully alive to the pressing danger with which he was menaced, and, intelligent general that he was, did his utmost to meet it. He withdrew at once from the Mein, and moved southwards in all haste to Heppenheim, half-way towards the Neckar, hoping almost against hope that he might combine with Wurmser and reach Heidelberg before it was too late. Pichegru's slowness saved the place, not Clairfayt's haste ; the French general had lingered three days in Mannheim, and when he advanced against Heidelberg it was timidly, by both banks of the Neckar, although Heidelberg lay all on the left, and he was beaten back without difficulty by Quasdanowich before Clairfayt arrived. This lamentable want of generalship on the part of Pichegru tended to jeopardise Jourdan seriously, seeing that his position suffered greatly from the vicious nature of the original plan of campaign. It was not his fault that the passage of the Rhine had been undertaken at two far distant extremities ; but now that Mannheim, in the very centre, had been captured, first errors might have been remedied, and the French armies could have operated most effectively from the new base, with its ample bridge accommodation for drawing supplies or securing retreat. Jourdan, in a conference with Pichegru, accordingly urged strongly and with sound judgment, an immediate advance of the whole Army of the Rhine from Mannheim along the Neckar, while Jourdan co-operated by crossing the Mein. Pichegru obstinately opposed this wise suggestion, some say through ignorance, others through disloyalty ; and it was at last agreed that instructions should be sought from Paris, Jourdan meanwhile besieging Mayence, and Pichegru demonstrating from Mannheim. But no large offensive movement was to be undertaken until Mayence and Ehrenbreitstein had fallen.

This decision, forced upon Jourdan against his better judgment, promised to bring about his speedy discomfiture. Wurmser had now arrived with a strong corps near Mannheim, which he proposed to recapture, and Clairfayt, relieved of all anxiety for his communications with colleague and base, gathered up all his strength to deal with Jourdan alone. Jourdan's position was, in truth, most critical. He was not weak in numbers, certainly, now that the 28,000 men investing Mayence were also under his control, but he occupied an extensive line ; his left was in the air, although nominally protected by the neutrality of Frankfort, and his supplies reached him with difficulty by a very circuitous route, if at all. His first successes had only brought him to this : that nothing could well save him but the seizure of Frankfort, after setting neutral restrictions at defiance, as he had done in crossing the Rhine, the concentration of all his forces to fight a decisive battle with Clairfayt, and in the event of defeat, retreat behind the river by the Neuwied bridge. While Jourdan hesitated, Clairfayt, less scrupulous, marched through the neutral territory, and bore with all his strength upon Jourdan's now exposed left. Pushing on from Aschaffenbourg he passed the Mein at Offenbach, and concentrated in strength behind the Nidda. Jourdan's right, under Kléber, was now in front of Mayence, his centre at Hœchst, his left extended to the mountains of Nassau. On the 11th the Austrians continued their outflanking movement, and Jourdan, hearing of it, had to decide whether he would raise the blockade of Mayence, concentrate all his strength to meet Clairfayt in the open field, or retreat before him.

A more daring general would have adopted the first course, which promised best; Napoleon, in similar circumstances, did so with marvellous success at Mantua a year later.

Jourdan preferred to call a council of war, at which all voices were opposed to fighting, and unanimously in favour of a retreat. Jourdan accepted this decision as inevitable. Kléber was directed to retire through Nassau on Montabauer, where he was to pick up Marceau, now relieved from besieging Ehrenbreitstein, and both were to cross the Rhine at Neuwied. The centre marched on Bonn, the left, led by Jourdan in person, passed through Altenkirchen to the Sieg, and thence to Düsseldorf. The retreat commenced on the night of the 16th of October. Clairfayt pursued on every line, but only with his light troops, and leisurely, partly because supplies were scanty, and partly because he had other operations in view. All the French columns withdrew without interference, but the right, under Kléber, narrowly escaped destruction.

Marceau had been instructed to resign the siege of Ehrenbreitstein, and to collect and destroy all the boats on this part of the river. This duty was entrusted to a captain of engineers, who, instead of sinking them, set them on fire ; some of the burning boats being carried down by the stream, made a breach in the bridge of Neuwied, and set it also on fire. Kléber, arriving on the heights above on the 19th of October, found the bridge in flames, and his means of retreat thus cut off. This disaster brought into strong relief the peculiar character of the two generals, Marceau and Kléber. The young general, impetuous and highly impressionable, was in despair. He blamed himself as really responsible for the accident which now jeopardised the safety of 25,000 men, and drawing a pistol, would have shot himself on the spot. An aide-de-camp tore the pistol from Marceau's hand, and Kléber coming up, reproved him sternly. "Rather seek death, young man," he said, "in defending the passage with your cavalry," and Marceau humbly obeyed. Kléber then, with great coolness and presence of mind, gave orders that the bridge should be repaired in all haste. The engineers asked for twenty-four hours; Kléber granted thirty, but said that, at their peril, the work must be completed then. At the same time he appealed to his troops to show a bold front, and by his fortitude and self-possession completely restored their confidence. Fortunately the enemy did not press him; Clairfayt was ignorant of the accident to the bridge, and only a few squadrons of hussars had followed Kléber to Neuwied. On the 20th his corps recrossed the Rhine.

Jourdan had now placed the great river between himself and his enemy, and it was still possible for him, although his line of retreat had been divergent, to combine with Pichegru by the left bank. Had the operations been controlled by a master mind, he would have been directed in all haste upon Bingen, where he would have been within easy reach of his colleague, and could have reinforced him at Mannheim with 60,000 men. There would have been no fear for Düsseldorf, for Clairfayt could not have advanced beyond the Sieg without exposing his communications, and a small force, moreover, could have been withdrawn from Holland to hold Düsseldorf.

Yet Jourdan must not be blamed for faulty dispositions, or neglected opportunities. He was not a free agent. The Committee of Public Safety arrogated to itself the supreme command of the armies in the field, and resolved to operate by fractions at points widely apart. Under its orders Jourdan was to remain chiefly about Düsseldorf, detaching a force by the Hundsruck on Mannheim to resume the offensive, whilst Pichegru was to be sent high up the river to cross at Kiel. These movements were, however, rendered impossible by the superior strategy of the Austrian generals. Clairfayt and Wurmser possessed the advantage of internal lines; in

other words, they could move in and around the centre, while
the French were on the circumference. Clairfayt, under the
advice of one of his staff officers, had determined to strike a
blow at Mayence, raise the blockade, and cutting in between
the French armies, roll them up separately to right and left.

In pursuance of this plan, Wurmser pursued Pichegru
hard and forced him back on Mannheim, which he now proposed to besiege with all his' strength. Clairfayt next
reinforced the garrison of Mayence, and issuing forth
suddenly from that fortress, drove the French out of their
lines with the loss of all their siege train. At the same
time, demonstrations had been made against Neuwied to
occupy Jourdan, while Wurmser on the left attacked
Pichegru in front of Mannheim, to prevent him from succouring the corps blockading Mayence. Clairfayt's only fault in
the execution of this brilliant operation, was that he collected
too few forces at the decisive point. More than twenty
thousand men were left on the right bank of the river, who
might have been more usefully employed in the movement
from Mayence. Nevertheless the Austrians obtained a
substantial success: its immediate effect was to force
Pichegru to withdraw behind the Pfrimm, and to intercept
his communications with Jourdan. That general, hearing
of the defeat at Mayence, had at once dispatched Marceau to
reinforce Poncet in the Hundsruck, with the intention of
relieving Pichegru if possible by a diversion, and of protecting
the right of his own line. Marceau, having some 15,000
men under his orders, pushed on beyond Stromburg as far
as Kreutznach, where he came into collision with the enemy,
dislodged him, but he could not make good his hold, and
retired again next day: a prudent resolve, seeing that the
Austrians were in great numbers hereabouts, and that they
soon returned to renew the attack in strength. Meanwhile,

Clairfayt was resolved to press Pichegru back from the Pfrimm ; while he held that line based upon Mannheim, no sufficient advantage could be obtained by the Austrians' advance. Accordingly Clairfayt, strongly reinforced, wheeled round, attacked Pichegru, and after a series of actions drove him back, first on Frankenthal and next behind the Queich. Pichegru's position was now nearly secure, his right on the river, his centre under the guns of Landau, and his left towards Pirmasens. Mannheim was thus isolated, and Clairfayt on the left bank, with Wurmser on the right, completed its investment. There was no hope for it except from Jourdan, and he was urgently pressed by the Directory, which had replaced the Committee of Public Safety, to attempt the relief of Mannheim at all costs. He had at first been confused by contradictory and unintelligible orders, but the news of Pichegru's discomfiture induced the Directory to leave Jourdan to act as he thought best, provided only he could attain success.

Accordingly he moved into the Hundsruck with 40,000 men in three columns, the left on Bingen, the centre on Kreuznach, the right, under Marceau, on Lautereck on the Glaine. The whole of his columns reached the Nahe on the 29th of Novembér, after a most distressing march in terrible weather, the troops suffering greatly from fatigue and scarcity of supplies. The Nahe was swollen by floods, and to bridge it was a difficult and costly affair, yet Marceau made good his passage, and the left and centre were established at the points indicated. Jourdan, in spite of serious obstacles, was preparing to continue his advance when news came that Mannheim had capitulated. This misfortune made it futile to proceed further; moreover, the possession of a secure passage permitted Wurmser to throw his army across the river and concern himself with watching and restraining Pichegru, while Clairfayt was released to act against Jourdan with all his force. Clairfayt's right was directed on Bingen, the main body on Kreuznach, the left was to pass the upper waters of the Glaine, and, pointing on Baumholder, turn Marceau's right flank. Marceau attacked on the 16th of December, but was driven back after a struggle behind the Nahe, and the whole of Jourdan's army fell back upon the Moselle, where the general-in-chief constructed an entrenched camp to secure his passage across that river. His position was far from satisfactory; Kléber, who was in command at Coblentz, had reason to fear that the Austrians would force the passage of the river below this city, and so turn the line of the Moselle. His left was hard pressed by Clairfayt in following through Bacharach, but his right disputed the ground obstinately with the Austrians on this side. The advantage was with Clairfayt, however, and he might have continued to press Jourdan disastrously, being greatly superior in numbers. But the season was far advanced, the weather most inclement, and the Austrian army was greatly harassed and worn out with fatigue. Clairfayt seems to have shrunk from entering winter quarters between the Rhine and the Moselle, exposed to constant irritating attacks by the French. He proposed an armistice therefore, which Jourdan accepted on condition that Pichegru's army should be included in the cessation of arms. This was agreed to, and further operations were postponed till the following spring.

CHAPTER XIV.

JOURDAN.

NEITHER of the opposing generals who had taken part in the armistice gained much thanks for their services in the campaign just ended. The Directory pretended to disapprove of a measure which actually saved the Army of the Sambre-et-Meuse from imminent disaster ; it declared that Jourdan had acted beyond his powers in agreeing to a cessation of arms ; it annulled the Convention with Clairfayt, but speedily re-enacted one exactly similar through delegates whom it named. Clairfayt, on the other hand, although received as a conqueror in Vienna, was condemned by the Aulic Council for having made terms with an adversary. Whether his success had raised him up enemies, or whether the Court was dissatisfied with the measure, will never certainly be known, but the fact remains that he was now superseded in his command by the Archduke Charles, a young general who had already given great promise in subordinate grades, and who was soon to establish a military reputation second to none of the Royal Princes of Austria. At the same time he was promoted to the rank of Field Marshal, and surrounded by able staff officers. Wurmser continued, for some months at least, to act as his colleague in the command of the Army of the Upper Rhine ; but ere long he was transferred to Italy, and the Archduke Charles obtained supreme control of the Imperial forces upon the Rhine.

Changes also took place in the French armies. Jourdan remained at the head of the Army of the Sambre-et-Meuse. Pichegru, whose loyalty and capacity were now more than suspected, was removed from his command, and replaced by Moreau, a general of the true Republican stamp, who had recently done good service in Holland, and who in after years, although his career was abruptly cut short, proved himself an able and energetic commander. Another new general, by name Napoleon Buonaparte, known rather for his restless energy than for his commanding genius, was destined in this year, 1796, to make his *début* in war, and his rapid and startling victories in Italy were not without their influence on the Rhine campaign.

The armistice, of which the Aulic Council had disapproved, was to terminate in May, but the Austrian Government made no preparations for recommencing hostilities with promptitude and vigour. Their forces were admirably situated for undertaking a vigorous offensive, and a speedy invasion of the country of Trèves promised the most excellent results. But nothing was done, and the French had ample time to reorganise and regain fresh strength and confidence, both on the Upper and Lower Rhine. It was not until Buonaparte was pressing Beaulieu hard in Northern Italy that the Archduke Charles was directed to create a diversion in his favour by advancing to the Moselle and the Sarre. His delay was the more incomprehensible when his numbers are considered, and that Beaulieu had assumed the initiative with far less strength. There was much, as has been said, in favour of the Archduke Charles's offensive ; he held his forces in a central position, and could concentrate to right and left against either Jourdan or Marceau. The first success, if he could gain it, would oblige his enemies to still further weaken their forces by throwing garrisons into all the fortresses. These could be so observed or masked by the Archduke Charles that he would still be greatly superior in the open field. Such reasons were sufficient to set the Austrians in movement, and the march on the Moselle was actually in progress when Beaulieu's reverses necessitated his reinforcement, and Wurmser was ordered to detach 5,000 men to save Mantua. These he was to follow in person, and assume the supreme command in Northern Italy.

This weakening of the Austrian forces on the Rhine was deemed sufficient to limit them to defensive operations. Yet they were still superior in numbers to the French, having 135,000 men, of whom 33,000 were superb cavalry, while the French had only 120,000, and of these only 16,000 were cavalry, badly armed and equipped. The Austrians also enjoyed the undoubted advantage of acting under a single and undivided command, Wurmser's departure having left the Archduke Charles supreme as commander-in-chief; the French, on the other hand, were operating in two distinct armies, and their plans were constantly liable to be injured or opposed by the want of unanimity of opinion, and lacked the vigorous impulsion that is imparted by a single mind. But the French, more enterprising than their enemies, were about to take the offensive, and might at least count upon the benefit that the initiative is always supposed to confer.

Towards the end of May, the army of the Archduke Charles held the line of the Nahe, facing Jourdan; his main body lay between Baumholder and Kreuznach; his right, under the Duke of Wurtemburg, was on the other bank of the Rhine in advance of the Lahn, one division was at

Neuwied, another at Ehrenbreitstein, two more at Alten-kirchen and the advanced posts on the Sieg. The Austrian left was composed of what had been Wurmser's army, but was now under the command of Latour; it faced Moreau, part of it being behind the Rhine, between Huningue and Philippsburg, part above Mannheim, and the remainder extending as far as Kayserslautern, where it lent a hand to the Archduke Charles. The right of Moreau's army was around Brisach and Strasbourg, the centre lower down the river about Gimmersheim, the left extended behind the Queich as far as Amweiler and the mountains of the Vosges. Jourdan occupied the Nahe on the opposite bank to the Austrians, and part of the Rhine. Marceau was in command of the right wing of the first-named river observing the Arch-duke Charles; in the centre, Jourdan himself watched the Hundsruck, having divisions behind Coblentz, Bonn, and Cologne; Kléber commanded the left at Düsseldorf. The plan of campaign imposed upon the French generals had Carnot for its author. It was based on his favourite device of attacking the flanks of an enemy's line rather than its centre, and in theory, at least, he proposed to throw his whole weight on one end, although in practice, he made the mistake of operating against both. Jourdan was instructed to keep his right in the Hundsruck, but to extend his left across the river at Düsseldorf, the only passage which the French at this time possessed. This operation was intended to facilitate Moreau's crossing, by obliging the Archduke Charles to abandon the left bank of the Rhine to protect his communications.

On receiving his orders, Jourdan proceeded to execute them without delay. The moment the ten days' notice to end the armistice had elapsed, Kléber passed the river at Düsseldorf and advanced in force against the Duke of Wurtemburg. On the 30th of May, he had passed the Witter, the next day he was on the Agger; the same day Lefebre overcame the Austrian advanced guard and seized the bridge at Siegburg. Wurtemburg had retrograded rapidly before Kléber, evacuating each position in turn until he reached Altenkirchen, where he was attacked with determination and driven back with loss. He continued to retreat on Montabauer, expecting Finck, who was at Neuwied, to join him there. But Finck had already evacuated Neuwied, and Wurtemburg resolved to withdraw behind the Lahn. Kléber followed and occupied the opposite bank, being reinforced by Grenier's division, which had crossed the Neuwied as soon as the Austrians had disappeared. Wurtemburg was fortunate in having escaped without more severe loss, but it was bad generalship on the part of the Archduke Charles to have left him alone and unsupported, at a distance of more than 120 miles, to sustain the whole brunt of the French advance. A mass of Austrians, some 60,000 in all, were thus paralysed between Mayence and Kreuznach, while 20,000 would have been more than sufficient to cover Mayence. The Archduke should rather have supported the Duke of Wurtemburg upon the Lahn with all his available forces, ready to offer a vigorous resistance to Jourdan, whenever his column appeared. Jomini is of opinion that a still wiser course for the Archduke to pursue, would have been to attack Jourdan on the Nahe while the French were divided by the Rhine. This operation was, it is true, forbidden by the orders from Vienna to remain on the defensive, but nevertheless the Archduke did not so limit himself, as we shall see when he faced Jourdan on the Lahn.

The first effect of Kléber's advance was to bring the Archduke from the left bank of the Rhine back to the right. He crossed on the 10th of June, and on the 14th arrived between Limburg and Wetzlar. Jourdan, the moment he heard of his adversaries' departure, followed also to the right bank, and extending his left, crossed at Neuwied to reinforce Kléber. Marceau was left with 20,000 men to watch Mayence. On the 14th, Jourdan was in position behind the Lahn; his right rested on the Rhine, a strong division invested Ehrenbreitstein,* the centre was at Limburg, Lefebre was on the left bank covered by Soult's brigade, who was in command at Herborn, with posts thrown out to Geissen.

The only safe course for Jourdan now was to force the passage of the Lahn, and attack vigorously all he found in front of him. This he might have done on the 15th, but he postponed it inadvisedly to the 17th, waiting till Lefebre occupied Wetzlar, and thus more effectually covered the left. This delay was the Archduke's opportunity; he had quickly penetrated the faults of Jourdan's position, occupying a line at right angles to a great river, and he saw his advantage in placing himself in strength upon the extreme left of the enemy's position.

Such a manœuvre would force Jourdan to sacrifice one of his wings or make a difficult change of front with the risk of fighting a great battle with the Rhine in his rear. The Archduke's project was sound and praiseworthy, his only fault lay in his not utilising greater numbers to overwhelm the French left. Thirty thousand men were left to hold the steep banks of the Lower Lahn, and it would have served his

---

* Jomini points out that Jourdan on several occasions detached 7,000 or 8,000 men to besiege this inaccessible fortress, with a garrison of no more than 2,500, when a force of the same strength would have sufficed to watch it. This blockade would have been safe from any vigorous sortie, for the commandant of a place can never employ more than half his troops in such an operation.

purpose better to have enticed the French across to his side instead of resisting their passage. However, he directed three columns on Wetzlar, where they crossed the Lahn on the 15th, and prepared to attack next day. Lefebre, as we have seen, was marching towards Wetzlar on the same day, and he was soon engaged with the Austrians. He was at first ignorant of the numbers opposed to him and maintained the fight obstinately, until the Archduke, appearing at Wetzlar in person, employed greater strength, and Lefebre was forced to retire. But this engagement aroused Jourdan to a sense of his danger. Next day, the 16th, the Austrian column continued to encircle the French left, and fresh columns were coming up and crossing the river. Jourdan, however, was already in full retreat; he was too late to assume the offensive, and he had rejected the alternative of a defensive battle under the peculiar dangers that threatened him.

He had achieved his object in drawing the Archduke towards the Lahn and preventing him from continuing with Wurmser (or more exactly, Latour) to oppose Marceau's passage of the Lower Rhine, and he decided to retreat directly he heard of Lefebre's engagement at Wetzlar. His right fell back on Montabauer, the centre on Mahlsbourg, and the left on Renderoth. These movements nearly sacrificed Soult on the extreme left; but through the dashing gallantry of Ney at the head of a squadron of hussars, Soult received intelligence of the retreat, and was able to extricate himself in time. The whole of the Archduke's army followed Jourdan without pause on Renderoth, Freilingen, and Montabauer. Jourdan, being hard pressed, determined to place the river between the enemy and a part of his forces. Three divisions were directed to cross the river at Neuwied, where a disaster not unlike that which had overtaken Kléber and Marceau, for a time threatened his right. The Austrians had sent down rafts and broken the bridge, which could not be re-paired without a dangerous delay ; Jourdan, however, showed a firm front, and was not attacked, although exposed to a destructive artillery fire.   Covered skilfully by Bernadotte's cavalry, Jourdan eventually crossed the river without the loss of a single man.   Meanwhile the Archduke, ignorant of Jourdan's passage, massed his forces at Hachem-borg to attack him, but he had only Kléber before him, who retired speedily upon the strong position of Uckrath, where he took upon himself to defend the passage of the Sieg. This was against Jourdan's orders, who had wished Kléber to withdraw without fighting, and the consequences might have been serious to the French had the Austrian general, Kray, acted less precipitately.   Kray was attacked in his turn but held his ground, and Kléber was forced to fall back in the night behind the Sieg.   A portion of these troops now crossed the river at Bonn, the remainder retired behind the Witter, but remained in a strong position on the right bank of the Rhine, covering Düsseldorf.   Jourdan had no longer any reason •to disturb himself about the Archduke ; news now reached the Austrians on the Lower Rhine that Moreau had crossed the River Kehl, and was menacing their communications along the Danube with Vienna.

Moreau's task had been more difficult than Jourdan's, and like that general he possessed no bridge across the river, but must force its passage in the teeth of the enemy.   He resolved to do this opposite Strasbourg, and accomplished it with great enterprise and skill.   The enemy had been led to suppose that Moreau's army would remain upon the defensive, and to encourage this idea the army under Jourdan had preceded it, as we have seen, in taking the field.   Moreau still further sought to deceive the Austrians by transferring his headquarters to Landau, as though he would operate against Mannheim, if he meant to operate at all. He went further, and demonstrated in strength in this direction, being more than once sharply engaged with the enemy in front of Mannheim. But now it was known that Wurmser had left for Italy with a part of his forces, Jourdan's retreat was also known, and Moreau was more than ever bound to cross the Rhine, if it was only to allow Jourdan time to make a fresh advance.

Strasbourg was the place selected for the passage, upon which Moreau rapidly countermarched his columns on the 23rd of June. That fortress was closed at once, preparations were secretly made, and during the night Desaix was thrown across the river to Kehl, which he held gallantly against all attack until reinforcements reached him by boat and by the bridge which was rapidly completed behind it. Latour at first thought that the crossing at Kehl was a feint to divert his attention from Mannheim, and he made no determined effort to meet Moreau; but all doubts were removed by the next day's news, and he concentrated as quickly as possible behind the line of the Murg. Marceau pushed forward from Kehl upon Wildstadt, and practically cut Latour's army in two; one half fell back behind the Kintzig, the other towards Renchen. The former was occupied by General Ferino, while Marceau, turning to his left, attacked the latter. It was in considerable danger, and as Marceau was now reinforced by his whole left wing, which had come from behind Mannheim and crossed at Kehl, he ought to have manœuvred against the communications of this Austrian corps so as to roll it up before supports could arrive. But the Austrians effected their retreat on Rastadt, where Latour came up on the 30th. The Archduke Charles, with all available forces, was also on the march from the Lahn, which he left on the 26th. The Austrians were not sufficiently strong upon the Murg to have opposed Moreau successfully had he now promptly and vigorously put forward all his strength, but he lost some days in irreparable inaction, and the action fought at Rastadt on the 5th of July, although it forced the Austrians to retreat, was by no means decisive.   Here Moreau remained on the 6th and 7th, and by this time he had the Archduke in front of him.

The Archduke having now to oppose the French advance, was called upon to decide whether he would fight a battle in the plains or extend his left into the mountains to cover his communications with the Neckar and Danube more effectually.   As he was superior in cavalry, he adopted the former course.   An engagement followed at Ellingen, the laurels of which were equally divided, but the Archduke's left at Wildbad having been defeated, he retired by a forced march on Pforzheim; in this position the Archduke came to a wise resolve, which was to govern his subsequent operations and bring him victory in the end.   He decided to fall back upon the Danube, disputing the ground step by step, but declining any decisive engagement.   At some point, far to the rear, he would reunite with Wartensleben, who had been directed to fall back similarly before Jourdan, and, thus concentrated, he would attack whichever of the two French armies offered him the best prospect of success.

The Austrians halted three days at Pforzheim to give time for the evacuation of the great artillery park at Heilbron; on the 14th May they again fell back, and on the 18th they were at Louisbourg on the Neckar, where they crossed the river and continued their retreat.   Moreau followed, his army occupying a very wide front, which extended from Stuttgart to Switzerland.   The Archduke had halted on the heights of Cannstadt, on the far side of the river, in order to give his waggon trains time to move on.   Moreau attacked him here, and might, had he held his troops more in hand, have overwhelmed the Austrian left; but the Archduke effected his retreat in good order on Wiesensteig, and continued it through Heidenheim and Neresheim on Nordlingen, which he reached on the 3rd of August.

In the pursuit, Moreau leant more to his right than to his left, a manifestly wrong direction, for it widened the distance between him and Jourdan, with whom he might have opened communications had he extended to Heilbron. Concentration on the left, moreover, would have had the effect of separating Wartensleben from the Archduke. Moreau's centre was in front of Neresheim, on the 10th; but now the Imperial army, instead of continuing to retreat, faced round with the intention of attacking its pursuers. The moment was ill chosen, for the Danube was at its back. Instead of fighting Moreau, the Archduke would have been wiser had he drawn to himself all the troops still on the right bank of the Danube, and, co-operating with Wartensleben who was now approaching, had fallen upon Jourdan's flank, while his lieutenant opposed him in front. An excuse has been made for him, that the battle of Neresheim was rendered necessary to gain time for the complete withdrawal of guns, munitions, and stores; but such a plea would hardly justify the risk his army ran.

The Archduke's attack was partially successful, for the French right wing was beaten, although the centre held its own. In the evening of this hard-fought day, Moreau, who had displayed great coolness and presence of mind, saw that he could neither hold his position nor safely retreat. He accordingly resolved to attack early next morning; but at six a.m. on the 12th the Austrians began to retire, and Moreau was glad to let them go. The Archduke's right again rested on Nordlingen, his left on the Danube at

Dillingen, the centre midway between. Next day he crossed the Danube, descended the right bank, breaking the bridges *en route*, as far as Donauwert, where he recrossed the river and marched forward against Jourdan.

Moreau, although now alive to the advantage of manœuvring by his left to lend a hand to his colleague, was forbidden to do so. He received positive orders from Paris to cross the Danube and operate by the right bank, to which he passed by Dillingen and Lauingen, on the 19th of August, and occupied first the line of the Zusam, and next that of the Lech. This decision was based on the idea that he would thereby facilitate the operations of the army in Italy. But Jourdan had actually more need for his co-operation, and the faulty directions given to Moreau at this juncture were the approximate cause of the disasters which were soon to overwhelm the Army of the Sambre-et-Meuse.

It is time now to return to Jourdan, who, the moment he heard that Moreau was across the Rhine, resumed the offensive and prepared to force a passage at Neuwied. Kléber was sent on the 27th of June on Düsseldorf, to advance on the Sieg, and occupy the whole of the enemy's attention. Kléber's three divisions arrived on the Sieg on the 30th, where they halted till the 2nd of July. On the 2nd, Jourdan, who was at Coblentz, had collected all available forces and concentrated three divisions opposite Neuwied. At two on the 3rd, Bernadotte crossed in boats; he was attacked by the enemy as soon as they had recovered from their first surprise, but repulsed them. By one a.m. a bridge had been thrown across at Neuwied, and the French columns passed over rapidly. The divisions of Bernadotte, Championnet, and Poncet were now pushed forward till their advanced posts were at Dierdorf. On this day Kléber, with the left wing, was at Uckrath, a few miles behind, and on the 4th the whole French army, with the exception of Marceau, who was left on the right bank, concentrated between Hachemborg and Montabauer. Lefebre lay some way to the left on the Upper Sieg.

The Austrians, under Wartensleben, who had in all but 40,000 men, including cavalry, were at this date much disseminated and a more energetic advance of the French army, which was now greatly superior in numbers, might have isolated various Austrian divisions and led to their defeat in detail. But Jourdan, who was incompletely informed of the enemy's position, tarried to collect stores, thus giving the Austrians time to withdraw behind the Lahn, a retreat which they effected by the 6th; they held this river from its junction with the Rhine through Limburg and Wetzlar, as far as Giessen, thus dispersing a weak force over a very wide front.

Jourdan now prepared to force the Lahn, operating, however, on a front as wide as that occupied by his enemy; a manifest error, which lost him all the advantages to be gained by pressing hard upon their centre or overwhelming their right by forcing them to show a front between two great rivers, the Rhine being at their back. The Lahn was passed without difficulty, as the Austrians continued to retire, and the French now advanced in three columns on the Maine. Marceau, with what was practically the French right, but still on the left bank of the river, observed Mayence; Kléber was on the left, and directed on Frankfort. Jourdan himself commanded the centre, moving in the open country between the mountains and the Maine. On the 9th, Jourdan came up with the enemy at Camberg, under Werneck, who fell back that night on Konigstein.

The same day, Kléber, advancing from Wetzlar, was engaged with Kray's division, Wartensleben's rearguard, on the plains of Butzbach.   The French were successful ; Wartensleben fell back on Friedberg, still covered by Kray ; on the 10th the enemy continued their retreat in good order. Jourdan still neglected the advantages offered by his superior numbers, and continued to follow along each line instead of concentrating on his left to outflank and crush the Austrian right.   The French front extended from Konigstein to Butzbach, beyond which was Lefebre's division.   On the extreme Austrian left, Wartensleben, although advised to avoid a pitched battle, had been directed by the Archduke Charles to defend the position of Friedbourg, and he came to the conclusion that the best means of effecting this would be by attacking the French.   He was preparing to fall on Kléber, when he became uneasy at the direction of Lefebre's march upon his right, and he retreated precipitately, first behind the Neider, then behind the Maine, which he crossed on the 11th at Offenbach, occupying Frankfort with a strong garrison.   Kléber followed, and on the 12th paused to summon that city, a needless delay, for it must have been evacuated, had Jourdan, concentrating 50,000 men at Hanau, marched at once on Aschaffenburg, thus striking at the communications of Wartensleben and effectually isolating Frankfort.

Jourdan lingered before Frankfort until it surrendered on the 16th, and by that date Wartensleben had occupied Aschaffenburg, and covered his march on Wurzburg. Jourdan, however, had sufficient generalship to see that he must follow the southern bank of the Maine in continuing his advance.   He should have pointed directly on Mergentheim and Rothenburg, a march which would have a doubly happy result.   By operating against Wartensleben's left, he would have effectually cut off that general from the Danube and the Archduke ; at the same time he would have opened up communications with Moreau, who at this date was about Heilbron on the Neckar, and distant only some 60 miles from the Maine. But here the Directory unhappily again interposed, and overlooking its original instructions to Moreau, and the incalculable value of uniting the two armies of the Rhine, directed Jourdan to manœuvre against Wartensleben's right flank, and follow the northern bank of the Maine.

The campaign was thus condemned by anticipation. The foundations were laid for that failure, which subsequent faulty orders to Moreau completed, and ended in Jourdan's disastrous retreat. Jourdan was fully alive to the mistake committed in thus manœuvring by two armies on exterior lines at a considerable distance from their base, and allowing the enemy to concentrate freely between. But he had not the fiery independence of character that would have prompted him to set erroneous instructions at naught, and he marched on Wurzburg as ordered. But now he deeply regretted his many lost opportunities, and saw his mistake in not having already overwhelmed Wartensleben when he had the chance. On the 25th of July the French were in Wurzburg, and the Austrians fell back first on Ziel, and then on Bamberg, behind the Rednitz. At this moment Jourdan fell ill, and the command for the time fell to Kléber.

Here for a moment a chance offered for reopening communications with Moreau. A force extended through Mergentheim, and Hall would have found him at Gmund on the march to Neresheim; and this movement, followed by a rapid concentration to right and left of both armies, would have had the effect of collecting upwards of 100,000 French troops at a central point, and of completing the separation between the two Austrian wings. But Kléber, like his chief, was obedient to the Directory, and he continued to march against Wartensleben's left, following both banks of the Maine.   On the 4th of August he occupied Bamberg, and the Austrians fell back behind the Rednitz on Forchheim.

Kléber came upon them on the 7th of August with their two wings divided by the Rednitz, but, by attacking on too wide a front, failed to gain a decisive victory.   Ney, by his impetuous gallantry, contributed mainly to the success of this day, and the Austrians fell back on Nuremberg. Jourdan, who now resumed command, followed by both banks of the Rednitz to fight with Wartensleben, who had fallen back again on Lauf, and so to Sulzbach.   Here Jourdan, instead of extending his right and leaning towards Moreau by way of Dittfurt on the Altmuhl, continued, pursuant to his instructions, to manœuvre by his left, and soon became involved in the difficult and mountainous country around the Rednitz.   Notwithstanding the great difficulties of his march, his columns cleared the defiles, and his advanced guard was engaged on the 16th with Kray, first at Neukirchen, and next at Sulzbach.   Kray covered Wartensleben, who had retired upon Amberg, a position he was directed to hold tenaciously until the Archduke, now on his northward march, could join him.   Fresh news reached him, however, of the Archduke's approach, and he withdrew behind the river Naab still covered by Kray, who occupied Amberg.   Jourdan followed, and drove Kray back on Wolfering, where he was again engaged and again beaten back on the 20th.   The French columns now approached the Naab, and on the 21st the left occupied Nabburg, the centre Schwarzenfeld and Schwandorf, while Bernadotte covered the right flank towards Neumarkt, watching the road to Ratisbon.   Only the river separated the opposing armies. This was the turning point in the campaign, the Austrian retreat was ended; it was now the fortune of the French to recoil. Wartensleben was about to be reinforced by the Archduke Charles, and the Austrians, becoming greatly superior in numbers, were to roll back the French in their turn.

CHAPTER XV.

JOURDAN.

**1796, JOURDAN'S RETREAT BEFORE THE ARCHDUKE CHARLES.
DEATH OF MARCEAU.**

THE Archduke Charles left Neuburg on the Danube on the
16th of August. Wartensleben, on the 18th, was standing
firm behind the line of Naab, while Jourdan lined the other
bank of this river, his front still extending from Nerburg
to Schwandorf; and to the right rear in front of Neumarkt,
Bernadotte remained, covering that flank. The Archduke
had sent several battalions to reinforce Nauendorf on this
side, and Bernadotte soon saw that he had a numerous, if not
a superior enemy, in front of him. Had the Archduke
promptly put forward his whole strength, he might have
crushed Bernadotte utterly, and compromised Jourdan's
retreat. But he forbore to avail himself fully of his advantages, and Bernadotte, after showing fight at Neumarkt, was
able to draw off to Altorf and thence on Lauf. He had sent
to warn Jourdan of impending danger, and the French
general-in-chief accepted the message with the news of
Bernadotte's retreat as the signal for the immediate evacuation
of the positions in the Naab. He withdrew in the evening
of the 23rd; next morning he was in full retreat, the left,

on Sulzbach; the centre, on Amberg; the right also, by
Castel; where it encountered the heads of the Archduke's
columns. Wartensleben had been instructed to pursue
Jourdan directly he showed any intention of retreating, and
accordingly on the 24th, he followed in three columns from
Schwartzenfeld and Schwandorf on Amberg, his left
column soon joining hands with the Archduke. Jourdan
did not hold Amberg, but fell back on Sulzbach, covered by
Ney in command of the rearguard. His direct line of retreat
lay through Nuremberg, on Wurzburg; but on this he now
found himself forestalled. The Archduke proposed to continually manœuvre against the French right flank; and already
on the 22nd, the Austrians, after beating back Bernadotte,
had stretched forward as far as Nuremberg, and driven him
off the main road. Bernadotte had been compelled therefore
to turn off and retire on Forchheim; Jourdan too, whose
position was becoming more critical, had to diverge from the
main route and adopt a more oblique cross-country road,
fortunately practicable for wheels, by Welden on Hildpold-
stein, also on Forchheim. Kléber, commanding the left wing,
was ordered to make a still wider detour, and the retreat,
proving most toilsome by these difficult roads, might have
ended most disastrously had the Archduke been more enterprising. Kléber was nearly cut off; however, he promptly
changed his route, and the whole of Jourdan's columns
reached Ebermannstadt beyond Forchheim, on the Bamberg
road, on the 26th and 27th of August. Throughout this
critical retrograde movement, Jourdan had been followed by
only one weak division: the main body of Austrians having
halted at Sulzbach. The Archduke's chief desire was to cut
the French off from the Wurzburg road; but as the head
of an Austrian column was at Nuremberg on the 24th, with
greater activity he might have reached Bamberg before them,

a far more disastrous affair for them. The occupation of Bamberg would have intercepted Jourdan's retreat on the Lahn, and interfered with his best, if not his only, chance of escape. To be forestalled at Wurzburg was a far less serious misfortune, seeing that Jourdan had the Maine between him and his enemy, and could follow the direct road through Schweinfurt, Gmunden, and Hanau, without being disturbed.

Jourdan reached Schweinfurt on the 31st August, and from that moment was safe. But of his own accord he went out of his way to court fresh danger. For some days past he had begun to realise that the enemy opposed to him was vigorous and determined; but he also thought that the best means of avoiding his difficulties would be to fight a general action. With this idea he had already, when retiring from Bamberg on Schweinfurt, sent his right flank to the south bank of the river, where it had been engaged with the Archduke's advanced columns. The action had been hazardous, but through the fault of the Austrian divisional generals, had done the French no great harm. Jourdan, however, on reaching Schweinfurt, resolved to turn southward on Wurzburg and again attack the enemy. The project was indefensible on strategic grounds, but Jourdan had some excuse for his hazardous undertaking. His hasty retreat had been forced upon him by unavoidable pressure; not the less was he loth to yield his ground, and eager to retrieve his position by some brilliant exploit. The Directory had, moreover, desired him to stand firm on the Rednitz, an order which reached him a little late in the day, but the instructions were clearly opposed to a continuous retreat.

Jourdan was compelled to fight by yet another and more honourable motive. Further retreat meant the abandonment of Moreau, who must extricate himself from the heart of

Bavaria as best he could, and this too just when he had offered to assist his colleague by assuming a vigorous offensive across the Iser. Accordingly, hearing on the 2nd of September that an Austrian division was close to Wurzburg, Jourdan determined to overwhelm it without delay. Hotze was attacked on the 2d of September by Bonnaud, who was supported by Bernadotte, and the whole French army, threading the defile of Kornach, took post in front of it. Starray had crossed at Kintzingen to support Hotze, and the Archduke Charles, hearing of Jourdan's march on Wurzburg, directed all his forces on Schwarzach, where they crossed the Maine on the evening of the 2nd.

Next morning a thick fog held the opposing forces inactive till 8 a.m., when Hotze drove the French before him through the ravine of Kornach ; but Jourdan sent Championnet, supported by Grenier, to turn the Austrian right under Starray. This movement was in progress when the Archduke's columns, debouching from the river, appeared on Championnet's left, and Jourdan now realised that he had to deal with the whole Austrian army. He sent back a pressing order to Lefebre, who had been left at Schweinfurt, to push forward in all haste ; but the enemy held all the intervening space, and no message reached Lefebre. Jourdan now found his left threatened by both Wartensleben and Kray in overwhelming strength. Grenier was driven back, but the Austrians, pausing to form up on two formal lines, did not profit by their advantage, and Jourdan, under cover of Championnet, was able to withdraw on Arnstein. Jourdan had been outnumbered at all points, but he had held his own with great tenacity, and had displayed much cool courage and tactical skill in the field.

The result of his defeat was that the enemy anticipated his retreat on the Hanau, and his columns were turned off towards the Fulda mountains, reaching Schluchtern on the 6th in great disorder, and continuing the retreat next day towards the Upper Lahn. On the 9th the army crossed that river at Wetzlar and Giessen. The army had suffered very severely during the retreat, supplies had been very scarce, and ammunition was running short, the peasantry were hostile, and harassed the French troops on every side, but Jourdan, having reached the Lahn, resolved to defend it with determination. He was joined here by Marceau from Mayence, thanks to the intelligence of that enterprising young soldier, who had divined the cause of his commander's difficulties, and hastened to reinforce him. Jourdan, after the Battle of Wurzburg, sent messenger after messenger desiring Marceau to raise the siege of Mayence and fall back on the Lahn, but none had reached him; and it was not until the 7th of September that small parties sent by Marceau to clear the woods of Spessart of marauders, came suddenly upon the heads of the Austrian columns, and were driven back with loss. Marceau at once concluded that the Army of the Sambre-et-Meuse was in full retreat, and he accordingly directed Hardy, who commanded on the left bank, to retire behind the Nahe; and, breaking all the bridges on the Maine, he himself retired rapidly to Limburg on the Lahn, which he reached on the 10th of September, and passed under Jourdan's command. He was entrusted with the defence of the Lower Lahn between Limburg and the Rhine. Bernadotte was next him at Runkel, then Championnet at Wielberg, Lefebre was at Wetzlar, and Grenier on the extreme left at Giessen.

The Archduke after Wurzburg had been called upon to decide whether he would still press Jourdan, or, letting him go, return and cut off Moreau. He was in a position to have struck at Stuttgart or Ulm, and, in conjunction with

Latour, could have surrounded Moreau's army. But he determined to follow Jourdan, and separate him if possible from the corps observing Mayence. This he might have effected had he used more dispatch ; but his pursuit at this critical time was far too leisurely. He entered Frankfort on the 8th, whence he marched in three columns on the Lahn. Kray, on the extreme right, was on the Upper Lahn on the 11th, when he attacked Grenier and seized Giessen. The Archduke himself marched on Friedbourg, Hotze towards Limburg, and Neu on the left towards the Lower Lahn. Kray's attack led Jourdan to suppose that the Archduke would operate against his left on the Upper Lahn, and with this in view, he reinforced Grenier by Lefebre, drawing Bernadotte towards Wetzlar, and occupying the line of the Dill by Championnet. The Archduke, however, proposed to make a feint only upon Wetzlar, and to direct his whole force upon Limburg and the Lower Lahn. Kray, however, again attacked Jourdan's left at Giessen on the 16th : an engagement undertaken with so much intention that it soon brought Jourdan to the spot with considerable forces to support Grenier.

The result of the action was that the French held their ground on this flank ; but the same day the Archduke had driven in Marceau's advanced posts from Mensfelden on Limburg and Dietz, and, following up with vigour, had made himself master of Limburg, from which he proposed to advance next morning to force the river. But Marceau that night learned that his right under Castelvardt, who occupied the line from Dietz to the Rhine, had fallen back without orders, thus exposing his right flank ; and Marceau had no alternative but to retire, which he did, on Molzberg, sharply pursued by the Austrian advanced guard. Jourdan now realised that the Austrian main attack was directed on

Marceau, and he accordingly sent Bernadotte on the 17th to reinforce him; but Marceau had already retired, and Bernadotte fell in with the right of the enemy's advancing columns instead of the left of his friend's. The French centre at Weilburg was in extreme danger; but Bernadotte, alive to this, boldly stayed the Austrian advance until the columns on his left could withdraw. On the 18th the left and centre of the French were retiring: Castelvardt was at Neuwied, Marceau at Molzberg, where he was attacked vigorously by the Archduke, but fell back fighting on Freilingen, and held out bravely to cover the retreat of the rest of the army. On the 19th, this retreat continued upon Hachemburg and Altenkirchen, and, thanks to Marceau's manœuvres, was safely performed. On the 20th, Poncet's division recrossed the Rhine at Bonn; the rest of the army withdrew behind the Sieg, and was no further molested by the Archduke.

Marceau had sacrificed himself to save his comrades. Nothing could surpass the skill and tenacity with which he disputed the Austrian advance; although he had with him barely 5,000 men, he struggled bravely to the last, occupying and making the most of every favourable position, and yielding his ground inch by inch only when overwhelmed by superior numbers. In this way he contested a few miles for more than a couple of days. Such timely boldness met with its reward; but in one of the last encounters Marceau unhappily lost his life. He was in occupation of the line of the Wiedbach, supported by Bernadotte on his left, with the cavalry reserve behind the centre of his position. Having placed a battery of artillery on a commanding height, Marceau rode forward to watch the enemy issuing from the woods of Hochtsbach before him, when a stray musket-shot, fired from the line of Austrian skirmishers, struck him in the thigh. The gallant young general fell from his horse mortally wounded, and news of the untoward event spread rapidly through the French ranks. Marceau was carried on a litter through the lines, amidst loud manifestations of grief and sympathy from his troops. His mind was still full of his duty; he was oppressed with care, not for his condition, but that he should be struck down before he had completed his task of covering the army's retreat.

" It kills me to think that I shall be forced to see our men retiring in disorder before the enemy," he said to Bernadotte, who was now at his side. " Comrade, let me be spared that anguish at least."

Bernadotte strove to reassure him, declaring that the French troops would fight with more desperate courage under the eyes of their dying chief; and, as a fact, just then the offensive was resumed, and the Austrian advance for the moment was stayed. Marceau, meanwhile, was carried to a house in Altenkirchen, where Jourdan himself hastened, and was overwhelmed with grief at finding there was no hope. Marceau could not even be removed, and, as the retreat still continued, it was imperative to abandon him. Jourdan took a last farewell of the gallant young spirit, cut off so prematurely, and left him with a couple of doctors, his aide-de-camp, and a letter addressed to the Austrian commander-in-chief, recommending the dying French general to the tender mercies of his foes.

The treatment he received at the hands of his generous enemies did them infinite honour, and is a bright spot in the dark annals of grim-visaged war. The Austrian general, Haddick, who soon occupied Altenkirchen, placed a guard upon the house in which Marceau lay; an equerry brought messages of condolence from the Archduke, and was accompanied by the Prince's chief physician. Austrian officers of the regiments against whom Marceau had been principally engaged, begged to be allowed to visit his bedside; among others came the gray-haired veteran, General Kray, who was deeply affected by the sufferings of the gallant young Frenchman. Marceau, racked with terrible anguish, was often delirious; he raved then of the retreat, talked of Limburg and the Lahn, and gave words of command to his troops. But he regained consciousness towards the end, and arranged his affairs. No one was forgotten. His meagre fortune was shared between the sister who had educated him, and his young brother. To his aides-de-camp, he left souvenirs, and to Jourdan his chief; to Kléber, who was fighting at a distance, and whom he was forbidden to see again in life, he bequeathed the best of his chargers. These dispositions exhausted him; he again became delirious, and towards six a.m., on the morning of the 21st, he died. Just after he had breathed his last, the Archduke, accompanied by generals and staff, arrived, and it is said that Charles looked long and with visible emotion on the corpse of his dead opponent, a youthful general of equal promise, and about his own age, just twenty-seven. The news of Marceau's death brought a flag of truce from the French to claim his body : the Austrians would have willingly paid him the last honours, but they surrendered his remains and sent them under a guard of honour, followed by Kray, Neu, and other general officers as mourners, as far as the bridge of Neuwied. On the 23rd, Marceau was buried within the entrenched camp of Coblentz; the French guns from the fortress sounded his requiem, and were echoed by Austrian salvoes from Ehrenbreitstein.

A subscription was at once set on foot in the Army of the Sambre-et-Meuse, to raise a suitable monument to Marceau's memory; and the design of this, a simple pyramid, was attributed to Kléber. It bore various inscriptions. On the northern face was a brief account of the manner in which Marceau met his death, and on the southern the same story was retold in still more simple words. "Here lies Marceau," it ran. "Born at Chartres: a private soldier at sixteen, a general at twenty-two, he died fighting for his country; whoever ye be, friend or foe, respect the ashes of this young hero."

Byron, in "Childe Harold," also wrote his epithet, using more poetic but nearly similar phrases:

> Honour to Marceau, on whose early tomb
> Tears, big tears, gushed from the rough soldier's lid!
> Brief, brave, and glorious was his young career.
> His mourners were two hosts, his friends and foes.

There was much that was heroic in the type of this gallant soldier, cut off at the moment of his brightest promise. Marceau seems to have richly merited the good opinion universally entertained of him. His character was of a kind to inspire affection and command respect. He won the former from all his comrades; his chiefs, his brother generals, his officers, his men. The latter he earned by right of his humanity, his chivalry, and disinterestedness. His conduct was always irreproachable; it "had the respectable tone," says one of his biographers, "of a man who had been well brought up, and was backed up with sound moral principles."

This judgment was endorsed by a magistrate of Coblentz, who paid him the compliment of declaring that he did not seduce their daughters nor was he a terror to husbands; he strove to lighten the burden of war on the inhabitants of a conquered province, to protect their trade, and always preserved the proprieties. In private life Marceau was known as an affectionate son and a devoted friend. Proud and quick-tempered if misunderstood, his heart was full

of generous impulses; his disposition tender and true.
All he possessed was freely offered to those he loved; his
purse was open to them; his carriages, horses, everything
was at their service. In his public career Marceau was
distinguished for many admirable qualities. Ever ardent,
impetuous, indefatigable, he could not tolerate any negligence
or want of zeal; but while he exacted a full performance of
duty from others, he never spared himself. His military
gifts must have been of the highest. He was an excellent
tactician, had a quick eye for country, an almost intuitive
penetration into an enemy's intentions, and he was peculiarly
ready to adapt himself to the varying fortunes of a fight.
Kléber, his fast friend and most appreciative colleague, had
the highest opinion of his capacity in this respect. "Others
might surpass Marceau," said Kléber, "in laying a siege,
but I have known no general his equal in changing a plan
of battle with sound judgment and self-possession on the
very field."

Marceau's death, and the severe losses incurred in the
long retreat, were not the only misfortunes which overtook
the French in this disastrous campaign. Moreau was also
compromised, and a brief summary of that general's later
operations will find fitting record here. He had hesitated
on first hearing of the Archduke's movement towards the
Naab; doubtful how to act, whether to operate on the left
bank of the Danube as the Directory wished, or cross
and give Jourdan immediate support. He decided at length
on the former and more erroneous course, proposing to cross
the Lech, attack Latour who had been left to "contain"
him, and then invade Bavaria. The plan was vicious, and
opposed to the true principles of strategy. Success on
this line could not save Jourdan; while Jourdan's retreat
.must of necessity bring Moreau back too. Here again the

Directory's unwise orders prevailed over Moreau's better judgment, and the consequences were what might have been foreseen. Moreau crossed the Lech and drove back Latour before him as far as the Iser. He then contemplated manœuvring against the Archduke's left, but learnt at length that the Army of the Sambre-et-Meuse had retreated, and that the Archduke Charles now menaced his communications dangerously. He was accordingly obliged to fall back, now pressed hard by Latour. But Latour was checked and badly beaten in the Battle of Biberach, and Moreau effected his retreat undisturbed upon Fribourg.

Latour's right now effected a junction with the Archduke, who had retrograded from the Lahn, reaching Homberg on the 17th October. Thus concentrated, the Austrians pressed forward to drive Moreau back across the Rhine. The French had halted on the Elz, but the position was soon seen to be insecure, and Moreau now resolved to fall back on Schliegen, there to await and resist attack with one portion of his army, while it covered the passage of the rest. A sharp engagement took place on the 25th October without decisive results, but the Austrians remained under arms, intending to renew the attack next day. That night, however, Moreau retired on Huningue, and used its bridge to withdraw the whole of his forces to the left bank.

Jourdan cannot well be blamed for the faults observable in the second campaign of 1796. In its earlier period, through the month of July, when advancing to the Lahn and the Maine, he erred, in not using his superior strength to crush Wartensleben; but for the false strategy which directed him against the wrong flank of the retreating Austrians, the Directory, as has been pointed out, was responsible. All that can be laid to Jourdan's charge was the want of moral courage to set injudicious orders at defiance. Being actually in presence of his foe, he must have penetrated his intentions; he must have been aware, from the direction of Wartensleben's retreat, that the two Austrian armies were manœuvring to join forces. This should have urged upon him with irresistible logic the paramount necessity for combining with Moreau. A stronger general at such juncture would have dared to be disobedient, and would have looked for pardon in the success that was his due. The chance was there, had he but seized his opportunity; but it did not return, and the whole of his subsequent misfortunes are directly traceable to his acceptance of instructions he knew to be wrong. He was, of course, thrown over by the masters whose contempt for the true principles of strategy had caused his misfortune. The Directory chose to ignore their own culpable mistake, and visited their sins upon Jourdan. When that general, at Schweinfurt, disheartened and disgusted at his want of success, placed his resignation in their hands, they eagerly accepted it, although no successor was nominated until Jourdan, on reaching the Lahn, renewed his application to be relieved of his command.

Then Beurnonville, a commander with no claims to generalship, and no military qualities but that of general courage, was sent to replace Jourdan. Beurnonville's incompetence was soon proved, as I shall show in a later chapter, and he was eventually superseded by Hoche. Jourdan meanwhile retired into comparative obscurity, from which he only emerged to take a part in the current political rather than military warfare. He became one of the Council of Five Hundred, under the Constitution of 1795, and was listened to with attention in the Chamber on military subjects.

When Hoche was attacked by one of the Council, and accused of misusing his position as general-in-chief of the Rhine to embezzle public funds, Jourdan defended him warmly. "For two years," said Jourdan, "I commanded 150,000 men. Well, never more than 10,000 rations were issued to us daily; the State paid for the whole number, but the balance was stolen by dishonest agents, the vampires who devour the substance of the people."

It was the same in Hoche's case, Jourdan declared, and his championship sufficed to save his successor on the Rhine from further malevolent persecution. Jourdan did a large service to his country, in introducing the law for conscription. Till 1797 the Government had been satisfied with extraordinary levies to replenish the ranks of the army; but this intermittent and occasional method of recruiting was most unsatisfactory. Jourdan proposed that the obligation of military service should be deemed compulsory on all Frenchmen between 20 and 45, and brought forward a scheme of classes, each of which should be called upon according to the emergency. His suggestion was readily accepted, and a year later, when war again threatened France, it was at Jourdan's instance that all conscripts were called to the colours. Jourdan commanded in another campaign, in which he was again worsted by the Archduke Charles; but this, with his subsequent career, belongs to the concluding chapter of his biography.

CHAPTER XVI.

HOCHE.

HOCHE'S INVASION OF IRELAND.

THE invasion of England had always been a favourite project with Hoche. Three years before, when only a staff officer at Dunkirk, he contemplated an undertaking of this kind. He wrote then to a member of the Committee of Public Safety, urging the measure with great fervour.

"From the beginning of this campaign I have never ceased to believe," he says, "that we should best fight the English by carrying the war into their own country. Six months' reflection has confirmed me in my opinion that there was nothing wild or impossible in the idea. Fifteen veteran battalions, as many more of the new levies, twelve or fifteen squadrons, some light artillery, and a small siege train would suffice. A brave man at the head of 40,000 comrades, could bring the country to submission. But as to sea transport, you will ask! Cover the sea with the shipping of your merchant marine, arm them as men-of-war, and make one long bridge from the French shore to that of haughty Albion. No manœuvres, no stratagem, nothing but iron, fire, and patriotism. If we are attacked in crossing the Channel, we will use red-hot shot. Why obey the rules of war with barbarians who fight us with poison, murder, and conflagration? I ask no rank, no appointment. I only wish to be the first to put my foot on this land of political brigands."

These ambitious aspirations returned with renewed force to Hoche when he was completing the pacification of the West. In May, 1796, when the insurgent Chouans were at last absolutely conquered, he began to prepare for a secret expedition beyond the sea.

A corps was organised under the name of the "Légion de France," officered and recruited by volunteers. Hoche had called for them in general orders, asking first for 40 officers, of approved courage and sound health, to undertake a special mission. Soon afterwards he called for 120 more, assuring rapid fortune and promotion to all who presented themselves; at the same time the legion raised numbered 2,000 men. It was intended to throw them into England, under the leadership of some daring chief, probably Humbert, and it was hoped that their own bold efforts would ensure them success. Carnot is said to have thus indicated their operations :

"Well armed, provided with abundant supplies, they would invade the country, declare war against the rich, recruit their ranks amongst the poor, gathering strength daily, organising forays, conducting a partisan warfare, and doing all the damage they could."

Nothing came of this wild scheme, which could only have originated in the minds of men utterly ignorant of the character of the country they rashly proposed to invade. It may be safely asserted that very few of these reckless adventurers, had they landed in England, would have lived to return to their own land. But while the preparations for this strange expedition were still in progress, a larger and more practicable enterprise presented itself.

Ireland, at the close of the last century, was even more disturbed than at this. A formidable insurrection was on the point of breaking out, and its leaders had severally sent agents to implore the assistance of France. Some of these made their way direct to Hoche, and offered him the most ample support if he would appear in Ireland at the head of a French army, to serve as the rallying point of the people. Hoche listened eagerly to these proposals, and then started for Paris to obtain the consent of the Directory to the expedition. He was received cordially, as a general who deserved well of his country; but the Directory, although they lavished encomiums and gifts on him, hesitated to accept his views about Ireland.

Yet Hoche talked them over, pointing out the manifest advantages to be obtained from supporting an Irish insurrection. It was paying off the English, he said, who had stirred up Brittany and La Vendée, in their own coin. It would oblige them to use all their resources in defending the integrity of their own soil, and divert them from fomenting and fostering the war on the Continent.

"Depend upon it," declared Hoche, "the shortest way to London is by Dublin."

The Directory yielded, and Hoche at once proceeded, in concert with Admiral Truguet, the Minister of Marine, to organise the expedition. Truguet—a sailor passionately devoted to his own arm of the service—had deeply grieved over the many reverses endured by the French navy, and he grasped eagerly at the chance of retrieving its reputation. He threw himself heart and soul into the preparations. Pressing orders were sent to Brest, to prepare for sea every ship and frigate that could float. He raised money by new loans on Dutch merchants, and enjoined the utmost activity on his subordinates. Unhappily for Hoche, and the success of an enterprise he had so deeply at heart, the French Admiral commanding at Brest was utterly opposed to the Irish expedition.

Admiral Villaret-Joyeuse had long been preparing a fleet destined to carry support to Tippoo Sahib, who was at that time struggling vainly against the British power in Madras. Villaret seems to have been loyally satisfied that the invasion of Ireland could not succeed; but there can be no doubt that he was also bitterly disappointed at the diversion of an expedition he was to have commanded in person, and resented being placed under the orders of Hoche.

Admiral Villaret-Joyeuse submitted himself, but with a bad grace, and sought covertly to oppose and hinder the preparations by every means in his power. According to him, the French naval resources were quite unequal to the demands put upon them. Hoche chafed impatiently at the delays and difficulties which his unwilling colleague continually threw in his way. The day of departure was repeatedly postponed : Villaret named two months hence, three months ; then he declared that he could fix no date ; the fleet wanted everything, it was without stores, without crews. Hoche insisted that the fitting out of the ships should be proceeded with, and for crews he offered soldiers specially selected for the work. To increase Hoche's annoyance, murmurs were now heard in the ranks of his army. The men openly vented their discontent, murmurs gained ground that the projected enterprise was too hazardous, and must end in the annihilation of the invading force. Hoche silenced these complaints by appealing to the better feelings of his troops. One of the liveliest causes of dissatisfaction had been the report, that the general himself meant to allow the expedition to start without him, that he would see it leave the port, but that he intended to avoid its dangers by remaining behind.

"Such cowardly suspicions should be appreciated as they deserve," says Hoche in an order of the day; "it is right, however, that the general, while assuring the troops, whom he has the honour to command, of his confidence in them, should remind them of the confidence with which they have so often honoured him. Never! no, never! will he abandon brave men destined to win new glory. His feelings would prompt him to this assurance, if even he had not received distinct orders from the Government on this head. He will be found, as on previous occasions, always in the foremost place!"

Further inquiry satisfied Hoche that these ideas had been fostered by the insidious and seditious proceedings of Admiral Villaret and many of his officers. He might have arrested his faithless colleague, but he preferred to report his conduct, and leave his condemnation to the Minister of Marine. Truguet was slow to believe evil of the admiral, and forbore to call him to account, thinking that perhaps Hoche was embittered against him on account of the unavoidable tardiness with which the expedition was being got under way. Hoche would not allow Villaret to escape, and inveighed against him in still stronger terms.

"Villaret," he again writes to Truguet, "has quite lost my confidence, I declare him unworthy of that of the nation; I would not even trust him with the command of a corvette. So long as he thought that a part of the fleet was to go to India, he assured me he could send fourteen ships of the line and nine frigates to sea; but now that he has learnt that I propose to employ the whole squadron in the expedition against Ireland, he falls back upon his former declaration, and will put only five ships at my disposal. And yet you allow this man to retain your confidence ! Oh ! minister, think of the Republic ! Five ships ! And the nine others, what will he do with them ? Use them as transports for India ?"

Truguet still refused to be convinced, he suggested to Hoche that it might be as Villaret declared ; other naval officers corroborated his opinion that only five ships were ready.

"What officers ?" asked Hoche in reply. "Five or six tradesmen of Lorient, who compose Villaret's surroundings. I have too much respect for the French navy to believe that they represent its spirit. Only give us a naval commander, and we will set out." These urgent representations at length convinced Truguet against his will. He yielded to Hoche, and Villaret was removed from his command, being succeeded by Admiral Morard de Galles, an officer advanced in years and not too active, but at least he was well disposed ; and from this moment the preparations proceeded apace. The shipping were got ready rapidly, the seamen flocked in in hundreds to take service. Hoche's delight was unbounded. It breaks out in his correspondence at this date. "I am choking with joy," he writes. "Ah ! my dear minister, how soundly I have slept these last three nights !" Truguet replied in similar spirit: "The dismissal of Villaret had clearly relieved him of a great burden," he writes Hoche. "The other day, you might have been all going to a funeral ; to-day, it seems certain that you are all marching to glory. Your presence, my dear Hoche, animates every one ; I expect the happiest results from your influence ; nothing seemingly can resist it."

Hoche's fiery energy, his intolerance of opposition, his fierce hatred of all who would not second his efforts with equal determination, must have greatly increased the number of his enemies. Already we have seen him exposed to the vilest machinations; his enemies now went further, and descended to dastardly and murderous attacks. As he was returning from the theatre with his brother-in-law and the chief of his staff, Hoche heard a shot behind him, and thought at first that it had been fired through carelessness. But the shouts of "Murderer! Seize him!" soon undeceived him.

The would-be assassin was arrested, and confessed that he had been offered fifty louis to kill General Hoche. Fuller investigation brought home the intended crime to Rossignol, a former Chouan leader, who was arrested, tried, and in due course guillotined. Nor was this all. Shortly afterwards Hoche's life was again in danger at Brest; he was seized with a mysterious malady after dinner, and his acute sufferings justified the suspicion that he had been poisoned. But he escaped with life, and, regaining strength, addressed himself with renewed vigour to the projected invasion. A proclamation to the Irish people was prepared and secretly printed at Angers, in which Hoche set forth his intentions of assisting them to escape from the tyranny of the English dominion; he pointed out to them the enormous benefits that must follow freedom, and at the same time promised to obtain it for them. He came armed, he said, by the generosity of the French Republicans seeking, by the zeal and integrity of his comrades, to establish Irish independence. England should no longer be able to paralyse the whole of the physical and moral resources of Ireland.

"Can there be a single well-informed Irishman," cries Hoche, "who is not aware of the advantages of the geographical position of his country, of the richness of its soil, of the activity, strength, and courage of its people, of the number, excellence, and convenient situations of its ports?" He ended his long harangue in the following impassioned terms : " People of Ireland, I have now informed you of the intentions of the French nation ; I have also expressed my personal sentiments with the frankness of a soldier whose glory depends upon the success of our common enterprise. Remember that all Europe watches you, and will judge whether you deserve to break your chains. Nothing can be easier if you bravely insist upon it. Rise unanimously, and in mass, at all points of your island. I and my brave brethren in arms will serve as a point on which to rally. Our imposing force must assure you of prompt and complete victory without striking a blow. Just as the reviving rays of the sun clear the earth of pestilential vapours, destroying the vermin they breed, so will the flames of your patriotism put tyranny to flight, and destroy its vile satellites, amidst united French and Irish shouts of ' Vive la Liberté ! Vive l'Égalité !'"

There can be no doubt that the Directory had brought themselves to hope much from the expedition to Ireland, and was encouraged in consequence to repel the overtures now made by Pitt. Lord Malmesbury had come to Paris to negotiate. Pitt certainly dreaded a French descent; he knew that Ireland was ripe for rebellion, and he was not deceived by the specious reports that the flotilla collecting at Brest was destined anywhere rather than for the coasts of the British Isles. The attitude of the English Ambassador was hardly conciliatory, but Hoche had given orders to sail even before Lord Malmesbury had been ordered to leave Paris. On the 14th of December the fleet prepared for sea. It was not supported by other French squadrons, but was sufficiently strong in itself. It consisted of fifteen sail of the line, twelve frigates, a few large transports and store vessels. Hoche had wisely decided not to embarrass himself with a large convoy of transports, and the troops of the expedition were mostly carried on board the men-of-war. The force numbered about 15,000 men; these landed, the ships were to return and make a second voyage with 10,000 more. Few guns or horses were on board the first flotilla, for it was hoped that both would be seized from the enemy after landing. The most minute and precise instructions were issued to all commanders, the best anchorages were indicated, and each captain carried sealed orders giving instructions as to the position his ship was to occupy when the disembarkation commenced. Hoche added fuller directions when the troops were once on board. The ships were to avoid any engagement with the enemy in crossing, but if action was unavoidable they were to lay alongside and board, using the troops for the purpose. His last words were addressed to the Minister of Marine : " The gales may come, but everything by land and sea seems entirely in our favour ; joy and security are on our brows, patriotism and confidence in our hearts."

Hoche, unhappily for himself, was not weatherwise. He could not read the elements, and there was no machinery at the close of the last century to convey to him the warning that a deep depression was approaching the French coasts. His fleet set sail in unconscious security, on the 15th of December, and for that day at least all went well ; no English cruisers were in sight, and the expedition got to. sea without opposition. But on the 16th it met contrary winds which rapidly increased to a hurricane, and the French ships, mistaking signals, and thrown into much distress by the storm, were soon separated from each other. On the morning of the 17th they were all dispersed.

With infinite pains Rear-Admiral Bouvet reassembled nine ships of the line and six frigates, with which he steered towards Cape Clear. Next day other ships came up, and all with one exception arrived in due course in Bantry Bay. This exception was the ship that carried Hoche and Admiral Morard des Galles. Precious moments were now lost irreparably in doubt and hesitation; Bouvet and General Grouchy, who was second in command of the troops, were uncertain how to act in the absence of their chiefs. Chèrin, chief of the staff, strongly urged Grouchy to disembark. Grouchy would not accept so grave a responsibility. In vain Chèrin protested and implored, nothing could shake Grouchy from his resolve, and there was a moment, so Chèrin confesses, when he was ready to throw Grouchy overboard as the only practical solution of this serious difficulty. All this time the weather continued tempestuous, and the French ships had more than once been obliged to put out to sea. It was during a momentary calm that the landing already referred to had been contemplated, but once again the sea and wind rose threateningly. The ships were in danger and many of them were obliged to put to sea, while others took refuge in the mouth of the Shannon. But now Bouvet, utterly discouraged, gave up all hope, and putting his ships about sailed back to France. He regained Brest on the 1st of January with five ships of the line and three frigates; others followed one by one, and last of all Hoche returned to France. His ship had been driven far out to the westward during the gale, but was at length making for Ireland when it encountered and was chased by an English cruiser and was still further delayed. Hoche reached Bantry Bay at last only to find that his fleet had disappeared. What had become of it? It is easy to imagine the general's surprise and dismay. Had they landed their freight and returned for the remainder of the French troops? At first Hoche thought he distinguished the French flag on shore, but now he was boarded by an Irish fishing-boat and learnt exactly what had occurred. The French ships had entered the bay, anchored, and remained there a few days, then sailed away again. Hoche in disgust immediately set sail for France, but on the voyage back he encountered fresh gales which drove him to the southward, and he eventually landed in a small boat near Rochefort, whence he started post haste for Paris. The Directory, already informed of the failure of his expedition, consoled Hoche by exonerating him .from all blame. As a proof of their unshaken confidence they at once offered him the command of the Army of the Sambre-et-Meuse, but Hoche at first declined ; he was wild to return to Ireland to keep faith as he said, as he insisted, with the Irish people.

But the Directory became more pressing, and he yielded to their desires that he should proceed to the Rhine. "My friend," he said to Truguet when they met, "we may be perhaps the most miserable people under the sun, but we shall be the most vile if we abandon the Irish people to the vengeance of their tyrants. Our enterprise is only post-poned, my friend ; re-equip your fleet, I shall be ready to re-embark. I have been entrusted with the command of the Army of the Sambre-et-Meuse. It is disorganised ; I will set all right. You for your part restore your navy ; write me when your arrangements are completed, then without delay I will let some general succeed me, and will instantly quit the banks of the Rhine to fly back to the shores of the ocean."

Speculation as to what might have occurred, but did not, is seldom profitable ; but we may with advantage pause to consider what might have been the consequence had Hoche effected his landing in Ireland. Napoleon, discussing probabilities long afterwards at St. Helena, was of opinion that he would have succeeded, because Hoche had "all the qualities that ensure success. He was accustomed to civil war, and had waged it with advantage ; he had pacified La Vendée, and he would have led the Irish intelligently, had he been at their head." Englishmen will scarcely be prepared to endorse the views of the great captain, and will hardly concede that the permanent conquest of Ireland was possible in 1796. England would have sent her last man and spent her last shilling before she would have submitted to such a loss ; but the struggle might have been long protracted, and it would certainly have made excessive demands upon the resources of the nation. Ireland, it must be remembered, was in a state of the most dangerous ferment at this time ; it was honey-combed by a vast conspiracy, organised with reckless daring, its members sworn to subvert the supremacy of the British Crown. The French, on landing, would have been welcomed with open arms. Some idea of the support awaiting them may be gathered from the correspondence of Wolfe Tone, although his urgent appeals to the Directory for help might have been couched in rather exaggerated terms. Wolfe Tone wrote to assure the French Government that Ireland contained three millions of Catholics trained up in hatred of the English name. An army of 200,000 could be as easily got together as one of 10,000; indeed, the Irish people would flock to the French standards in such numbers as to be almost embarrassing. The militia, moreover, to which the defence of the island was chiefly entrusted, were mainly Roman Catholics, and might be expected to go over to Hoche to a man.

This uncertain and untrustworthy force was the only enemy the French would encounter. Not only men, but money, provisions, support of every kind, would have been so freely accorded to the invaders, that their success, if only for a time, seems more than probable. Hoche ought to have established himself firmly, he might even have carried all before him, at first. In any case he must have effectually recalled the attention of England, as he had intended, from foreign enterprises to matters of far deeper moment at home. With a bold enemy under a most capable general, securely planted in the midst of the most turbulent province, she would have had but little heart for Continental wars, small sympathy, scant support from foreign allies. Every effort must have been concentrated upon revindicating the integrity of the British dominions, and compassing the expulsion of Hoche at all hazards and at all costs.

Nor can we dismiss the subject without a passing reference to the dangerous facility with which the preliminaries to invasion were accomplished. Neither the command of the sea, fortified by recent naval successes, nor the friendly alliance of the elements, unchained as it were expressly to safeguard our shores, could prevent the arrival of the hostile expedition in Bantry Bay; it was no vigilant cruisers nor yet the recurrence of hostile winds that stopped the disembarkation, but the simple accident of an absent leader in one missing ship that marred the operation and gave Great Britain safety from attack. It is clear, then, that no absolute reliance could at all times be placed upon our insular position and the navy, our so-called first line of defence.

CHAPTER XVII.

HOCHE.

BEURNONVILLE, the general appointed to supersede Jourdan, had proved a conspicuous failure. He was utterly unable to cope with the distress and want of discipline of an army worn out by a long harassing retreat. Dismayed at the excesses of the troops, disheartened at the supposed luke-warm support of apathetic subordinates, he weakly gave way to despair, and overwhelmed his army with unmeasured abuse.

When one or two of his discontented generals desired to resign, he threatened to have them shot publicly as traitors who wished to desert. Yet, when the Directory refused his piteous appeals for colleagues and chiefs to share with him the responsibility of command, Beurnonville, too, begged to resign.

In reply he was ordered peremptorily to advance upon the Lahn and the Rednitz, to help Moreau by a new diversion. Again his desperate pessimism was heard protesting despondingly :

"The Lahn ! Yes, I might get there if I had bread to eat in crossing the intervening desert, and transport trains to carry off my wounded from the forests and the crows. But the Rednitz ! No, Citizen Minister, I cannot do that. I am without bread, without meat, without hay. I am quite unable to push on as far as the Rednitz. Entrust the work to some one who is not afraid of being beaten. Appoint Kléber, Scherer, Hoche. You will be the death of me if you persist in obliging me to undertake this arduous pilgrimage."

A creature of this kind was clearly unfit to lead a Re-publican army, as the Directory at length admitted, and Kléber was named to succeed Beurnonville. Kléber, how-ever, declined. Then Hoche returned disheartened from his Irish fiasco, and the Government, as we have seen, sent him to take command of the Army of the Sambre-et-Meuse.

Hoche was received with joy by that army; he was well known to it, personally and by reputation. Many still served in its ranks who had been with him in the Vosges in 1793, and all had heard of his recent successes in the west of France. The failure of the Irish expedition was not laid at his door; it was attributed, and rightly, to causes beyond his control. His great popularity with the army was not difficult to understand. In the three short years since he had left the banks of the Rhine he had seen much and learned more. He had gained great experience in warfare ; had become a more skilful leader, a more practised adminis-trator; he had acquired a deep insight into character, and was more fitted, more capable for command.

General Gouvion St. Cyr, who served under his orders in this campaign, and who was not a too friendly critic, renders him full justice, nevertheless, in his "Memoirs." St. Cyr describes him as greatly changed since 1793. His hot-headedness had calmed down, his political bias was more moderate; he was no longer a fierce partisan of the Mountain, nor did he affect the outrageously simple uniform which he had worn in his first campaign. He now seemed greatly impressed with the dignity and importance of his position as commander-in-chief. The studied simplicity of the Republican citizen was replaced by the ostentatious display of the great general. He was accompanied by a numerous staff, and made a show of luxury hitherto un-known in the armies of the frontier. There was every reason to hope great things from his leadership. His high military qualities, his boundless energy, his unflagging self-reliance, and his great natural aptitude for the science of war, were now generally admitted alike by friends and foes.

Another of his lieutenants, destined in after years to win great fame for himself, was at this time on the Rhine, and believed in him thoroughly. This was Soult, who, from his own personal observation, was satisfied that Hoche possessed all the qualities of the great captain, emphasized by the most seductive personal traits. " While his noble majestic bearing," says Soult, " his open and engaging countenance, won him confidence at first sight, his deportment on the field of battle gained him general admiration. His coup-d'œil was prompt and unerring ; his character so bold and enterprising that no difficulty could check him ; he was actuated by the purest and most elevated motives ; and he ever displayed extreme kindliness to his comrades and a constant solicitude for his men."

He now found under his orders many generals whose fortunes he had laid, and whose friendship he knew how to secure. The army, generally chafing at inaction and eager to retrieve the misfortunes of the previous year, viewed the appointment of this young, enterprising, and sympathetic leader as a sure augury of coming success.

Directly Hoche arrived on the Rhine he addressed himself vigorously to the reorganisation of his army. Since La Vendée he had become an adept in administration, and he knew only too well the crying evils of the infamous system in force throughout the French service. The armies in the field were absolutely at the mercy of its rascally agents ; fraud and peculation prevailed on every side; the troops were constantly robbed of their food ; the army horses suffered severely from the misappropriation of forage ; the peasantry, from whom supplies were purchased, were grossly swindled in the prices paid; the public treasury also suffered by false statements of the liabilities it had to meet. Dishonesty was more particularly rife in the transport service; requisitions made upon the conquered districts for horses and carriages were intercepted by a company got together for the purpose, who let them out at exorbitant rates to the army. Other contractors contrived to waylay funds sent from Paris to feed, clothe, and equip the troops, and divert large sums into their own pockets. Hoche was not long in laying bare these villanies ; he traced them directly to the rapacious agents and *employés* who taxed the helpless troops to increase their ill-gotten gains. " I know all about it now," cried Hoche to the Directory ; "I wondered what mines of inexhaustible wealth could meet the scandalous extravagance of some of our officers, the superb establishments of contractors, the grand houses of commissaries and clerks of all classes. Why should I have been surprised? The whole fortune of the State passes into their hands, and in the midst of all their gorgeous display the country's defenders go barefooted, they are without the commonest necessaries in the hospitals, and die for want of medicines and soup."

Hoche set himself to work to rid the army of these

vampires; he entirely reorganised the system of supply, he maintained the principle of requisitions, and declared that the conquered provinces should still contribute to the support of the troops; but he persuaded the Directory to sweepaway the civil officials by which these unhappy countries had been governed, and to substitute a military administration working under his own eye. "I will do it at half the price," he said; "my system shall not cost you more than 15,000 francs a year, all told. But no one shall make his fortune out of us on pain of being shot; on the other hand, the army will benefit by local subsidies, and the inhabitants will no longer be piteously robbed." Hoche selected his men, choosing only those whose honesty was proved and irreproachable, and, when once appointed, he made them independent of himself. Their duties, after all, were only to supervise and control; the actual levies for supplies were entrusted to the local authorities, civil and clerical, who had managed the country before the arrival of the French. These measures were rapidly and entirely successful; the military chest was soon replenished; the supply service worked readily; the troops were properly paid, well fed, and sufficiently clothed. Hoche found means even to remount the cavalry and artillery, and provided fresh horses for the transport trains; so self-supporting and independent did his army become, that he was able to decline his share of the million sent by Buonaparte from his Italian indemnity, and allowed Moreau to have the whole sum.

Hoche's reorganisation was not limited to the civil departments of his army; he rearranged the *personnel* as well as the *matériel*. He had now some 80,000 men under his orders. These he divided into three corps, of two divisions each: the right was entrusted to Lefebre; the centre to Grenier; and the left to Championnet. He made a new arrangement of his cavalry, which had hitherto been split up into small bodies and attached to the various infantry divisions; all the cavalry regiments were collected together by arms, each of which, constituted in a single division, was attached to an army corps: the hussars, under Ney, were attached to the right; the chasseurs, under Richepanse, were with the centre; the dragoons, under Klein, with the left. There was besides a reserve of heavy cavalry, under d'Hautpoult, and this was joined to the infantry reserve under Watrin, which was intended eventually to invest Mayence. The whole army was in excellent order, the cavalry was numerous and effective, the artillery well horsed, well served and equipped. Hoche was naturally eager to commence the campaign. The Army of Italy was already engaged. Moreau only delayed, being without boats to cross the Rhine. But Hoche would not wait for him, and sent him word that, with or without him, he meant to take the field on the 17th of April.

The point he had selected for passage was the bridge of Neuwied, but to distract the enemy from his intention, he directed Championnet to cross at Düsseldorf, and push on at once beyond the Sieg. This Championnet effected on the 17th, the date fixed by Hoche. Werneck, who commanded the Austrians, hesitated to relinquish his hold on Neuwied, where Kray occupied a strong position on the right bank, and Championnet was allowed to approach Altenkirchen without opposition. There Werneck proposed to face him with all his forces, Kray being also drawn towards him, leaving only a few battalions at Neuwied. Werneck hoped, after disposing of Championnet, to return towards Neuwied and meet any advance in that direction. On the 17th of April, he had his right at Neukirch, his centre at Dierdorf, which place Kray was also approaching with the left. Werneck's dispositions were extremely faulty, holding as he did an extensive front of nearly fifty miles with barely 30,000 men. The whole of Championnet's corps threatened his centre, and on his extreme left at Neuwied, his line of retreat might be cut off by Hoche, who could cross at this point with 36,000 men, or more than Werneck's total force. He would more wisely have retreated at once behind the Lahn.

Hoche, although ignorant of his opponent's errors, proceeded to carry out a plan well calculated to overwhelm him. On the 18th of April, at 3 a.m., the two divisions of the right wing, preceded by its cavalry, crossed the Neuwied bridge and took post in the plain below the *tête du pont*, the centre followed, and last of all the reserves. These operations were effected without opposition in full sight of the detachments left behind by Kray. But now Werneck, fearing for his left flank, told Kray to countermarch and face Hoche by reoccupying the lines opposite Neuwied. Hoche's forces were well across by 8 a.m., and were at once directed upon the Austrian position : its left rested at Zollengers, near the Rhine; its right on Hettersdorf, a fortified village ; the front was covered with strong redoubts, armed with heavy artillery. Lefebre was sent against the left, Grenier against the right; and the attack was made with such strength that the result could hardly be in doubt. Lefebre drove all before him, and his cavalry pushed on as far as Montabauer ; Grenier had at first been equally successful, but the obstinate defence of a single redoubt at Hettersdorf gave Kray time to withdraw. The French were, however, completely successful along the whole line. Hoche now swiftly followed up his victory, and advanced to Dierdorf, where he effected his junction with Championnet. Together they fell upon Werneck. That night the Austrian general found himself defeated, driven back at all points, and his beaten columns were in full retreat through Hachemburg on Neukirch. Next morning, Hoche pursued, but in the wrong direction, continuing to press against the Austrian right towards Hachemburg, when the reinforcement of Lefebre and an advance against the Austrian left, by cutting the enemy off the Lahn, would undoubtedly have led to its annihilation.

Lefebre, however, marched towards Limburg, on the Lahn, and sent his scouts across the river, far on the road towards Mayence. Werneck, meanwhile, finding a halt at Neukirch impossible, fell back in the night on Wetzlar; Hoche next morning advanced to attack him, but, finding no enemy, could only follow, and having failed to cut his enemy off from the Lahn, forestall him, if possible, on the Maine. Lefebre was directed on Frankfort, Hoche himself proposing to press still against the Austrian right. He hoped Werneck would hold fast at Friedberg, or at least at Bergen, and give him a chance of seizing Hanau first, and with it the line of retreat through Aschaffenburg. With this object he continued to manœuvre against Werneck's right, and the Austrian general was in a position of great peril on the 22nd April, surrounded on almost every side by greatly superior French forces, and having his communications in danger. But on this date, Lefebre, who was close to Frankfort, received news of the armistice concluded between the Emperor of Austria and Buonaparte ; and the preliminaries to peace commenced at Leoben. Lefebre passed on the courier to his commanding officer, and awaited Hoche's instructions. The French general was naturally somewhat loth to allow Werneck to escape from the toils; but a temporary suspension of hostilities could not be avoided, and Hoche and Werneck accordingly came to terms.

It must have been a deep disappointment to Hoche to allow Werneck to escape. But he had no alternative, and agreed to a suspension of arms, even though it checked him just when a decisive victory seemed close at hand. He would not admit, however, that peace was absolutely certain, and held his forces ready to resume operations at once should the negotiations fail. He established his own headquarters at Friedberg, and sent his troops into cantonments along the Lahn. Like a prudent soldier he made them his first care; and, whether war or peace was close at hand, was equally resolved to improve the discipline and efficiency of his army. The period of inaction was to be diligently employed in drill; regiments were to be kept constantly under arms, and to be continually instructed and practised in manœuvres and the minor operations of war; officers of all ranks were desired also to improve themselves, more especially by devoting themselves to acquiring a knowledge of the surrounding country, its general features, mountains, roads, rivers, and resources. At the same time his carefully elaborate system for obtaining and controlling supplies was extended to the localities now newly occupied, and with most satisfactory results. The Army of the Sambre-et-Meuse became more efficiently organised day by day. "You have no conception," writes Hoche to the War Minister, "of the excellence and perfection of my army. It now wants nothing, either in clothing or equipment; I will not say that all wear precisely the same uniform; but it is a fact, nevertheless, that misery and nakedness have quite disappeared. Discipline, moreover, is perfect." The pardonable satisfaction Hoche felt found voice in his general orders. After reviewing and inspecting all his divisions he published a glowing encomium upon their appearance, complimenting each particular corps in turn, and presenting his most promising officers with swords, pistols, belts, and so forth, as proofs of his appreciation and esteem. His popularity at this time had reached the highest pitch ; he was beloved by all ranks, and the whole army was ready to follow him wherever he might lead.

It was this, no doubt, that marked him out to the Directory as one of the generals on whose assistance it could reasonably rely. Political dissensions loomed near, and armed intervention seemed inevitable if the Republic was to survive. The Directory had turned already to Napoleon ; but his victorious legions were distant, while Hoche with the Army of the Sambre-et-Meuse was much closer at hand. It is probable, too, that Barras, the moving spirit of the Directory, distrusted the more ambitious spirit of Buonaparte, and preferred to employ Hoche, who now was summoned to Paris to confer with the Government. The ostensible object of his visit was to discuss the chances of a new invasion of Ireland, a project which Hoche still favoured. He had but just visited Holland, in fact, to examine into the resources of its marine, and had withdrawn large detachments from his army, directing them across France upon Brest, where they were to form the nucleus of a new expedition.

Hoche's appearance in Paris gave rise to rumours of all kinds. It was reported that the Directory had broken with Buonaparte ; that Hoche was to be dispatched forthwith to Italy to supersede him. These stories were absolutely without foundation. Barras was still in communication, but now through Hoche, with the general commanding the Army of Italy, and Hoche himself was at great pains to express openly his esteem and friendship for Buonaparte. He published a letter addressed to the Minister of Police, in which he indignantly denied the false and ridiculous rumours in circulation, and this letter, full of glowing eulogy, throws an agreeable light on Hoche's character. It seems clear that he was above small jealousies; he could rejoice heartily in a colleague's success, without fearing his rivalry or being consumed with envy, hatred, and all uncharitableness. How far later events might have modified his opinion of Napoleon cannot well be estimated. Hoche was a staunch Republican, and he probably would have resented Napoleon's seizure of despotic power. But at this date and up to the time of his death, Hoche's sentiments towards Napoleon were those of genuine admiration; one successful general could appreciate another's triumphs, and Hoche recognised in Buonaparte a great master in war.

When Hoche reached Paris, the ceaseless intrigues of the Royalists imperilled the Republic, and threatened its very existence. They had a majority in the two Councils, that of "Ancients" and "Five Hundred," and all laboured strenuously to bring about a restoration.

Attempts were made to win over Hoche : his persecution under Robespierre, the moderation he had displayed in putting down the Western insurrections, the spirit of forbearance and toleration which avowedly animated him, all warranted the Royalists in hoping to secure him. They openly promised him the most liberal rewards, and tried to dazzle him with the offer of high rank and station under the restored monarchy.

But Hoche, whether or not he was still unshaken in his loyalty to the Republic, certainly distrusted the party from whom these overtures came. The Royalist camp contained too many of his personal enemies. It included Pichegru, Villaret-Joyeuse, and others with whom he had had serious differences, and he was too prudent a man to trust himself to the generosity of his old foes. It is probable, too, that he saw greater safety, more solid advantage, possibly, from the unwavering support of the existing régime. In any case he readily ranged himself upon the Republican side, and freely offered his services to the Directory with those of his army, now entirely devoted to him.

Throughout July he was in constant, close communication with Barras, who made him his confidant, and tried to make him his tool. At Barras' instance Hoche halted not far from Paris a portion of his troops on the way through to Brest. This raised a storm amidst the Royalist partisans, who saw the dangers it threatened. By the Constitution of 1795, no troops were permitted to approach within a certain distance of Paris, and this limit had now been transgressed. Explanations were demanded by Pichegru in the council of the "Five Hundred" and the Directory, some of whose members had Royalist leanings, called Hoche strictly to account. Carnot accused him of treachery, and talked darkly of arrest. Meanwhile Barras, who was really responsible for what Hoche had done, sat silent with downcast eyes, meanly declining to defend his agent. Another member of the Directory, however, Larevellière-Lepeaux, although in the dark as to what was going on, took up the cudgels for Hoche and silenced Carnot. He bade Hoche take no notice of vain threats; "the enemies of liberty," he said, "no more spared the generals than the magistrates who defended it."

Hoche after this incident lost all confidence in Barras, and he wrote him next day to decline the post of Minister of War which the Directory had offered him, and declared his intention of returning to his command. He had halted his men on the march, but retained them at Rheims, where they would be still close at hand if required in Paris. Hoche himself proceeded with his family to Wetzlar, where he established his headquarters. He was safe there from personal interference, but he could not escape the calumnies of his enemies. Vile accusations were hurled at him from Paris. Now he was said to be meditating flight into Switzerland, to escape just retribution for his crimes; now charged with fraud and the wholesale embezzlement of public funds. To these foul aspersions Hoche replied indignantly, and at length, in the public journals; but revenge, independent of himself, was close at hand. Barras, after Hoche's departure, had reopened communications with Buonaparte, who already seems to have contemplated the creation of a military dictatorship.

The ambitious young leader of the victorious Army of Italy was still loud, however, in his protestations of his devotion to the Republic, and readily lent the Directory the aid it required. He sent Augereau, a rough, ruthless soldier and an uncompromising Republican, to act as the Government's strong right arm. Augereau's irruption into the "Corps Législatif" at the head of his soldiers, and his forcible arrest of Pichegru and all the Royalist leaders, speedily extinguished the hopes of that party.

The news of their arrest reached Hoche at Wetzlar, and filled him with joy; he had returned ill from Paris, pale and suffering, hacked perpetually by a dry cough, and with fever in his veins. He felt, he said, as though enveloped perpetually in the garment of Nessus, and the pains in his chest and agonising spasms, accompanied by a constant nervous irritation, gave his friends cause for serious alarm. But the news from Paris seemed to give him instant relief;

it did him more good, as he told the doctor, than all his remedies, and he rose from bed anxious to devote himself again to his duties.

But he had clearly overrated his strength; there was no convalescence in him; on the contrary, his worst symptoms continued and grew more grave. The doctors declared that complete rest was indispensable. Hoche asked for any other remedy—not inaction merely, but some medicine to cure fatigue. He could not rest: they had ordered him to Metz to try peace and quiet at a distance from work and worry, but he would not go. "His army was his life," he said; "to be separated from it meant his death from impatience and anxiety." Now, too, his responsibilities had been increased. The Directory had added Moreau's army to his command. Hoche was now supreme along the Rhine; he had a new task in administration, fresh troops to bring into perfect discipline. It was not a time to suffer the forces of the Republic to deteriorate; it was not yet absolutely safe; the strife of parties might yet be kindled into civil war.

Patient and doctors could not agree. They came, therefore, to a compromise. A short period of activity should be followed by a complete cessation from work; then Hoche was to be allowed to start for Strasbourg to commence the reorganisation of the Army of the Rhine. This treatment, accompanied by such harmless distractions as a visit to Frankfort Fair, benefited Hoche greatly. He grasped eagerly, too, at the promises of speedy cure held out by some quack without condemning him to further rest, and, feeling better already, deserted his regular medical attendant to return to Wetzlar.

There, however, his illness reappeared in an aggravated form, and his doctor was again called in, to find Hoche quite beyond hope. The dread verdict could not be concealed from the dying man. Yet the news of the general's condition had spread rapidly through the army, and, as the doors of the sick chamber were no longer closed, his friends and colleagues had come to express their sympathy at his bedside. Hoche received them calmly, talked long and with interest on the exciting topics of the hour, then bade them farewell without emotion, although it was for the last time.

That night a temporary improvement showed itself, followed by a most painful crisis, and, after some hours of intense agony he died, in the flower of his youth and hopes, at the early age of twenty-nine.

This sudden death of a young man, commonly believed to enjoy the most robust health, could not pass without arousing suspicions of foul play. The report that Hoche had been poisoned spread rapidly, and has never been categorically and finally disproved. A post-mortem examination revealed the presence of numerous black spots in the intestines, which the medical science of the day could neither account for nor explain away. Nor were the distressing symptoms of Hoche's last malady altogether at variance with the supposition that his death had not been due to natural causes. Yet no positive evidence has been adduced to even hint at the motives for such a crime, or to bring home the guilt to any person.

Hoche had many enemies in the West; and there were those who declared that the seeds of his mysterious malady and premature death were sown in that violent sickness that attacked him one night after dinner at Brest. But he does not seem to have complained in the interval of more than a year between that illness and his death, and it is hardly likely that all this time the fell poison was insidiously working its way. Nor is there any ground for bringing home

motives for murder to Hoche's political rivals and foes.   At
the time of his death Barras appears to have been anxious
to reopen communications with him.

Grave doubts were already entertained of Buonáparte,
whose ambitious designs were now but imperfectly veiled.
It is generally believed that Barras would gladly have used
Hoche as a counterweight to Napoleon in the dangers that
seemed approaching, and this assumption is so probable
that it disposes of any suspicion that Barras or any of his
party were concerned in Hoche's death.   There remains
Napoleon himself, on whom doubts afterwards rested, although it is but fair to say, without foundation.   Napoleon
knew of them and laughed them to scorn.   He told Las
Cases, at St. Helena, that he had been accused of poisoning
Hoche, just as he had been charged with compassing Kléber's
assassination and Desaix's suicide; and he would hardly
have referred thus coolly to crimes in which he had really
had a hand.

There remains a more plausible explanation of Hoche's
death.   He had no doubt greatly overtried his strength;
he possessed strong passions, and was greatly addicted to
pleasure; he was of a very emotional character notwithstanding his strength of mind, and there can be no doubt
that he felt deeply the agitation and opposition experienced
in his last visit to Paris.   His extreme delight at the sudden
clearing off of political storms brought a reaction, and his
health gave way under the shock.

The news of his death spread grief throughout France.   In
Paris they were celebrating the anniversary of the foundation
of the Republic; the Directory, the Ministers, the chief public
functionaries, many military leaders, and great crowds of people,
were collected together on the Champs de Mars, when they
heard that Hoche was dead.   The *fête* ended sadly, as the death

of this young soldier was felt by all to be a national loss. Next day the Corps Législatif decreed that Hoche should have a public funeral, and that the ceremony should be observed as a day of mourning at the headquarters of all the armies of the Republic. But already he had been buried at Coblentz, within the entrenched camp, by the side of intrepid young Marceau, who had preceded him by only a few short months to the grave. The funeral was an imposing military spectacle ; the *cortége* left Wetzlar, followed by the generals, the staff, numbers of officers, and detachments from every corps in the Army of the Sambre-et-Meuse. As it passed the fortress of Ehrenbreitstein the Austrian commandant turned out his garrison upon the glacis and saluted the corpse of his former foe. As he approached the Rhine, the mourners increased in number every mile ; the funeral procession crossed the Rhine in the presence of an imposing French force, and entered the entrenched camp. Hoche was laid to his rest 'amidst the thunder of artillery from the neighbouring forts, the rattle of musketry, and the eloquent tributes of his sorrowing comrades. Generals Lefebre, Championnet, and Grenier, all pronounced funeral orations at his grave. Championnet rose almost to eloquence in expressing his heartfelt sorrow. " Virtue, genius, talent—pitiless death has devoured them all." Such was the burden of his speech. " What did I say ? A great man never dies ; he may descend into the tomb, but there immortality begins. Supported by numerous triumphs, the name of Hoche will survive to the most distant posterity. His glory extends to a hundred different places ; the plains of Weissenberg, the walls of Landau, the rocks of Quiberon, the shores of the Rhine, are eternal monuments which will bear witness through centuries of the braveness of his courage and the depth of his conception. Military talent was not Nature's only gift; as skilful in conciliation as he was masterly in manœuvre, he extinguished that horrible war kindled by fanaticism and fanned by foreign gold that so long desolated the most beautiful parts of France. He gave back home to thousands of estranged Frenchmen, and restored them to spots from which they seemed exiled for ever. He richly deserved the epithet of ' peacemaker.' So many brilliant deeds, such eminent public services performed in so short a time, all these have established his claim to the gratitude and admiration of coming generations. But how much deeper must be our grief, we the comrades who lived with him, at this his premature end. He was the friend no less than the leader of his men, and his unceasing thoughts were for their needs. . . . . Comrades, weep for a dear father worthy of all our affection; mingle your tears with those that friendship sheds on his tomb. You owe him your sincerest regrets, for you were first in his heart, he lived only for you and France. His last thoughts were devoted to you : ' My country, my comrades,' these were the last words that passed his dying lips."

A single incident will serve to show how deeply Hoche was mourned by his troops. As the funeral was about to retire from the grave a grenadier stepped forward, and presenting arms, threw a crown of laurels upon the coffin, with the impassioned words: " Hoche, in the name of the whole army, I offer you this crown ! "

Funeral honours as decreed were paid to Hoche with great pomp and ceremony both in Paris and elsewhere. The President of the Directory, in eloquent terms, expressed the national sorrow, and he was followed by Daunou, who pronounced a warm eulogium upon the general's life, while hundreds of voices chanted patriotic hymns, and mourners came in crowds to lay branches of oak-leaves upon the monumental bier. It was the same in the country, more particularly in the West, where Hoche was universally regretted. A citizen residing at Maine-et-Loire offered more substantial proof of his regard for Hoche's memory ; hearing that Hoche's aged father was left in great distress, he generously promised him a home for the rest of his days.

The verdict of posterity has fully endorsed the high opinion entertained of Hoche by his contemporaries. He is undoubtedly one of the greatest figures in the revolutionary epoch. His services were great and varied, even in his short career. He reformed and reorganised armies, and led them to victory ; he was a politician in La Vendée ; a naval officer at Brest ; and an administrator on the Rhine. There is no saying what he might have become had he lived. He might have opposed Napoleon, whom he rivalled in reputation, although he was, probably, not his equal in genius. More probably, he would have yielded to the irresistible influence of the greater mind, and would have become one of Napoleon's greatest lieutenants. Napoleon himself, feeling that he might have had a rival in Hoche, was at pains to consider in after years which of them was the best man. Napoleon always fancied that he had the advantage of Hoche first, through his better education and the more profound knowledge it gave him ; next, in his great patience. "Hoche," said Napoleon, "could not wait for the best moment to act. I, on the contrary, have been guided always by circumstances." Hoche, again, Napoleon thought, was incapable of forming a strong party or of securing the unswerving devotion, as did Napoleon, of a large circle of followers. This judgment is scarcely supported by facts, but beyond doubt Napoleon had the highest opinion of Hoche. When some one remarked that the Republican general, although so young, had given great promise, Napoleon replied: " He did more; he fulfilled it!" and he summed up his verdict by declaring that Hoche had especially won the esteem of every one by his able pacification of La Vendée. Hoche had undoubtedly a great future before him, and his early death was a grave misfortune to himself and his country. Thiers points out, with justice, that Hoche was decidedly an unlucky man. At moments when his star seemed most in the ascendant he met with most serious rebuffs. Triumphant at Weissenberg, the young general, who had but just led the French troops to victory, was disgraced and imprisoned in the Conciergerie; having pacified La Vendée and started on an expedition that augured well for so ambitious and enterprising a leader, he was baffled by tempests and forbidden to land in Ireland; once more victorious on the Rhine, he had Werneck in his grip, and ought to have destroyed him, when peace unexpectedly saved his victim; last of all, supreme leader of the Armies of the Rhine and the Moselle, he awaited only the resumption of hostilities to invade Germany and carry all before him, when death, premature death, pitilessly intervened.

CHAPTER XVIII.

JOURDAN.

JOURDAN'S CAMPAIGN OF 1799.

THE formation of a new coalition in 1798, again threatened France with war. Austria was now backed up by Russia, and by England as before ; she was well prepared for a new campaign, having at her disposal a numerous and well-disciplined army, supported by an immense quantity of material. Three Austrian armies were ready to take the field : one was cantoned behind the Lech, in Bavaria ; a second occupied the Tyrol ; and the third was on the Adige. Each of these numbered from 70,000 to 80,000 men, making a total of 240,000, and 60,000 Russians could at any time be counted upon in support. Austria, nevertheless, was indisposed to take the offensive, preferring to leave the odium of a rupture upon the French ; and the latter, although considerably inferior in numbers and less well-prepared for war, were ready enough to strike the first blow. The plan of campaign proposed by the Directory was originated, it is said, by a subordinate staff officer ; but Jourdan, who was named to command the bulk of the forces, endorsed it, and is in a measure responsible for it.

According to this plan, the Army of Mayence, 45,000 strong, was to cross the Rhine at Kehl, traverse the Black Forest, and march on Bregenz. Jourdan was entrusted with this operation, and his orders were to push on, and if possible, forestall the Austrians in Bavaria upon the Upper Lech; he was at the same time to facilitate the invasion of the Tyrol, by a second army of 30,000 men under Massena. Jourdan was to be assisted by Bernadotte, who, with 48,000 men, was to blockade Mannheim and Phillipsburg, and demonstrate against the Austrian right. Both Bernadotte and Massena were under Jourdan's command. The fourth army, that of Italy, 50,000 strong, was to operate against the Austrians upon the Adige, and force them back behind the Brenta, and the Piave. The fifth army, under MacDonald, was to complete the conquest of the kingdom of Naples.

This scheme was far beyond the means of the French armies. They covered an immense front, extending from the Adige to Mayence, and they numbered barely 170,000 men all told. Their forces were split up into several fractions, with incomplete intercommunication between, and having separate aims. Jourdan at Bregenz could only join hands with Massena through Feldkirch, and this was still in the hands of the enemy. Moreover, the Austrians were masters of the valley of the Adige, through which lay the only means of communication between the Army of Italy and Massena. But the chief error of the campaign was, that it frittered away the French armies along an interminable line, instead of concentrating to strike a decisive blow at a central point. Even had the plan been perfect, the French forces were far too weak to carry it out. Only 128,000 men were really ready to come into line; the cavalry was weak and badly mounted, the artillery short of horses: all arms alike had deteriorated during the two years' peace. Ill-devised retrenchment had reduced the cadres of officers to a mere handful, and discontent was rife amongst those who still served. Yet the Directory rushed into the war recklessly, and without pausing to consider why they could prosecute it with any reasonable hopes of success.

On the 1st of March, 1799, Jourdan and Bernadotte were already across the Rhine. This, under the Treaty of Campoformio, was in itself a *casus belli;* but France did not actually declare war. Jourdan crossed at Kehl and Valles, and, advancing through the Black Forest, occupied a line from Rothweil to Tollingen, on the 6th. He had only 38,000 men in all, 8,000 of whom were cavalry.

Bernadotte crossed the Rhine on the same day with 8,000 men, and laid siege to Mannheim and Phillipsburg; the enemy retiring before him to Heilbronn, on the Neckar.

The Archduke Charles was before Jourdan, and, on hearing of the French advance, threw forward his main body to Biberach, reinforced the garrisons of Ulm and Ingolstadt on the Rhine, and directed a strong force under Starray to watch Bernadotte.

Meanwhile Massena had also assumed the initiative and invaded the Grisons, acting with such promptitude and vigour that the enemy retired before him.

Jourdan, hearing of Massena's success, decided to continue his advance on the 12th of March. On the day following he crossed the Danube : his left occupied Mengen; his centre was at Pfullendorf; and his right at Salmansweiler. But he was not strong enough to attack the Archduke, who had retired concentrating before him. Jourdan's great desire was to communicate with Massena, whom he pressed to manœuvre to his left.

Massena was fully alive to the necessity of effecting a junction with his chief, and he made repeated efforts to seize Feldkirch, but always without success, and, in the last engagement, with serious loss to himself. These disasters were, however, counterbalanced by the successes of the French generals operating from the Adige.

On the 19th March Jourdan heard that war was definitely declared. He was at the same time urged strongly by the Directory to assume the offensive, and attack the Archduke Charles. With this object, and to assist by a diversion Massena's operations against Feldkirch, Jourdan advanced to Ostrach and Mengen, where he took up a somewhat extended division, detaching Vandamme to Sigmaringen, on the left bank of the Danube.

Unfortunately a false report was circulated to the effect that the Archduke had turned the French left, whereupon Vandamme fell back towards the Neckar, and ceased to be of effective service in the actions now close at hand.

Jourdan's adversary was not disposed to surrender the advantage of the initiative; and having left Biberach on the 18th, he drove in the French outposts behind the Ostrach on the following day. His vigorous advance warned Jourdan that he must be prepared to fight, and the French general preferred to accept battle in a position however faulty to being attacked in retreat. On the night of the 20th, the Archduke made his dispositions, resolving to use all his strength along the roads that end in Ostrach. A sharp engagement followed on the 21st; Lefebre, who was at first single-handed in the defence of Ostrach, and reinforced too late, could not contain the Austrians at this point, and with the loss of Ostrach Jourdan felt it imperative to retreat on Pfullendorf.

Jourdan had no desire to risk a second engagement here or elsewhere, until he had concentrated all his forces. This he effected first round Stockach on the 22nd, then between Tutlingen and Engen on the 23rd. The Archduke pursued very leisurely; on the 23rd he was still at Pfullendorf, and he did not occupy Stockach till the following day, when his advanced guard was more or less seriously engaged all along the line. The opposing generals now arrived simultaneously at the same decision; each resolved to attack the other. The Archduke was anxious to penetrate Jourdan's intentions. Was his adversary about to withdraw without fighting by Schaffhausen, so as to join hands with Massena? A reconnaissance in force which might develop into a general action, would probably decide this. At the same moment Jourdan, impressed with the importance of Stockach, which he could only abandon at the cost of sacrificing his communication with Massena, had resolved to resume the offensive and capture it. He wished to anticipate the Archduke, and soon after daybreak on the 25th, set all his columns in motion. Two of these, moving by the right, were to unite before Stockach, while two others consisting of St. Cyr, supported by Soult, formed the left attack. The advanced guard on the right obtained the first success, and Jourdan, thinking the Austrians were in full retreat, directed St. Cyr to make a long detour by Moeskirch by himself. This was a grave error; the Archduke rapidly reinforced his right, which was already engaged with Soult about Liptigen, and was on the point of yielding. But Jourdan had no reserves to utilise, and instead of drawing St. Cyr towards him, he hastened that general's march to Moeskirch.

The fight at Liptigen was obstinately contested for some

time, and might have ended in favour of the French had their cavalry charged at the moment Jourdan wished ; but d'Hautpoult tarried, and his horsemen were too late to save the day.   Jourdan was driven back from Liptigen, but kept up a desultory fire during the night. St. Cyr, meanwhile, hearing of Jourdan's reverse, saw his peril, and retrograded rapidly on Sigmaringen, where he recrossed the Danube, and continued his retreat by the left bank.   The French centre and right had been more successful, but they were unable to dislodge the Austrians in front of them, and were separated by a dangerous interval from Jourdan.   The results of the day's fighting were decidedly unfavourable to the French, although the Austrians had achieved no great success. Jourdan's army, greatly reduced in numbers, however, was now divided into three detachments at great distances from each other; he was compelled, therefore, to renounce all hope of co-operating with Massena, and he had no alternative but to effect a concentration by retreat.   He might have entered Switzerland by Schaffhausen ; but this meant a dangerous flank march in the presence of a victorious enemy particularly strong in cavalry, and the abandonment of St. Cyr on his left.   Jourdan, moreover, was hourly expecting strong reinforcements from France, and he judged it wisest to withdraw behind the Black Forest. This retreat was effected on the 26th, and was not interfered with by the enemy, although the dispersion of the French forces gave the Archduke a fine opportunity. But the Archduke did not pursue till the 28th, and then only leisurely;   the appearance of his cavalry about Rothweil having the effect of sending Jourdan still further to the rear.   On the 31st he was approaching the valley of the Rhine.   On the 3rd of April the Austrian advanced guard penetrated between the centre and right of the French army; but General Ernouf, who was in command during Jourdan's absence through illness, extricated his columns, and on the 5th and 6th recrossed the Rhine, the right at Brissac, the left at Kehl. The Archduke Charles might have crushed the Duke in this precipitous retreat, but prompt action was forbidden him by peremptory orders from Vienna to look first to the safety of the Tyrol. Jourdan's retreat rendered Bernadotte's imperative, and that general raised the siege of Phillipsburg and recrossed the Rhine.

The blame for this most unsatisfactory and unsuccessful campaign was visited upon Jourdan, although it was directly traceable to the faultiness of the general plan as sketched out by the Directory. The French Government did not choose to see that a few fractions of French troops could not hope to triumph over twice the number of concentrated Austrians. Yet their defeat would have been far more decisive but for the interference of the Aulic Council with the plans of the Archduke Charles.

The whole bulk of the Directory's displeasure fell upon Jourdan, whose resignation was eagerly accepted, and the command of the Armies of the Rhine was united in the person of Massena. Jourdan, for a moment, retired from active military employment, and his career as a Republican general ended from that time. The French Republic was indeed approaching its term, and the establishment of the Consulate was shortly to vest supreme power in other hands. The advent of the Buonaparte régime was not calculated to push Jourdan much further to the front.

There is every reason to suppose that Napoleon never forgave Jourdan his opposition to the 18th Brumaire. In any case, Jourdan received no new command for some years to come. His language to Jourdan, however, was always flattering; he had written him in 1799 that he had the greatest wish to see the conqueror of Fleurus on the high road which leads to the organisation of true liberty and happiness.

"I beg," he adds, "you will never doubt the friendship I bear you."

In 1804, however, he was appointed commander-in-chief of the Army in Italy, only to be superseded by Massena the following year.

Yet it has been asserted that this change was made on public grounds and not from personal dislike to Jourdan. Napoleon gave reasons in writing to Prince Eugène which support this view. "I cannot entrust Jourdan," he says, "with so vital a command in the present important juncture; he does not know Italy well enough; he is not sufficiently active, and is said to be too easily discouraged." Napoleon even wrote apologetically to Jourdan himself; he told him that he had the highest opinion of his talents and was quite satisfied with his conduct; "but," he went on, "I want a general in the most robust health, one who is thoroughly well at home in the locality, and who, like Massena, knows every position from the Riviera to the Adige."

A few years later, Napoleon selected Jourdan to act as his brother Joseph's chief of the staff in Spain. He called Jourdan then an honest man; but he was profoundly disgusted with him after the loss of the Battle of Talavera, and took him bitterly to task for his want of candour in endeavouring to gloss over that defeat. As a matter of fact, Jourdan was the only Marshal of France whom Napoleon never advanced to high titular rank. He never received a dukedom like his comrades, and when the promotion was pressed upon

Napoleon by Joseph, he excused himself by saying, " If I were to give Jourdan the rank of Duke of Fleurus and a settled fortune, he would want to leave Spain and return to Paris." But with native duplicity, Napoleon hinted that he had ten duchies to give away, and told Joseph that this bribe would secure him Jourdan's adhesion for some time to come. In the end, however, Jourdan survived the Napoleonic régime, and died, after the Bourbon Restoration, full of honours, a Count, a Senator, and Marshal of France.

THE END.

CHARLES DICKENS AND EVANS, CRYSTAL PALACE PRESS.

INDEX.

T

11, Henrietta Street, Covent Garden, W.C

October, 1890.

A

Catalogue of Books

PUBLISHED BY

CHAPMAN & HALL,

LIMITED.

FOR

Drawing Examples, Diagrams, Models, Instruments, etc.,

ISSUED UNDER THE AUTHORITY OF

THE SCIENCE AND ART DEPARTMENT, SOUTH KENSINGTON,

FOR THE USE OF SCHOOLS AND ART AND SCIENCE CLASSES,

See separate Illustrated Catalogue.

BOOKS

PUBLISHED BY

CHAPMAN & HALL, LIMITED.

ABLETT (T. R.)—
WRITTEN DESIGN. Oblong, sewed, 6d.

ABOUT (EDMOND)—
HANDBOOK OF SOCIAL ECONOMY; OR, THE
WORKER'S A B C. From the French. With a Biographical and Critical
Introduction by W. FRASER RAE. Second Edition, revised. Crown 8vo, 4s.

AFRICAN FARM, STORY OF AN. By OLIVE SCHREINER
(Ralph Iron). New Edition. Crown 8vo, 1s.; in cloth, 1s. 6d.

ANDERSON (ANDREW A.)—
TWENTY-FIVE YEARS IN A WAGGON IN THE
GOLD REGIONS OF AFRICA. With Illustrations and Map. Second Edition.
Demy 8vo, 12s.

AGRICULTURAL SCIENCE (LECTURES ON), AND
OTHER PROCEEDINGS OF THE INSTITUTE OF AGRICULTURE,
SOUTH KENSINGTON, 1883-4. Crown 8vo, sewed, 2s.

AVELING (EDWARD), D.Sc., Fellow of University College, London—
MECHANICS AND EXPERIMENTAL SCIENCE.
As required for the Matriculation Examination of the University of London.
MECHANICS. With numerous Woodcuts. Crown 8vo, 6s.
Key to Problems in ditto, crown 8vo, 3s. 6d.
CHEMISTRY. With numerous Woodcuts. Crown 8vo, 6s.
Key to Problems in ditto, crown 8vo, 2s. 6d.
MAGNETISM AND ELECTRICITY. With Numerous Woodcuts.
Crown 8vo. 6s.
LIGHT AND HEAT. With Numerous Woodcuts. Crown 8vo, 6s.
Keys to the last two volumes in one vol. Crown 8vo, 5s.

BADEN-POWELL (GEORGE)—
STATE AID AND STATE INTERFERENCE. Illus-
trated by Results in Commerce and Industry. Crown 8vo, 9s.

BAILEY (JOHN BURN)—
MODERN METHUSELAHS; or, Short Biographical
Sketches of a few advanced Nonagenarians or actual Centenarians who were
distinguished in Art, Science, or Philanthropy. Also brief notices of some
individuals remarkable chiefly for their longevity. With an Introductory Chapter
on "Long-Lasting." Demy 8vo, 10s. 6d.

BARTLEY (G. C. T.)—
A HANDY BOOK FOR GUARDIANS OF THE POOR.
Crown 8vo, cloth, 3s.

BAYARD: HISTORY OF THE GOOD CHEVALIER,
SANS PEUR ET SANS REPROCHE. Compiled by the LOYAL SERVITEUR.
With over 200 Illustrations. Royal 8vo, 21s.

BEATTY-KINGSTON (W.)—
A JOURNALIST'S JOTTINGS. 2 vols. Demy 8vo.

MY "HANSOM" LAYS: Original Verses, Imitations, and
Paraphrases. Crown 8vo, 3s. 6d.

THE CHUMPLEBUNNYS AND SOME OTHER
ODDITIES. Sketched from the Life. Illustrated by KARL KLIETSCH. Crown
8vo, 2s.

A WANDERER'S NOTES. 2 vols. Demy 8vo, 24s.

BEATTY-KINGSTON (W.)—*Continued*—

MONARCHS I HAVE MET. 2 vols. Demy 8vo, 24s.

MUSIC AND MANNERS: Personal Reminiscences and Sketches of Character. 2 vols. Demy 8vo, 30s.

BELL (JAMES, Ph.D., &c.), Principal of the Somerset House Laboratory—

THE CHEMISTRY OF FOODS. With Microscopic Illustrations.

PART I. TEA, COFFEE, COCOA, SUGAR, ETC. Large crown 8vo, 2s. 6d.
PART II. MILK, BUTTER, CHEESE, CEREALS, PREPARED STARCHES, ETC. Large crown 8vo, 3s.

BENSON (W.)—

UNIVERSAL PHONOGRAPHY. To classify sounds of Human Speech, and to denote them by one set of Symbols for easy Writing and Printing. 8vo, sewed, 1s.

MANUAL OF THE SCIENCE OF COLOUR. Coloured Frontispiece and Illustrations. 12mo, cloth, 2s. 6d.

PRINCIPLES OF THE SCIENCE OF COLOUR. Small 4to, cloth, 15s.

BINGHAM (CAPT. THE HON. D.)—

THE MARRIAGES OF THE BOURBONS. With Illustrations. 2 vols. Demy 8vo, 32s.

A SELECTION FROM THE LETTERS AND DESPATCHES OF THE FIRST NAPOLEON. With Explanatory Notes. 3 vols. Demy 8vo, £2 2s.

THE BASTILLE. With Illustrations. 2 vols. Demy 8vo, 32s.

BIRDWOOD (SIR GEORGE C. M.), C.S.I.—

THE INDUSTRIAL ARTS OF INDIA. With Map and 174 Illustrations. New Edition. Demy 8vo, 14s.

BLACKIE (JOHN STUART), F.R.S.E.—

THE SCOTTISH HIGHLANDERS AND THE LAND LAWS. Demy 8vo, 9s.

ALTAVONA: FACT AND FICTION FROM MY LIFE IN THE HIGHLANDS. Third Edition. Crown 8vo, 6s.

BLENNERHASSETT (LADY)—

MADAME DE STAEL: Her Friends, and Her Influence in Politics and Literature. Translated from the German by J. E. GORDON CUMMING. With a Portrait. 3 vols. Demy 8vo, 36s.

BLEUNARD (A.)—

BABYLON ELECTRIFIED: The History of an Expedition undertaken to restore Ancient Babylon by the Power of Electricity, and how it Resulted. Translated from the French by F. L. WHITE, and Illustrated by MONTADER. Royal 8vo, 12s.

BLOOMFIELD'S (BENJAMIN LORD), MEMOIR OF—

MISSION TO THE COURT OF BERNADOTTE. With Portraits. 2 vols. Demy 8vo, 28s.

BONVALOT (GABRIEL)—

THROUGH THE HEART OF ASIA OVER THE PAMIR TO INDIA. Translated from the French by C. B. PITMAN. With 250 Illustrations by ALBERT PÉPIN. Royal 8vo, 32s.

BOULGER (DEMETRIUS C.)—

GENERAL GORDON'S LETTERS FROM THE CRIMEA, THE DANUBE, AND ARMENIA. 2nd Edition. Crown 8vo, 5s.

BOWERS (G.)—
  HUNTING IN HARD TIMES. With 61 coloured
  Illustrations. Oblong 4to, 12s.
BRACKENBURY (COL. C. B.)—
  FREDERICK THE GREAT. With Maps and Portrait.
  Large crown 8vo, 4s.
BRADLEY (THOMAS), of the Royal Military Academy, Woolwich—
  ELEMENTS OF GEOMETRICAL DRAWING. In Two
  Parts, with Sixty Plates. Oblong folio, half bound, each Part 16s.

MRS. BRAY'S NOVELS AND ROMANCES.
New and Revised Editions, with Frontispieces. 3s. 6d. each.

THE WHITE HOODS.
DE FOIX ; a Romance of Bearn.
FITZ OF FITZFORD ; a Tale of Destiny.
HENRY DE POMEROY.
TRELAWNY OF TRELAWNE.
A FATHER'S CURSE AND A
  DAUGHTER'S SACRIFICE.

TRIALS OF THE HEART.
THE TALBA ; or, The Moor of Portugal.
THE PROTESTANT.
WARLEIGH ; or, The Fatal Oak.
COURTENAY OF WALREDDON.
HARTLAND FOREST AND ROSE-
  TEAGUE.

BRIDGMAN (F. A.)—
  WINTERS IN ALGERIA. With 62 Illustrations. Royal
  8vo, 10s. 6d.
BRITISH ARMY, THE. By the Author of "Greater Britain,"
  " The Present Position of European Politics," etc. Demy 8vo, 12s.
BROADLEY (A. M.)—
  HOW WE DEFENDED ARABI AND HIS FRIENDS.
  A Story of Egypt and the Egyptians. Illustrated by FREDERICK VILLIERS.
  Demy 8vo, 12s.
*BROCK (DR. J. H. E.), Assistant Examiner in Hygiene, Science and Art
  Department—*
  ELEMENTS OF HUMAN PHYSIOLOGY FOR THE
  HYGIENE EXAMINATIONS OF THE SCIENCE AND ART
  DEPARTMENT. Crown 8vo, 1s. 6d.
BROMLEY-DAVENPORT (the late W.), M.P.—
  SPORT : Fox Hunting, Salmon Fishing, Covert Shooting,
  Deer Stalking. With numerous Illustrations by General CREALOCK, C.B.
  New Cheap Edition. Post 8vo, 3s. 6d.
  ————— Small 4to, 21s.
BUCKLAND (FRANK)—
  LOG-BOOK OF A FISHERMAN AND ZOOLOGIST.
  With numerous Illustrations. Fifth Thousand. Crown 8vo, 5s.
BUCKMAN (S. S.), F.G.S.—
  JOHN DARKE'S SOJOURN IN THE COTTESWOLDS
  AND ELSEWHERE : A Series of Sketches. Crown 8vo, 3s. 6d.
BROWN (J. MORAY)—
  POWDER, SPEAR, AND SPUR : A Sporting Medley.
  With Illustrations by G. D. GILES and EDGAR GIBERNE from Sketches by the
  Author. Crown 8vo, 10s. 6d.
BURCHETT (R.)—
  DEFINITIONS OF GEOMETRY. New Edition. 24mo
  cloth, 5d.

BURCHETT (R.)—Continued—
LINEAR PERSPECTIVE, for the Use of Schools of Art.
New Edition. With Illustrations. Post 8vo, cloth, 7s.
PRACTICAL GEOMETRY: The Course of Construction
of Plane Geometrical Figures. With 137 Diagrams. Eighteenth Edition. Post
8vo, cloth, 5s.

BURGESS (EDWARD)—
ENGLISH AND AMERICAN YACHTS. Illustrated
with 50 Beautiful Photogravure Engravings. Oblong folio, 42s.

BUTLER (A. J.)—
COURT LIFE IN EGYPT. Second Edition. Illustrated.
Large crown 8vo, 12s.

CAFFYN (MANNINGTON)—
A POPPY'S TEARS. Crown 8vo, 1s.; in cloth, 1s. 6d.

CARLYLE (THOMAS), WORKS BY.—See pages 29 and 30.
THE CARLYLE BIRTHDAY BOOK. Compiled, with
the permission of Mr. Thomas Carlyle, by C. N. WILLIAMSON. Second Edition.
Small fcap. 8vo, 3s.

CARSTENSEN (A. RIIS)—
TWO SUMMERS IN GREENLAND: An Artist's
Adventures among Ice and Islands in Fjords and Mountains. With numerous
Illustrations by the Author. Demy 8vo, 14s.

CHALDÆAN AND ASSYRIAN ART—
A HISTORY OF ART IN CHALDÆA AND ASSYRIA.
By GEORGES PERROT and CHARLES CHIPIEZ. Translated by WALTER ARMSTRONG,
B.A. Oxon. With 452 Illustrations. 2 vols. Imperial 8vo, 42s.

CHAPMAN & HALL'S SHILLING SERIES.

Bound in Cloth, 1s. 6d.

A POPPY'S TEARS. By MANNINGTON CAFFYN.
NOTCHES ON THE ROUGH EDGE OF LIFE. By LYNN CYRIL D'OYLE.
WE TWO AT MONTE CARLO. By ALBERT D. VANDAM.
WHO IS THE MAN? A Tale of the Scottish Border. By J. S. TAIT.
THE CHILD OF STAFFERTON: A Chapter from a Family Chronicle. By CANON
    KNOX LITTLE.
THE BROKEN VOW: A Story of Here and Hereafter. By CANON KNOX LITTLE
THE STORY OF AN AFRICAN FARM. By OLIVE SCHREINER.
PADDY AT HOME. By BARON E. DE MANDAT-GRANCEY.

CHARLOTTE ELIZABETH, LIFE AND LETTERS OF,
Princess Palatine and Mother of Philippe d'Orléans, Regent of France, 1652-1722.
Compiled, translated, and gathered from various Published and Unpublished
Sources. With Portraits. Demy 8vo, 10s. 6d.

CHARNAY (DÉSIRÉ)—
THE ANCIENT CITIES OF THE NEW WORLD.
Being Travels and Explorations in Mexico and Central America, 1857—1882.
Translated from the French by J. Gonino and Helen S. Conant. With upwards of
200 Illustrations. Super Royal 8vo, 31s. 6d.

CHURCH (PROFESSOR A. H.), M.A. Oxon.—
FOOD GRAINS OF INDIA. With numerous Woodcuts.
Small 4to, 6s.
ENGLISH PORCELAIN. A Handbook to the China
made in England during the Eighteenth Century, as illustrated by Specimens
chiefly in the National Collection. With numerous Woodcuts. Large crown
8vo, 3s.

CHURCH (PROFESSOR A. H.)., M.A. Oxon. (Continued)—
ENGLISH EARTHENWARE. A Handbook to the
Wares made in England during the 17th and 18th Centuries, as illustrated by Specimens in the National Collections. With numerous Woodcuts. Large crown 8vo, 3s.
PLAIN WORDS ABOUT WATER. Illustrated. Crown
8vo, sewed, 6d.
FOOD : Some Account of its Sources, Constituents, and
Uses. A New and Revised Edition. Large crown 8vo, cloth, 3s.
PRECIOUS STONES : considered in their Scientific and
Artistic Relations. With a Catalogue of the Townsend Collection of Gems in the South Kensington Museum. With a Coloured Plate and Woodcuts. Large crown 8vo, 2s. 6d.

CLINTON (R. H.)—
A COMPENDIUM OF ENGLISH HISTORY, from the
Earliest Times to A.D. 1872. With Copious Quotations on the Leading Events and the Constitutional History, together with Appendices. Post 8vo, 7s. 6d.

COBDEN, RICHARD, LIFE OF. By the RIGHT HON. JOHN
MORLEY, M.P. With Portrait. New Edition. Crown 8vo, 7s. 6d.
Popular Edition, with Portrait, 4to, sewed, 1s.; cloth, 2s.

COLLINS (WILKIE) and DICKENS (CHARLES)—
THE LAZY TOUR OF TWO IDLE APPRENTICES ;
NO THOROUGHFARE; THE PERILS OF CERTAIN ENGLISH PRISONERS. With 8 Illustrations. Crown 8vo, 5s.
*** These Stories, which originally appeared in "Household Words," are now reprinted for the first time complete.

COOKERY—
THE PYTCHLEY BOOK OF REFINED COOKERY
AND BILLS OF FARE. By MAJOR L——. Fourth Edition. Large crown 8vo, 8s.
BREAKFASTS, LUNCHEONS, AND BALL SUPPERS.
By MAJOR L——. Crown 8vo. 4s.
OFFICIAL HANDBOOK OF THE NATIONAL
TRAINING SCHOOL FOR COOKERY. Containing Lessons on Cookery; forming the Course of Instruction in the School. Compiled by "R. O. C." Twentieth Thousand. Large crown 8vo, 6s.
BREAKFAST AND SAVOURY DISHES. By "R. O. C."
Ninth Thousand. Crown 8vo, 1s.
HOW TO COOK FISH. Compiled by "R. O. C."
Crown 8vo, sewed, 3d.
SICK-ROOM COOKERY. Compiled by "R. O. C."
Crown 8vo, sewed, 6d.
THE ROYAL CONFECTIONER : English and Foreign.
A Practical Treatise. By C. E. FRANCATELLI. With numerous Illustrations. Fifth Thousand. Crown 8vo, 5s.
THE KINGSWOOD COOKERY BOOK. By H. F.
WICKEN. Crown 8vo, 2s.

COOPER-KING (LT.-COL.)—
GEORGE WASHINGTON. Large crown 8vo. With
Portrait and Maps. *[In the Press.*

COURTNEY (W. L.), M.A., LL.D., of New College, Oxford—
STUDIES NEW AND OLD. Crown 8vo, 6s.
CONSTRUCTIVE ETHICS : A Review of Modern Philo-
sophy and its Three Stages of Interpretation, Criticism, and Reconstruction. Demy 8vo, 12s.

CRAIK (GEORGE LILLIE)—
ENGLISH OF SHAKESPEARE. Illustrated in a Philological Commentary on his "Julius Cæsar." Eighth Edition. Post 8vo, cloth, 5s.
OUTLINES OF THE HISTORY OF THE ENGLISH LANGUAGE. Eleventh Edition. Post 8vo, cloth, 2s. 6d.

CRAWFURD (OSWALD), Her Majesty's Consul at Oporto—
ROUND THE CALENDAR IN PORTUGAL. With numerous Illustrations by Mrs. H. M. STANLEY (DOROTHY TENNANT), Mrs. ARTHUR WALTER, Mr. TRISTRAM ELLIS, Miss WOODWARD, Miss THOMSON, Mr. A. LEE, and the Author. Royal 8vo. *[In the Press.*
BEYOND THE SEAS; being the surprising Adventures and ingenious Opinions of Ralph, Lord St. Keyne, told by his kinsman, Humphrey St. Keyne. Second Edition. Crown 8vo, 3s. 6d.

CRIPPS (WILFRED JOSEPH), M.A., F.S.A.—
COLLEGE AND CORPORATION PLATE. A Handbook for the Reproduction of Silver Plate. [*In the South Kensington Museum, from celebrated English collections.*] With numerous Illustrations. Large crown 8vo, cloth, 2s. 6d.

DAIRY FARMING—
DAIRY FARMING. To which is added a Description of the Chief Continental Systems. With numerous Illustrations. By JAMES LONG. Crown 8vo, 9s.
DAIRY FARMING, MANAGEMENT OF COWS, etc. By ARTHUR ROLAND. Edited by WILLIAM ABLETT. Crown 8vo, 5s.

DALY (J. B.), LL.D.—
IRELAND IN THE DAYS OF DEAN SWIFT. Crown 8vo, 5s.

DAUBOURG (E.)—
INTERIOR ARCHITECTURE. Doors, Vestibules, Staircases, Anterooms, Drawing, Dining, and Bed Rooms, Libraries, Bank and Newspaper Offices, Shop Fronts and Interiors. Half-imperial, cloth, £2 12s. 6d.

DAVIDSON (ELLIS A.)—
PRETTY ARTS FOR THE EMPLOYMENT OF LEISURE HOURS. A Book for Ladies. With Illustrations. Demy 8vo, 6s.

DAVITT (MICHAEL)—
LEAVES FROM A PRISON DIARY. Crown 8vo, sewed, 1s. 6d.

DAY (WILLIAM)—
THE RACEHORSE IN TRAINING, with Hints on Racing and Racing Reform, to which is added a Chapter on Shoeing. Sixth Edition. Demy 8vo, 9s.

DAS (DEVENDRA N.)—
SKETCHES OF HINDOO LIFE. Crown 8vo, 5s.

DE AINSLIE (GENERAL)—
A HISTORY OF THE ROYAL REGIMENT OF DRAGOONS. From its Formation in 1661 to the Present Day. With Illustrations. Demy 8vo, 21s.

DE CHAMPEAUX (ALFRED)—
TAPESTRY. With numerous Woodcuts. Cloth, 2s. 6d.

DE FALLOUX (THE COUNT)—
MEMOIRS OF A ROYALIST. Edited by C. B. PITMAN. 2 vols. With Portraits. Demy 8vo, 32s.

D'HAUSSONVILLE (VICOMTE)—
SALON OF MADAME NECKER. Translated by H. M. TROLLOPE. 2 vols. Crown 8vo, 18s.

DE KONINCK (L. L.) and DIETZ (E.)—
PRACTICAL MANUAL OF CHEMICAL ASSAYING,
as applied to the Manufacture of Iron. Edited, with notes, by ROBERT MALLET.
Post 8vo, cloth, 6s.

DE LESSEPS (FERDINAND)—
RECOLLECTIONS OF FORTY YEARS. Translated
from the French by C. B. PITMAN. 2 vols. Demy 8vo, 24s.

DE LISLE (MEMOIR OF LIEUTENANT RUDOLPH),
R.N., of the Naval Brigade. By the Rev. H. N. OXENHAM, M.A. Third
Edition. Crown 8vo, 7s. 6d.

DE MANDAT-GRANCEY (BARON E.)—
PADDY AT HOME; OR, IRELAND AND THE IRISH AT
THE PRESENT TIME, AS SEEN BY A FRENCHMAN. Translated from the French.
Fifth Edition. Crown 8vo, 1s. ; in cloth, 1s. 6d.

D'OYLE (LYNN CYRIL)—
NOTCHES ON THE ROUGH EDGE OF LIFE.
Crown 8vo, 1s. ; in cloth, 1s. 6d.

DE STAËL (MADAME)—
MADAME DE STAËL: Her Friends, and Her Influence
in Politics and Literature. By LADY BLENNERHASSETT. Translated from the
German by J. E. GORDON CUMMING. With a Portrait. 3 vols. Demy 8vo, 36s.

DE WINDT (H.)—
FROM PEKIN TO CALAIS BY LAND. With nume-
rous Illustrations by C. E. FRIPP from Sketches by the Author. Demy 8vo, 20s.

DICKENS (CHARLES), WORKS BY—See pages 31—37.
THE LETTERS OF CHARLES DICKENS. Two
vols. uniform with "The Charles Dickens Edition" of his Works. Crown 8vo, 8s.

THE LIFE OF CHARLES DICKENS—*See "Forster."*

THE CHARLES DICKENS BIRTHDAY BOOK.
With Five Illustrations. In a handsome fcap. 4to volume, 12s.

THE HUMOUR AND PATHOS OF CHARLES
DICKENS. By CHARLES KENT. With Portrait. Crown 8vo, 6s.

DICKENS (CHARLES) and COLLINS (WILKIE)—
THE LAZY TOUR OF TWO IDLE APPRENTICES;
NO THOROUGHFARE: THE PERILS OF CERTAIN ENGLISH
PRISONERS. With Illustrations. Crown 8vo, 5s.
* These Stories are now reprinted in complete form for the first time.

DILKE (LADY)—
ART IN THE MODERN STATE. With Facsimile.
Demy 8vo, 9s.

DINARTE (SYLVIO)—
INNOCENCIA: A Story of the Prairie Regions of Brazil.
Translated from the Portuguese and Illustrated by JAMES W. WELLS, F.R.G.S.
Crown 8vo, 6s.

DIXON (CHARLES)—
IDLE HOURS WITH NATURE. With Frontispiece.
Crown 8vo.

ANNALS OF BIRD LIFE: A Year-Book of British
Ornithology. With Illustrations. Crown 8vo, 7s. 6d.

DOUGLAS (JOHN)—
SKETCH OF THE FIRST PRINCIPLES OF PHYSIO-
GRAPHY. With Maps and numerous Illustrations. Crown 8vo, 6s.

DOWN WITH ENGLAND. Translated from the French.
With Maps. Crown 8vo, 1s.

DRAYSON (MAJOR-GENERAL A. W.), Late R.A., F.R.A.S.—
THIRTY THOUSAND YEARS OF THE EARTH'S
PAST HISTORY. Large Crown 8vo, 5s.
EXPERIENCES OF A WOOLWICH PROFESSOR
during Fifteen Years at the Royal Military Academy. Demy 8vo, 8s.
PRACTICAL MILITARY SURVEYING AND
SKETCHING. Fifth Edition. Post 8vo, cloth, 4s. 6d.
DREAMS BY A FRENCH FIRESIDE. Translated from the
German by MARY O'CALLAGHAN. Illustrated by Fred Roe. Crown 8vo, 7s. 6d.

DUCOUDRAY (GUSTAVE)—
THE HISTORY OF ANCIENT CIVILISATION. A
Handbook based upon M. Gustave Ducoudray's "Histoire Sommaire de la
Civilisation." Edited by REV. J. VERSCHOYLE, M.A. With Illustrations. Large
crown 8vo, 6s.

DUFFY (SIR CHARLES GAVAN), K.C.M.G.—
THE LEAGUE OF NORTH AND SOUTH. An Episode
in Irish History, 1850-1854. Crown 8vo, 8s.

DYCE (WILLIAM), R.A.—
DRAWING-BOOK OF THE GOVERNMENT SCHOOL
OF DESIGN; OR, ELEMENTARY OUTLINES OF ORNAMENT. Fifty
selected Plates. Folio, sewed, 5s.; mounted, 18s.
ELEMENTARY OUTLINES OF ORNAMENT. Plates I.
to XXII., containing 97 Examples, adapted for Practice of Standards I. to IV.
Small folio, sewed, 2s 6d.
SELECTION FROM DYCE'S DRAWING BOOK.
15 Plates, sewed, 1s. 6d.; mounted on cardboard, 6s. 6d.
TEXT TO ABOVE. Crown 8vo, sewed, 6d.

EDWARDS (H. SUTHERLAND)—
FAMOUS FIRST REPRESENTATIONS. Crown 8vo, 6s.

EGYPTIAN ART—
A HISTORY OF ART IN ANCIENT EGYPT. By
G. PERROT and C. CHIPIEZ. Translated by WALTER ARMSTRONG. With over
600 Illustrations. 2 vols. Imperial 8vo, £2 2s.

ELLIS (A. B., Major 1st West India Regiment)—
THE EWE-SPEAKING PEOPLE OF THE SLAVE
COAST OF WEST AFRICA. With Map. Demy 8vo, 10s. 6d
WEST AFRICAN STORIES. Crown 8vo, 6s.
THE TSHI-SPEAKING PEOPLES OF THE GOLD
COAST OF WEST AFRICA: their Religion, Manners, Customs, Laws,
Language, &c. With Map. Demy 8vo, 10s. 6d.
SOUTH AFRICAN SKETCHES. Crown 8vo, 6s.
THE HISTORY OF THE WEST INDIA REGI-
MENT. With Maps and Coloured Frontispiece and Title-page. Demy 8vo, 18s.
THE LAND OF FETISH. Demy 8vo, 12s.

ENGEL (CARL)—
MUSICAL INSTRUMENTS. With numerous Woodcuts.
Large crown 8vo, cloth, 2s. 6d.

ESCOTT (T. H. S.)—
POLITICS AND LETTERS. Demy 8vo, 9s.
ENGLAND: ITS PEOPLE, POLITY, AND PURSUITS.
New and Revised Edition. Demy 8vo, 3s. 6d.

EUROPEAN POLITICS, THE PRESENT POSITION OF.
By the Author of "Greater Britain." Demy 8vo, 12s.

FANE (VIOLET)—

AUTUMN SONGS. Crown 8vo, 6s.

THE STORY OF HELEN DAVENANT. Crown 8vo, 3s. 6d.

QUEEN OF THE FAIRIES (A Village Story), and other Poems. Crown 8vo, 6s.

ANTHONY BABINGTON: a Drama. Crown 8vo, 6s.

FARR (WILLIAM) and THRUPP (GEORGE A.)—

COACH TRIMMING. With 60 Illustrations. Crown 8vo, 2s. 6d.

FIELD (HENRY M.)—

GIBRALTAR. With numerous Illustrations. Demy 8vo, 7s. 6d.

FIFE-COOKSON (LIEUT-COL. J. C.)—

TIGER-SHOOTING IN THE DOON AND ULWAR, AND LIFE IN INDIA. With numerous Illustrations by E. Hobday, R.H.A. Large crown 8vo, 10s. 6d.

FITZGERALD (PERCY), F.S.A.—

THE HISTORY OF PICKWICK. Demy 8vo.

THE CHRONICLES OF BOW STREET POLICE OFFICE. With numerous Illustrations. 2 vols. Demy 8vo, 21s.

FLEMING (GEORGE), F.R.C.S.—

ANIMAL PLAGUES: THEIR HISTORY, NATURE, AND PREVENTION. 8vo, cloth, 15s.

PRACTICAL HORSE-SHOEING. With 37 Illustrations. Fifth Edition, enlarged. 8vo, sewed, 2s.

RABIES AND HYDROPHOBIA: THEIR HISTORY, NATURE, CAUSES, SYMPTOMS, AND PREVENTION. With 8 Illustrations. 8vo, cloth, 15s.

FORSTER (JOHN)—

THE LIFE OF CHARLES DICKENS. Uniform with the Illustrated Library Edition of Dickens's Works. 2 vols. Demy 8vo, 20s.

THE LIFE OF CHARLES DICKENS. Uniform with the Library Edition. Post 8vo, 10s. 6d.

THE LIFE OF CHARLES DICKENS. Uniform with the "C. D." Edition. With Numerous Illustrations. 2 vols. 7s.

THE LIFE OF CHARLES DICKENS. Uniform with the Household Edition. With Illustrations by F. Barnard. Crown 4to, cloth, 5s.

FORSTER, THE LIFE OF THE RIGHT HON. W. E.
By T. Wemyss Reid. With Portraits. Fourth Edition. 2 vols. Demy 8vo, 32s.
FIFTH EDITION, in one volume, with new Portrait. Demy 8vo, 10s. 6d.

FORSYTH (CAPTAIN)—

THE HIGHLANDS OF CENTRAL INDIA: Notes on their Forests and Wild Tribes, Natural History and Sports. With Map and Coloured Illustrations. A New Edition. Demy 8vo, 12s.

FORTESCUE (THE HON. JOHN)—

RECORDS OF STAG-HUNTING ON EXMOOR. With 14 full page Illustrations by Edgar Giberne. Large crown 8vo, 16s.

FORTNIGHTLY REVIEW (see page 40)—
FORTNIGHTLY REVIEW.—First Series, May, 1865, to Dec. 1866. 6 vols. Cloth, 13s. each.
New Series, 1867 to 1872. In Half-yearly Volumes. Cloth, 13s. each.
From January, 1873, to the present time, in Half-yearly Volumes. Cloth, 16s. each.
CONTENTS OF FORTNIGHTLY REVIEW. From the commencement to end of 1878. Sewed, 2s.

FORTNUM (C. D. E.), F.S.A.—
MAIOLICA. With numerous Woodcuts. Large crown 8vo, cloth, 2s. 6d.
BRONZES. With numerous Woodcuts. Large crown 8vo, cloth, 2s. 6d.

FOUQUÉ (DE LA MOTTE)—
UNDINE: a Romance translated from the German. With an Introduction by JULIA CARTWRIGHT. Illustrated by HEYWOOD SUMNER. Crown 4to, 5s.

FRANCATELLI (C. E.)—
THE ROYAL CONFECTIONER: English and Foreign. A Practical Treatise. With Illustrations. Fifth Edition. Crown 8vo, 5s.

FRANCIS (FRANCIS), JUNR.
SADDLE AND MOCASSIN. 8vo, 12s.

FRANKS (A. W.)—
JAPANESE POTTERY. Being a Native Report, with an Introduction and Catalogue. With numerous Illustrations and Marks. Large crown 8vo, cloth, 2s. 6d.

FROBEL, FRIEDRICH; a Short Sketch of his Life, including Fröbel's Letters from Dresden and Leipzig to his Wife, now first Translated into English. By EMILY SHIRREFF. Crown 8vo, 2s.

GALILEO AND HIS JUDGES. By F. R. WEGG-PROSSER. Demy 8vo, 5s.

GALLENGA (ANTONIO)—
ITALY: PRESENT AND FUTURE. 2 vols. Dmy. 8vo, 21s.
EPISODES OF MY SECOND LIFE. 2 vols. Dmy. 8vo, 28s.
IBERIAN REMINISCENCES. Fifteen Years' Travelling Impressions of Spain and Portugal. With a Map. 2 vols. Demy 8vo, 32s.

GASNAULT (PAUL) and GARNIER (ED.)—
FRENCH POTTERY. With Illustrations and Marks. Large crown 8vo, 3s.

GILLMORE (PARKER)—
THE HUNTER'S ARCADIA. With numerous Illustrations. Demy 8vo, 10s. 6d.

GIRL'S LIFE EIGHTY YEARS AGO (A). Selections from the Letters of Eliza Southgate Bowne, with an Introduction by Clarence Cook. Illustrated with Portraits and Views. Crown 4to, 12s.

GLEICHEN (COUNT), Grenadier Guards—
WITH THE CAMEL CORPS UP THE NILE. With numerous Sketches by the Author. Third Edition. Large crown 8vo, 9s.

GORDON (GENERAL)—
  LETTERS FROM THE CRIMEA, THE DANUBE,
  AND ARMENIA. Edited by DEMETRIUS C. BOULGER. Second Edition.
  Crown 8vo, 5s.

GORST (SIR J. E.), Q.C., M.P.—
  An ELECTION MANUAL. Containing the Parliamentary
  Elections (Corrupt and Illegal Practices) Act, 1883, with Notes. Third Edition.
  Crown 8vo, 1s. 6d.

GOWER (A. R.), Royal School of Mines—
  PRACTICAL METALLURGY. With Illustrations. Crown
  8vo, 3s.

GRAHAM (SIR GERALD), V.C., K.C.B.—
  LAST WORDS WITH GORDON. Crown 8vo, cloth, 1s.

GRESWELL (WILLIAM), M.A., F.R.C.I.—
  OUR SOUTH AFRICAN EMPIRE. With Map. 2 vols.
  Crown 8vo, 21s.

GRIFFIN (SIR LEPEL HENRY), K.C.S.I.—
  THE GREAT REPUBLIC. Second Edition. Crown 8vo,
  4s. 6d.

GRIFFITHS (MAJOR ARTHUR), H.M. Inspector of Prisons—
  FRENCH REVOLUTIONARY GENERALS. Large
  crown 8vo.   [*In the Press.*
  CHRONICLES OF NEWGATE. Illustrated. New
  Edition. Demy 8vo, 16s.
  MEMORIALS OF MILLBANK : or, Chapters in Prison
  History. With Illustrations by R. Goff and Author. New Edition. Demy 8vo,
  12s.

HALL (SIDNEY)—
  A TRAVELLING ATLAS OF THE ENGLISH COUN-
  TIES. Fifty Maps, coloured. New Edition, including the Railways, corrected
  up to the present date. Demy 8vo, in roan tuck, 10s. 6d.

HAWKINS (FREDERICK)—
  THE FRENCH STAGE IN THE EIGHTEENTH
  CENTURY. With Portraits. 2 vols. Demy 8vo, 30s.
  ANNALS OF THE FRENCH STAGE : FROM ITS
  ORIGIN TO THE DEATH OF RACINE. 4 Portraits. 2 vols. Demy 8vo, 28s.

HILDEBRAND (HANS), Royal Antiquary of Sweden—
  INDUSTRIAL ARTS OF SCANDINAVIA IN THE
  PAGAN TIME. With numerous Woodcuts. Large crown 8vo, 2s. 6d.

HILL (MISS G.)—
  THE PLEASURES AND PROFITS OF OUR LITTLE
  POULTRY FARM. Small 8vo, 3s.

HOLBEIN—
  TWELVE HEADS AFTER HOLBEIN. Selected from
  Drawings in Her Majesty's Collection at Windsor. Reproduced in Autotype, in
  portfolio. £1 16s.

*HOLMES (GEORGE C. V.), Secretary of the Institution of Naval Architects,
  Whitworth Scholar—*
  MARINE ENGINES AND BOILERS. With Sixty-nine
  Woodcuts. Large crown 8vo, 3s.

HOPE (ANDRÉE)—
  CHRONICLES OF AN OLD INN ; or, a Few Words
  about Gray's Inn. Crown 8vo, 5s.

HOUSSAYE (ARSÈNE)—
BEHIND THE SCENES OF THE COMÉDIE FRAN-
CAISE, AND OTHER RECOLLECTIONS. Translated and Edited, with
Notes, by ALBERT D. VANDAM. Demy 8vo, 14s.
HOVELACQUE (ABEL)—
THE SCIENCE OF LANGUAGE: LINGUISTICS,
PHILOLOGY, AND ETYMOLOGY. With Maps. Large crown 8vo, cloth, 5s.
HOZIER (H. M.)—
TURENNE. With Portrait and Two Maps. Large crown
8vo, 4s.
HUEFFER (F.)—
HALF A CENTURY OF MUSIC IN ENGLAND.
1837—1887. Demy 8vo, 8s.
HUNTLY (MARQUIS OF)—
TRAVELS, SPORTS, AND POLITICS IN THE EAST
OF EUROPE. With Illustrations by the Marchioness of Huntly. Large
Crown 8vo, 12s.
INDUSTRIAL ARTS: Historical Sketches. With numerous
Illustrations. Large crown 8vo, 3s.
IRELAND IN THE DAYS OF DEAN SWIFT. By J. B.
DALY, LL.D. Crown 8vo, 5s.
IRISH ART OF LACEMAKING, A RENASCENCE OF
THE. Illustrated by Photographic Reproductions of Irish Laces, made from
new and specially designed Patterns. Introductory Notes and Descriptions. By
A. S. C. Demy 8vo, 2s. 6d.
IRON (RALPH), (OLIVE SCHREINER)—
THE STORY OF AN AFRICAN FARM. New Edition.
Crown 8vo, 1s.; in cloth, 1s. 6d.
ITALY, FROM THE ALPS TO MOUNT ETNA. Translated
by FRANCES ELEANOR TROLLOPE, and Edited by THOMAS ADOLPHUS TROLLOPE.
Illustrated with upwards of 100 full-page and 300 smaller Engravings. Imperial 4to.
JACKSON (FRANK G.), Master in the Birmingham Municipal School of Art—
DECORATIVE DESIGN. An Elementary Text Book of
Principles and Practice. With numerous Illustrations. Crown 8vo, 7s. 6d.
JAMES (HENRY A.), M.A.—
HANDBOOK TO PERSPECTIVE. Crown 8vo, 2s. 6d.
PERSPECTIVE CHARTS, for use in Class Teaching. 2s.
JARRY (GENERAL)—
OUTPOST DUTY. Translated, with TREATISES ON
MILITARY RECONNAISSANCE AND ON ROAD-MAKING. By Major-
Gen. W. C. E. NAPIER. Third Edition. Crown 8vo, 5s.
JEANS (W. T.)—
CREATORS OF THE AGE OF STEEL. Memoirs of
Sir W. Siemens, Sir H. Bessemer, Sir J. Whitworth, Sir J. Brown, and other
Inventors. Second Edition. Crown 8vo, 7s. 6d.
JONES (CAPTAIN DOUGLAS), R.A.—
NOTES ON MILITARY LAW. Crown 8vo, 4s.
JONES. HANDBOOK OF THE JONES COLLECTION
IN THE SOUTH KENSINGTON MUSEUM. With Portrait and Wood-
cuts. Large crown 8vo, 2s. 6d.
JUNKER (DR. WM.)—
TRAVELS IN AFRICA. With 38 Full-page Plates and
125 Illustrations in the Text and Map. Translated from the German by
Professor KEANE. Demy 8vo, 21s.

KENNARD (EDWARD)—
 NORWEGIAN SKETCHES: FISHING IN STRANGE
 WATERS. Illustrated with 30 beautiful Sketches. Second Edition. Oblong
 folio, 21s. A Set of Ten Hand-coloured Plates, £3; in Oak Frames, £4 10s.
 Smaller Edition. 14s.

KENT (CHARLES)—
 HUMOUR AND PATHOS OF CHARLES DICKENS.
 Crown 8vo, 6s.

KING (LIEUT.-COL. COOPER)—
 GEORGE WASHINGTON. Large crown 8vo. [*In the Press.*

KLACZKO (M. JULIAN)—
 TWO CHANCELLORS: PRINCE GORTCHAKOF AND
 PRINCE BISMARCK. Translated by MRS. TAIT. New and cheaper Edition, 6s.

KNOLLYS (MAJOR HENRY), R.A.—
 SKETCHES OF LIFE IN JAPAN. With Illustrations.
 Large crown 8vo, 12s.

LACORDAIRE'S JESUS CHRIST; GOD; AND GOD AND
 MAN. Conferences delivered at Notre Dame in Paris. New Edition.
 Crown 8vo, 6s.

LAINÉ (J. M.), R.A.—
 ENGLISH COMPOSITION EXERCISES. Crown 8vo,
 2s. 6d.

LAING (S.)—
 PROBLEMS OF THE FUTURE AND ESSAYS.
 Fifth Thousand. Demy 8vo, 3s. 6d.

 MODERN SCIENCE AND MODERN THOUGHT.
 With a Supplementary Chapter on Gladstone's "Dawn of Creation" and Drummond's
 "Natural Law in the Spiritual World." Ninth Thousand. Demy 8vo, 3s. 6d.

 A MODERN ZOROASTRIAN. Fourth Thousand. Demy
 8vo, 3s. 6d.

LAVELEYE (ÉMILE DE)—
 THE ELEMENTS OF POLITICAL ECONOMY.
 Translated by W. POLLARD, B.A., St. John's College, Oxford. Crown 8vo, 6s.

LANDOR (W. S.)—
 LIFE AND WORKS. 8 vols.
  VOL. 1. WALTER SAVAGE LANDOR. A Biography in Eight Books. By
   JOHN FORSTER. Demy 8vo, 12s.
  VOL. 2. Out of print.
  VOL. 3. CONVERSATIONS OF SOVEREIGNS AND STATESMEN, AND
   FIVE DIALOGUES OF BOCCACCIO AND PETRARCA.
   Demy 8vo, 14s.
  VOL. 4. DIALOGUES OF LITERARY MEN. Demy 8vo, 14s.
  VOL. 5. DIALOGUES OF LITERARY MEN (*continued*). FAMOUS
   WOMEN. LETTERS OF PERICLES AND ASPASIA. And
   Minor Prose Pieces. Demy 8vo, 14s.
  VOL. 6. MISCELLANEOUS CONVERSATIONS. Demy 8vo, 14s.
  VOL. 7. GEBIR, ACTS AND SCENES AND HELLENICS. Poems.
   Demy 8vo, 14s.
  VOL. 8. MISCELLANEOUS POEMS AND CRITICISMS ON THEO-
   CRITUS, CATULLUS, AND PETRARCH. Demy 8vo 14s.

*LE CONTE (JOSEPH), Professor of Geology and Natural History in the Uni-
 versity of California—*

 EVOLUTION AND ITS RELATIONS TO RELIGIOUS
 THOUGHT. Crown 8vo, 6s.

LEFÈVRE (ANDRÉ)—
  PHILOSOPHY, Historical and Critical. Translated, with
  an Introduction, by A. W. KEANE, B.A. Large crown 8vo, 7s. 6d.
LE ROUX (H.)—
  ACROBATS AND MOUNTEBANKS. With over 200
  Illustrations by J. GARNIER. Royal 8vo, 16s.
LESLIE (R. C.)—
  OLD SEA WINGS, WAYS, AND WORDS, IN THE
  DAYS OF OAK AND HEMP. With 135 Illustrations by the Author. Demy
  8vo, 14s.
  LIFE ABOARD A BRITISH PRIVATEER IN THE
  TIME OF QUEEN ANNE. Being the Journals of Captain Woodes Rogers,
  Master Mariner. With Notes and Illustrations by ROBERT C. LESLIE. Large
  crown 8vo, 9s.
  A SEA PAINTER'S LOG. With 12 Full-page Illustrations
  by the Author. Large crown 8vo, 12s.
LETOURNEAU (DR. CHARLES)—
  SOCIOLOGY. Based upon Ethnology. Large crown
  8vo, 10s.
  BIOLOGY. Translated by WILLIAM MacCALL. With 83
  Illustrations. A New Edition. Demy 8vo, 3s. 6d.
LILLY (W. S.)—
  ON RIGHT AND WRONG. Demy 8vo, 12s.
  A CENTURY OF REVOLUTION. Second Edition.
  Demy 8vo, 12s.
  CHAPTERS ON EUROPEAN HISTORY. With an
  Introductory Dialogue on the Philosophy of History. 2 vols. Demy 8vo, 21s.
  ANCIENT RELIGION AND MODERN THOUGHT.
  Second Edition. Demy 8vo, 12s.
LITTLE (THE REV. CANON KNOX)—
  THE CHILD OF STAFFERTON : A Chapter from a
  Family Chronicle. New Edition. Crown 8vo, boards, 1s.; cloth, 1s. 6d.
  THE BROKEN VOW. A Story of Here and Hereafter.
  New Edition. Crown 8vo, boards, 1s.; cloth, 1s. 6d.
LITTLE (THE REV. H. W.)—
  H. M. STANLEY : HIS LIFE, WORKS, AND
  EXPLORATIONS. Demy 8vo, 10s. 6d.
LLOYD (COLONEL E.M.), R.E., late Professor of Fortification at the Royal
  Military Academy, Woolwich—
  VAUBAN, MONTALEMBERT, CARNOT : ENGINEER
  STUDIES. With Portraits. Crown 8vo, 5s
LLOYD (N. N.), late 24th Regiment—
  ON ACTIVE SERVICE. Printed in Colours. Oblong
  4to, 5s.
  LIFE IN INDIA. Printed in Colours. 4to, 6s.
LONG (JAMES)—
  DAIRY FARMING. To which is added a Description of
  the Chief Continental Systems. With numerous Illustrations. Crown 8vo, 9s.
LOW (WILLIAM)—
  TABLE DECORATION. With 19 Full Illustrations.
  Demy 8vo, 6s.
LYTTON (ROBERT, EARL)—
  POETICAL WORKS—
    FABLES IN SONG. 2 vols. Fcap. 8vo, 12s.
    THE WANDERER. Fcap. 8vo, 6s.
    POEMS, HISTORICAL AND CHARACTERISTIC. Fcap. 6s.

McCOAN (J. C.)—
> EGYPT UNDER ISMAIL: a Romance of History.
> With Portrait and Appendix of Official Documents. Crown 8vo, 7s. 6d.

MACDONALD (FREDERIKA)—
> PUCK AND PEARL: THE WANDERINGS AND WONDER-
> INGS OF TWO ENGLISH CHILDREN IN INDIA. By FREDERIKA MACDONALD.
> With Illustrations by MRS. IRVING GRAHAM. Second Edition. Crown 8vo, 5s.

MALLESON (COL. G. B.), C.S.I.—
> PRINCE EUGENE OF SAVOY. With Portrait and
> Maps. Large crown 8vo, 6s.

> LOUDON. A Sketch of the Military Life of Gideon
> Ernest, Freiherr von Loudon, sometime Generalissimo of the Austrian Forces.
> With Portrait and Maps. Large crown 8vo, 4s.

MALLET (ROBERT)—
> PRACTICAL MANUAL OF CHEMICAL ASSAYING,
> as applied to the Manufacture of Iron. By L. L. DE KONINCK and E. DIETZ.
> Edited, with notes, by ROBERT MALLET. Post 8vo, cloth, 6s.

MARCEAU (SERGENT)—
> REMINISCENCES OF A REGICIDE. Edited from
> the Original MSS. of SERGENT MARCEAU, Member of the Convention, and
> Administrator of Police in the French Revolution of 1789. By M. C. M. SIMPSON,
> Author of the "Letters and Recollections of Julius and Mary Mohl." Demy 8vo,
> with Illustrations and Portraits, 14s.

MASKELL (ALFRED)—
> RUSSIAN ART AND ART OBJECTS IN RUSSIA.
> A Handbook to the Reproduction of Goldsmiths' Work and other Art Treasures.
> With Illustrations. Large crown 8vo, 4s. 6d.

MASKELL (WILLIAM)—
> IVORIES: ANCIENT AND MEDIÆVAL. With nume-
> rous Woodcuts. Large crown 8vo, cloth, 2s. 6d.

> HANDBOOK TO THE DYCE AND FORSTER COL-
> LECTIONS. With Illustrations. Large crown 8vo, cloth, 2s. 6d.

MAUDSLAY (ATHOL)—
> HIGHWAYS AND HORSES. With numerous Illustra-
> tions. Demy 8vo, 21s.

MECHELIN (SENATOR L.)—
> FINLAND AND ITS PUBLIC LAW. Translated by
> CHARLES J. COOKE, British Vice-Consul at Helsingfors. Crown 8vo, 2s. 6d.

GEORGE MEREDITH'S WORKS.

A New and Uniform Edition. Crown 8vo, 3s. 6d. each.

DIANA OF THE CROSSWAYS.
EVAN HARRINGTON.
THE ORDEAL OF RICHARD FEVEREL.
THE ADVENTURES OF HARRY RICHMOND.
SANDRA BELLONI.
VITTORIA.
RHODA FLEMING.
BEAUCHAMP'S CAREER.
THE EGOIST.
THE SHAVING OF SHAGPAT; AND FARINA.

MERIVALE (HERMAN CHARLES)—

BINKO'S BLUES. A Tale for Children of all Growths.
Illustrated by EDGAR GIBERNE. Small crown 8vo, 5s.

THE WHITE PILGRIM, and other Poems. Crown 8vo, 9s.

*MILLS (JOHN), formerly Assistant to the Solar Physics Committee, and author
of "Alternative Elementary Chemistry"—*

ADVANCED PHYSIOGRAPHY (PHYSIOGRAPHIC
ASTRONOMY). Designed to meet the Requirements of Students preparing for
the Elementary and Advanced Stages of Physiography in the Science and Art
Department Examinations, and as an Introduction to Physical Astronomy.
Crown 8vo, 4s. 6d.

ELEMENTARY PHYSIOGRAPHIC ASTRONOMY.
Crown 8vo, 1s. 6d.

ALTERNATIVE ELEMENTARY PHYSICS. Crown
8vo, 2s. 6d.

MILLS (JOHN) and NORTH (BARKER)—

QUANTITATIVE ANALYSIS (INTRODUCTORY
LESSONS ON). With numerous Woodcuts. Crown 8vo, 1s. 6d.

HANDBOOK OF QUANTITATIVE ANALYSIS. Crown
8vo, 3s. 6d.

MOLESWORTH (W. NASSAU)—

HISTORY OF ENGLAND FROM THE YEAR 1830
TO THE RESIGNATION OF THE GLADSTONE MINISTRY, 1874.
Twelfth Thousand. 3 vols. Crown 8vo, 18s.

ABRIDGED EDITION. Large crown, 7s. 6d.

MOLTKE (FIELD-MARSHAL COUNT VON)—

POLAND: AN HISTORICAL SKETCH. An Authorised
Translation, with Biographical Notice by E. S. BUCHHEIM. Crown 8vo, 4s. 6d.

MORLEY (THE RIGHT HON. JOHN), M.P.—

RICHARD COBDEN'S LIFE AND CORRESPON-
DENCE. Crown 8vo, with Portrait, 7s. 6d.

Popular Edition. With Portrait. 4to, sewed, 1s. Cloth, 2s.

MUNTZ (EUGENE)—

RAPHAEL: his Life, Works, and Times. Illustrated with
about 200 Engravings. A new Edition, revised from the Second French Edition
by W. ARMSTRONG, B.A. Oxon. Imperial 8vo, 25s.

MURRAY (ANDREW), F.L.S.—

ECONOMIC ENTOMOLOGY. APTERA. With numerous Illustrations. Large crown 8vo, 7s. 6d.

NECKER (MADAME)—

THE SALON OF MADAME NECKER. By VICOMTE
D'HAUSSONVILLE. 2 vols. Crown 8vo, 18s.

NESBITT (ALEXANDER)—

GLASS. With numerous Woodcuts. Large crown 8vo,
cloth, 2s. 6d.

NEVINSON (HENRY)—

A SKETCH OF HERDER AND HIS TIMES. With
a Portrait. Demy 8vo, 14s.

NICOL (DAVID)—

THE POLITICAL LIFE OF OUR TIME. Two vols.
Demy 8vo, 24s.

NILSEN (CAPTAIN)—

LEAVES FROM THE LOG OF THE "HOMEWARD
BOUND"; or, Eleven Months at Sea in an Open Boat. Crown 8vo, 1s.

NORMAN (C. B.)—

TONKIN; OR, FRANCE IN THE FAR EAST. With
Maps. Demy 8vo, 14s.

O'BYRNE (ROBERT), F.R.G.S.—

THE VICTORIES OF THE BRITISH ARMY IN
THE PENINSULA AND THE SOUTH OF FRANCE from 1808 to 1814.
An Epitome of Napier's History of the Peninsular War, and Gurwood's Collection
of the Duke of Wellington's Despatches. Crown 8vo, 5s.

O'GRADY (STANDISH)—

TORYISM AND THE TORY DEMOCRACY. Crown
8vo, 5s.

OLIVER (PROFESSOR D.), F.R.S., &c.—

ILLUSTRATIONS OF THE PRINCIPAL NATURAL
ORDERS OF THE VEGETABLE KINGDOM, PREPARED FOR THE
SCIENCE AND ART DEPARTMENT, SOUTH KENSINGTON. With
109 Plates. Oblong 8vo, plain, 16s.; coloured, £1 6s.

OLIVER (E. E.), Under-Secretary to the Public Works Department, Punjaub—

ACROSS THE BORDER; or, PATHAN AND BILOCH.
With numerous Illustrations by J. L. KIPLING, C.I.E. Demy 8vo, 14s.

OXENHAM (REV. H. N.)—

MEMOIR OF LIEUTENANT RUDOLPH DE LISLE,
R.N., OF THE NAVAL BRIGADE. Third Edition, with Illustrations.
Crown 8vo, 7s. 6d.

PAYTON (E. W.)—

ROUND ABOUT NEW ZEALAND. Being Notes from
a Journal of Three Years' Wandering in the Antipodes. With Twenty Original
Illustrations by the Author. Large crown 8vo, 12s.

PERROT (GEORGES) and CHIPIEZ (CHARLES)—

A HISTORY OF ANCIENT ART IN SARDINIA,
JUDÆA, SYRIA, AND ASIA MINOR. With 395 Illustrations. 2 vols.
Imperial 8vo, 36s.

A HISTORY OF ANCIENT ART IN PHŒNICIA
AND ITS DEPENDENCIES. Translated from the French by WALTER
ARMSTRONG, B.A. Oxon. Containing 644 Illustrations in the text, and 10 Steel
and Coloured Plates. 2 vols. Imperial 8vo, 42s.

PERROT (GEORGES) and CHIPIEZ (CHARLES)—Continued—

A HISTORY OF ART IN CHALDÆA AND ASSYRIA.
Translated by WALTER ARMSTRONG, B.A. Oxon. With 452 Illustrations. 2 vols.
Imperial 8vo, 42s.

A HISTORY OF ART IN ANCIENT EGYPT. Trans-
lated from the French by W. ARMSTRONG, B.A. Oxon. With over 600 Illustrations. 2 vols. Imperial 8vo, 42s.

PETERBOROUGH (THE EARL OF)—

THE EARL OF PETERBOROUGH AND MON-
MOUTH (Charles Mordaunt): A Memoir. By Colonel FRANK RUSSELL, Royal
Dragoons. With Illustrations. 2 vols. demy 8vo. 32s.

PHŒNICIAN ART—

A HISTORY OF ANCIENT ART IN PHŒNICIA
AND ITS DEPENDENCIES. By GEORGES PERROT and CHARLES CHIPIEZ.
Translated from the French by WALTER ARMSTRONG, B.A. Oxon. Containing
644 Illustrations in the text, and 10 Steel and Coloured Plates. 2 vols. Imperial
8vo, 42s.

PILLING (WILLIAM)—

LAND TENURE BY REGISTRATION. Second Edition
of "Order from Chaos," Revised and Enlarged. Crown 8vo, 5s.

PITT TAYLOR (FRANK)—

THE CANTERBURY TALES. Selections from the Tales
of GEOFFREY CHAUCER rendered into Modern English, with close adherence
to the language of the Poet. With Frontispiece. Crown 8vo, 6s.

POLLEN (J. H.)—

GOLD AND SILVER SMITH'S WORK. With numerous Woodcuts. Large crown 8vo, cloth, 2s. 6d.

ANCIENT AND MODERN FURNITURE AND
WOODWORK. With numerous Woodcuts. Large crown 8vo, cloth, 2s. 6d.

POOLE (STANLEY LANE), B.A., M.R.A.S.—

THE ART OF THE SARACENS IN EGYPT. Pub-
lished for the Committee of Council on Education. With 108 Woodcuts. Large
crown 8vo, 4s.

POYNTER (E. J.), R.A.—

TEN LECTURES ON ART. Third Edition. Large
crown 8vo, 9s.

PRINSEP (VAL), A.R.A.—

IMPERIAL INDIA. Containing numerous Illustrations
and Maps. Second Edition. Demy 8vo, £1 1s.

PURCELL (the late THEOBALD A.), Surgeon-Major, A.M.D., and Principal
Medical Officer to the Japanese Government)—

A SUBURB OF YEDO. With numerous Illustrations.
Crown 8vo, 2s. 6d.

RADICAL PROGRAMME, THE. From the *Fortnightly*
Review, with additions. With a Preface by the RIGHT HON. J. CHAMBERLAIN,
M.P. Thirteenth Thousand. Crown 8vo, 2s. 6d.

RAE (W. FRASER)—

AUSTRIAN HEALTH RESORTS THROUGHOUT
THE YEAR. A New and Enlarged Edition. Crown 8vo, 5s.

RAMSDEN (LADY GWENDOLEN)—
A BIRTHDAY BOOK. Illustrated. Containing 46 Illustrations from Original Drawings, and numerous other Illustrations. Royal 8vo, 21s.

RANKIN (THOMAS T.), C.E.—
SOLUTIONS TO THE QUESTIONS IN PURE MATHEMATICS (STAGES 1 AND 2) SET AT THE SCIENCE AND ART EXAMINATIONS FROM 1881 TO 1886. Crown 8vo, 2s.

RAPHAEL: his Life, Works, and Times. By EUGENE MUNTZ. Illustrated with about 200 Engravings. A New Edition, revised from the Second French Edition. By W. ARMSTRONG, B.A. Imperial 8vo, 25s.

REDGRAVE (GILBERT)—
OUTLINES OF HISTORIC ORNAMENT. Translated from the German. Edited by GILBERT REDGRAVE. With numerous Illustrations. Crown 8vo, 4s.

REDGRAVE (RICHARD)—
MANUAL OF DESIGN, compiled from the Writings and Addresses of RICHARD REDGRAVE, R.A. With Woodcuts. Large crown 8vo, cloth, 2s. 6d.

ELEMENTARY MANUAL OF COLOUR, with a Catechism on Colour. 24mo, cloth, 9d.

REDGRAVE (SAMUEL)—
A DESCRIPTIVE CATALOGUE OF THE HISTORICAL COLLECTION OF WATER-COLOUR PAINTINGS IN THE SOUTH KENSINGTON MUSEUM. With numerous Chromo-lithographs and other Illustrations. Royal 8vo, £1 1s.

REID (T. WEMYSS)—
THE LIFE OF THE RIGHT HON. W. E. FORSTER. With Portraits. Fourth Edition. 2 vols. Demy 8vo, 32s.
FIFTH EDITION, in one volume, with new Portrait. Demy 8vo, 10s. 6d.

RENAN (ERNEST)—
THE FUTURE OF SCIENCE. Demy 8vo.

HISTORY OF THE PEOPLE OF ISRAEL TILL THE TIME OF KING DAVID. Demy 8vo, 14s.

HISTORY OF THE PEOPLE OF ISRAEL. From the Reign of David up to the Capture of Samaria. Second Division. Demy 8vo, 14s.

RECOLLECTIONS OF MY YOUTH. Translated from the original French, and revised by MADAME RENAN. Crown 8vo, 8s.

REYNARDSON (C. T. S. BIRCH)—
SPORTS AND ANECDOTES OF BYGONE DAYS in England, Scotland, Ireland, Italy, and the Sunny South. With numerous Illustrations in Colour. Second Edition. Large crown 8vo, 12s.

DOWN THE ROAD: Reminiscences of a Gentleman Coachman. With Coloured Illustrations. Large crown 8vo, 12s.

RIANO (JUAN F.)—
THE INDUSTRIAL ARTS IN SPAIN. With numerous Woodcuts. Large crown 8vo, cloth, 4s.

RIBTON-TURNER (C. J.)—

A HISTORY OF VAGRANTS AND VAGRANCY AND BEGGARS AND BEGGING. With Illustrations. Demy 8vo, 21s.

ROBINSON (JAMES F.)—

BRITISH BEE FARMING. Its Profits and Pleasures. Large crown 8vo, 5s.

ROBINSON (J. C.)—

ITALIAN SCULPTURE OF THE MIDDLE AGES AND PERIOD OF THE REVIVAL OF ART. With 20 Engravings. Royal 8vo, cloth, 7s. 6d.

ROBSON (GEORGE)—

ELEMENTARY BUILDING CONSTRUCTION. Illustrated by a Design for an Entrance Lodge and Gate. 15 Plates. Oblong folio, sewed, 8s.

ROCK (THE VERY REV. CANON), D.D.—

TEXTILE FABRICS. With numerous Woodcuts. Large crown 8vo, cloth, 2s. 6d.

ROGERS (CAPTAIN WOODES), Master Mariner—

LIFE ABOARD A BRITISH PRIVATEER IN THE TIME OF QUEEN ANNE. Being the Journals of Captain Woodes Rogers, Master Mariner. With Notes and Illustrations by ROBERT C. LESLIE, Author of "A Sea Painter's Log." Large crown 8vo, 9s.

ROOSE (ROBSON), M.D., F.C.S.—

THE WEAR AND TEAR OF LONDON LIFE. Second Edition. Crown 8vo, sewed, 1s.

INFECTION AND DISINFECTION. Crown 8vo, sewed, 6d.

ROLAND (ARTHUR)—

FARMING FOR PLEASURE AND PROFIT. Edited by WILLIAM ABLETT. 8 vols. Crown 8vo, 5s. each.
   DAIRY-FARMING, MANAGEMENT OF COWS, etc.
   POULTRY-KEEPING.
   TREE-PLANTING, FOR ORNAMENT OR PROFIT.
   STOCK-KEEPING AND CATTLE-REARING.
   DRAINAGE OF LAND, IRRIGATION, MANURES, etc.
   ROOT-GROWING, HOPS, etc.
   MANAGEMENT OF GRASS LANDS, LAYING DOWN GRASS, ARTIFICIAL GRASSES, etc.
   MARKET GARDENING, HUSBANDRY FOR FARMERS AND GENERAL CULTIVATORS.

SARDINIAN ART: HISTORY OF ANCIENT ART IN SARDINIA, JUDÆA, SYRIA, AND ASIA MINOR. By GEORGES PERROT and CHARLES CHIPIEZ. With 395 Illustrations. 2 vols. Imperial 8vo, 36s.

SCIENCE AND ART: a Journal for Teachers and Scholars. Issued monthly. 3d. See page 38.

SCHREINER (OLIVE), (RALPH IRON)—

THE STORY OF AN AFRICAN FARM. Crown 8vo,
1s. ; in cloth, 1s. 6d.

SCHAUERMANN (F. L.)—

HANDBOOK ON WOOD-CARVING. With numerous
Illustrations. Imperial 8vo.

SCOTT (JOHN)—

THE REPUBLIC AS A FORM OF GOVERNMENT ;
or, The Evolution of Democracy in America. Crown 8vo, 7s. 6d.

SCOTT (LEADER)—

THE RENAISSANCE OF ART IN ITALY : an Illus-
trated Sketch. With upwards of 200 Illustrations. Medium quarto, 18s.

SCOTT-STEVENSON (MRS.)—

ON SUMMER SEAS. Including the Mediterranean, the
Ægean, the Ionian, and the Euxine, and a voyage down the Danube. With a
Map. Demy 8vo, 16s.

OUR HOME IN CYPRUS. With a Map and Illustrations. Third Edition. Demy 8vo, 14s.

OUR RIDE THROUGH ASIA MINOR. With Map.
Demy 8vo, 18s.

SEEMAN (O.)—

THE MYTHOLOGY OF GREECE AND ROME, with
Special Reference to its Use in Art. From the German. Edited by G. H.
BIANCHI. 64 Illustrations. New Edition. Crown 8vo, 5s.

SETON-KARR (H. W.), F.R.G.S., etc.—

TEN YEARS' TRAVEL AND SPORT IN FOREIGN
Lands ; or, Travels in the Eighties. Second Edition, with additions and Portrait
of Author. Large crown 8vo, 5s.

SHEPHERD (MAJOR), R.E.—

PRAIRIE EXPERIENCES IN HANDLING CATTLE
AND SHEEP. With Illustrations and Map. Demy 8vo, 10s. 6d.

SHIRREFF (EMILY)—

A SHORT SKETCH OF THE LIFE OF FRIEDRICH
FROBEL ; a New Edition, including Fröbel's Letters from Dresden and Leipzig
to his Wife, now first Translated into English. Crown 8vo, 2s.

HOME EDUCATION IN RELATION TO THE
KINDERGARTEN. Two Lectures. Crown 8vo, 1s. 6d.

SHORE (ARABELLA)—

DANTE FOR BEGINNERS : a Sketch of the " Divina
Commedia." With Translations, Biographical and Critical Notices, and Illustrations. With Portrait. Crown 8vo, 6s.

SIMKIN (R.)—

LIFE IN THE ARMY : Every-day Incidents in Camp,
Field, and Quarters. Printed in Colours. Oblong 4to, 5s.

SIMMONDS (T. L.)—

ANIMAL PRODUCTS : their Preparation, Commercial
Uses, and Value. With numerous Illustrations. Large crown 8vo, 7s. 6d.

SIMPSON (M. C. M.)—

REMINISCENCES OF A REGICIDE. Edited from the Original MSS. of Sergent Marceau, Member of the Convention, and Administrator of Police in the French Revolution of 1789. Demy 8vo, with Illustrations and Portraits, 14s.

SINGER'S STORY, A. Related by the Author of "Flitters, Tatters, and the Counsellor." Crown 8vo, sewed, 1s.

SINNETT (A. P.)—

ESOTERIC BUDDHISM. Annotated and enlarged by the Author. Sixth and cheaper Edition. Crown 8vo, 4s.

KARMA. A Novel. New Edition. Crown 8vo, 3s. 6d.

SINNETT (MRS.)—

THE PURPOSE OF THEOSOPHY. Crown 8vo, 3s.

SMITH (MAJOR R. MURDOCK), R.E.—

PERSIAN ART. With Map and Woodcuts. Second Edition. Large crown 8vo, 2s.

SMITH (S. THEOBALD)—

A RAMBLE IN RHYME IN THE COUNTRY OF CRANMER AND RIDLEY. Illustrated by HAROLD OAKLEY from Sketches by the Author. Crown 8vo, 2s. 6d.

STANLEY (H. M.): HIS LIFE, WORKS, AND EXPLORA- TIONS. By the Rev. H. W. LITTLE. Demy 8vo, 10s. 6d.

STOKES (MARGARET)—

EARLY CHRISTIAN ART IN IRELAND. With 106 Woodcuts. Demy 8vo, 7s. 6d.

STORY (W. W.)—

ROBA DI ROMA. Seventh Edition, with Additions and Portrait. Crown 8vo, cloth, 10s. 6d.

CASTLE ST. ANGELO. With Illustrations. Crown 8vo, 10s. 6d.

SUTCLIFFE (JOHN)—

THE SCULPTOR AND ART STUDENT'S GUIDE to the Proportions of the Human Form, with Measurements in feet and inches of Full-Grown Figures of Both Sexes and of Various Ages. By Dr. G. SCHADOW, Member of the Academies, Stockholm, Dresden, Rome, &c. &c. Translated by J. J. WRIGHT. Plates reproduced by J. SUTCLIFFE. Oblong folio, 31s. 6d.

SYMONDS (JOHN ADDINGTON)—

ESSAYS, SPECULATIVE AND SUGGESTIVE. 2 vols. Crown 8vo, 18s.

TAINE (H. A.)—

NOTES ON ENGLAND. Translated, with Introduction, by W. FRASER RAE. Eighth Edition. With Portrait. Crown 8vo, 5s.

TAIT (J. S.)—

WHO IS THE MAN? A Tale of the Scottish Border. Crown 8vo, 1s. ; in cloth, 1s. 6d.

TANNER (PROFESSOR), F.C.S.—

HOLT CASTLE; or, Threefold Interest in Land. Crown 8vo, 4s. 6d.

JACK'S EDUCATION; OR, HOW HE LEARNT FARMING. Second Edition. Crown 8vo, 3s. 6d.

TAYLOR (EDWARD R.), Head Master of the Birmingham Municipal School of Art—
ELEMENTARY ART TEACHING: An Educational and Technical Guide for Teachers and Learners, including Infant School-work; The Work of the Standards; Freehand; Geometry; Model Drawing; Nature Drawing; Colours; Light and Shade; Modelling and Design. With over 600 Diagrams and Illustrations. Imperial 8vo, 10s. 6d.

TEMPLE (SIR RICHARD), BART., M.P., G.C.S.I.—
COSMOPOLITAN ESSAYS. With Maps. Demy 8vo, 16s.

THRUPP (GEORGE A.) and FARR (WILLIAM)—
COACH TRIMMING. With 60 Illustrations. Crown 8vo, 2s. 6d.

THRUPP (THE REV. H. W.), M.A.—
AN AID TO THE VISITATION OF THOSE DISTRESSED IN MIND, BODY, OR ESTATE. Crown 8vo, 3s. 6d.

TOPINARD (DR. PAUL)—
ANTHROPOLOGY. With a Preface by Professor PAUL BROCA. With 49 Illustrations. Demy 8vo, 3s. 6d.

TOVEY (LIEUT.-COL., R.E.)—
MARTIAL LAW AND CUSTOM OF WAR; or, Military Law and Jurisdiction in Troublous Times. Crown 8vo, 6s.

TRAHERNE (MAJOR)—
THE HABITS OF THE SALMON. Crown 8vo, 3s. 6d.

TRAILL (H. D.)—
THE NEW LUCIAN. Being a Series of Dialogues of the Dead. Demy 8vo, 12s.

TROLLOPE (ANTHONY)—
THE CHRONICLES OF BARSETSHIRE. A Uniform Edition, in 8 vols., large crown 8vo, handsomely printed, each vol. containing Frontispiece. 6s. each.

THE WARDEN and BARCHESTER TOWERS. 2 vols.	THE SMALL HOUSE AT ALLINGTON. 2 vols.
DR. THORNE.	LAST CHRONICLE OF
FRAMLEY PARSONAGE.	BARSET. 2 vols.

LIFE OF CICERO. 2 vols. 8vo. £1 4s.

TROUP (J. ROSE)—
WITH STANLEY'S REAR COLUMN. With Portraits and Illustrations. Demy 8vo.

VANDAM (ALBERT D.)—
WE TWO AT MONTE CARLO. Second Edition. Crown 8vo, 1s.; in cloth, 1s. 6d.

VERON (EUGENE)—
ÆSTHETICS. Translated by W. H. ARMSTRONG. Large crown 8vo, 7s. 6d.

VERSCHOYLE (REV. J.), M.A.—
THE HISTORY OF ANCIENT CIVILISATION. A Handbook based upon M. Gustave Ducoudray's "Histoire Sommaire de la Civilisation." Edited by REV. J. VERSCHOYLE, M.A. With Illustrations. Large crown 8vo, 6s.

WALFORD (MAJOR), R.A.—
PARLIAMENTARY GENERALS OF THE GREAT CIVIL WAR. With Maps. Large crown 8vo, 4s.

WALKER (MRS.)—
UNTRODDEN PATHS IN ROUMANIA. With 77 Illustrations. Demy 8vo, 10s. 6d.

WALKER (MRS.)—Continued—
EASTERN LIFE AND SCENERY, with Excursions to Asia Minor, Mitylene, Crete, and Roumania. 2 vols., with Frontispiece to each vol. Crown 8vo, 21s.

WARD (JAMES)—
ELEMENTARY PRINCIPLES OF ORNAMENT. With 122 Illustrations in the text. 8vo, 5s.

WATSON (JOHN)—
BRITISH SPORTING FISHES. With Frontispiece. Crown 8vo, 3s. 6d.

WATSON (WILLIAM)—
LIFE IN THE CONFEDERATE ARMY: being the Observations and Experiences of an Alien in the South during the American Civil War. Crown 8vo, 6s.

WEGG-PROSSER (F. R.)—
GALILEO AND HIS JUDGES. Demy 8vo, 5s.

WELLS (HENRY P.)—
CITY BOYS IN THE WOODS; or, A Trapping Venture in Maine. With upwards of 100 Illustrations. Royal 8vo.

WHITE (WALTER)—
A MONTH IN YORKSHIRE. With a Map. Fifth Edition. Post 8vo, 4s.

A LONDONER'S WALK TO THE LAND'S END, AND A TRIP TO THE SCILLY ISLES. With 4 Maps. Third Edition. Post 8vo, 4s.

WILL-O'-THE-WISPS, THE. Translated from the German of Marie Petersen by CHARLOTTE J. HART. With Illustrations. Crown 8vo, 7s. 6d.

WORKING MAN'S PHILOSOPHY, A. By "ONE OF THE CROWD." Crown 8vo, 3s.

WORNUM (R. N.)—
ANALYSIS OF ORNAMENT: THE CHARACTER-ISTICS OF STYLES. An Introduction to the History of Ornamental Art. With many Illustrations. Ninth Edition. Royal 8vo, cloth, 8s.

WRIGHTSON (PROF. JOHN), M.R.A.C., F.C.S., &c.; President of the College of Agriculture, Downton, near Salisbury, &c., &c.
PRINCIPLES OF AGRICULTURAL PRACTICE AS AN INSTRUCTIONAL SUBJECT. With Geological Map. Second Edition. Crown 8vo, 5s.

FALLOW AND FODDER CROPS. Crown 8vo, 5s.

WORSAAE (J. J. A.)—
INDUSTRIAL ARTS OF DENMARK, FROM THE EARLIEST TIMES TO THE DANISH CONQUEST OF ENGLAND. With Maps and Woodcuts. Large crown 8vo, 3s 6d.

YOUNGE (C. D.)—
PARALLEL LIVES OF ANCIENT AND MODERN HEROES. New Edition. 12mo, cloth, 4s. 6d.

YOUNG OFFICER'S "DON'T"; or, Hints to Youngsters on Joining. 32mo, 1s.

SOUTH KENSINGTON MUSEUM SCIENCE AND ART HANDBOOKS.

Handsomely printed in large crown 8vo.

Published for the Committee of the Council on Education.

MARINE ENGINES AND BOILERS. By GEORGE C. V. HOLMES, Secretary of the Institution of Naval Architects, Whitworth Scholar. With Sixty-nine Woodcuts. Large crown 8vo, 3s.

EARLY CHRISTIAN ART IN IRELAND. By MARGARET STOKES. With 106 Woodcuts. Crown 8vo, 4s.
A Library Edition, demy 8vo, 7s. 6d.

FOOD GRAINS OF INDIA. By PROF. A. H. CHURCH, M.A., F.C.S., F.I.C. With Numerous Woodcuts. Small 4to, 6s.

THE ART OF THE SARACENS IN EGYPT. By STANLEY LANE POOLE, B.A., M.A.R.S. With 108 Woodcuts. Crown 8vo, 4s.

ENGLISH PORCELAIN: A Handbook to the China made in England during the 18th Century, as illustrated by Specimens chiefly in the National Collections. By PROF. A. H. CHURCH, M.A. With numerous Woodcuts. 3s.

RUSSIAN ART AND ART OBJECTS IN RUSSIA: A Handbook to the reproduction of Goldsmiths' work and other Art Treasures from that country in the South Kensington Museum. By ALFRED MASKELL. With Illustrations. 4s. 6d.

FRENCH POTTERY. By PAUL GASNAULT and EDOUARD GARNIER. With Illustrations and Marks. 3s.

ENGLISH EARTHENWARE: A Handbook to the Wares made in England during the 17th and 18th Centuries, as illustrated by Specimens in the National Collection. By PROF. A. H. CHURCH, M.A. With numerous Woodcuts. 3s.

INDUSTRIAL ARTS OF DENMARK. From the Earliest Times to the Danish Conquest of England. By J. J. A. WORSAAE, Hon. F.S.A., &c. &c. With Map and Woodcuts. 3s. 6d.

INDUSTRIAL ARTS OF SCANDINAVIA IN THE PAGAN TIME. By HANS HILDEBRAND, Royal Antiquary of Sweden. With numerous Woodcuts. 2s. 6d.

PRECIOUS STONES: Considered in their Scientific and Artistic relations, with a Catalogue of the Townsend Collection of Gems in the South Kensington Museum. By PROF. A. H. CHURCH, M.A. With a Coloured Plate and Woodcuts. 2s. 6d.

INDUSTRIAL ARTS OF INDIA. By Sir GEORGE C. M. BIRDWOOD, C.S.I., &c. With Map and Woodcuts. Demy 8vo, 14s.

HANDBOOK TO THE DYCE AND FORSTER COLLECTIONS in the South Kensington Museum. With Portraits and Facsimiles. 2s. 6d.

INDUSTRIAL ARTS IN SPAIN. By JUAN F. RIAÑO. With numerous Woodcuts. 4s.

GLASS. By ALEXANDER NESBITT. With numerous Woodcuts. 2s. 6d.

GOLD AND SILVER SMITHS' WORK. By JOHN HUNGERFORD POLLEN, M.A. With numerous Woodcuts. 2s. 6d.

TAPESTRY. By ALFRED DE CHAMPEAUX. With Woodcuts. 2s. 6d.

BRONZES. By C. DRURY E. FORTNUM, F.S.A. With numerous Woodcuts. 2s. 6d.

SOUTH KENSINGTON MUSEUM SCIENCE & ART HANDBOOKS—*Continued.*

PLAIN WORDS ABOUT WATER. By A. H. CHURCH, M.A. Oxon. With Illustrations. Sewed, 6d.

ANIMAL PRODUCTS: their Preparation, Commercial Uses, and Value. By T. L. SIMMONDS. With Illustrations. 7s. 6d.

FOOD: Some Account of its Sources, Constituents, and Uses. By PROFESSOR A. H. CHURCH, M.A. Oxon. New Edition, enlarged. 3s.

ECONOMIC ENTOMOLOGY. By ANDREW MURRAY, F.L.S. APTERA. With Illustrations. 7s. 6d.

JAPANESE POTTERY. Being a Native Report. With an Introduction and Catalogue by A. W. FRANKS, M.A., F.R.S., F.S.A. With Illustrations and Marks. 2s. 6d.

HANDBOOK TO THE SPECIAL LOAN COLLECTION of Scientific Apparatus. 3s.

INDUSTRIAL ARTS: Historical Sketches. With Numerous Illustrations. 3s.

TEXTILE FABRICS. By the Very Rev. DANIEL ROCK, D.D. With numerous Woodcuts. 2s. 6d.

JONES COLLECTION IN THE SOUTH KENSINGTON MUSEUM. With Portrait and Woodcuts. 2s. 6d.

COLLEGE AND CORPORATION PLATE. A Handbook to the Reproductions of Silver Plate in the South Kensington Museum from Celebrated English Collections. By WILFRED JOSEPH CRIPPS, M.A., F.S.A. With Illustrations. 2s. 6d.

IVORIES: ANCIENT AND MEDIÆVAL. By WILLIAM MASKELL. With numerous Woodcuts. 2s. 6d.

ANCIENT AND MODERN FURNITURE AND WOOD- WORK. By JOHN HUNGERFORD POLLEN, M.A. With numerous Woodcuts. 2s. 6d.

MAIOLICA. By C. DRURY E. FORTNUM, F.S.A. With numerous Woodcuts. 2s. 6d.

THE CHEMISTRY OF FOODS. With Microscopic Illustrations. By JAMES BELL, Ph.D., &c., Principal of the Somerset House Laboratory. Part I.—Tea, Coffee, Cocoa, Sugar, &c. 2s. 6d. Part II.—Milk, Butter, Cheese, Cereals, Prepared Starches, &c. 3s.

MUSICAL INSTRUMENTS. By CARL ENGEL. With numerous Woodcuts. 2s. 6d.

MANUAL OF DESIGN, compiled from the Writings and Addresses of RICHARD REDGRAVE, R.A. By GILBERT R. REDGRAVE. With Woodcuts. 2s. 6d.

PERSIAN ART. By MAJOR R. MURDOCK SMITH, R.E. With Map and Woodcuts. Second Edition, enlarged. 2s.

CARLYLE'S (THOMAS) WORKS.

THE ASHBURTON EDITION.

An entirely New Edition, handsomely printed, containing all the Portraits and Illustrations, in Seventeen Volumes, demy 8vo, 8s. each.

THE FRENCH REVOLUTION AND PAST AND PRESENT. 2 vols.
SARTOR RESARTUS; HEROES AND HERO WORSHIP. 1 vol.
LIFE OF JOHN STERLING—LIFE OF SCHILLER. 1 vol.
LATTER-DAY PAMPHLETS—EARLY KINGS OF NORWAY—
ESSAY ON THE PORTRAIT OF JOHN KNOX. 1 vol.
LETTERS AND SPEECHES OF OLIVER CROMWELL. 3 vols.
HISTORY OF FREDERICK THE GREAT. 6 vols.
CRITICAL AND MISCELLANEOUS ESSAYS. 3 vols.

LIBRARY EDITION COMPLETE.

Handsomely printed in 34 vols., demy 8vo, cloth, £15 3s

SARTOR RESARTUS. With a Portrait, 7s. 6d.

THE FRENCH REVOLUTION. A History. 3 vols., each 9s.

LIFE OF FREDERICK SCHILLER AND EXAMINATION
OF HIS WORKS. With Supplement of 1872. Portrait and Plates, 9s.

CRITICAL AND MISCELLANEOUS ESSAYS. With Portrait.
6 vols., each 9s.

ON HEROES, HERO WORSHIP, AND THE HEROIC
IN HISTORY. 7s. 6d.

PAST AND PRESENT. 9s.

OLIVER CROMWELL'S LETTERS AND SPEECHES. With
Portraits. 5 vols., each 9s.

LATTER-DAY PAMPHLETS. 9s.

LIFE OF JOHN STERLING. With Portrait, 9s.

HISTORY OF FREDERICK THE SECOND. 10 vols.,
each 9s.

TRANSLATIONS FROM THE GERMAN. 3 vols., each 9s.

EARLY KINGS OF NORWAY; ESSAY ON THE POR-
TRAITS OF JOHN KNOX; AND GENERAL INDEX. With Portrait
Illustrations. 8vo, cloth, 9s.

CHEAP AND UNIFORM EDITION.

23 vols., Crown 8vo, cloth, £7 5s.

THE FRENCH REVOLUTION: A History. 2 vols., 12s.

OLIVER CROMWELL'S LET-TERS AND SPEECHES, with Elucidations, &c. 3 vols., 18s.

LIVES OF SCHILLER AND JOHN STERLING, 1 vol., 6s.

CRITICAL AND MISCELLANEOUS ESSAYS. 4 vols., £1 4s.

SARTOR RESARTUS AND LECTURES ON HEROES. 1 vol., 6s.

LATTER-DAY PAMPHLETS. 1 vol., 6s.

CHARTISM AND PAST AND PRESENT. 1 vol., 6s.

TRANSLATIONS FROM THE GERMAN OF MUSÆUS, TIECK, AND RICHTER. 1 vol., 6s.

WILHELM MEISTER, by Göethe. A Translation. 2 vols., 12s.

HISTORY OF FRIEDRICH THE SECOND, called Frederick the Great. 7 vols., £2 9s.

PEOPLE'S EDITION.

37 vols., small crown 8vo, 37s.; separate vols., 1s. each.

SARTOR RESARTUS. With Portrait of Thomas Carlyle.

FRENCH REVOLUTION. A History. 3 vols.

OLIVER CROMWELL'S LET-TERS AND SPEECHES. 5 vols. With Portrait of Oliver Cromwell.

ON HEROES AND HERO WORSHIP, AND THE HEROIC IN HISTORY.

PAST AND PRESENT.

CRITICAL AND MISCELLANEOUS ESSAYS. 7 vols.

THE LIFE OF SCHILLER, AND EXAMINATION OF HIS WORKS. With Portrait.

LATTER-DAY PAMPHLETS.

WILHELM MEISTER. 3 vols.

LIFE OF JOHN STERLING. With Portrait.

HISTORY OF FREDERICK THE GREAT. 10 vols.

TRANSLATIONS FROM MUSÆUS, TIECK, AND RICHTER. 2 vols.

THE EARLY KINGS OF NOR-WAY; Essay on the Portraits of Knox.

Or in sets, 37 vols. in 18, 37s.

CHEAP ISSUE.

THE FRENCH REVOLUTION. Complete in 1 vol. With Portrait. Crown 8vo, 2s.

SARTOR RESARTUS, HEROES AND HERO WORSHIP, PAST AND PRESENT, AND CHARTISM. Complete in 1 vol. Crown 8vo, 2s.

OLIVER CROMWELL'S LETTERS AND SPEECHES. Crown 8vo, 2s. 6d.

CRITICAL AND MISCELLANEOUS ESSAYS. 2 vols. 4s.

WILHELM MEISTER. 1 vol. 2s.

SIXPENNY EDITION.

4to, sewed.

SARTOR RESARTUS. Eightieth Thousand.

HEROES AND HERO WORSHIP.

ESSAYS: Burns, Johnson, Scott, The Diamond Necklace.

The above in 1 vol., cloth, 2s. 6d.

DICKENS'S (CHARLES) WORKS.

ORIGINAL EDITIONS.

In demy 8vo.

THE MYSTERY OF EDWIN DROOD. With Illustrations by S. L. Fildes, and a Portrait engraved by Baker. Cloth, 7s. 6d.

OUR MUTUAL FRIEND. With Forty Illustrations by Marcus Stone. Cloth, £1 1s.

THE PICKWICK PAPERS. With Forty-three Illustrations by Seymour and Phiz. Cloth, £1 1s.

NICHOLAS NICKLEBY. With Forty Illustrations by Phiz. Cloth, £1 1s.

SKETCHES BY "BOZ." With Forty Illustrations by George Cruikshank. Cloth, £1 1s.

MARTIN CHUZZLEWIT. With Forty Illustrations by Phiz. Cloth, £1 1s.

DOMBEY AND SON. With Forty Illustrations by Phiz. Cloth, £1 1s.

DAVID COPPERFIELD. With Forty Illustrations by Phiz. Cloth, £1 1s.

BLEAK HOUSE. With Forty Illustrations by Phiz. Cloth, £1 1s.

LITTLE DORRIT. With Forty Illustrations by Phiz. Cloth, £1 1s.

THE OLD CURIOSITY SHOP. With Seventy-five Illustrations by George Cattermole and H. K Browne. A New Edition. Uniform with the other volumes, £1 1s.

BARNABY RUDGE: a Tale of the Riots of 'Eighty. With Seventy-eight Illustrations by George Cattermole and H. K. Browne. Uniform with the other volumes, £1 1s.

CHRISTMAS BOOKS: Containing—The Christmas Carol; The Cricket on the Hearth; The Chimes; The Battle of Life; The Haunted House. With all the original Illustrations. Cloth, 12s.

OLIVER TWIST and TALE OF TWO CITIES. In one volume. Cloth, £1 1s.

OLIVER TWIST. Separately. With Twenty-four Illustrations by George Cruikshank. Cloth, 11s.

A TALE OF TWO CITIES. Separately. With Sixteen Illustrations by Phiz. Cloth, 9s.

*** *The remainder of Dickens's Works were not originally printed in demy 8vo.*

DICKENS'S (CHARLES) WORKS.—*Continued.*

LIBRARY EDITION.

In post 8vo. With the Original Illustrations, 30 vols., cloth, £12.

				s.	d.
PICKWICK PAPERS	43 Illustrns.,	2 vols.		16	o
NICHOLAS NICKLEBY	39	,,	2 vols.	16	o
MARTIN CHUZZLEWIT	40	,,	2 vols.	16	o
OLD CURIOSITY SHOP & REPRINTED PIECES	36	,,	2 vols.	16	o
BARNABY RUDGE and HARD TIMES	36	,,	2 vols.	16	o
BLEAK HOUSE	40	,,	2 vols.	16	o
LITTLE DORRIT	40	,,	2 vols.	16	o
DOMBEY AND SON	38	,,	2 vols.	16	o
DAVID COPPERFIELD	38	,,	2 vols.	16	o
OUR MUTUAL FRIEND	40	,,	2 vols.	16	o
SKETCHES BY "BOZ"	39	,,	1 vol.	8	o
OLIVER TWIST	24	,,	1 vol.	8	o
CHRISTMAS BOOKS	17	,,	1 vol.	8	o
A TALE OF TWO CITIES	16	,,	1 vol.	8	o
GREAT EXPECTATIONS	8	,,	1 vol.	8	o
PICTURES FROM ITALY & AMERICAN NOTES	8	,,	1 vol.	8	o
UNCOMMERCIAL TRAVELLER	8	,,	1 vol.	8	o
CHILD'S HISTORY OF ENGLAND	8	,,	1 vol.	8	o
EDWIN DROOD and MISCELLANIES	12	,,	1 vol.	8	o
CHRISTMAS STORIES from "Household Words," &c.	14	,,	1 vol.	8	o

Uniform with the above, 10s. 6d.

THE LIFE OF CHARLES DICKENS. By JOHN FORSTER. With Illustrations.

A NEW EDITION OF ABOVE, WITH THE ORIGINAL ILLUSTRA-TIONS, IN LARGE CROWN 8vo, 30 VOLS. IN SETS ONLY.

THE "CHARLES DICKENS" EDITION.

In Crown 8vo. In 21 vols., cloth, with Illustrations, £3 16s.

			s.	d.
PICKWICK PAPERS	8 Illustrations		4	o
MARTIN CHUZZLEWIT	8	,,	4	o
DOMBEY AND SON	8	,,	4	o
NICHOLAS NICKLEBY	8	,,	4	o
DAVID COPPERFIELD	8	,,	4	o
BLEAK HOUSE	8	,,	4	o
LITTLE DORRIT	8	,,	4	o
OUR MUTUAL FRIEND	8	,,	4	o
BARNABY RUDGE	8	,,	3	6
OLD CURIOSITY SHOP	8	,,	3	6
A CHILD'S HISTORY OF ENGLAND	4	,,	3	6
EDWIN DROOD and OTHER STORIES	8	,,	3	6
CHRISTMAS STORIES, from "Household Words"	8	,,	3	6
SKETCHES BY "BOZ"	8	,,	3	6
AMERICAN NOTES and REPRINTED PIECES	8	,,	3	6
CHRISTMAS BOOKS	8	,,	3	6
OLIVER TWIST	8	,,	3	6
GREAT EXPECTATIONS	8	,,	3	6
TALE OF TWO CITIES	8	,,	3	o
HARD TIMES and PICTURES FROM ITALY	8	,,	3	o
UNCOMMERCIAL TRAVELLER	4	,,	3	o

Uniform with the above.

THE LIFE OF CHARLES DICKENS. Numerous Illustrations. 2 vols. 7 o
THE LETTERS OF CHARLES DICKENS 2 vols. 7 o

DICKENS'S (CHARLES) WORKS.—*Continued.*

THE ILLUSTRATED LIBRARY EDITION.
(WITH LIFE.)

Complete in 32 Volumes.   Demy 8vo, 10s. each; or set, £16.

This Edition is printed on a finer paper and in a larger type than has been employed in any previous edition.   The type has been cast especially for it, and the page is of a size to admit of the introduction of all the original illustrations.

No such attractive issue has been made of the writings of Mr. Dickens, which, various as have been the forms of publication adapted to the demands of an ever widely-increasing popularity, have never yet been worthily presented in a really handsome library form.

The collection comprises all the minor writings it was Mr. Dickens's wish to preserve.

SKETCHES BY "BOZ."   With 40 Illustrations by George Cruikshank.

PICKWICK PAPERS.   2 vols.   With 42 Illustrations by Phiz.

OLIVER TWIST.   With 24 Illustrations by Cruikshank.

NICHOLAS NICKLEBY.   2 vols.   With 40 Illustrations by Phiz.

OLD CURIOSITY SHOP and REPRINTED PIECES.   2 vols.   With Illustrations by Cattermole, &c.

BARNABY RUDGE and HARD TIMES.   2 vols.   With Illustrations by Cattermole, &c.

MARTIN CHUZZLEWIT.   2 vols.   With 40 Illustrations by Phiz.

AMERICAN NOTES and PICTURES FROM ITALY.   1 vol.   With 8 Illustrations.

DOMBEY AND SON.   2 vols.   With 40 Illustrations by Phiz.

DAVID COPPERFIELD.   2 vols.   With 40 Illustrations by Phiz.

BLEAK HOUSE.   2 vols.   With 40 Illustrations by Phiz.

LITTLE DORRIT.   2 vols.   With 40 Illustrations by Phiz.

A TALE OF TWO CITIES.   With 16 Illustrations by Phiz.

THE UNCOMMERCIAL TRAVELLER.   With 8 Illustrations by Marcus Stone.

GREAT EXPECTATIONS.   With 8 Illustrations by Marcus Stone.

OUR MUTUAL FRIEND.   2 vols.   With 40 Illustrations by Marcus Stone.

CHRISTMAS BOOKS.   With 17 Illustrations by Sir Edwin Landseer, R.A., Maclise, R.A., &c. &c.

HISTORY OF ENGLAND.   With 8 Illustrations by Marcus Stone.

CHRISTMAS STORIES.   (From "Household Words" and "All the Year Round.")   With 14 Illustrations.

EDWIN DROOD AND OTHER STORIES.   With 12 Illustrations by S. L. Fildes.

LIFE OF CHARLES DICKENS.   By John Forster.   With Portraits.   2 vols. not separate.)

DICKENS'S (CHARLES) WORKS.—*Continued.*

THE POPULAR LIBRARY EDITION
OF THE WORKS OF
CHARLES DICKENS,

In 30 *Vols., large crown 8vo, price £6; separate Vols.* 4*s. each.*

An Edition printed on good paper, each volume containing 16 full-page Illustrations, selected from the Household Edition, on Plate Paper.

SKETCHES BY "BOZ."
PICKWICK. 2 vols.
OLIVER TWIST.
NICHOLAS NICKLEBY. 2 vols.
MARTIN CHUZZLEWIT. 2 vols.
DOMBEY AND SON. 2 vols.
DAVID COPPERFIELD. 2 vols.
CHRISTMAS BOOKS.
OUR MUTUAL FRIEND. 2 vols.
CHRISTMAS STORIES.
BLEAK HOUSE. 2 vols.
LITTLE DORRIT. 2 vols.

OLD CURIOSITY SHOP AND REPRINTED PIECES. 2 vols.
BARNABY RUDGE. 2 vols.
UNCOMMERCIAL TRAVELLER.
GREAT EXPECTATIONS.
TALE OF TWO CITIES.
CHILD'S HISTORY OF ENGLAND.
EDWIN DROOD AND MISCELLANIES.
PICTURES FROM ITALY AND AMERICAN NOTES.

HOUSEHOLD EDITION.
(WITH LIFE.)

In 22 *Volumes. Crown* 4*to, cloth, £*4 8*s.* 6*d.*

MARTIN CHUZZLEWIT, with 59 Illustrations, 5s.
DAVID COPPERFIELD, with 60 Illustrations and a Portrait, 5s.
BLEAK HOUSE, with 61 Illustrations, 5s.
LITTLE DORRIT, with 58 Illustrations, 5s.
PICKWICK PAPERS, with 56 Illustrations, 5s.
OUR MUTUAL FRIEND, with 58 Illustrations, 5s.
NICHOLAS NICKLEBY, with 59 Illustrations, 5s.
DOMBEY AND SON, with 61 Illustrations, 5s.
EDWIN DROOD; REPRINTED PIECES; and other Stories, with 30 Illustrations, 5s.
THE LIFE OF DICKENS. BY JOHN FORSTER. With 40 Illustrations, 5s.
BARNABY RUDGE, with 46 Illustrations, 4s.
OLD CURIOSITY SHOP, with 32 Illustrations, 4s.
CHRISTMAS STORIES, with 23 Illustrations, 4s.
OLIVER TWIST, with 28 Illustrations, 3s.
GREAT EXPECTATIONS, with 26 Illustrations, 3s.
SKETCHES BY "BOZ," with 36 Illustrations, 3s.
UNCOMMERCIAL TRAVELLER, with 26 Illustrations, 3s.
CHRISTMAS BOOKS, with 28 Illustrations, 3s.
THE HISTORY OF ENGLAND, with 15 Illustrations, 3s.
AMERICAN NOTES and PICTURES FROM ITALY, with 18 Illustrations, 3s.
A TALE OF TWO CITIES, with 25 Illustrations, 3s.
HARD TIMES, with 20 Illustrations, 2s. 6d.

DICKENS'S (CHARLES) WORKS.—*Continued.*

THE COMPLETE WORKS OF CHARLES DICKENS,

ENTITLED

THE CROWN EDITION,

Is now being PUBLISHED MONTHLY.

The Volumes contain ALL THE ORIGINAL ILLUSTRATIONS,

And the Letterpress printed from Type expressly cast for this Edition.

LARGE CROWN OCTAVO.
PRICE FIVE SHILLINGS EACH.

The Volumes Now Ready are:

1.—**THE PICKWICK PAPERS.** With Forty-three Illustrations by SEYMOUR and PHIZ.

2.—**NICHOLAS NICKLEBY.** With Forty Illustrations by PHIZ.

3.—**DOMBEY AND SON.** With Forty Illustrations by PHIZ.

4.—**DAVID COPPERFIELD.** With Forty Illustrations by PHIZ.

5.—**SKETCHES BY "BOZ."** With Forty Illustrations by GEO. CRUIKSHANK.

6.—**MARTIN CHUZZLEWIT.** With Forty Illustrations by PHIZ.

7.—**THE OLD CURIOSITY SHOP.** With Seventy-five Illustrations by GEORGE CATTERMOLE and H. K. BROWNE.

8.—**BARNABY RUDGE**: a Tale of the Riots of 'Eighty. With Seventy-eight Illustrations by GEORGE CATTERMOLE and H. K. BROWNE.

9.—**OLIVER TWIST** and **TALE OF TWO CITIES.** In One Volume. [*October 27th.*

10.—**CHRISTMAS BOOKS.** With Forty-three Illustrations by LANDSEER, MACLISE, STANSFELD, LEECH, etc. [*November 25th.*

11.—**BLEAK HOUSE.** With Forty Illustrations by PHIZ. [*December 30th.*

12.—**LITTLE DORRIT.** With Forty Illustrations by PHIZ.

13.—**OUR MUTUAL FRIEND.** With Forty Illustrations by MARCUS STONE.

ETC. ETC. ETC.

A CHRISTMAS CAROL, with the Original Coloured Plates.
Being a reprint of the Original Edition. With red border lines. Small 8vo, red cloth, gilt edges, 5s.

DICKENS'S (CHARLES) WORKS.—*Continued.*

THE CABINET EDITION.

In 32 vols. small fcap. 8vo, Marble Paper Sides, Cloth Backs, with uncut edges, price Eighteenpence each.

Each Volume contains Eight Illustrations reproduced from the Originals.

In Sets only, bound in blue cloth, with cut edges, £2 8s.

CHRISTMAS BOOKS.
MARTIN CHUZZLEWIT, 2 vols.
DAVID COPPERFIELD, 2 vols.
OLIVER TWIST.
GREAT EXPECTATIONS.
NICHOLAS NICKLEBY, 2 vols.
SKETCHES BY "BOZ."
CHRISTMAS STORIES.
THE PICKWICK PAPERS, 2 vols.
BARNABY RUDGE, 2 vols.
BLEAK HOUSE, 2 vols.
AMERICAN NOTES AND PIC-TURES FROM ITALY.
EDWIN DROOD; AND OTHER STORIES.
THE OLD CURIOSITY SHOP, 2 vols.
A CHILD'S HISTORY OF ENGLAND.
DOMBEY AND SON, 2 vols.
A TALE OF TWO CITIES.
LITTLE DORRIT, 2 vols.
MUTUAL FRIEND, 2 vols.
HARD TIMES.
UNCOMMERCIAL TRAVELLER
REPRINTED PIECES.

CHARLES DICKENS'S CHRISTMAS BOOKS.
REPRINTED FROM THE ORIGINAL PLATES.

Illustrated by JOHN LEECH, D. MACLISE, R.A., R. DOYLE, C. STANFIELD, R.A., etc.

Fcap. cloth, 1s. each.   Complete in a case, 5s.

A CHRISTMAS CAROL IN PROSE.

THE CHIMES: A Goblin Story.

THE CRICKET ON THE HEARTH: A Fairy Tale of Home.

THE BATTLE OF LIFE. A Love Story.

THE HAUNTED MAN AND THE GHOST'S STORY.

SIXPENNY REPRINTS.

READINGS FROM THE WORKS OF CHARLES DICKENS.

As selected and read by himself and now published for the first time. Illustrated.

A CHRISTMAS CAROL, AND THE HAUNTED MAN. By CHARLES DICKENS. Illustrated.

THE CHIMES: A GOBLIN STORY, AND THE CRICKET ON THE HEARTH. Illustrated.

THE BATTLE OF LIFE: A LOVE STORY, HUNTED DOWN, AND A HOLIDAY ROMANCE. Illustrated.

The last Three Volumes as Christmas Works,
In One Volume, red cloth, 2s. 6d.

DICKENS'S (CHARLES) WORKS.—*Continued.*

A NEW EDITION, ENTITLED

THE PICTORIAL EDITION,

Now being issued in MONTHLY PARTS, royal 8vo, at

ONE SHILLING EACH.

Each Part will contain 192 pages of Letterpress, handsomely printed, and, besides full-page Plates on plate paper, about 24 Illustrations inserted in the Text.

The Edition will be completed in about THIRTY-SEVEN PARTS, of which Thirteen are now ready, and will contain in all—

UPWARDS OF NINE HUNDRED ENGRAVINGS.

The Volumes now ready are:

DOMBEY AND SON. 3s. 6d.	BARNABY RUDGE. 3s. 6d.
DAVID COPPERFIELD. 3s. 6d.	OLD CURIOSITY SHOP. 3s. 6d.
NICHOLAS NICKLEBY. 3s. 6d.	MARTIN CHUZZLEWIT. *[Now being issued in Parts.*

PROSPECTUSES AND SHOWCARDS ON APPLICATION.

THE TWO SHILLING EDITION.

Each Volume contains a Frontispiece.   Crown 8vo, 2*s.*

The Volumes now ready are—

DOMBEY AND SON.	BLEAK HOUSE.
MARTIN CHUZZLEWIT.	OLD CURIOSITY SHOP.
THE PICKWICK PAPERS.	BARNABY RUDGE.

MR. DICKENS'S READINGS.

Fcap. 8vo, sewed.

CHRISTMAS CAROL IN PROSE. 1s.	STORY OF LITTLE DOMBEY. 1s.
CRICKET ON THE HEARTH. 1s.	POOR TRAVELLER, BOOTS AT THE HOLLY-TREE INN, and MRS. GAMP. 1s.
CHIMES: A GOBLIN STORY. 1s.	

SCIENCE AND ART.

A Journal for Teachers and Students.

The Official Organ of the Science and Art Teachers' Association.

MONTHLY, THREEPENCE; POST FREE, FOURPENCE.

The Journal contains contributions by distinguished men; short papers by prominent teachers; leading articles; correspondence; ahswers to questions set at the May Examinations of the Science and Art Department; and interesting news in connection with the scientific and artistic world.

PRIZE COMPETITION.

With each issue of the Journal, papers or drawings are offered for Prize Competition, extending over the range of subjects of the Science and Art Department and City and Guilds of London Institute.

There are thousands of Science and Art Schools and Classes in the United Kingdom, but the teachers connected with these institutions, although engaged in the advancement of identical objects, are seldom known to each other except through personal friendship. One object of the Journal is to enable those engaged in this common work to communicate upon subjects of importance, with a view to an interchange of ideas, and the establishment of unity of action in the various centres.

TERMS OF SUBSCRIPTION.

ONE YEAR'S SUBSCRIPTION (including postage)	**4s.**	**0d.**
HALF „ „ „	**2s.**	**0d.**
SINGLE COPY „		**4d.**

Cheques and Post Office Orders to be made payable to

Messrs. CHAPMAN & HALL, Limited,

Agents for the Science and Art Department of the Committee of Council on Education.

SOLUTIONS TO THE QUESTIONS IN PURE MATHE-MATICS—Stages 1 and 2—SET AT THE SCIENCE AND ART EXAMINATIONS from 1881 to 1886. By THOMAS T. RANKIN, C.E., Rector of the Gartsherrie Science School, and West of Scotland Mining College. Crown 8vo, 2s.

SOLUTIONS TO THE QUESTIONS SET IN THE FOLLOWING SUBJECTS AT THE MAY EXAMINATIONS OF THE SCIENCE AND ART DEPARTMENT ANTERIOR TO 1887.

1. Animal Physiology ... From 1881 to 1886.
2. Hygiene ... ... ,, 1884 to 1886 { with Notes and Index.
3. Building Construction ... ,, 1881 to 1886.
4. Machine Construction ... ,, 1881 to 1886.
5. Agriculture ... ... ,, 1881 to 1886.
6. Magnetism and Electricity ,, 1881 to 1886.
7. Physiography ... ... ,, 1881 to 1886.
8. Sound, Light, and Heat ,, 1881 to 1886.

Each Subject will be dealt with in a Separate Volume, which will contain Complete Answers to the Elementary and Advanced Papers for the Years noted.

Price 1s. 6d. each.

ANSWERS TO QUESTIONS, 1887, 1888, & 1889.

1890 IN THE PRESS.

SOLUTIONS TO THE QUESTIONS (*Elementary and Advanced*) *set at the Examinations of the Science and Art Department of May, 1887, 1888, and 1889, are published as under, each subject and year being kept distinct, and issued in pamphlet form separately.   Crown 8vo, 3d. each.*

1. ANIMAL PHYSIOLOGY. By J. H. E. Brock, M.D., B.S. (Lond.), F.R.C.S. (Eng.), D.P.H. (Univ. of Lond.)

2. BUILDING CONSTRUCTION. By H. Adams, C.E., M.I.M.E.

3. THEORETICAL MECHANICS. By J. C. Fell, M.I.M.E., E. Pillow, M.I.M.E., and H. Angel.

4. INORGANIC CHEMISTRY (Theoretical). By Rev. F. W. Harnett, M.A., and J. J. Pilley, F.C.S., F.R.M.S.

5. Ditto, ALTERNATIVE COURSE. By J. Howard, F.C.S.

6. MAGNETISM AND ELECTRICITY. By W. Hibbert, F.I.C., A.I.E.E.

7. PHYSIOGRAPHY. By W. Rheam, B.Sc., and 'W. S. Furneaux, F.R.G.S.

8. PRACTICAL PLANE AND SOLID GEOMETRY. By H. Angel.

9. ART—THIRD GRADE. PERSPECTIVE. By A. Fisher and S. Beale.

10. PURE MATHEMATICS. By R. R. Steel, F.C.S., and H. Carter, B.A.

11. MACHINE CONSTRUCTION AND DRAWING. By H. Adams, C.E., M.I.M.E.

12. PRINCIPLES OF AGRICULTURE. By H. J. Webb, Ph.D., B.Sc.

13. SOUND, LIGHT, AND HEAT. By C. A. Stevens and F. Carrodus, Assoc. N.S.S.

14. HYGIENE. By J. J. Pilley, F.C.S., F.R.M.S.

15. INORGANIC CHEMISTRY (Practical). By J. Howard, F.C.S.

16. APPLIED MECHANICS. For 1888 and 1889 only. By C. B. Outon, Wh.Sc.

17. ALTERNATIVE ELEMENTARY PHYSICS. By W. Hibbert, F.I.E., A.S.I.E. For 1889 only.

Price of each Pamphlet (*dealing with both Elementary and Advanced Papers for a single year*), *3d. net, postage included.*